Death by Deception

Death by Deception

The Shepherd Sisters Mysteries

Tracy Gardner

TULE
PUBLISHING

Dedication

For Joe, my always and most
And for Katy, Joey, and Halle, my heartbeat

Dear Reader,

First, thank you for reading my book! I know you haven't yet, but it's in your hands and you're ready to begin. I appreciate you more than you know.

For those of you who are new to the Shepherd sisters, welcome! I am so excited you're here. For readers who are already acquainted with my sister trio and their quaint but murder-prone lakeside town, welcome back!

This first book now has a brand-new, gorgeous cover and title and has undergone a few minor changes. The cute pup on the front is modeled after our beloved family dog, Fonzie, who really believed he was one of our kids. I love seeing him on the cover, as he is the constant companion to main character Savanna Shepherd throughout the five-book series.

Did I really just say *five-book series*? I figured you'd catch that! The Shepherd Sisters Mystery series now encompasses five books so far. These sisters, their close-knit family, and their small Lake Michigan town are close to my heart. I am lucky. Writing these books often feels like hanging out with longtime friends. I hope you love diving in and spending time with the sisters as they work to unravel local murder mysteries while navigating the joy and heartache of love and family drama. The sisters are also lucky. They are surrounded by a nurturing, supportive family, another facet of the stories that I loved living within while writing. After all, the Shepherd family always has room for one more at their Sunday evening dinners—or even at weekly Wednesday lunch dates at Fancy Tails and Treats.

A little about me before you begin. I've always been a reader. I was that kid stumbling home from the library with a stack of books too high to see over, only to return them a day or two later for more. I've been writing stories since I was six. I started writing my first novel when my kids were babies. They were nearly adults when I landed my first book contract. I spent many, many years, tears, and sleepless nights clinging to hope—hope that a great literary agent would decide to represent me, hope that an amazing publisher would fall in love with my work, hope that my books would one day make into readers' hands and onto bookstore shelves.

I don't like to think in terms of numbers. Numbers can get too overwhelming too fast... how many query letters I wrote, how many rejections I received, how many manuscripts died, unseen, in the dreaded "drawer," how many people told me no. I prefer to see things more broadly. Like most worthwhile endeavors, writing to become published is a journey, and I've been on this journey a while.

A more sensible person might have given up long before now. I never claimed to be sensible. When I did finally connect with that great literary agent who champions my books like crazy and the amazing publisher who fell so in love with the Shepherd Sisters that they're publishing all five books in one wild year, the long journey begins to seem more like an incredible adventure with plenty of side quests.

I am so grateful to each person who has picked up one of my books, shared it, talked about it, reviewed it, messaged me to say they can't put it down, or continued to think about the story and characters long after finishing. I hope you love the book. Thank you for reading!

Tracy

Carson, Michigan

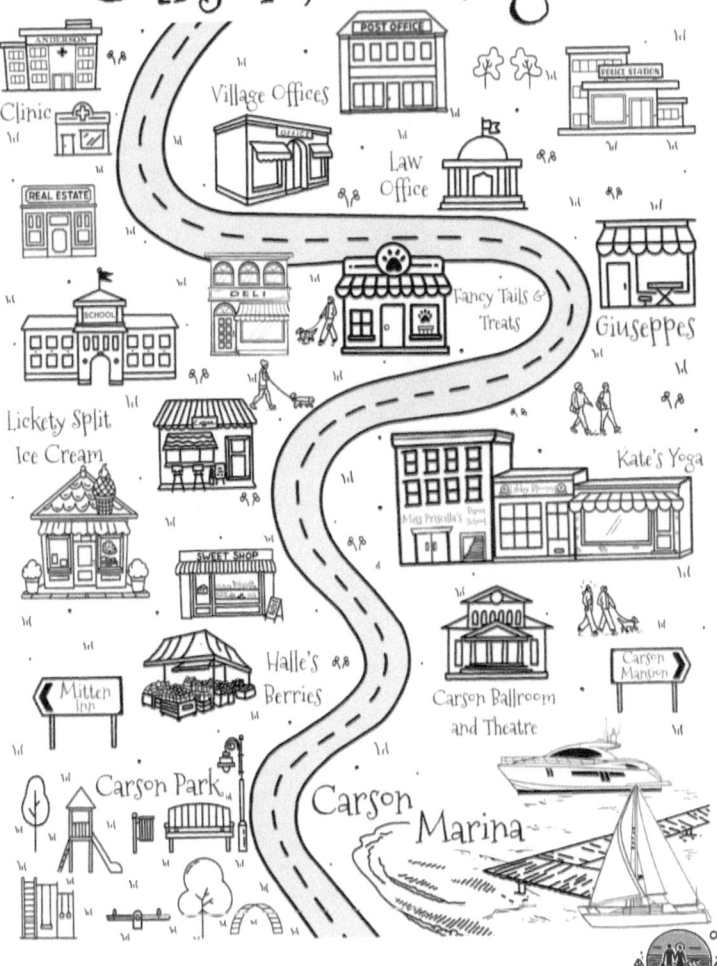

Clinic

ANDERSON

Village Offices

POST OFFICE

POLICE STATION

REAL ESTATE

Law Office

SCHOOL

DELI

Fancy Tails & Treats

Giuseppes

Lickety Split Ice Cream

Miss Priscilla's

Kate's Yoga

SWEET SHOP

Halle's Berries

Carson Ballroom and Theatre

Carson Mansion

Mitten Inn

Carson Park

Carson Marina

Chapter One

S AVANNA SHEPHERD BREATHED deeply, closing her eyes for a moment to savor the crisp fall air that was somehow sweeter on this side of Lake Michigan. Those vast blue waves with beautiful whitecaps made it seem more like an ocean than a lake; she'd never tire of it. It was good to be home.

Savanna let the poodles lead her down the sandy sidewalk. They were tiny and well-mannered and knew the way by heart. Even though she'd grown up here, Savanna was still acclimating to her little beach town after over a decade spent in Chicago. At the age of thirty, it was strange to think about her old life, due west across the lake. Her twelfth-floor apartment, her job as art authenticator for a prestigious gallery, and her fiancé, Rob, had been replaced with a small pink room at her sister's house in Carson, an elementary art teacher job, and her Boston terrier, Fonzie, as her most constant companion.

Despite the whiplash feeling from so many changes in such a short time, Savanna was grateful. She'd been lucky to fall into a teaching position just as the school year was starting. Younger sister Sydney happily offered up her spare bedroom while she figured things out. She'd missed her sisters. In the middle, with Skylar two years older and

Sydney two years younger, Savanna was surprised to realize how much she'd missed their close-knit little trio the last several years.

Savanna bent to untangle the leashes; as they approached Caroline's house, Duke pranced in circles around Princess. The poodles were primped and fluffed and smelled like a flower shop, courtesy of Sydney's grooming salon, Fancy Tails and Treats. Along with the poodles, Savanna was delivering a little paper sack of gourmet dog biscuits Sydney had made herself. After Savanna's very first day at Carson Elementary School, she'd stopped by the salon to bring her sister a coffee and had ended up volunteering to return the poodles to Caroline Carson.

The Shepherd sisters had grown up thinking Caroline was their grandmother. Even after they were old enough to understand that the families were just close friends, Savanna remembered spending Sunday afternoons and long summer days on Caroline's wraparound porch and the beach beyond. Spotting the pillars of the wide front entrance, Savanna could almost smell the lemonade and sunscreen from her youth. The Carson mansion was gorgeous and stately, the rear of the house overlooking the lake and its rolling dunes.

Princess and Duke were having trouble containing their exuberance, as Savanna tried to sidestep them on the way up the wide porch steps. She hadn't seen Caroline in almost five years. She'd wanted to come home for the funeral when Mr. Carson had passed last year, but she couldn't get away from work. She was equally excited and nervous, and underneath that, Savanna couldn't wait to see what had changed in the

Carsons' art collection. The beautiful pieces on the walls of this house were largely what had inspired Savanna to go into art authentication. She'd always enjoyed doodling and painting, but she'd found her niche in college, learning about world-renowned artists and their techniques, minoring in early education but majoring in studio art to earn her BFA.

The poodles scrambled wildly onto the porch, pulling Savanna smack into a tree. Well, not a tree, but an impossibly tall stranger just stepping out onto Caroline's porch. Savanna looked up to find herself staring into the bluest eyes she'd ever seen. She watched them crinkle at the corners, making her suddenly aware she was standing there, gawking, mute. He had a shock of unruly black hair, cut close but longer on top, and a few faint freckles across his cheeks.

"Hello." His voice was deep and quiet. He placed one large hand lightly on her upper arm, steadying her as she stepped back.

After tripping over a leash, Savanna regained her balance. She looked down and found the poodles had taken the opportunity to weave themselves in and around both her and the stranger's ankles.

She laughed, trying to extricate herself. "Here." She finally scooped up Duke. "Would you mind?" She handed the poodle to the man and he took it, smiling at her and making her more flustered. What was she doing? Why would she assume this man would just hold a random dog? Too late now, she thought, unclipping Duke's leash and unwrapping it from their legs while Princess sprung into the air, pawing at Duke.

"Oh, jeez," Savanna murmured, capturing a squirming Princess and glancing up at the man again. "I'm so sorry!"

"Don't be." He laughed. "I love these two."

She frowned at him without meaning to. She knew everyone in town; who was this man on Caroline's porch, claiming to know Caroline's poodles? And why was his smile making her all warm and stupid inside?

"I'm Aidan. And you are…not Sydney."

Savanna shook her head, disconcerted. How did he know Sydney? Aidan who? "I'm not. I'm Savanna. Shepherd," she added.

Understanding dawned on him. "Ah-ha! The third Shepherd sister!"

"Yes. How do you know my sisters?"

"We take our dog to Fancy Tails. And I've crossed paths with your sister picking up Caroline's poodles before. And your other sister, Skylar, is my attorney. Not that I need a lawyer," he interrupted himself. "Just, y'know, for things that come up. Nothing bad. Financial stuff. She's great. They're both great," he finished awkwardly.

Savanna heard one thing in Aidan's explanation, and it had nothing to do with him needing Skylar's services—*we*. As in, *"We" take our dog to Fancy Tails.* This ridiculously hot man was taken—of course. How could he not be?

"Your sisters must be happy to have you back."

"I'm thrilled to be home. I haven't seen Caroline yet, so I offered to deliver these two." She gestured at the little dogs, now back on their leashes.

He nodded, stepping aside and holding the door open

for her. "It was nice meeting you." The deep timbre of his voice sent a pleasant little zing through her.

Again, she wondered—Aidan who? But Savanna's mother had raised her with good manners. There was no polite way she could ask him to define who he was to Caroline. "Nice meeting you too, Aidan." She took his offered hand, large and warm, noting as she let go that he held on just a beat longer.

"Maybe I'll see you around." He turned and headed down the front steps.

Savanna stood in the doorway and watched his retreat. Okay, she'd have to sneak details out of Caroline. She was pretty sure he was married. She mentally kicked herself for not noticing if he wore a ring. And, on the heels of that, kicked herself again for even wondering. After everything Rob had put her through, she'd sworn she was done with men—for a good while anyway.

Savanna reached outside and rang the doorbell before closing the door and unclipping the poodles. She didn't want to just walk in and startle an old woman. "Hello? Caroline?"

"Hello, dear. In here," the familiar voice called.

Savanna peeked into each room as she made her way to the back of the enormous house, knowing she'd find Caroline in the parlor. The best room in the mansion, it spanned the entire west wing and had more windows than Sydney's whole house. Sunset on Lake Michigan was breathtaking, just as Savanna remembered it. She stood for a moment in the doorway, basking in the orange and pink light spilling over Caroline's wingback chair. If she lived here, she'd never leave this room.

Caroline rose, reaching for her cane as she spoke. "Now, Sydney, you must take this. You do such good work with my babies." She turned toward Savanna with cash in hand, registering happy surprise.

"Not Sydney," Savanna said for the second time today, smiling and wrapping Caroline in a warm hug.

"Oh, my! I'd heard whispers… I'm so glad to see you, Savanna!" Caroline carried her age well. She must be ninety. She was still tall, though not quite as tall as she'd been when Savanna was a child. There was a regal air about her, in her mannerisms, her gait, the way she spoke. Savanna spied *The New York Times* crossword on the table beside Caroline's chair; she was obviously as sharp as ever.

"I've missed you so much!" Savanna gave her one extra little squeeze before letting go. "You look exactly the same, Caroline. How can that be?"

The older woman chuckled. "You always were a good fibber." She held Savanna at arm's length and looked her up and down. "Lovely, my dear. You look wonderful. It seems leaving the city and that idiot man has been just what you needed."

Savanna's eyebrows went up in surprise. "Sydney told you?"

"Skylar told me. She'd like to find him and give him a piece of her mind, you know."

Savanna laughed. "Oh, no." She shook her head. Rob wouldn't know what hit him. "My sisters weren't too happy when he broke off the engagement. Well, that's not true. I think they actually are happy it's over; they never liked him. They weren't great at hiding it. But I'm all right. I promise."

"Of course you are. I think he did you a favor." She leaned in, curling one arm loosely through the crook of Savanna's elbow. "You belong here, with your sisters. I'm glad you're home. Now, how about a refresher? We've acquired some exquisite work since I last saw you; let me show you, and you can tell me what you know from your worldly fine art pedigree. I want to hear all about Chicago."

Caroline kept her arm linked through Savanna's and they began in the library, Princess and Duke following closely. Dark cherrywood was everywhere Savanna looked, and stacks of books reached far over her head. An imperial staircase led up both sides of the room to a catwalk stretching across it. The whole presentation was breathtaking, even to Savanna, who'd grown up devouring the Nancy Drew and Hardy Boys collections on these shelves. The railing along the catwalk above gleamed, and just below it, Savanna was stunned to see an actual Minkov hung on the wall. She gasped.

Caroline followed her gaze up to the painting.

"Is that a Sergei Minkov?" Savanna already knew the answer, but she had to ask. She'd only ever seen his work in books. It was so beautiful in person.

"It is. Everett fell in love instantly, the same as you. He had to have it." She chuckled and lowered her voice in a poor imitation of her late husband. "'I don't care what it costs, Caroline. That piece belongs in our library.'"

"Wow," Savanna breathed. "I've never actually seen one.

May I take a closer look?"

"Of course."

Savanna left Caroline to rest a moment at a reading table, a few books scattered across the top. She moved as close as she could to the painting, a good size even in the huge library. It was exquisite. Most Minkovs were valued in the hundreds of thousands or higher, and that wasn't taking into consideration the year, the period, the size, or the individual piece. Even for collectors such as Everett and Caroline, even in a town known for its long history of an esteemed art community, this was an incredible acquisition. She doubted if any of her peers in Chicago had ever seen a real-life Minkov in person.

"There's another in the dining room," Caroline said. "Come, I'll show you."

Savanna was seriously impressed. Another? She listened as they passed through the living room and Caroline pointed out two paintings Savanna recognized, one a Monet and the other by an early nineteenth-century artist, Francois Laurant. The Minkov in the dining room was smaller than the painting in the library, but no less amazing.

"I hope these are well insured, Caroline," Savanna murmured. "I'm not sure you realize what you have here."

Caroline gave Savanna's arm a little squeeze. "Absolutely, don't worry. Your sister handles all of that for me—insurance, copies of paperwork, everything. Everett was always so smart about finances and legal things, and Skylar has been a big help in recent years."

They circled around back toward the parlor, passing the

grand staircase, and Savanna noticed three faded rectangular outlines, bare spots, on the wall on the way up the stairs. "What was there?"

"Ah! That was a...Matisse, I believe, and a Rothman, and an early Laurant—a painting of the Roman canals. I have trouble keeping them all straight. There are too many." She glanced at Savanna. "I've begun some cleaning since losing Everett. We found a new home for the Rothman that was there and moved the other two for now while the stairway is redone. My neighbor Maggie has her husband helping with construction." She gestured in the direction of the house next door.

Back in the parlor, Savanna shook her head. "You're busier now than when I left ten years ago." She smiled at Caroline. "Why are you renovating? Your house is gorgeous."

Caroline clapped her hands suddenly, excited. "Oh, my, I just realized. You don't even know, do you? You have to come. We're planning a grand party here for my ninetieth birthday next month!"

Savanna's face lit up. "Really? I came home just in time then, didn't I?"

Back in the parlor, Caroline leaned forward in her chair. "Savanna. I wonder if you might consider doing me a favor? At least think about it."

"Anything."

"A mural. Might I commission you to paint me a mural? That wall." She nodded toward the north end of the room. "Everett and I always felt it should have a seascape. After all the years here, it almost seems I can see it. It would complement our view." She glanced out at Lake Michigan. "And you have the talent—I remember your artwork. Would you do it?"

Savanna was taken aback. She hadn't painted—not seriously—in years. She'd messed around a little, but Rob had made her feel as if it were a waste of time, and she'd stopped making the time to do it. She'd dabbled a little since coming back to Carson, but…the idea of a mural was both exciting and daunting. "Caroline, I'm flattered. But—you haven't seen my work in ten years. I'm not sure I can meet your expectations. Why not just hire it out?"

"Because I want you to do it."

Savanna wasn't sure what to say. The quiet, firm demeanor of the woman sitting across from her was exactly what had made Caroline Carson such a shrewd businesswoman through the course of her life. Savanna wasn't about to tell her no. "How about if I bring my portfolio for you to look at? I have some pieces from school, and one I started recently when I came home. Then you can tell me if you're still sure."

"Perfect," Caroline agreed.

SAVANNA WAS WALKING into the grooming salon before she realized she'd forgotten to ask about that handsome stranger on Caroline's porch. Well, she'd see the woman tomorrow. If she was even still curious, she firmly told herself.

She handed Sydney two crisp hundred-dollar bills, flouncing down onto the comfy aqua couch her sister kept in a little seating area for customers. The shop was split into two sides, the smaller nook with only a desk, laptop, and file cabinet that held each of Sydney's grooming customers' specifics: dog's name, breed, color, preferred services, style of grooming, allergies, and medical issues. The doorway behind the desk led to a large soundproofed horseshoe with six holding areas, the bathing and grooming facilities in the center. The larger opposite end of the shop, through a wide daisy-decorated archway, housed a long glass display case, filled with an assortment of gourmet pet treats. On first glance, the goodies in the case could be assumed to be delicious concoctions for people; they were all so pretty and unique. A second smaller shelving unit displayed animal-themed collars, bows, leashes, sweaters, booties, and a small selection of cruelty-free hygiene and grooming products that smelled delightful. The front corner of the shop was dedicated to making her patrons feel at home while they shopped or waited for a quick canine trim: an overstuffed couch and chair, a red and chrome retro round table with vintage matching chairs, a mini-fridge with complimentary drinks, and a huge basket of dog toys. Fancy Tails and Treats sat at the end of Main Street, with Sydney's house in the back. She'd bought the place specifically so Harlan could turn the defunct beauty salon in the front into Fancy Tails. Savanna loved that she was already just as comfortable in the shop as she was in the guest bedroom at Sydney's.

Sydney rolled her eyes. "You're not supposed to take her

money. I told you!"

Savanna laughed. "Right, like she listens when you tell her no?"

"Never," Sydney agreed. "I've told her over and over not to do that. This is twice what the fee would be for her poodles. She's so stubborn."

"Are you almost finished? I can help you close up."

Sydney moved behind the gourmet treat counter. "Just about. Here, you can sweep." She handed Savanna a broom. Sydney's red hair fell in a loose braid down her back, beads interwoven here and there catching the light. Savanna's own hair was darker, more auburn; she'd never have the nerve to dress it up the way her sister wore hers, but it looked natural on Syd.

Sydney moved to the bulletin board near the entrance, swapping out last week's yoga schedule for this week's. She taught a class twice a week for her friend Kate, who owned the studio across the street. She glanced over her shoulder at Savanna. "Are you going to come tomorrow? Even Skylar finds time now and then. What are you afraid of?"

Savanna smiled sweetly at her persistent sister. "I have a date with Caroline, or I definitely would. I swear!"

"Uh-huh."

It was no secret that Syd was the athletic one in their family. Savanna knew she'd eventually have to make an appearance in her sister's class, but she was not nearly as bendy as the rest of the yogis. She much preferred the walks she'd started taking along the beach since coming home to Carson. Lake Michigan might as well be an ocean, for its beauty and size. There was just something calming about being close to the sand, water, and sky.

Savanna was certain Skylar benefitted from attending a class now and then. Her older sister hadn't slowed down after having her son three years ago. She was now full partner in the largest law firm in western Michigan, running the Carson office and commuting to Lansing twice a week. She'd always been super-stress-Skylar when it came to school or work; yoga was probably great for keeping her balanced.

Savanna was reaching for the light switch when the bell over the door jingled. Her little nephew burst into the shop, singing and skipping, Skylar close behind him. Nolan threw himself at Sydney and she caught him, swinging him around. He kissed his aunt on the cheek and peeked out from around her shoulder at Savanna. She was still new, and he was shy.

Sydney carried him over to Savanna, dipping him a bit toward her and then pulling him back, making the toddler giggle. "What about Auntie Savanna?"

Nolan gave her the cutest, most dimpled grin ever, and then buried his face in Sydney's neck.

Savanna poked him lightly in the ribs. "Auntie Savanna still sees you, silly boy!"

He turned his face, peering at her with one eye, and then whipped around, arms out, and she grabbed him from Sydney. He squeezed his chubby arms around her neck in a hug, his white-blond hair tickling her nose. His mother's hair was the exact same shade, cut into a no-nonsense bob.

"He's had dinner, *and* dessert." Skylar raised one well-shaped brow at her son. "So don't let him tell you any sob stories. Travis will pick him up before nine tomorrow morning." Skylar shifted her briefcase, weighed down with that plus a messenger bag, purse, and overnight bag. She handed Sydney Nolan's Pokémon backpack.

Savanna was thrilled to now be a part of the Wednesday-night routine; Nolan slept over at Sydney's house once a week or so, when Skylar had early court mornings in Lansing. It helped both Skylar and her husband, Travis, and Nolan was so much fun to spoil.

"How was your first day of school?" Skylar turned to Savanna.

"It was awesome. Seriously," she added when Skylar looked at her skeptically. "I loved it. Everyone is so nice. Oh, and Caroline's grandson Jack is the school librarian. And the kids…they were amazing." Elementary art was a hard left turn in her career path, but Savanna hoped it was the right choice.

"You started school, Auntie? I just started too!"

"Then we're both lucky!"

They parted ways outside, Skylar leaning in to kiss each sister's cheek and give Nolan one more hug.

Savanna jostled Nolan on her hip, winking at Sydney beside her. "So, Nolan, did you know that where I used to live, we have *second dessert*? Are you in?"

Chapter Two

THE NEXT DAY after school, Savanna dove into her boxes in Sydney's basement, looking for the few pieces of her own work she'd brought from Chicago. She was due at the Carson house tonight at 7:30. Caroline had even told her to bring Fonzie to get acquainted with her Princess and Duke.

Savanna located her original portfolio and flipped through it. Some of these were from her junior year in college, eight or nine years ago. She pulled out three of her least favorite, replacing them with newer copies of ones she'd done just before starting at the gallery for Rob's family. Savanna had sorely neglected her painting passion. When she'd finally picked up the brush again, just last week, it had been too long a hiatus. She didn't realize how much better she felt painting until she was doing it again.

Sydney had let her set up space to paint in the sunroom. It was the perfect spot, the room facing south, so the light in the room shifted throughout the day. The rising and setting sun would cast a slightly different light on whatever was on the easel, and sometimes it'd give Savanna a whole new perspective on the piece. It reminded her a little of the time spent examining work for the gallery, the various methods she'd used to view works of art, the medium, the brushstrokes and palette, the signature techniques of each individual artist, the material beneath, looking for the smallest details, any sign of authenticity or forgery. The process was painstaking, one that could fool a novice. Early in college, a professor had introduced them to pentimento—a trace of an earlier painting beneath the current layer or layers of paint on a canvas—and then had expounded on never jumping to conclusions, as many artists painted over their own work, unable to afford the cost of new canvas each time. The skill was in learning to detect true work from the artist versus excellent forgeries. And for Savanna, the fun in her career had been two-fold: recognizing and acquiring genuine works of art for the museum, and using her sharp eye to find the flaws, whether they were trademark signs from the real artist or clues to a forgery.

She popped into the sunroom and took her current piece from a few days ago off the easel, wanting to show Caroline, as it had some of the color palette they'd discussed for her mural. Packing that and her portfolio into her car, Savanna opened the door for Fonzie to hop into his spot in the passenger seat, his head out the window, ready. He loved car rides—he hadn't minded the trip home from Chicago at all.

Arriving on Caroline's front porch, Savanna was struck with what a busy house the older woman had. Tonight, there were three new cars in the driveway, and she could hear some kind of construction going on around the back of the house. The front door opened before Savanna could ring the bell, and she was greeted by a middle-aged woman wearing a green Happy Family Grocery Delivery apron and carrying a clipboard.

"Oh! Sorry," the woman said, pulling the visor lower on her cap and trotting down the front steps.

So Caroline apparently had a grocery delivery service? Savanna wasn't surprised. She hadn't imagined Caroline relying on family to do her shopping, but she supposed grocery shopping at eighty-nine might not be easy. Of course she'd have found a smart solution.

Savanna poked her head into the open door, not wanting to just walk in. "Hello?" No answer. She stepped back out onto the porch and rang the bell, hearing footsteps a moment later.

A pretty young woman descended the staircase just through the foyer. "Come in! Grams is expecting you. She's been talking about it all day. Oh! I'm Lauren, her granddaughter." She needn't have clarified that; the resemblance was striking. Lauren was tall and thin with pale blue eyes that matched Caroline's exactly. She shifted the serving tray she held to her other hip, teacups and small plates clattering together. "You don't remember me, do you?"

Savanna stared at her. Yes. She did remember! "I do—you were here in the summers, right? A few times, when we were kids?" Savanna estimated the woman to be around her own age. She recalled out-of-state family visiting, extra children playing on the beach and the porch.

"We moved back last year after my grandfather passed," she explained. "Grams just needs a little help. She's so excited about the mural you're painting for her."

Savanna followed her through to the parlor. "She's pretty

persuasive."

Lauren tossed a look over her shoulder. "That's a nice word." She must have caught Savanna's surprised expression, as she added, "I just mean, she knows what she wants, and she doesn't take no for an answer. Right?"

Savanna felt her cheeks warm. Lauren wasn't wrong, but her irritation had given her voice a hard edge. How could Savanna agree without sounding like she was dissing the woman who'd taught her everything she knew about her creative side?

Lauren stopped just outside the parlor, a hand on Savanna's arm. "I'm sorry. It's just been a long day." She sighed. "Sometimes I need two of me to manage this house plus my own. Don't listen to me."

Savanna nodded. It must be difficult, being Caroline's caretaker on top of her own commitments. "You're doing such a wonderful thing," she said, her voice quiet. "I can only imagine how much Caroline appreciates it!"

"I know she does. Thank you, Savanna. It's really good to see you again. Grams is thrilled you're back."

Lauren left Savanna at the entryway to the parlor and went the other way toward the kitchen, presumably to take care of the dishes and the groceries from Happy Family.

Juggling her portfolio and the new work-in-progress piece, Savanna spoke without looking up as she entered the parlor. "I brought several for you, Caroline; this one is a lake scene, but it's done in acrylics, which we wouldn't use for—" Savanna stopped midsentence, realizing she was interrupting some sort of meeting. Seven or eight women were seated around the room, each with the same book in their lap. "Oh! Hello. Book club? I'll come back another time," she offered.

"Don't be silly. We were just finishing up," Caroline said. "I think we can all agree we need to go in a different direction for next month's choice?"

The women around the room murmured their agreement.

Caroline held a hand out to Savanna, and she went to the woman's side. "Far too much description, dear, and very dry. I wouldn't recommend it." She tapped the book in her lap. She addressed the group. "Eleanor and I will go through your suggestions, and we'll email you with the selection for October. Savanna, meet my book club."

Caroline made introductions as the ladies took their cue and began shuffling out.

"Next month, the second Thursday in October," Caroline called as the last couple of women exited, "and don't forget to bring your appetites!" She turned toward Savanna and the one woman left sitting in the wingback chair to her right. "Savanna, this is my good friend Eleanor Pietila. Eleanor, Savanna Shepherd. Eleanor and I choose the next book from the suggestion list after each meeting. Sit, please! I'm dying to see what you brought."

Savanna took the chair beside Eleanor, resting her portfolio against her legs.

Eleanor was focused intently on the laptop that sat on a folding table in front of her. She browsed some unseen website, jotting down titles on a notepad occasionally, while Savanna went through the portfolio with Caroline. Lauren flitted around the room, picking up plates and cups here and there and carrying them out to the kitchen.

Savanna walked over to the wide wall the mural was meant for. She rested her current half-finished canvas against the wall and backed up to Caroline's chair, tilting her head, squinting.

"I think you're right. Those are the colors. The water, at least. The sky will be lighter, though, right?"

"Yes, the sky should be as it was last night, just before sunset."

Lauren popped back into the room, dishwasher running now in the kitchen and the parlor restored to order. "Would anyone like something to drink before I head home? Grandmother, maybe some tea or an evening claret?"

"Why don't you surprise us? Either sounds lovely."

The doorbell rang, and Lauren left to get it, returning a few minutes later with three short goblets of red wine. She distributed them. "Amber brought this claret with the Happy Family delivery. It's in such a pretty bottle—it has gold vines wrapped around it, some kind of import. I'm sure it'll be good. Oh, and that was Dr. Gallager at the door. He had to adjust something with your transmitter upstairs—I told him to just go up."

"Thank you, Lauren." Caroline took her glass, setting it on the table beside her, and patted her granddaughter's arm. "He's so conscientious. I'm sure it could have waited until the appointment next week."

Lauren leaned down and hugged Caroline goodbye. "Love you, Grams. Princess and Duke are in for the night, and your towels are in the dryer. I'll take care of them tomorrow." Princess and Duke were indeed in for the night, curled up with Fonzie in front of the fireplace at the other end of the room.

After Lauren had gone, Caroline's eyes shimmered. "That girl… I'm very fortunate to have her."

"Lovely girl," Eleanor murmured, sipping her wine. The laptop was closed now, her notebook on top of it with a short list of book titles scrawled across the paper.

"Caroline." Savanna leaned forward in her chair, unable to hide her concern. "I hope you don't mind me asking, but why do you have a doctor checking on you? What transmitter—is there something wrong?"

"No, no." Caroline waved a dismissive hand in the air. "I was having a few flutters, some little thing with my heart, and he's making me wear a monitor for a while. I'm sure everything is fine."

Her fears completely unappeased with that explanation, Savanna rose, leaving her claret untouched alongside Caroline's. She went to the enormous picture window, looking out into the darkness over the dunes and lake. In spite of appearances, some things had changed. Caroline wasn't invincible. And now she had a doctor making house calls to check on her heart.

Caroline surprised Savanna, joining her at the window. She linked an arm through Savanna's. "My dear girl. I don't want you to worry. This is just routine, I promise. And Dr. Gallager is excellent. He worked in the cardiothoracic department at New York Presbyterian before coming to

Carson. If there is anything wrong, he'll find it and fix it."

The woman was a mind reader. Savanna put an arm around Caroline in a light hug. "Okay. If you aren't worried, I'm not worried. I hope this doctor is as good as you say he is."

"Even better." The deep voice came from behind Savanna, making her jump.

She whipped around, shocked to see the tall stranger from Caroline's porch yesterday. His frame filled the doorway to the parlor. This was Caroline's doctor? But he was too young. Somehow, Savanna had imagined an older, grayer, country-doctor type, the kind who carried a little black bag and wore wire spectacles... How was this thirtysomething guy qualified to keep Caroline's heart running like clockwork?

"Savanna, this is Dr. Aidan Gallager. Dr. Gallager, meet my Savanna." Caroline moved back to her chair. "Would you like to join us in an evening claret?"

Aidan shook his head. "No, thank you. Nice to see you again, Savanna."

She smiled widely at him before she could stop herself. "We met yesterday, when I brought your poodles back," Savanna told Caroline.

"Oh, how nice! Is everything all right now with that box upstairs? I've got all the little wires on, I promise."

Dr. Gallager nodded. "I reset the transmitter and changed the frequency; it wasn't connecting at the other end."

"Thank you for taking care of that. See?" Caroline

nudged Savanna. "I told you I'm in good hands."

At that moment, movement caught Savanna's eye, and she turned to watch Eleanor's empty glass slide out of her hand, hit the floor, and shatter. Caroline and Savanna moved to help the woman, but Dr. Gallager made it to her chair first, kneeling beside her, one hand on her wrist.

Eleanor was slumping to one side, and Aidan gently eased her onto the floor, grabbing a pillow and placing it under her legs, his stethoscope at Eleanor's chest while he pulled a small flashlight from his breast pocket.

He briefly looked up at Savanna. "Call an ambulance."

Savanna's phone was already in hand.

Everything that happened next was a blur. Savanna escorted Caroline out of the room, the woman leaning heavily on her as the sirens approached. Two men and a woman dressed in the county medical response team navy blue uniforms entered through the front door, carrying a large duffel bag, two official-looking black cases, and a collapsible stretcher. Poor Eleanor must have suffered a heart attack or something sudden. She'd seemed fine until moments ago.

Caroline's house phone rang from the kitchen, startling Savanna. She looked at Caroline, but the older woman just shrugged, worry painting her features. Savanna went to the kitchen to answer it, surprised to hear Lauren on the other end.

"Hello? Er—Savanna?" Lauren sounded startled, confused. "You're still there? Is Grandmother all right?"

When Savanna filled her on Eleanor's sudden collapse, saying Dr. Gallager and paramedics were with her now,

Lauren hung up immediately, saying she was on her way.

Savanna sat with Caroline in the living room, waiting for Lauren to arrive. The trio of dogs followed them, spooked by the crash and upset. Duke was curled against Caroline's side, while Princess and Fonzie sat at her feet. Dogs could sense when something was wrong. Savanna could hear, faintly from the parlor, frantic activity and then quiet, the three attendants discussing among themselves and Dr. Gallager in low tones. She held Caroline's hand, neither of them speaking.

Savanna stared at the painting across from her until her eyes blurred. She blinked, hard, and again, trying to clear her vision: there was something wrong with the upper-left corner of the Laurant. The dark edge of the man's hairline was offset by the bright background, except for one spot. The area was discolored, appearing one-dimensional. Laurant took painstaking efforts to add depth and texture to his work using a chiaroscuro technique. Savanna rose and moved closer to the painting; it hung above Caroline's piano on the east wall, the frame perfectly complementing the deep mahogany of the well-preserved upright Baldwin. That abrupt change in the painting from dark to light was off, didn't fit with the rest of the portrait.

Or did it? Looking up at the piece from only a few feet away now, Savanna didn't see the discordant spot.

"Savanna?" Caroline's voice startled her from her musings. "Do you think... Should we try to go back in there?"

"No. Caroline, no. If there's anything to be done to help Eleanor, Dr. Gallager and his team in there will do it."

Savanna returned to the couch and held Caroline's hand, covering it with her other one. The Laurant across from her looked unremarkable. She was overtired, or stressed, or both, seeing things that weren't there.

Savanna could have hugged Lauren when she finally arrived. She was so out of her depth, and she had no idea how to handle things with Caroline if Eleanor wasn't all right. She rose, then sat. Then stood again, moving to the doorway. She should go try to help.

Before Savanna could get all the way down the dark hall to the parlor, Aidan appeared in the doorway. His suit jacket gone and shirtsleeves rolled up, Aidan's head was down as he took off his gloves. He ran a hand over the top of his head, leaving it at the back of his neck. He stood still for a long time before looking up to find Savanna watching him.

He silently shook his head.

Oh. Poor Eleanor. Poor Caroline. Savanna resumed walking and met him halfway.

"I have to tell her," he said, his voice low.

Savanna didn't have any words. What could she say? There was sweat on his brow and pain in his eyes. He looked...defeated. "I'm sorry," she said in a whisper. "Eleanor was in her eighties. You did everything you could to save her."

Aidan shook his head. "I just don't get it. I don't think it was her heart. The EKG didn't reflect that. I've never seen anything like it."

Savanna frowned. What was he saying?

"I don't know," he said, as if reading her mind. "But I

have to tell Caroline. The paramedics will take Eleanor out the back, and the medical examiner will call her family from the hospital."

Savanna watched him walk slowly to the living room.

Returning home to Sydney's that night, finally, near midnight, Savanna had never been so happy to see the cotton-candy-pink bedroom. She threw the bright yellow throw pillows on the floor, grabbed the unicorn-kitty stuffed animal Nolan had given her for safekeeping, and crawled into her cozy bed, pulling the comforter up over her head. Fonzie turned in circles until he'd settled himself tight against her legs. She dreamed of Caroline in her mural, on a sailboat, far out to sea on stormy waters.

Chapter Three

"NOT TOO MUCH," Harlan Shepherd cautioned. "You'll kill it if you overdo it."

Savanna hovered over a steaming casserole dish on the stove in her parents' kitchen. She added a little more honey Dijon to the dish, glancing at her dad before putting it back in the oven for the last few minutes.

"Like that?" She realized Holy Yum Baked Chicken might have been a bit too ambitious for her meager cooking skills. But she knew her dad would step in to help—it was her turn, after all, and she'd missed a decade's worth of turns.

Sunday dinners were Shepherd family tradition, with everyone alternating coming up with unique dishes. Sydney's choices tended to be vegan, organic, ultrahealthy meals; Skylar always found loopholes, making standard meat-and-potato fare but with a twist, like her Italian meatloaf last week; Charlotte, Savanna's mother, had declared long ago that she'd leave the cooking to her talented husband, and Harlan was famous for his knack with the grill. It was probably just an excuse to be outdoors, but nobody complained, as he came up with the most delicious, inimitable concoctions.

Savanna had used Google. She was out of practice with her family's tradition, but the Holy Yum Baked Chicken had looked delicious online. With the dish back in the oven now, she turned to the island countertop to finish frosting her brownies, her own specialty she could never screw up.

Out of nowhere, Nolan appeared, climbing up onto one of the stools. "We can have two desserts today?"

Savanna laughed. "Oh, boy, Nolan, I don't think so. We only have two desserts on Wednesdays, and only at Sydney's house."

He sighed, seeming to accept the explanation. He was such a sweet boy.

"But," she whispered, "you can be my taste tester, okay?" She cut a tiny corner out of the brownie pan, placing it on a napkin and letting it cool.

Skylar walked in with Travis just as Nolan popped the brownie in his mouth. "Bad influence." She scowled at Savanna. Even out of her business attire, dressed in jeans and a crisp pink button-down blouse, Skylar looked professional, like Casual Friday Barbie fresh out of the box.

"I don't know what you're talking about. Nolan is an important part of my kitchen team."

Skylar cracked a smile. "I'm sure." Her phone buzzed and she quickly swiped the screen to answer the call.

"Dinner's ready," Harlan said. He went around the polished concrete countertop and scooped up Nolan with one hand, tossing him over his shoulder as the little boy shrieked in delight. Her father stood six-two and still had the build of a linebacker at fifty-five. His thick, wavy brown hair had a hint of gray at the temples now, and his crow's feet were a little deeper than Savanna remembered, but Harlan Shepherd would always be the foundation of this family. He was the best man she knew.

They were seated around the table, passing a basket of rolls, when Skylar rejoined them, taking her seat next to her husband, Travis. Savanna hadn't spent much time around him yet, but Travis seemed like the perfect husband. He'd already set Nolan up with his plate, in his booster seat, and was tucking a napkin into the toddler's shirt. Travis and Skylar had met while working opposing sides on a commercial property case a few years ago. Travis was a civil engineer for a company in Muskegon, just north of Carson. He somehow worked his schedule around Skylar's, limiting the time Nolan had to spend with a sitter and handling most of the cooking.

Savanna thought she'd found the perfect partner in Rob, but she'd been wrong. She and Rob had been engaged for almost two years, and now, looking back, he was the reason they'd never set an actual date. Every time she'd brought it up, Rob had had another excuse to wait. Savanna was still mad at herself for not seeing the signs.

The only empty chair now was where Charlotte belonged. Their mother was due back tonight from Boston, but Savanna knew she didn't always have control over where and when her job took her.

"I thought Mom would be home by now," Sydney spoke up.

"She'll make it for dessert, don't worry," Harlan said.

The family dove in—Savanna's Holy Yum Baked Chicken was delicious, thanks to a silent assist from her dad. The sauce had turned out great, the perfect combination of spicy and sweet. Fresh asparagus, rice, garlic bread, and a dry, locally produced white wine complemented the meal.

"Savvy, you learned to cook in Chicago! This is so good," Syd said, reaching for another helping. Her silver bracelets jangled musically as she ladled the pasta onto her plate.

"Hey. I could always cook."

"You just hid it well," Skylar cracked.

Travis elbowed his wife. "Pot, meet kettle."

"What? I cook!"

Travis smirked and took another bite. "Okay then. This is really good."

Skylar rolled her eyes for the second time that night. "I *can* cook. You just usually beat me to it," she told Travis.

At that moment, the front door opened and snapped shut, and Charlotte appeared, breathless, in the dining room doorway. Her cheeks were flushed from the chill in the air. Her wavy auburn hair, the same color as Savanna's, was pulled up into a messy bun, tendrils spiraling down to brush the shoulders of her smart taupe suit, crisp white collar peeking out above the lapels. Harlan rose and went to her, taking her bags out of her hands. She hugged him, and Savanna watched her dad's arm remain around Charlotte's waist when she let go.

She looked up at him. "I told you I'd make it."

Savanna's dad planted a kiss on her. "Yes, you did." He smiled.

That was it, Savanna thought. That was what she wanted. A man who'd look at her like her dad looked at her mother—like, no matter what else was going on in his life, nothing was complete until she was back in his arms. Rob had never looked at her that way.

"Oh, my, honey," her mother exclaimed after her first bite. "This is quite a comeback act. Delicious."

"Mom," she said, "did you hear about what happened at Caroline's when I was there Friday?"

"Your father told me," Charlotte replied. "Poor Mrs. Pietila. And poor Caroline."

"Yes. She was so upset. I still don't know what happened."

"What do you mean? I thought she had a heart attack?"

Sydney shook her head. "I don't buy that. That woman walked her dog almost a full mile into town and back every single day. Her collie loved the doggie ice cream I've started making. Mrs. Pietila would come in and have some tea while she let Mr. Wags eat his ice cream. She always seemed totally fine. How could it have been her heart?"

"Dr. Gallager even thought something didn't add up with the way she died," Savanna added. One minute, Eleanor had been fine, looking up book titles, and the next minute she'd dropped her claret and was gone. Savanna had seen the shattered glass on the floor, Aidan at Eleanor's side... What if it was a reaction to the wine? She'd finished hers, but Savanna and Caroline hadn't touched theirs yet. No. That just didn't make sense.

Charlotte looked up from her plate. "Dr. Gallager was

there when it happened?"

"Yes, he came by to check on something with Caroline—did you know she has a heart monitor? Why has she not told us about that?"

Skylar spoke up. "She did. I knew about it. It's no big deal. Her doctor is just being cautious."

Sydney frowned at her older sister. "You knew the woman we think of as our grandmother had something going on with her heart, and you didn't think to tell the rest of us?"

Skylar's eyebrows went up. "Relax. She told me because she wanted to make sure her will was up to date."

"What?" Savanna couldn't keep her volume down. "Her will? And this heart monitor thing is no big deal? You can't keep that kind of thing from us, Skylar! Caroline is even older than Mrs. Pietila, who just died of a heart attack."

"Alleged heart attack," Sydney muttered.

Charlotte spoke up. "All right, girls, that's enough." Slight and petite, Charlotte didn't look intimidating. But as much as Harlan was the foundation, Charlotte was the ruling force, and all three sisters knew it. "Skylar was doing her job as Caroline's attorney. Caroline's health is privileged information, unless she chooses to tell us herself. Which she hasn't, which must mean that she isn't worried. Which means we shouldn't worry. And, Savanna, your imagination has always been overactive. Eleanor's obituary says she passed away due to heart disease; if her family is fine with that consensus, I'm sure that's what it was."

"You all need to remember that Caroline is tough," Harlan added. "And she's in very good hands if Dr. Gallager is looking after her."

Savanna shook her head. "Okay, who even is this guy? I keep hearing how amazing he is, but he's super young. Where did he come from? How does everyone know he's so great?"

"He's been running the practice in town for at least six or seven years," Harlan said. "I know because I built the addition when Dr. Milano sold it to him."

Skylar nodded. "He is good, Savanna. He's more than qualified to handle Caroline's health."

"He moved here so his wife would be closer to her family," Charlotte said. "When she passed two years ago, he stayed."

"Oh." Savanna was quiet. Dr. Gallager was a widower. She suddenly felt guilty for being so critical of him.

"You don't need to worry," Skylar said. "He's got great credentials, and he seems like a good guy. I helped him with some legal and financial matters after his wife died."

"He isn't dating anyone," Sydney said, her singsongy voice giving her away as she wiggled her eyebrows at Savanna.

"I don't think he's dated since losing Olivia, and we are not playing matchmaker," Charlotte said sternly to Sydney. "Savanna is just fine on her own for now."

Savanna's mother understood. She wasn't even a full month out from a crushing breakup with her fiancé. The last thing she needed was a new man.

Sydney sighed. "You guys are no fun at all."

"I am!" Nolan chimed in. "I'm fun at all! We can have

dessert now?"

The room erupted in laughter, and Savanna went to fetch the brownies. Nolan was so good at making the family lighten up. She carried over a tray of frosted chocolate chunk brownies along with a carton of French vanilla ice cream and a stack of bowls, giving Nolan a wink as she passed him. Every day presented one more reason Savanna was grateful to be back in Carson—today, Sunday night dinner and Nolan were two reasons. She'd happily compete with Sydney for the favorite aunt title.

MONDAY MORNINGS WERE different now that Savanna was heading four blocks away to the redbrick elementary school, rather than making the mad rush to the train in Chicago amid throngs of other commuters. The weather in Carson was perfect for the short walk from Sydney's house. She'd probably have to start driving when fall turned to winter, but for now she thoroughly enjoyed the crisp, sunny autumn air. She popped her earbuds in and hit play on the *Hamilton* musical cast recording; she had a constantly rotating playlist of Broadway soundtracks. She'd been in a *Hamilton* mood lately; before that, it had been *Mamma Mia!* nonstop.

She'd chosen a royal blue dress with a Peter Pan collar and A-line skirt today, her hair pinned back on one side to reveal small gold earrings. She'd almost never worn dresses in Chicago; attire at the museum was stuffy and masculine. The one time she'd tried to have a little fun with her wardrobe, wearing a red dress with a sparkling Santa Claus on the front last December, Rob had pulled her aside and asked what she thought she was doing. Her appearance promoted an unprofessional atmosphere, he'd said. Well, as an elementary art teacher, Savanna would wear whatever made her happy. Today, the swishy blue skirt and her matching embroidered flats did the job.

Savanna stopped in the teacher's lounge for coffee before heading to her classroom. The room was buzzing with gossip.

"Caroline Carson saw it happen?"

"No, I heard she wasn't even there. She found her that way!"

"Maybe it was a home invasion!"

"I heard there was broken glass everywhere."

"I heard paramedics had to break the door down to get in!"

"Did she die instantly?"

"My neighbor said she died on the way to the hospital."

"Are you sure it was Mrs. Pietila?"

"I heard she and Caroline Carson hated each other!"

Savanna quietly drifted to the back of the room and poured herself a coffee. What the heck?

"Shhh!"

"Hush," a whispered voice near Savanna spoke, and she turned, thinking they were all quieting because they'd noticed she'd arrived. How would they even know she was there at Caroline's when it had happened?

The cluster of six or seven teachers at the break table

were looking toward the door, where Jack Carson, Caroline's grandson, had just entered. Jack was the librarian; Savanna's classroom sat right next to the library.

"Morning," he addressed the group.

The room remained uncomfortably quiet as Jack joined Savanna at the counter, pulling his coffee mug from the hook over the sink. As he poured himself a cup, she read the caption on the mug, below the picture of a stack of multicolored books: *I like my coffee strong and my books long.*

He turned to face the room, steaming cup in one hand. A pair of glasses was tucked into the breast pocket of his pale blue button-down shirt, and he smelled of aftershave. He appeared tense; Savanna could see the muscle in his jaw pulsing as he contemplated the group. "My grandmother was with Mrs. Pietila when she died. They loved each other. They'd been friends since grade school. There was no home invasion, no foul play, no broken-down door. We believe it was a heart attack. Mrs. Pietila didn't suffer—though that doesn't seem to be what you're all worried about." He raised his eyebrows.

Savanna was instantly reminded of the one pitfall of living in a small town: everyone knew everyone else's business. Bad news traveled twice as fast as good and was almost always inaccurate. She watched Jack exit through the door of the lounge, hanging back in her spot against the counter. She wondered if she'd been part of the gossip before arriving, but this group seemed to have no idea she'd even witnessed the events of Friday night—probably a good thing. She figured someone here must have gotten a little misinformation from one of the responding medical team and had embellished the story from there.

Savanna didn't see Jack Carson the rest of the day until he handed off the after-school pick-up lane to her. She took the orange and yellow safety vest from him, dropping it over her head and waving a few cars through. Savanna stopped him as he was turning to head back into the school. "I was with your grandmother Friday when Mrs. Pietila died," she said. "I hope she's okay?"

He looked surprised. "You were?"

She nodded. "She has me doing a mural. We were going over details. It was pretty awful. Caroline was so upset."

"She's been through a lot lately. Losing my grandfather took its toll on her. And now her own medical issues are cropping up." Jack spoke haltingly, seeming uncomfortable with discussing the details of his grandmother's health.

Savanna frowned. "She mentioned that. She's always seemed so strong. I really hope she's all right." She and Jack didn't really know each other. He was Lauren's cousin, a few years her senior, and had gone away to school when Savanna was still young.

"Anyway," he said, "thank you for being there. I'm glad she wasn't alone when it happened."

Savanna shuddered. "Oh, yes. I'm glad too. She's very special to me and my sisters. I was supposed to start the mural tonight, but I think I'll wait until after the funeral."

"Good idea. She isn't quite herself. I'll be checking on her and so will Lauren."

"Give her my love, please. Let me know if there is anything I can do." She'd do anything to help Caroline.

"Will do," he said, heading back into the building.

Jack Carson was sure tough to read. Savanna watched him go, wondering if he meant to come off as abrupt as he did or if it was just how he typically interacted. Caroline had two children—Elizabeth and Thomas—seven grandchildren, and Savanna didn't know how many great-grandchildren. Jack was an only child and belonged to Caroline's daughter, Elizabeth; Lauren was one of six children. The entire family was involved in one way or another in Everett Carson's successful tri-state real estate development business, except for Jack, Savanna realized. She wondered what had led him into education instead. Savanna doubted she'd ever learn the story behind that decision. As nice as he was, the man seemed intensely guarded and private. But she was glad he'd defended Caroline and put a stop to the shallow school gossip.

Chapter Four

SAVANNA AND FONZIE arrived at Caroline's house promptly after school on Thursday. She'd offered to delay the mural, as Eleanor's funeral had been just yesterday, but Caroline wouldn't hear it.

Lauren ushered Savanna into what was, once again, a busy house. She heard the hum of an electric drill or sander close by and saw she was right when they passed the grand staircase: a large bearded man was near the top, a bucket of plaster on the step by his feet and a small electric sander in one hand. He paused, glancing down as he saw them and giving a funny little salute. He wore denim coveralls, marked with various paint colors from what must be years of use on projects like this one.

Lauren gestured up the stairs. "Savanna, this is Bill Lyle, Grandmother's neighbor. He's helping spruce things up around here for the party next month. Bill, this is Savanna, a friend of the family."

Savanna waved. "You do great work. It looks amazing so far!" The spindles on the main railing were in the process of being stained and refinished, and the ones that were done gleamed. The handrail was gone, leaving the length of the stairway looking strangely bare, and Bill was patching over nicks and holes in the wall.

He grinned, the corners of his eyes crinkling. "Thanks. The boss lady keeps a close eye on me."

"He means Maggie, his wife," Lauren murmured to Savanna, "not Grams."

She laughed. "I can't wait to see it all finished."

"We'll let you get back to work. Oh! And I'll unlock the garage for you in case you plan on working on the handrail today," Lauren called up the stairs. To Savanna, as they continued toward the parlor, she said, "Maggie heard we were having some work done and she volunteered her husband. I think it works out for them as well as it does for us. We know he'll do a good job, and Grams wouldn't accept his bid; she insists on paying more."

"Of course she does." Savanna smiled, remembering the ridiculous overpayment to Sydney for her poodles' grooming services.

Caroline rose from her chair, meeting Savanna halfway across the room with a hug. Fonzie and the poodles pranced around each other, reacquainting themselves from the other day.

Savanna drew back, looking at her. "How are you?"

"I'm fine. All of you need to stop worrying about me. Yesterday was very sad. I'll miss Eleanor terribly. We were lucky to have had such a long-lasting friendship. But this is part of life. Now, I want to see what you can bring out of that boring space." She gestured at the bare wall, Savanna's canvas. The large ornate mirror and buffet table that had previously adorned the wall were now temporarily stored in the hallway for Bill to take out to the garage.

Savanna shook her head, rolling her eyes at the woman. Always pragmatic, always irreverent. "All right. I'm glad to see you're fine."

She kissed Caroline on the cheek and dropped her huge, heavy bag of supplies in the corner, getting to work laying out a large, worn, paint-spattered drop cloth along the wall. She pulled paints, brushes, pans, and palettes and more from the bag; once everything was set up, she turned to find Caroline sipping tea in her wingback chair, observing. Princess had wedged herself into the little space next to her, and Duke was curled at her feet.

"Don't mind me," Caroline said. "I'm just fascinated. I never possessed an ounce of artistic talent. Would you like me to leave? I can go, if you feel uncomfortable."

Oh, boy. Savanna was not about to tell Caroline to leave her own parlor. "Nope, you're fine! But...I normally have music on. Do you mind?" She held up her phone with earbuds plugged in.

"My goodness, no. I would never interfere with your process." Caroline waved a hand at her, turning toward the lake out the window and pointedly holding a book in front her face. "Pretend I'm not here."

Savanna laughed, choosing the *Dear Evan Hansen* original cast recording in her playlist and pouring her base coat into the pan. She saw Fonzie climb into a corner of her large, empty carrying bag, turning in one circle after another, until he settled in and closed his eyes. He was used to this now; he kept her company at Sydney's when she was painting.

When Savanna finally set down her brush, she realized the room was now brightly lit from ceiling lamps, and night had fallen outside. The world seemed to disappear when she was really immersed in a project, and so far, she was loving this one. The lower wall was primed, and she'd done the pale blue trim along the bottom, and then had sketched lightly in charcoal, laying the groundwork for the seascape, the waves, and two sailboats dotting the horizon.

She turned, half expecting to find Caroline still watching her. The room was empty—how much time had passed? Even Fonzie had deserted her. Someone, probably Lauren, had left a plate of little sandwiches and a glass of lemonade on the side table near her bag. Savanna checked her phone, pulling the earbuds out and wrapping them up. It was almost eight p.m.! She grabbed a sandwich, ravenous, and gulped down the lemonade. She left her supplies, wanting to find Caroline and ask about a ladder for next time before she headed home.

It was oddly quiet as Savanna wandered toward the front of the house. She saw that Bill Lyle was gone for the day, his tools and supplies stacked neatly near the top of the staircase. The mirror and table were cleared out of the hallway. The landscapers who'd been working outside when she'd arrived earlier were all gone now. Caroline certainly had efficient help.

Lauren was out front with the dogs, Savanna saw through the living room window. Fonzie leaped back and forth between the poodles, and she could see they were already great friends.

"Caroline?" She felt strange walking through the house alone. She must be here somewhere. Savanna found her in the dining room with a compact, well-dressed gentleman.

"Savanna!" Caroline held an arm out, beckoning her in. "Here she is, my own personal fine art expert! Felix, this is Savanna Shepherd, my granddaughter in spirit. Savanna, meet Felix Thiebold, gallerist." Caroline beamed at them both.

Felix took Savanna's extended hand, shaking it and then not letting go. He was quite handsome, sharply dressed in a three-piece suit, even on this warm Thursday evening. Silver hair was combed back, and he wore a tasteful silver mustache. Savanna guessed him to be in his sixties. "Caroline speaks highly of you," he said. "I understand you came from the Kenilworth Museum in Chicago?"

"Yes, you know it?" Stupid question, Savanna thought. Everyone knew Kenilworth. Rob's family made certain the museum was known internationally.

"Of course. Impressive, I must say. I helped broker a deal for Kenilworth a few years ago, procuring a Renoir from a private party in Paris. Your curator was lovely to work with."

Kenilworth's curator was Savanna's would-be sister-in-law. A pang hit her. Sometimes the world was too small. She'd loved Rob's family. She remembered the Renoir deal. The name Thiebold had jogged her memory, and now she knew why—Felix Thiebold was quite a well-known gallerist in the art world.

"Felix was one of Everett's closest friends," Caroline spoke up. "He helped us add some stunning work to our collection. With Everett gone, I'm hoping to find new homes for several of the pieces. I put calls in to Felix and a couple of the other gallerists who brokered deals for us. You've been so generous with your time," she said to Felix. "I so appreciate your help."

"I still can't talk you out of it, I suppose? The beauty in the pieces Everett chose is timeless, exquisite. You might find you miss them once they're gone."

Caroline sighed. "Yes, I know I will. Though, at some point, one just doesn't have quite the need for such abundance." She glanced at Savanna. "I'm liquidating some of the collection to spare my family the hassle. I am nearly ninety after all."

"Caroline, you'll be around another decade at least," Savanna said firmly. "But…what about the Minkov? In the library? You aren't selling that one, are you?"

"I don't think so. That was one of Everett's favorites. It seems to be yours, as well." She paused. "How is the mural coming? You've been at it for hours! I've commissioned Savanna for an original piece in the parlor," Caroline told Felix, pride in her voice.

Savanna blushed. "I've only just started. Oh," she remembered, "do you think Mr. Lyle would bring a ladder in for me from your garage? That ceiling must be eighteen or twenty feet."

"I'll put it on his list. He's indispensable lately. As is this gentleman." Caroline patted Felix's arm fondly.

"I should let you two have the evening," Felix said. "I'll have Ryan stop by next weekend to pick up the Laurant we discussed. We'll get things taken care of, no worries." He kissed Caroline on the cheek and took Savanna's hand once more. "It was delightful to meet you, Savanna."

Once he was gone, Caroline turned to Savanna, eyes sparkling. "Isn't he a gem? Every time I see him, it almost makes me feel like Mr. Carson is still here."

Savanna nodded. "I can certainly understand that. You're blessed with such good friends and family, Caroline."

"That I am."

They made their way back to the parlor. The front door snapped open and shut, and the three dogs skittered into the room, yipping and tackling each other.

"Savanna," Caroline said, picking up a jeweled change purse from the table near her chair, "I'm hoping you won't mind...when you see your sister next, could you pick up more of those little treats for my Princess and Duke? Sydney knows which ones."

Savanna promised to bring the treats Saturday morning when she returned. She and her sisters were meeting for lunch the next day at Fancy Tails and Treats, so it'd be an easy task.

ON FRIDAY, SAVANNA claimed the big overstuffed chair in the corner of Sydney's boutique before Skylar arrived. Syd was finishing a sale at the counter. She had a knack for this, chatting with her patrons, making each of them feel important and valued. Her long red hair was loose today, and

Savanna spotted narrow braids here and there interwoven with brightly colored macramé thread. Syd followed the customer to the door, bidding him goodbye, and then slid the Open sign out of its slotted frame, replacing it with her lunchtime sign, a cartoon of a big, drooling St. Bernard with the words: *Never trust a dog to watch your food. We don't! Closed for lunch.*

Savanna handed Sydney the cash Caroline had forced on her and tucked the bag of organic dog biscuits into her purse so she'd have it tomorrow for the poodles. "You've got every dog in town addicted to these things." Savanna laughed. "Aren't they, like, kale and green beans and tofu or something? How do you even get them to eat that stuff?"

"Hey, don't make fun of my talent. I'm keeping Carson's dogs healthy! And they love it." She opened a doggie ice cream cup and set it on the floor for Fonzie. "See?"

Savanna was grateful that Sydney let her little Boston terrier hang out at the shop all day. This life was so different for him than Chicago, where his sad little face would tug at her heart each morning while running out to work and he'd be waiting at the door each night when she returned. Now he had people to greet and other dogs to boss around and endless treats as payment for his hard work.

The bell over the door jingled as Skylar arrived, bearing a large brown paper bag from the deli, just two blocks down, next to her office. She deposited it on the table where her sisters sat, unpacking sandwiches, freshly baked potato chips, three large chocolate chip cookies, and three bottles of Mary Ann's soda—ginger beer flavor for herself, strawberry for

Savanna, and cranberry for Sydney.

"Oh, wow, I missed this." Savanna set the bottle down after a long swallow. "This is such a Michigan drink. And I swear, that deli makes the best club sandwiches."

"No blueberry today?" Sydney frowned at Skylar, peering at her bottle of pop.

"Nope, sorry," Skylar said. The artisanal, seasonal soda company distributed out of Detroit, and the deli's supply was always changing.

"Well, this is just as good." Sydney smacked her lips.

The three of them fell quiet as they dug in. Savanna was on her lunch hour, which was actually only forty-five minutes. She forced herself to slow down. She still had plenty of time, and it was only a five-minute walk back to school.

Sydney spoke around a mouthful of ham on rye, telling them about her date tonight. He was a fireman, blond, tough, but with the biggest sweet tooth, just like Sydney. This was to be their first date, although they'd been flirting every morning at the coffee shop. Savanna laughed; while Syd was on her date with her fireman, she would be in the middle of her school's two-hour Open House fair, surrounded by kids and parents. Skylar confessed she couldn't wait to cuddle up with Travis on the couch for an *NCIS* marathon later tonight.

"So," Skylar said, setting her sandwich down. "You guys were such freaks about Eleanor Pietila's death, I decided to see what I could find out. You know, to prove you wrong."

"What did you find? How did you even get any information? Did you use secret lawyer resources?" Savanna leaned forward, elbows on the little round table.

"I have ways. Listen, I'm not ever going to do anything shady based on one of your hunches, you know that, right? You aren't Nancy Drew."

Savanna sat back, crossing her arms and glaring at her older sister. "Very funny. I'm not a kid anymore, even if you still want to treat me like one, Skylar. I wouldn't have said a word about how she died, but it was strange. Even Caroline's doctor thought so."

Skylar put her hands up defensively. "I know! That's why I kept thinking about it. Sheesh." She looked at Sydney, as if for help. "I'm trying to say, I think maybe you were right. Something is weird about the way she died."

Savanna was still pouting. Just because she'd grown up devouring every mystery she could get her hands on, just because she was always fascinated with what wasn't easily seen, just because she'd made a living off of looking for hidden signs that could betray the truth in works of art, didn't mean she was irrational. Sometimes Skylar could be her greatest ally, but sometimes she could be an annoyingly arrogant big sister.

Sydney intervened. "Knock it off, you guys. Thank you, Skylar, for checking into it. You're seriously awesome. What did you find?"

"Suck-up," Savanna muttered.

Sydney kicked Savanna's foot under the table, making her jump. Syd wore sturdy boots to work with the dogs. Savanna had ballet flats on. "What did you find? And be nice."

Savanna stuck her tongue out at Sydney.

"The only reason I can tell you this is because death certificates are public record. Just so you know," Skylar clarified. "I had to go through Eleanor's will with her son, who's the executor, and on the death certificate—which still has to be filed, since some of the autopsy items are pending—they have 'sudden cardiac death' listed as cause of death. That's not a heart attack. And I can tell you, Eleanor's son is a mess. He says she never had any trouble with her heart. Even her cholesterol and blood pressure values were great. She had an EKG last year as part of her physical, and everything was perfect. He confirmed what you said, Syd, that Eleanor walked nearly a mile every day. So it's definitely weird that her heart would suddenly stop beating, without her having an arrhythmia or being electrocuted or something."

Savanna sat back, mind spinning. "Well, we were all right there. She wasn't electrocuted. She was fine, and then she wasn't."

"Maybe something will come of it, since you said Dr. Gallager also felt like the way she died was odd," Skylar said.

Savanna pushed her chocolate chip cookie across the table to Skylar. "I officially apologize for being a brat. You're impressive. I can't believe you were able to find all that out."

Sydney picked up the cookie and took a bite. "What? I already ate mine. So, what does this mean?"

Skylar took the cookie out of Sydney's hand. "Mom should teach you how to share. I don't know what it all means, except it doesn't seem like she died of a heart attack. There's no way of knowing what she actually died from. It doesn't really matter—she was in a good place, with friends, happy I'd assume. Knowing that maybe the death certificate is wrong doesn't change anything."

Skylar was right. Savanna felt deflated, and she wasn't even sure why.

Sydney shrugged, shaking her head. "Poor Eleanor."

"Poor Eleanor," Savanna agreed.

Chapter Five

WHY WERE THERE so many different types of crackers? Savanna stood studying the multitude of flavors and brands in aisle seven at Happy Family. She put the bright orange box of cheddar flavor back on the shelf and instead grabbed the triangle-shaped sea salt crackers. And then a second box. And then, thinking better of it, put that one back on the shelf and selected one of the sun-dried tomato variety to add to her cart.

She knew it wasn't about crackers. Tonight was her very first school open house, in her very first teaching job. With all of her experience at Kenilworth in Chicago, her fine art degree, even her respectable age of thirty, she shouldn't feel so nervous.

But. She was a newbie, the most recent addition to her school. She had no track record. Parents in this town talked; they knew each other, and most knew the teachers. Give her a classroom of eight-year-olds any day—in fact, give her five classrooms of little kids every day of the week, as she current-ly was responsible for the art education of 284 children—and she was just fine. But the thought of spending two hours tonight waiting for parents to enter her classroom and find out she was a rookie? Savanna shook her head, trying to dissipate her anxiety. Jack Carson had assured her these open houses were easy. They were mainly a way to welcome families back to school for the year and allow parents to see where their kids would be spending their time. Raffle baskets and bake sale tables had already been set up in the gym, Savanna's classroom was decorated with the paintings her students had done the first week of school, and Jack would be on the other side of her classroom wall, running the book fair, just in case she needed anything. Okay. She could handle this.

She put all three boxes of crackers back on the shelf. The school had advised against teachers buying their own snacks and goodies to offer anyway, as there would be a four-dollar pizza or hot dog dinner in the cafeteria. Savanna was looking for something to make her room a little more inviting, but crackers were lame. They'd just sit out and get stale. She rounded the corner into the candy aisle, spotting packages of miniature chocolate bars. Sure, why not?

And fruit, Savanna thought. To balance the chocolate; couldn't have only unhealthy snacks. Armed with two bags of shiny red apples and one large bag of assorted flavors of minis, she was heading toward checkout when she caught a familiar name: Mrs. Carson.

She stopped, halfway down the paper goods aisle, near the remote-order pick-up area. Voices drifted over the top of the wall of paper toweling to her.

"She let that granddaughter take over, and she forgets to tip me half the time. I should still be running our diner. I would be, if it weren't for her rotten husband. Everett

Carson cost me everything. And now I'm the one who has to bring her groceries? I've just about had it, I'm telling you."

Savanna stood rooted to the spot. What in the world?

"Listen"—now a different, higher female voice—"I get it. I loved your diner, Amber. You guys had the best omelets in Carson. Are you wishing you didn't sell to him?"

"We shouldn't have. I wish old man Carson never made Roy the offer!"

"But...I thought you were going under. Isn't that why you sold when you had the chance?"

Savanna heard a frustrated groan. "We would have pulled out of the slump. The whole deal just made Roy spiral out of control."

"I'm sorry, honey. You've had an awful year. Losing your house is just the worst thing I can imagine! I know Roy would hate to see you so miserable."

"Yeah, well, he can't see me at all from jail, can he? He never meant for all of this to happen; none of it was his fault. It's Carson Realty's fault. I'm sure none of the Carsons even care what happened to us."

Savanna became aware of another cart in her peripheral vision. Embarrassed to be caught obviously eavesdropping, Savanna quickly scooted her cart to one side and turned toward the paper plates, picking up two packages and trying to look deeply involved in her price comparison.

As the shopper passed her, Savanna caught the tail end of what Amber was saying. "—doesn't matter now anyway. She'd better realize, what goes around, comes around, you know?"

There was some sort of murmured reply from the other woman.

That had to be the grocery delivery person Savanna had seen at Caroline's the other day...the day Eleanor had died. What on earth had happened that she hated the late Everett Carson so much? Savanna knew he'd been a shrewd businessman, but the Everett she remembered was boisterous, fair, and kind.

In the silence from the other side of the paper products, Savanna moved into the checkout line. She wasn't sure what she'd just heard. She turned and spied the delivery woman—Amber—in her green Happy Family apron and cap, loading a portable cart with groceries. The woman helping her was younger, around twenty or so. Her Happy Family apron was orange, like the person behind the remote-order counter. They weren't talking anymore; Amber loaded each bag with quick, jerky movements, frowning, visibly angry.

"Ma'am?"

The clerk pulled Savanna's attention back to the checkout. "I'm sorry," she murmured, swiping her card for her apples and candy, and the plates she hadn't meant to bring with her to the counter.

The conversation stayed with Savanna as she fussed over the candy bowl and basket of apples in her classroom. She felt sad for that woman, Amber. From the little she'd heard, she couldn't see how Everett Carson had caused Amber's life to fall apart. It seemed like Amber's husband was responsible for their hardships and had landed in jail because of it. But Savanna knew that blame wasn't always placed where it belonged. Amber had sounded furious at Carson Realty. She'd have to subtly try to get an idea of what Lauren thought of Amber...or see if Syd or Skylar knew anything about Amber and her husband. She didn't even know the woman's last name. But she was betting one of her sisters would be able to figure it out.

Fortunately, she was forced to push the odd overheard comments to the back of her mind as the first parents entered her room. With so many students, she didn't know them all by name, but she'd been studying the nametag photos she'd attached to each child's artwork folder, and she knew this was Parker, accompanied by both his parents. She went to welcome them, smiling as Parker led them over to his painting strung on the wall. Savanna found his folder and joined them, handing them Parker's self-portrait, a template of a person on a blank piece of paper that each child had filled in and decorated however they imagined themselves, complete with any glued on, sparkly, bright-colored, interestingly textured items they could find in the cubbies she kept filled with such things. Parker and his parents served to break the ice for Savanna; as the next few sets of people drifted in and out, her enthusiasm for the projects she'd planned this year eclipsed any nervousness still left.

Savanna's sweet, jovial principal made rounds throughout the evening, greeting parents and checking on teachers. Mr. Clay was awesome. He even brought Savanna a fresh cup of coffee halfway through, telling her to hang in there. He'd been the one to hire her, sitting across from her at his desk he'd probably inhabited for the last forty years and agreeing that even though she was inexperienced, she'd give the children a fantastic art education this year.

Nearly two hours later, Savanna was able to laugh at her own nerves; the evening had gone fine. It was so interesting meeting the families of her students, hearing about which one had an uncle who was an amazing painter or a grandmother who designed her own jewelry, and seeing the more relaxed, after-hours personalities of some of the kids. She'd even reacquainted with a few of her former classmates and friends, an odd sensation seeing them over a decade later, and now as parents of her students.

Jack Carson popped in, leaning in her doorway holding his coffee cup. He wore a tan sports coat tonight with his usual khakis and button-down, and a tie with books running the length of it. Savanna briefly imagined a closet full of nothing but khakis and ties with literary references; he seemed to wear almost the same thing every day. Jack's short sandy-brown hair was perpetually messy, but it looked good on him. "So," he said, "not as bad as you expected?"

"Not at all. Just a repeat of first-day jitters, I guess. It was actually kind of fun!"

"If you think this is fun, wait until parent-teacher conferences next month. We have it a little nicer than the K through fivers though. At least with the noncore classes, I don't end up getting kids grounded for skipping their math homework." Jack taught an intro to computer class to every third, fourth, and fifth grader at Carson Elementary.

"Definitely. I can see the perks of not teaching core," she said, though part of her envied the close relationship some of the kids seemed to have with their classroom teachers. Since starting this job, she'd been pleasantly surprised to learn that she loved working with children.

"You can probably start closing up," he told her. "Things are winding down."

Savanna moved about her classroom, turning chairs upside down on desktops for the custodial staff. She couldn't wait to get home and shed the heeled suede ankle boots she'd chosen for today. She never wore heels, but the cropped slim black pants and tailored blazer didn't look as good with anything else. "The price of beauty," Sydney had said, voicing her approval at Savanna's ensemble that morning before work, adjusting her aqua infinity scarf for her.

Price of beauty, my eye, Savanna thought. Her feet were killing her. She either needed to wear hip, trendy shoes more often to get used to them, or only wear ballet-flat appropriate outfits.

"I think we're a little late."

Savanna spun around at the deep voice behind her, startled; Jack's classical music through the wall had stopped, and the hallways were quiet. She'd thought she was alone. The last person she expected to see in her doorway was Dr. Aidan Gallager.

And Mollie...Gallager. Of course, Mollie Gallager. The little girl held tight to Aidan's hand, half hidden behind his tall frame. Sheesh, how had that slipped right by her? Mollie Gallager was in one of her first-grade classes. She should have made the connection. But it had never occurred to her that Aidan could be a dad.

Aidan looked as startled as Savanna felt. "Mrs. Shepherd," he said, glancing down at the classroom guide in his hand.

"Ms.," she automatically corrected. "I mean, Savanna." She laughed. "Um, I mean Ms. Shepherd." She smiled at Mollie by his side. Aidan looked somehow different tonight than the doctor she'd met at Caroline's house last week. His suit and tie were now replaced with dark denim jeans, a blue John Varvatos button-down with sleeves rolled up, and brown oxfords.

Aidan laughed with her. "Well, I'm a little behind on my parenting points. I'm not sure how I didn't know the name of my daughter's art teacher until just now."

Savanna smiled at the girl. Though it was only the second week of school, she did know Mollie Gallager. The child was sweet, and so quiet and shy that Savanna always spent at least a few minutes each class period working one-on-one with her, trying to make her more comfortable. So far, the girl had warmed up a bit, but Savanna noticed a little stutter every time Mollie spoke. "Would you like to show your dad your painting?"

Following Mollie to her artwork displayed near her desk, Savanna couldn't help doing the math in her head; Mollie would have been just four years old or so when she'd lost her mother. Savanna couldn't begin to imagine what Mollie and Aidan had been through.

"Mollie is my best sculptor," Savanna said. She moved to her desk and returned with a tiny clay bunny. Mollie had shaped it the first day of class and had left it stacked on her pile of clay when the children had filed out to their regular classroom. Savanna had set it aside to give her when she returned, but Mollie had shrugged and pushed it back into Savanna's hand to keep. The bunny now sat next to the stapler on Savanna's desk. It was two inches high with perfectly formed ears and a tail. Mollie had even used one of the toothpicks to create whiskers. Savanna loved it.

She motioned for Aidan and Mollie to take a seat at the nearby table and placed the bunny in Aidan's open palm.

Aidan examined it. "You made this, Mol?"

The girl nodded at her dad.

"What's his name?"

"She's a girl, not a boy!" Mollie's voice was loud and clear, something Savanna had never heard from the girl before.

"I'm so sorry, ma'am!" Aidan addressed the rabbit in his hand. "Of course I know you're a girl. I was just testing my daughter here," he explained to the clay figure.

Mollie was squinting at him. A few long strands of wispy strawberry-blond hair had come loose from her bluebird barrette, and she brushed them back off her forehead impatiently. "Daddy, she can't hear you."

He glanced sideways at her. "Are you sure about that? Her ears are e-*nor*-mous."

Mollie giggled, a high-pitched, lovely sound. "She can only hear me, Daddy. Her name is Mrs. FluffyPants."

Savanna was amazed. She'd never seen this side of the girl during school.

Aidan laughed. "That is a very respectable name. Does

she like living here on Ms. Shepherd's desk?"

"Yes, she has to stay here."

Both Aidan and Savanna raised their eyebrows at that. Savanna started to protest—Mollie could take her bunny home anytime she liked. But Aidan spoke first.

"Why is that? Why does she have to stay?"

Mollie leaned over and whispered in her dad's ear, Savanna watching curiously.

He sat back, stretching and crossing one long leg over the other, obviously uncomfortable in the small chair; Savanna caught a flash of rainbow-colored fabric between the hem of his jeans and his shoes, and then he smoothed the denim and it disappeared. The idea of this well-dressed man wearing some type of bright, silly socks made Savanna smile to herself.

Aidan glanced at his daughter before meeting Savanna's eyes. "It all makes sense now." He placed the bunny back in Savanna's hand, his fingertips brushing her skin. "Mrs. FluffyPants has to stay here so you don't get scared at night when all the kids go home."

Savanna remembered being Mollie's age and thinking all teachers lived at the school. "Makes perfect sense," she said. "Mollie, if Mrs. FluffyPants ever wants to take a little vacation at your house, that would be fine with me. Okay?"

"Okay," she said. "But not tonight."

There was absolutely no trace of any stutter this entire conversation, Savanna noticed. The minds of children. She had no idea there was so much going on in there.

"We should let you get home," Aidan said. "I'm sure

you've had a long day. I'm sorry we were late."

"It's no problem," she said. "I'm glad to see you. I mean, I'm glad you both made it. Before I left." Savanna looked up at him. She was beginning to have trouble meeting those intense blue eyes. They crinkled at the corners as he smiled at her, making her look away, her cheeks warm.

"It was great to see you again, Savanna," Aidan said, then corrected himself. "Ms. Shepherd." He took her hand in both of his. "Thank you for all you do for Mollie. She likes you a lot."

Savanna's cheeks burned. From the compliment, she told herself, not the contact. She forced herself to meet his gaze and felt her heartbeat race. *Stop it, Savanna,* she thought. She would not nurture a silly crush on this man, not after just being dumped by a man she'd thought she'd marry, and especially not on the father of one of her students.

That night at Sydney's house, Savanna couldn't sleep. She turned from one side to the other in the twin bed in her cotton-candy-pink bedroom. Fonzie kept repositioning as she tossed and turned, finally giving up and opting for his dog bed instead. She stretched out, forcing her eyes to stay closed, but her brain wouldn't shut off. It was too hot in here. Savanna got up and opened the window, flipping the switch for the ceiling fan before climbing back into bed. It was already past midnight. She'd told Caroline she'd be there at nine a.m. sharp to continue working on the mural. Now, still wide awake, she wished she'd left time to sleep in. The red digital numbers on the clock next to the bed mocked her.

12:49

1:34

2:16

She was going to be so tired tomorrow. She squeezed her eyes shut, determined not to watch the clock. It was the coffee, darn Mr. Clay and his hospitality. She knew better than to drink coffee at night. It had to be the coffee.

Chapter Six

SAVANNA WAS HIGH up on scaffolding in Caroline's parlor by ten the next morning. She hadn't needed the ladder after all; she'd woken up that morning with a better idea. She'd caught her dad about to hit the golf course and convinced him to accompany her to Caroline's first and bring scaffolding from his supplies. Savanna had helped Harlan with the quick setup, which would now easily allow her to work on the entire wall.

Caroline had insisted on serving Savanna and her dad coffee and freshly baked muffins before letting Harlan leave. Savanna couldn't refuse, despite having just thrown together scrambled eggs and bacon for herself and Sydney an hour earlier.

"Oh, wow, these are good," she'd commented around a mouthful of muffin. "Did Lauren make them?"

Caroline had looked surprised, pushing the plate of blueberry muffins across the kitchen table to Harlan. "I made them. Lauren doesn't handle everything around here. I've still got all my marbles."

"Of course! I guess I just assumed... I thought she came every day to help out."

"She has her own affairs to manage too; I don't want her

to get too frazzled. I told her I would be fine for the weekend." Savanna had remembered Lauren's fatigued attitude the evening Eleanor died; she was sure the woman needed a break.

Harlan had finished his cup of coffee and sat back. "Thanks for that, Caroline. We'd love to have you for dinner sometime. It's been too long. Charlotte's going to call you."

Savanna's dad had left with an overloaded plate of muffins, leaning down to plant a kiss on Caroline's cheek. He'd called back over his shoulder, "Watch yourself on that platform, little girl. No more superhero leaps."

She'd rolled her eyes. "Oh my God, Dad, I'm not six anymore. I can handle it."

Her family would never let her forget her Wonder Woman obsession, and the time she'd jumped out of her tree house, fresh off watching a Saturday morning *Justice League* marathon. She'd been convinced she could do it; she'd even had a pinned-on cape for good measure. The broken arm she'd sustained hadn't been nearly as bad as the two decades of razzing.

Fonzie was again curled up, half in and half out of Savanna's huge canvas art supply tote, near the base of the scaffolding. She could hear him snoring while she worked on the skyline near the ceiling. She thought of her music and earbuds, way down in the bag, but the windows were open, bringing in a nice breeze and the distant sound of waves—a different kind of music.

Time always ran away from Savanna when she was painting. She was jolted back to reality by voices coming from outside: a woman's high-pitched, shrill voice, undercut with lower tones, an argument from the sound of it. Curious, Savanna moved to the other side of the platform, where she could see through the windows to the wide lower deck at the back of the house. She recognized Bill, the handyman she'd met the other day, standing at the railing with his back to her. She was too high up to spot the woman he was talking with.

Bill jerked his cap off and slapped it against his leg, obviously aggravated. "I took care of it! What do you want from me, Maggie?"

Savanna wiped her paint-spattered hands on faded, paint-spattered jeans and climbed down the scaffolding, looking around for Caroline. She'd started out in her usual spot, her wingback chair, observing Savanna's work, but she was gone. Duke and Princess had migrated to the sun spot on the floor in front of the windows, where Savanna now stood. She saw Maggie Lyle, at the far side of the wide property. She vaguely recognized Caroline's neighbor; it had been so many years.

Savanna stood sideways, half behind the curtain, watching, not wanting to be caught eavesdropping. The couple's voices carried as they argued.

"You know what I want! You can't ever do anything right!"

Bill threw his hands up, putting his cap back on. "That's it. I'm trying to work here. Quit badgering me! Go home!"

"I am home," she shouted back at him, and Savanna saw her take a few steps back, onto the easement that separated their lot from Caroline's.

Bill whipped around in a huff, his face in a scowl as he stormed toward the house. The kitchen entrance sat just off the parlor; he'd see that Savanna was spying. She scurried over to her painter's bag, disturbing Fonzie, and pulled out a new palette, three pint-size paint cans, and a small box of paintbrushes. She set to work mixing the colors she wanted as she heard Bill come in the kitchen door and head through to the front of the house.

She straightened up, about to climb back up on the scaffolding, as the doorbell rang. Savanna waited, thinking Caroline would get it. When it rang again, she moved through the hallway and past the stairway. Bill was around the other side of the wall, kneeling on the floor and removing the molding one nail at a time. Painstaking work.

"Should I get it?" she stopped to ask him.

"Oh! Sure, I guess. Where's Lauren?"

Savanna shrugged. "Not here today." She continued on to the front entrance and was surprised to find Sydney, arms full with a large brown paper bag and a bottle of lemonade.

"I thought you might be hungry." She smiled. "Where's Caroline?"

"I have no idea. Come on in." Savanna led her toward the kitchen, Sydney stopping at the staircase.

"Oh, hey, Bill," Sydney said. "Would you like some?" She held up the lemonade. "Or some salad? I've got plenty."

"How about just the lemonade? Maggie'll kill me if I ruin my dinner."

Sydney laughed. "Okay, don't want to get you in trouble!"

Savanna found a note from Caroline on the kitchen counter. She held it up for Sydney. "She's crazy. This says she's out looking at new rugs for the foyer for her party. And that there's a Happy Family delivery coming today, Bill will be in and out, and Felix's assistant might stop by for a painting."

"Who?"

"Her art dealer. But I think it's just been Bill so far." Savanna had been absorbed in her work for a good four hours; it was past two now. She'd only heard Bill and Maggie because they'd been shouting at each other.

"Caroline's unbelievable. She never slows down!" Sydney moved around the kitchen, obviously just as comfortable in Caroline's house now as she was when they were kids. She pulled three glasses from the cupboard, pouring and handing one to Savanna. "Here, can you give this to Bill, and I'll set up our salads?"

The handyman was at the entrance to the front room now, still on the floor, a collection of tiny nails in a small cup beside him. Caroline was apparently replacing the chipped and time-worn molding. Savanna set the lemonade on the floor next to him. The wide grand staircase was now finished, Savanna had noticed this morning, the long, curved handrail back on and gleaming.

"The stairway looks beautiful," she told him.

"Thanks," he said. "Just finished it last night."

Savanna joined Sydney at the kitchen counter. "I want to hear about your date. The fireman? How did it go?"

Sydney tipped her head to one side and then the other. "Great! Brad is super fun. He's taking me out on his boat tomorrow. Oh, hey, want me to see if he has a friend? I could set you up."

Savanna laughed. "That's okay, I'm good."

Sydney groaned at her sister. "You can't mourn Rob forever, you know."

"I'm not mourning anything!" Savanna said defensively. "I need a little time. I'm not sad we broke up. I know now that there was something missing."

"Chemistry," Sydney said, swallowing a bite of her salad. "He was a snoozefest."

Savanna laughed. "You only met him once. But okay."

Syd set her fork down and stared at Savanna. "Come on. You're telling me you were happy? Rob set your soul on fire?"

"Rob was controlling and unreliable. Our issues had nothing to do with chemistry."

"Because there was none."

"Syd, chemistry is overrated. It wears off. It's not what matters."

"Okay, I have to respectfully disagree. Chemistry is the spark that keeps the flame burning in the long run. Even after kids and bills and years together. Look at Mom and Dad. You think they don't have chemistry?"

"Ew. Do we have to go there?"

"I'm just saying. The week I stayed with you and Rob in Chicago, anyone could have mistaken you for good friends. Or maybe cousins."

"Ew!" Savanna laughed. "Gross! I'm trying to eat!"

"I'm just glad he called it off. You deserve better." She reached across the counter and squeezed Savanna's arm. "Like, 'hot fireman' better."

Savanna rolled her eyes at Sydney.

"Okay, okay. I'll drop it. But when you're ready, let me know. I have connections."

"I know you do." Savanna chuckled, taking one last bite of her salad and then going to the sink to rinse the plate.

"Where's Lauren today?"

"Right? So it's not just me? She's always here. Caroline said she sent her home for the weekend. She's worried about overworking her."

"Huh."

Bill Lyle walked through the kitchen, weighted-down tool bag slung over one shoulder. "All set for today. Could you tell Mrs. Carson I'll be back on Monday with the new molding?"

"Sure." Savanna said, thinking he didn't look too thrilled to be heading home, but it could be her imagination.

She and Sydney ate in silence. Savanna poured them each more lemonade. Her sister had her thinking about the chemistry—or lack thereof—in her relationship with Rob over those five years. The more time that passed since leaving Chicago, the more Savanna could see how wrong she and Rob had been for each other. Why had she believed they were a good match? Maybe she'd tried too hard to believe it. She'd always wanted what her parents had. And then Skylar getting married had just cemented that wish.

Caroline appeared at the back door off the kitchen, arms loaded with packages. Sydney jumped up to let her in. "I'm so excited." She dropped her car keys and three large bags on the counter, her cane hooked over her forearm. "I found new curtains for the front room and the most gorgeous decorations for my party! Mmm, Michigan Cherry salad?" Caroline lifted the plastic lid on the salad container.

"Yes, I'll make you a plate," Savanna said. "I hope you don't mind us using your kitchen."

"Of course not!" Caroline went around the counter, pouring herself a half glass of lemonade. "I just want to change; the waistband is pinching on these pants. Too many muffins, I think." She set her glass down and headed out of the kitchen, now smartly using the cane.

"We want to see what you bought!" Sydney called after her.

"Back in a jiffy," Caroline called over her shoulder.

The sisters watched her go.

Savanna said it first. "I can't believe her energy."

"For real. I hope I still want to run around shopping for new rugs and curtains when I'm her age!"

Sydney arranged Caroline's salad on a plate, drizzling raspberry vinaigrette dressing over it and setting a place with a napkin and fork for her at the kitchen table. Savanna added the glass of lemonade.

"Can I see the mural so far?"

Savanna and Sydney stood staring up at the work in progress behind the scaffolding.

"She wants it to mirror her view"—Savanna gestured out

the panels of windows at Lake Michigan—"at sunset."

"I can see that already," Sydney said. "You've still got it, Savvy."

"I hope I do. I have a long way to go. It's a little scary, painting something this big, and especially for Caroline. But she seems happy with the concept."

Sydney bent to scratch Fonzie behind the ears. "How long do you think—"

Her words broke off as they heard a loud crash from the entryway. Savanna looked at Sydney, wide-eyed, and they ran toward the sound.

Fonzie, Princess, and Duke made it there first. Sydney rounded the corner into the foyer, Savanna right behind her, and gasped. Caroline was sprawled near the top of the staircase, hanging on to the hand railing, which had come away from the wall. Both sisters raced up the stairs. When they reached Caroline, the dogs were milling around her, whining and helpless.

Savanna sat down on the step and helped Caroline to an upright position, being careful not to jostle her too much. "Are you okay? What in the world happened?" She glanced at the handrail, which Sydney was now inspecting. One long screw still hung from the fixture on the railing, and she saw a couple more in small piles of debris and drywall dust on the steps below.

Caroline was clearly shaken up. "I—I'm not sure." She gingerly cupped her elbow, and then placed a hand on her right knee. "I don't know what happened. I hit my arm as I fell, and my leg got caught underneath me. My ankle..."

Her right ankle was already puffing up. Her hand trembled as she reached out, but stopped, not wanting to touch it. "Oh, it hurts."

"I'm calling 911." Sydney's phone was already out.

"No, no, I'm fine. I'm fine, girls! There's no need."

Savanna frowned at Caroline. "We're not moving you. Not with your ankle looking like that. It's okay—we need to get you some help."

"I'm not going to the hospital. I'm sure it's just sprained. Call my doctor; he'll come to the house."

"Caroline. Look how swollen it is already. Even if it is only sprained, he'll still want you to get an X-ray. Let us call an ambulance," Sydney pleaded.

"No! Call Dr. Gallager. He can take care of this." Caroline sat up straighter, looking at each of them in turn, expression stern. She pointed at Sydney with her good hand that was cradling her sore elbow. "You are *not* to call an ambulance. Call Dr. Gallager. You can find his number in the Google thing."

Savanna and Sydney exchanged exasperated glances. "Does anything else hurt?"

Caroline shook her head, stretching out her right arm and moving it around, turning it this way and that. "No. I think I'm okay. Except for this." She waved a shaking hand at her ankle.

"You're lucky, Caroline," Savanna murmured, looking at the handrail. "This could have been much worse. You could have landed at the bottom."

Chapter Seven

AIDAN GALLAGER ARRIVED at Caroline's within minutes of Sydney's call. Savanna heard his car door shut and left Sydney sitting on the stairs with Caroline to go let him in.

She met him in the driveway.

"Why didn't you call an ambulance?" His tone was curious rather than accusatory.

Savanna rolled her eyes at him, shaking her head as they walked up the front steps. "Have you met Caroline Carson? She is the most stubborn woman alive. We tried."

"You and your sister couldn't overrule an injured eighty-nine-year-old woman?"

"She seriously would not let us. She insisted we only call you."

"Sounds like Caroline. I'm glad you called."

On the stairway, Aidan set his black doctor's bag on a step and kneeled on one knee in front of Caroline, carefully examining her right ankle. He questioned her, using his own foot to show her the different motions. "Can you move it like this? How about like this? Can you point your toes toward the ceiling?"

Caroline nearly left the step, her body tense, as a short,

high-pitched cry left her lips.

Aidan carefully set her foot back down. "Well. You need an X-ray. There's no other way to know if it's broken. There are twenty-eight bones in your lower leg and foot. Any one of them, or more than one, could be fractured and possibly displaced. I'm calling an ambulance. They'll come stabilize your leg to take you in."

Caroline heaved a sigh, her shoulders drooping. "Fine," she said quietly, defeated.

Savanna felt terrible for her. "We can go with you," she said, her arm around Caroline's shoulders. "I can call Lauren. Or your kids or Jack, whoever you want."

Aidan descended the stairs, moving away from them to give the dispatcher the information.

Caroline didn't answer. She pulled at a new tear in her burgundy slacks, winding the loose threads around one finger.

Savanna looked at Sydney.

"Caroline? You're going to be okay," Sydney told her. "This is just a little blip on the radar. It was an accident. It could have happened to anyone."

"I should have kept my cane with me," she said. "I've never fallen before. Old ladies fall." She looked up at Sydney and then Savanna.

"You didn't fall," Savanna said. "The handrail gave way, Caroline. It would just as easily have happened to Lauren or anyone else coming down the stairs. It has nothing to do with your age," she said firmly.

Caroline looked somewhat bolstered by that. "You're

right."

"We have to get Bill back over here. He needs to see this," Savanna said, unable to conceal the anger and frustration in her voice. For goodness' sake, she hoped all of his workmanship wasn't this shoddy. Caroline should have hired her dad instead...but Savanna knew he was up to his ears in much larger projects at the moment.

"Could you call Lauren, please?" Caroline nodded at Sydney, her phone still in hand. "And Savanna, would you run up and grab my sweater? It's on the back of the chair by my bed. I'll also need my purse. Be careful on those stairs!"

By the time they heard the sirens, too reminiscent of two weeks ago when Eleanor had passed, Caroline was sitting on the step, now put together with her pearl-detailed cardigan and floral scarf, purse beside her and one shoe on her good foot. Savanna and Sydney flanked her, and Dr. Gallager stood at the foot of the stairs, waiting. Lauren was on her way. Having dressed Caroline for her trip to the hospital, Savanna became suddenly aware of her own appearance: faded, paint-stained jeans with holes worn in the knees, an old, too-tight Harry Potter shirt bearing the words *I solemnly swear that I am up to no good* across the front, her hair piled up in crazy waves on top of her head, several pieces hanging loose from a day spent painting and climbing on scaffolding.

Sydney leaned back and tapped Savanna's arm behind Caroline's back; Caroline was on the phone with her son, Lauren's dad. "Are we going to the hospital with her?" Syd whispered.

Savanna groaned. "Yes, of course we're going. But look

at me, I'm a hot mess. I hope I don't embarrass anyone. I look awful!"

"You do not! This whole carefree, artsy, rock-and-roll vibe you've got going on is super sexy, trust me."

Savanna's eyes widened, and she glanced down the steps to make sure Aidan hadn't overheard that comment. She hadn't been aiming for sexy; she'd been trying to avoid getting paint on her nicer clothes.

"Wait, hold on," Sydney said. She reached into her pocket and handed Savanna a pink bubble-gum-scented lip gloss. "Here. You might want to use this."

Savanna scowled at Syd but ducked behind Caroline to apply the lip gloss. She passed it back on the step.

Sydney smirked at her, silent.

"Shut. Up. I mean it," Savanna warned.

"What, dear?" Caroline turned to Savanna.

"I was just saying, I think I hear the ambulance getting closer," Savanna lied, ignoring her sister on the other side of Caroline. She could see Sydney's smug expression in her peripheral vision.

The front door opened and Lauren burst in, making a beeline up the steps to Caroline. "Grams, what the heck happened?" She embraced Caroline tightly.

Caroline patted her back. "I'm all right, Lauren. This is so much fuss over nothing."

Lauren stood back and stared at Caroline's swollen ankle. "It doesn't look like nothing!"

In the foyer below, three paramedics entered, along with equipment and a rolling stretcher.

"This is ridiculous," Caroline said. "I'm not riding on that thing. Help me up." She reached for Lauren, bracing one hand on Savanna's knee.

Lauren shook her head, hands on her hips and a worried expression painting her features.

"Brad!" Sydney exclaimed, trotting down the steps and giving one of the men a quick hug. She turned and pointed at Caroline. "Tell her to be still, would you?"

Sydney's suitor from the other night grinned at Syd. "Are you stalking me? You could have just called, you know. Kel"—he turned to his coworker, a petite woman with two long blond braids, and handed her a red canvas bag—"vitals first, then we move."

Sydney punched him in the shoulder, which she was about eye level with. His coworker was already on her way up the steps with the bag, reassuring Caroline that she must let them help her, for her own safety.

Outside in the driveway, Lauren followed the gurney into the ambulance. She leaned forward as Brad was packing up the equipment, addressing Savanna, Sydney, and Dr. Gallager. "Thank you so much. Grandmother fired me for the weekend. She wouldn't listen, no matter how much I told her I don't mind helping her. She thinks I need a break. You know what I was doing when you called?" She turned to Caroline behind her. "I was folding laundry. Laundry waits, Grams. You need to stop being so stubborn. You could have been really hurt."

Caroline moved around on the stretcher, sitting up with some difficulty, her face pinched in pain as she did. "That's enough, Lauren. You couldn't have prevented this. That railing wasn't attached correctly."

"Right. But I'd have gone upstairs to get your outfit for you, and you wouldn't have fallen." Caroline opened her mouth to argue further, and Lauren held up a hand, sounding very serious. "Grandmother! You are eighty-nine years old, and I want you around to see ninety! So please, just hush and let people help you. You're not allowed to fire me anymore."

Caroline sighed. "You're right. I'm sorry, to all of you." She looked past Lauren to Savanna, Sydney, and Aidan standing around the open ambulance doors. She took Lauren's hand and Lauren covered it with her other one.

"Thank you," Lauren said again to the trio in the driveway, tears in her eyes. "This could have been so much worse."

"Is there anyone else we should call? I work with Jack and I have his number. I'm sure he could let his mother know," Savanna offered.

"No," Lauren said quickly. "There's some... Well, it's a little stressful right now, that part of the family. No need to call them. I'm sure she'll be fine."

"Of course. Good luck, we'll be thinking of you, Caroline," she called. She hoped everything was all right where Jack was concerned; in just a few weeks, she'd already grown to like him.

"I'll be right behind you." Aidan nodded to the crew in the ambulance before they closed the doors.

As the ambulance departed, lights and sirens off at Caroline's request, Savanna replayed her words, the same ones she herself had said to Caroline. Today really could have been terrible, with Caroline seriously injured, or worse. "I've got to pack up my supplies." She looked at Aidan and her sister, wanting an excuse to go back into the house.

"I should take care of the dogs in case they're gone awhile," Syd added, heading back inside.

"I'm glad you called me," Aidan said. "She's stubborn, but that's part of why she manages so well."

"Do you think her ankle is broken?" Savanna self-consciously tucked one long curl behind her ear, now noticing Aidan looked like total Saturday Dad: navy athletic pants with dual white stripes running down the sides, gray hoodie, and Vans sneakers. He'd obviously dropped what he was doing and come right over when they'd called. Savanna imagined him at a barbecue grill, cooking burgers…standing in green grass, pushing Mollie on a swing set… Wait, where was Mollie?

"It's hard to say. If not, it's a bad sprain."

"Where's Mollie today? We didn't even ask what plans we were interrupting."

"Mollie's at soccer practice with her grandpa. Or maybe"—he glanced at his watch—"she's having ice cream by now. Don't worry. I'm always here for Caroline."

"Thank you," Savanna said. "I know she's in good hands."

Aidan slung his black bag over one shoulder, fishing his car keys out of his pocket. "I'm going to meet the ambulance. You know, see that she doesn't give them too much trouble in the ER." He grinned.

Savanna laughed. "Yeah, you'd better. She'll convince them to let her hobble out of there without an X-ray, knowing Caroline. Sydney and I will lock up here, and then I think we'll come up to check on her."

Aidan rested a hand on Savanna's upper arm momentarily. "She'll appreciate that. You and your sisters mean a lot to her. It's a good thing you were here."

Savanna watched Aidan climb into his vehicle, a dark gray SUV, and pull out of the drive. Back inside, instead of heading to the parlor to pack up from the day spent painting, Savanna climbed the staircase.

She'd seen the railing this morning, had noticed it because Bill had just finished putting it back up. It had looked fine. She ran her fingers over the cracked and broken drywall where the railing had detached. A whole chunk of hardened drywall mud was on the step directly below where the railing was attached; Savanna picked at the wall, finding the tract where two of the screws had been. She could see, from the one long screw still hanging in the bracket on the handrail, that they'd gone not just into the drywall, but into the plaster behind it; Caroline's turn-of-the-century house had undergone a major renovation when Savanna was a kid. The place was solid. She picked up a screw and tried fitting it into the hole; it slid around loosely, too much play to hold it.

"Syd!" Sydney would tell her if she was seeing connections where there were none.

"What!" Her sister's voice came from the back of the house.

"Come here!"

"Ugh! I'm feeding the dogs, hold on!"

Savanna sat down on the step, pushing the hand railing back up against the wall. The metal bracket wouldn't line up now.

Sydney appeared at the foot of the stairs. "What's up?"

"I don't know. Don't you think that was weird?"

"What's weird?"

"The railing. The handrail coming off and almost killing Caroline."

"Oh. I don't know." Sydney climbed the steps and bent to check out the hole in the wall where the railing had come loose. She knocked on the wall around it. "I mean, it's an old house."

"But this shouldn't have happened," Savanna said, moving down the stairs to the next bracket and giving it a tug, and then the next one. "These are all fine. It's just the top bracket that gave way."

Syd tipped her head at Savanna. "Maybe that Bill guy isn't as good as Caroline thinks."

Savanna was quiet.

"Or maybe he was trying to hurt her? Maybe he sabotaged his own work?"

Savanna frowned at Sydney. "When you say it like that, it sounds ridiculous."

"Well, why would anyone want to hurt Caroline?" Sydney gathered her hair into a long red ponytail, securing it with a hair tie from her wrist. "It was probably just the handyman rushing the job."

"Okay, but then if you add what happened to Eleanor..."

Now Sydney was quiet.

"You said yourself that the woman was tough. She walked to Fancy Tails every day." Defensiveness crept into Savanna's voice. "So, how did she just suddenly have a heart attack?"

"Savvy...I know what I said. Eleanor's death does seem strange. And this"—Sydney gestured to the handrail—"is strange too, since everything was just put back together and the rest of it seems secure. But I don't see how the two things could possibly be related."

Savanna shook her head. "I guess I don't either. It just strikes me as odd. Do you want to come to the hospital with me? I'd like to make sure Caroline's okay."

"I should, but I think it's better if I take Princess and Duke back to the salon. Who knows if they're going to send her home tonight. They can't stay here alone. Give her my love."

Savanna pulled on her jacket. "I will. Can you just drop me at the hospital and then you can take all the dogs home? I'll find a way home later, or maybe Dad can pick me up."

"Sure. I need to stop at Mom and Dad's later. It's my turn for dinner tomorrow night and I need to see if they have a couple of my ingredients," Sydney said. "Plus, I want to find out if they know much about Bill and Maggie Lyle."

Chapter Eight

CAROLINE'S LAUGHTER CARRIED down the hallway as the emergency department nurse escorted Savanna to her room. Anderson Memorial was a small, recently updated two-story hospital, adequate for the small town of Carson. Anything Anderson couldn't handle was transferred to the gigantic Ingham County Medical Center an hour away in Lansing. Most of Carson had visited for one thing or another at some point in their lives. Savanna did a double take as she passed Aidan on a framed poster, looking very doctorly in lab coat and serious expression. The caption underneath read *Put Your Trust in Anderson Memorial, Home of Renowned Cardiothoracic Surgeon Dr. Aidan Gallager.*

The ER nurse took stock of the group in the small holding room with Caroline and muttered something about having too many visitors. Aidan, Lauren, and Lauren's father stood around Caroline's bed, laughing at a great joke or something Savanna must have just missed.

"No worries," Aidan spoke, following the nurse into the hallway. "We'll clear out soon. Just keeping her company while she waits for the X-ray."

"Sure, Dr. Gallager, it's fine." The nurse softened.

"Maybe you could check on when that might be?" His

hospital name badge was clipped to his hoodie, making his Saturday Dad outfit look slightly professional.

"I'll call Radiology right now," she said, moving to the nurses' station in the center of the block of rooms.

Lauren made introductions. Savanna remembered Caroline's son, Thomas. As a child, he'd seemed old to her. Now that she was older, he seemed less so; she knew he and her dad were friends from childhood. He must be around Harlan's age, late fifties. Thomas was Jack's uncle, and Savanna could see the family resemblance.

Caroline held a hand out, and Savanna took it. "Dear girl, you needn't have come. I'm fine. In fact, it's feeling a little better." She gestured at her puffy purple ankle. "I'm sure it's only sprained."

"Looks like we're about to find out," Aidan said as a tech in green scrubs appeared in the doorway.

"There's a short wait," the man said, "but we can head down to Radiology. One family member can go with her."

"They'll both be coming with me," Caroline said firmly, looking at Lauren and her father.

The tech's gaze went to Aidan, who shrugged, nodding.

"Choose your battles," he said to Savanna once they'd left the room, the tech pushing the gurney followed by Lauren and Thomas. "Some things aren't worth arguing with her over."

"Oh, I know," she said. "I'm surprised she's letting you check her heart with that monitor you've got at the house."

"She's stubborn, but she isn't reckless. She knows it's important. Like the X-ray she doesn't think she needs. This will take a little while," he said. "Do you have time to grab a cup of coffee with me?"

Once in the cafeteria, the cashier waved them through, smiling at Dr. Gallager.

"Mmm," Savanna said, breathing in the rich aroma. "Fancy coffee, very nice." Savanna set her cup on the table by the window Aidan found for them.

"Yes," he agreed. "It's the real reason I keep coming here."

Savanna closed her hands around her steaming cup. She couldn't stop thinking about the strange happenings at Caroline's house. Should she get Aidan's opinion? What if he thought she was paranoid?

"Hey." He leaned on the table. "Don't worry. She'll be fine."

"I'm not worried. Well, not too much. I was just thinking about the accident."

Aidan tipped his head, curious. "What do you mean?"

"The handrail coming loose; Caroline's neighbor had just stained and glazed it. He'd painted and patched the entire stairway wall, and he reattached the railing just last night. I noticed it this morning. I thought he'd done a good job."

"Well, I'm sure it looked like he did, but it's a very old house. Maybe the screws just pulled loose."

"Maybe," Savanna said. "Sydney and I went back and looked at the spot where it came out of the wall."

Aidan's eyebrows went up. "Did you notice anything out of the ordinary?"

"There were large pieces of crumbled plaster lying on the

steps, and a few of the screws seemed not to fit well where they'd been secured. It doesn't make sense."

"Hmmm." He sat back, looking at her. "Well, to put it in perspective, two ambulances at her house in two weeks doesn't make sense either. First Eleanor, then Caroline."

Savanna stared at him. "Do you suspect something? Like...foul play?" The words felt ridiculous on her tongue.

His expression remained serious. "Do you?"

"I'm not sure," she admitted.

"But who would want to hurt Caroline? What would the neighbor—or anyone else—have against her?"

Savanna shook her head. "I have no idea. Everyone loves her; the whole town knows her family."

"She does seem to be well loved," Aiden said. "But...I'm sure the Carson estate is worth quite a lot. Money can make people do crazy things sometimes. So, what do we really know, after today's unfortunate accident?"

Savanna mused, "We know the handrail looked to be installed properly, but it wasn't. Oh! And we know that Bill's wife, Maggie, is the one who convinced Caroline to hire him, and Maggie was pretty irritated with Bill this morning over something," Savanna recalled, thinking of the argument she'd inadvertently eavesdropped on. What was that about? "And we know that Caroline could have been much more seriously hurt. Or worse. She could have wound up like Eleanor."

"But, to be fair, Eleanor collapsed. Her heart stopped. Caroline was the victim of faulty hardware."

"Faulty installation of hardware," Savanna corrected.

"By the neighbor, Caroline's handyman," Aidan said, lowering his voice.

"Well, the handrail failing doesn't have anything to do with Eleanor's heart stopping."

"True. But...I still don't have an explanation for how that happened. Nothing was consistent with a typical cardiac arrest, not the EKG, not her cardiac enzymes. I listed sudden cardiac death for the legal record—the death certificate. But it doesn't make any sense, medically. I can't betray patient confidentiality," he added quickly.

Savanna smiled at him, thinking of the conversation with Skylar. "Of course. I'd never ask you to."

"I wouldn't," he said somberly. "But now I'm wondering if the rest of Eleanor's pathology is back yet. It can take two to three weeks."

"What, like more lab work?"

Aidan hesitated, pensive. "An autopsy is done routinely on anyone who dies before reaching the hospital. The pathology report can include a variety of things, from a tox screen looking for foreign substances, to gastrointestinal contents, to tissue samples, dental findings, other stuff. It just depends on what we run. In a case like Eleanor's, the attending physician might check for substances in the system that don't belong there, something that might have contributed to sudden cardiac arrest."

"I see," Savanna said. "So, you're still waiting to receive Eleanor's report?"

"To be honest, I'd been watching for it. I'm still bothered by how she died. But I haven't checked in a few days."

"Well, Sydney swears Eleanor was super healthy. How could someone like that just keel over?"

"It's possible, though not very likely," Aidan said, frowning. "Had she eaten or drank anything out of the ordinary that night? Anything that you two didn't have?"

Savanna began to shake her head again, and then stopped. "The claret. The red wine that Lauren brought—"

"Lauren? You don't think that she—"

"No! No…I guess I can't imagine her doing anything to hurt her grandmother—or Eleanor. But I did wonder something." Savanna took a long swallow of her coffee. The hospital's French vanilla creamer was pretty good.

"You're killing me with suspense," Aidan joked.

"I'm sorry. I always thought it was weird how Lauren called after she'd left that night. She was so surprised that I was still there, and then she immediately asked if Caroline was all right. I remember thinking that was odd. Why wouldn't Caroline be all right?"

"Okay, but what about the red wine?"

"Lauren offered to get us each a drink before she left. Me, Caroline, and Eleanor. Eleanor was the only one who actually drank the wine."

Aidan stared at her. "Red wine…what kind? Did you see the bottle?"

"No. But I wondered if maybe Lauren had…" Savanna felt foolish now, giving voice to her thoughts. "I wondered if Lauren had possibly tried to hurt Caroline. It's such a stupid idea, I know." She glanced at Aidan, rushing on. "And I don't believe it. She loves her. You saw her today in the ambulance. She was terrified something could have happened to her grandmother. Lauren isn't capable of hurting anyone," Savanna said firmly.

Aidan was quiet. "She is very devoted."

"But the claret came from Happy Family. That's why Lauren chose it. She said the delivery had included a fancy-looking bottle that she thought Caroline would like to try."

Aidan looked disappointed. "I don't think it was the wine. Even if it was meant for Caroline but Eleanor drank it, why would someone from the grocery store want to poison Caroline?"

"You're going to think this sounds crazy."

Aidan looked at her. "*All* of this sounds crazy. So tell me. I trust your instincts, Savanna. You're seeing all these little details that might add up to something. I've heard you worked as an art authenticator in Chicago, right? So it was basically your job to find incongruities in what you're seeing. I'd like to hear your thoughts. If someone is trying to hurt Caroline, we need to know."

Savanna took a deep breath and told Aidan about the conversation she'd overheard the other day at Happy Family, between the grocery delivery woman and the clerk at the store. "Amber was so angry. She made it sound as if Everett Carson cost her family everything. She really sounded as if she wanted to do something about it."

"Okay. And Amber is the one who brought the wine. I can see how you're connecting the dots." He nodded. "But then…the railing…" He finished his coffee, frowning. "That was just an accident, maybe?"

Savanna shrugged. "I don't know. Maybe Amber has help? Or maybe it wasn't Amber at all. Maybe she just brought the wine with the groceries, and something happened to it once it was there."

Aidan stood abruptly. "Come with me."

Back in the emergency room, Savanna leaned in the doorway of a little alcove filled with computers. Aidan's back was to her as he worked. Caroline's room was still empty; she must still be down in X-ray.

"Eleanor's reports are back," Aidan said triumphantly, turning just as the printer to Savanna's right started spitting out sheets of paper. Aidan waited until they finished, six in all, and then grabbed them, scanning through them until he found what he was looking for on page three. He met Savanna's eyes. "I need to get these to the police," he said quietly, looking rattled.

"Whoa, what?" Savanna said, staring at him. What on earth had jumped out at him in that report?

At that moment, Caroline rolled by on the gurney. She waggled her fingers at Aidan and Savanna. "There's my wonderful doctor! The X-ray report is in, Dr. Gallager, good sir. You can check it and confirm that I'm right as rain!"

"They gave Grams more pain medication," Lauren said by way of explanation. "She's feeling *fine*."

Caroline snickered, patting her son's hand on the gurney railing as the tech continued pushing her toward her room. "Thomas, your daughter's tone is quite snarky; I think she thinks the medicine has made me loopy. But she's wrong!" Caroline rolled her head on the pillow back toward Lauren, grinning widely as they turned into her room.

"Oh, boy." Savanna giggled. "She sure is feeling fine."

Aidan was back on the computer, scrolling through screens. "No break. She guessed right," he told Savanna. "Let's go give her the good news."

Aidan informed Caroline that she'd be getting a walking cast to wear for two weeks, as a precaution, and he urged her to stay overnight because her blood pressure was elevated; he promised she could go home first thing in the morning.

"I'm staying with her," Lauren announced, waving a hand to shush Caroline when she protested.

"They'll be taking you up to your room soon, and then Ortho will be in to look at your ankle and fit the boot. Okay?"

Savanna said her goodbyes to Caroline and stepped into the hall to call Sydney for a ride. Aidan was waiting for her.

"I've got to get this report into the right hands. Would you like to be part of that conversation? If not, I can drop you off at your place...you said Sydney took the car?"

"I'm absolutely coming with you! What do you think is going on? Is she actually in danger?"

"She might be. This is just very strange." He looked at the folded papers in his hand. "Not what I expected. And even if you don't come with me, I'm sure whoever looks into it will be calling you with questions. You were there the night Eleanor died."

"Oh, wow," Savanna breathed. Did he mean someone had poisoned Eleanor? Aidan looked spooked.

In his car, as they pulled into the parking spot at the Carson police station, Aidan paused before getting out. "Savanna, you need to think about how this all affects you. We don't know anything yet, but I'm not sure whether Caroline is safe. I'm worried about both of you; you're there all the time. Just—be careful. Please."

She felt warm tingles rush through her, down to her fingertips and toes. Aidan was concerned about her safety. "I will, don't worry," she told him.

But worry a little, she thought, loving the unsolicited attention from Dr. Aidan Gallager.

Chapter Nine

S AVANNA SLEPT IN Sunday morning later than she had in
months. Yesterday was exhausting. The visit to Carson
Village police department had left a lot to be desired and had
left Savanna with the unsettled feeling that Aidan's pathology report might just sit on the detective's desk, untouched,
for who knew how long.

Savanna padded to Sydney's front door, Fonzie close at
her heels; who would be ringing the doorbell on a Sunday at
ten a.m.?

Skylar handed Savanna a heavy casserole dish with a
handful of Hershey's kisses scattered in the bottom, moving
past her into Sydney's kitchen. "Does she have coffee? She
never did before, only that organic decaf stuff that tastes like
dirt, but I figure maybe you've converted her?" Skylar was
pulling open cupboards and drawers and had discovered the
coffee before Savanna could even jump in to help.

"Why are you here so early?" Savanna set the dish down
and grabbed a banana from the bowl on the counter.
"What's with the kisses?"

Skylar set up the coffee maker on the counter, taking out
two cups and spooning sugar into one of them for Savanna.
"Syd needed the pan for her dinner tonight," Skylar said over

her shoulder, her perfectly straight, shiny blond hair just brushing the collar of the tailored, crisp white blouse she wore with fitted navy jeans. "And you know Mom says it's bad form to return an empty dish. The kisses are from Nolan."

Savanna rubbed her eyes and gathered her long hair into a high ponytail, yawning. "I hope you made it strong." She nodded at the coffeemaker.

Skylar joined Savanna on a stool at the counter. "Obviously."

"Where is Syd? I don't think she's here." Savanna glanced back toward the hallway to the bedrooms. Her little sister never slept in. She wouldn't still be in bed.

"She texted me from yoga."

"Oh my God, who does yoga this early on a Sunday?"

Skylar smiled at Savanna. "Our sister. And apparently a bunch of other people too. She said her classes have been overfull lately so she added a couple. I think she gets a lot of crossover from Fancy Tails."

"Our entrepreneur sister. Bringing Zen and wellness to all, one dog lover at a time." Savanna laughed. She unwrapped a chocolate kiss and popped it in her mouth.

"Breakfast?" Skylar raised an eyebrow at Savanna.

"Breakfast?" Savanna looked at Skylar's black coffee.

Skylar shrugged. "Maybe not. I was just dropping off the casserole dish. Travis was making breakfast when I left."

"Um. Okay, invitation accepted, let's go." Savanna finished her coffee and hopped off the stool, heading to her bedroom. "Let me change. Hey, maybe we can take my adorable nephew to the park later, and I'll tell you about my run-in with the police?"

"The police, Savanna? What the heck?"

By noon, Skylar and Savanna were seated comfortably in the sun on a red-and-blue-painted bench, full of pancakes and watching Nolan scoop sand into a bucket with a cute little girl in pigtails. The town park was a huge grassy rectangle of land at the west end of town, one block past the four corners where Main Street met Parkway Drive. September in Michigan was unpredictable; fifty degrees and rainy yesterday could give way to seventy and sunny today, perfect park weather. Savanna peeled off her denim jacket, turning her face up toward the sun.

"Okay, so I don't think I'm getting it," Skylar said. "Tell me again what happened with Aidan and the police station."

Savanna had started at the beginning over the delicious breakfast Travis made, but by the time she'd made it to she and Aidan meeting with the police detective, Nolan was screeching about wanting his kite for the park, the dishwasher was running, and Travis was on the phone. "Not much happened, actually. Aidan had the pathology report from Eleanor's autopsy and he said we needed to turn it in to the police. It showed a toxic level of Attendall in her system."

"*What?*" Skylar turned and started at Savanna on the bench. "Attendall? The ADD medication for kids?"

"Yes! It doesn't make sense, right?"

Skylar was shaking her head. "And Aidan told you this?"

"No," Savanna quickly replied, "he couldn't. But when they finally let us talk to the detective on duty, George

Taylor, he read it aloud off the report. He sounded surprised that Attendall showed up, but he acted like maybe Eleanor was just taking it on her own or something."

"Oh, jeez." Skylar rolled her eyes. "Like Eleanor would take something like that just for fun. Couldn't Aidan confirm what medications she was on? He was her doctor."

"He did," she said. "He gave the detective a complete list. She was only on a few things, and Attendall wasn't one of them."

"Taylor is a little green," Skylar said. "He might be out of his depth. He only made detective last year. Maybe I can try to put a word in," she mused.

"How?" Savanna couldn't see how Skylar could help.

"I deal with that division a lot in civil cases. I know all three of Carson's detectives—it's not a big precinct. I might be able to mention Eleanor's report to Jordan. He's the most reliable. I can say I'm checking on it as part of settling Eleanor's estate and life insurance. They should technically be contacting me if they suspect any kind of suspicious death, but I'll beat them to it."

Savanna hugged Skylar. "That would be so great. I went with Aidan because we both thought it might help, since I was there when Eleanor died. We thought the detective might have questions for me. But Taylor basically took the report, agreed that the Attendall was odd, and then kind of gave Aidan a funny look—like an 'okay, sure, buddy' kind of look—when he suggested it could have been slipped to her and made her heart stop. He didn't ask me anything about that night. I tried to tell him about the claret, but I think he thought we were nuts."

Skylar patted Savanna's knee. "Jordan will call you, I'm positive. He's going to want to know exactly what happened—how the wine got there, who served it, everything. I wonder if she still has the bottle. This whole thing is scary. Where is Caroline now?"

"She's probably home now. Aidan made her stay overnight because her blood pressure was up, but no wonder!"

"You need to be careful, Savanna," Skylar warned. "If Eleanor died because someone is trying to take Caroline out of the picture, and then Caroline just narrowly missed a bad fall all the way down that staircase, you could be hurt too."

"I know...I'll be careful. Aidan mentioned that too."

Skylar's mouth went up on one side in a crooked smile. "Really now."

"Well, yes! We both feel something questionable is going on over there."

"How nice that he's worried about you," Skylar said.

"Yes." Savanna glanced at her and then back at Nolan. "Just like he's worried about Caroline, I'm sure."

"Mm-hmm."

"I think Nolan needs help." Savanna got up abruptly and went over to the sandbox. Nolan most definitely did not need help; he was filling his shirt with sand one scoop at a time, little face screwing up with frustration every time he saw it spill out the bottom. As Savanna approached, he finally figured out how to tuck his shirt into his waistband so he wouldn't lose the sand. Smart boy. Dirty and dusty, but smart. Savanna smiled to herself.

"Nolan, want me to push you on the swing?"

Sydney must have been talking to Skylar; Savanna could tell by the knowing look on her older sister's face. There was nothing to know. Aidan was just a nice guy. It made total sense that he'd be concerned about her...and anyone else who might be in a potentially dangerous situation. Besides, he was very obviously devoted to his daughter and his work, and Savanna had come home to heal, to rediscover what was important to her, not to find a new man.

Skylar joined her at the swing set, on the opposite side. They pushed Nolan back and forth, and not another word was spoken about Aidan. Savanna and Skylar took turns overreacting every time Nolan swung toward them through the air, acting as if he might knock them down, and her nephew's delighted high-pitched giggles were music to Savanna's ears. She'd trade the whole decade in Chicago for time spent like this with family.

As they were packing up to leave the park, Skylar to deal with a phone conference and Savanna to work on the canvas in Syd's sunroom, a young boy and his mother approached them.

Savanna looked up from tying Nolan's shoe. She recognized the boy from one of her art classes...a second or third grader. She couldn't recall his name.

The child's mother spoke. "Ms. Shepherd?"

"Yes?"

"Parker wanted to say hello." The woman looked down at her son, who had a death grip on his mom's hand.

"Hi, Ms. Shepherd." His voice was so quiet Savanna had

to strain to hear. Now she remembered him. Second grade, left front table in her class. He was obsessed with *The Very Hungry Caterpillar*.

Savanna smiled at the boy and his mom. "Hi, Parker! I'm so excited for you to finish your caterpillar this week. I can't wait to see what other foods he'll eat." She looked up at the woman. "We're using magazines to make a collage; the assignment was to come up with a piece based on our favorite book. Parker is so creative!"

His mother's face lit up. "He loves your class. I have to say, this is the first year he's ever been excited to go to school. Whatever you're doing, Ms. Shepherd, please keep it up. We're lucky to have you!"

The random, unexpected compliment warmed Savanna's heart and stayed with her all day.

She made a detour on her way back home and stopped at Caroline's house; she was right in thinking she'd catch Lauren there. She motioned her out onto the porch, not wanting to talk in front of Caroline. "How is she?"

"She's doing well," Lauren said. "She actually feels pretty good. She won't take any of the pain pills they gave her, but I'm giving her Tylenol and keeping ice on her ankle. Her blood pressure came down by this morning."

"I'm so glad she's feeling okay," Savanna said. "She's impressive. Not much slows her down."

"I can't thank you enough for taking care of her yesterday. If you and Sydney hadn't been here—" Lauren shook her head. "I don't even want to think about it."

"Listen," Savanna said, lowering her voice and looking

past Lauren through the screened front door. She was sure Caroline wouldn't hear. "I was going to call you, but this is easier to explain in person. I'm a little worried… Dr. Gallager and I are a little worried about her, and her safety. It's just…" Savanna stopped, at a loss for words. How could she warn Lauren to keep Caroline safe without scaring her or making her think she was crazy? Could she even be trusted?

"What's the matter?" Lauren frowned, worry lines appearing between her eyebrows.

"Well, yesterday's accident, and only two weeks after the awful incident with Eleanor…it just seems like a lot of bad luck. I'm worried…we're worried…about the possibility that someone may be trying to hurt your grandmother."

Lauren's eyes widened. "Really? I never thought of that. I mean, it's been a little crazier than usual around here, but do you really think she's in danger?"

Savanna wasn't sure how much to say. "Dr. Gallager is looking into Eleanor's death. He isn't sure it was due to natural causes. And I know the railing coming loose was an accident, but all the same, it's probably a good idea to keep a close eye on her."

Lauren sighed. "I'll try. But Grams is the biggest obstacle to me being here even more to help her. She's so stubborn. At least now, with that bulky walking cast on, we have an excuse to keep close tabs on her until she's able to take it off. Thank you, Savanna. I appreciate you worrying."

"Of course. Oh—I meant to ask you. That red wine you served the other night was so good. Do you remember what brand it was? I'd love to pick up a bottle." Savanna tried to sound only mildly interested, as if it was an afterthought. She studied Lauren's features for any reaction.

"You know, it's the strangest thing. Grandmother mentioned the other day that she never got to try hers. It was such a pretty bottle, short and round with gold vines wrapped around the neck. I don't remember the brand—I couldn't have pronounced it. I went to pour us a glass, but the bottle is gone. We keep an organized kitchen. I'd find it if we still had it. All I can think is that someone must have thrown it out." Her response gave nothing away; she looked truly puzzled over where the claret could have gone.

"Well, maybe it'll turn up. You'll have to let me know if it does." Savanna felt certain Lauren had Caroline's best interests at heart. If she'd tampered with the drinks, wouldn't she have simply said they'd all finished the bottle, rather than saying it was missing?

"Absolutely."

By the time Savanna made it home Sunday afternoon, all she wanted was a hot shower and dinner with her family. Fonzie greeted her happily at the door and curled up on the bathroom rug when she climbed into the shower. Syd must have come and gone while she was out; the casserole dish was no longer on the kitchen counter, only a small pile of kisses.

Savanna towel-dried and combed through her hair, forgoing the hairdryer, a style Rob had never liked. It would dry into loose waves, leaving a little colic at her left temple. Sydney called it her beach hair, and Savanna liked that. At least, she had, until Rob had felt comfortable enough to insert his opinion. Well, she told the Savanna in the mirror, running her fingers through damp waves, who needed Rob's opinion? Certainly not her, and not for the multitude of choices she'd made in the last month. She applied lipstick and mascara and pulled on a short-sleeved, rose-colored A-line dress, mentally picking out the bell-sleeved navy sheath dress for Monday morning.

Once they were at her parents' house, Fonzie ran ahead of her inside, barking as he went at a big orange tabby hanging out on the front porch. The aroma of garlic wafted to Savanna as she made her way through the house to the kitchen. Sydney was at the stove, with Harlan next to her, slicing zucchini.

Charlotte looked up from the nook by the window, papers spread out in front of her. "Honey, come sit! I'm so glad you're here early."

Savanna joined her mother at the table, glancing at the papers. "What's this?"

"Ah, just work." Charlotte began collecting it one at a time, organizing it into piles that made sense to her; to Savanna, it looked daunting. Her mother was amazing. "I'll finish up tomorrow. I'll have time on the flight."

"Where to this time?"

"Japan for four days," she said, smiling. "I'm trying to get your father to come with me."

Harlan picked up the cutting board and slid the zucchini into the frying pan with his knife. He dropped the utensils into the sink and rinsed his hands, drying them on his jeans. "Can't," he said. "We've got too much work right now. Once snow comes and we slow down, Char, I'll be right there with you."

"I'll hold you to that, you know," Charlotte warned.

"You can hold me any way you want, my dear," Harlan growled, stooping on his way past the kitchenette to plant a kiss on her ear.

Charlotte pushed her chair back, gathering up the stack of papers. "I'm going to run upstairs and change, but I want to hear all about your excitement yesterday, Savanna. And I love your hair that way!"

Syd looked up from the frying pan she was minding as Charlotte left. "Ten minutes. It's almost ready."

"It smells delicious," Savanna said. "What are we having?"

"Vegetarian linguine with organic vegetables from Fred Wilson's produce stand on Maple Street. And fresh parmesan from a client of mine who has a dairy farm."

Savanna leaned on the kitchen counter and swiped a spot of the sauce from the side of the pan, tasting it. "Oh, wow, Syd. So good! Stop raising the stakes. You know I can't compete with this."

"Oh, I know." Sydney smiled sweetly, batting her eyelashes at Savanna.

"Snot." Savanna picked up a fork and speared a noodle and a piece of red bell pepper before Sydney could stop her.

"Out! Mom!" Sydney called. "Make her stop stealing. It's not ready yet."

"Tattletale." Savanna moved to the long dining table and began putting out place settings. "I'm just helping. Chill out."

When Charlotte reappeared, wearing a beige-flowered wrap dress, her hair tidied up into a French twist, she shook her head at both sisters. "I swear, put the two of you together in this kitchen and you instantly regress to eight-year-olds."

Skylar spoke up from the doorway. "More like five-year-olds. When are we eating? I'm starving."

With everyone finally seated around the table, heaping portions of colorful vegetarian linguine on each plate, Savanna swallowed her first delicious bite and asked the question she'd been waiting to ask of her parents. "What do you guys know about Bill and Maggie Lyle?"

"The Lyles? Caroline's neighbors, right? I know Maggie through my bridge club," Charlotte said. "Your dad probably knows Bill better than I do."

"Bill used to work for me," Harlan said.

"Wait, what? He did? What happened?"

"Yeah," Syd spoke up. "Did you fire him for something?"

Harlan chuckled. "No, he got work at the factory. They work so much overtime, he wasn't much use to my team after that."

"Well," Savanna said, "what kind of worker was he? Did he kind of slack off on things, or was he pretty good?"

"He was a hard worker," Harlan said. "Bill learned fast. I never had to show him twice how to do something."

"Maggie is nice enough," Charlotte said. "A little chilly, but I think that's just her way. Why do you ask? Were they involved in your trip to the police station yesterday?"

Savanna brought her family up to speed, with help from Sydney, both of them taking care not to say anything alarming in front of Nolan. Savanna tried talking in code, mentioning the night that Eleanor "fell asleep" after drinking the claret. She covered the argument she'd witnessed between Bill and Maggie Lyle, Maggie yelling at Bill for "never doing anything right," or something along those lines. She included the overheard complaints from the grocery delivery woman, Amber, last week when she'd been in Happy Family picking up snacks for her classroom. She finished with Caroline's close call on the stairs with the newly installed hand railing.

Harlan set his fork down, rubbing the back of his neck with one large hand. "Bill would know how to properly install a stair railing. There's no doubt in my mind. The screws must not have made it into the stud. But...he'd have been able to find the stud, so I don't know how that could have happened." Those twin lines between his eyebrows had appeared, letting Savanna know he was perplexed. Harlan didn't usually let go of something until he'd figured it out.

"What about the property dispute, Harlan? They'd been feuding over that for years. Maybe decades," Charlotte spoke up.

"What property dispute?" Savanna looked from her mother to her dad.

"It was an easement issue," Harlan said, "if I remember right. Bill's tried a few times to hire me to put up a privacy fence on that end of the property."

Skylar hit the table, open-palmed, making all of them jump. "Sorry. But yes. The Lyles say the easement that runs between the two pieces of property belongs to them. The Carsons have always maintained that it's Carson land. With the easement where it is, the Lyles can't split their land; they own just shy of twenty acres, I think." Skylar looked up toward the ceiling, trying to remember. "And the use laws in our township say property must have a minimum footage of frontage in order to be split and sold. Neither Caroline nor the Lyles have adequate frontage to piece sell their land without that easement. Not that Caroline wants to sell, but the Lyles have wanted to cash in on their land for years. They could split it four ways and sell off three; property values must have quadrupled since they originally bought. They've never been able to sell. They're in my office at least once a year asking about loopholes and trying to find a way to gain ownership of the easement. Everett would never sell to them, and it didn't matter, because the Lyles would never accept that the easement was on Carson property. We even had a surveyor out to mark property lines. The only way the Lyles can get the money out of their land is if Caroline sells them the easement...or if she dies."

Savanna's gasp expressed what each of them seemed to be thinking. Did Bill Lyle sabotage his own work in an attempt to get rid of Caroline?

Chapter Ten

CANARY YELLOW. IT was Savanna's chosen mood for Monday, and she dressed to match. What with Caroline's near miss this weekend, the hospital, the trip to the police station with Aidan, and fretting about the Lyles, Savanna barely slept last night. In the shower this morning, she decided she needed a pick-me-up. She paired a bright yellow midi skirt with a black and white polka-dot blouse, a yellow bow securing her hair into a low side-ponytail. She topped it off with only mascara and a cheerful red lipstick.

Sitting in the teachers' lounge during her prep period, scrolling through project ideas on her laptop, Savanna swore the yellow skirt was working on her mood. She and Aidan had done everything possible to make sure Caroline was safe. The police had the information about Eleanor's lab work. Lauren would act as safeguard at the house. Caroline would be okay—enough—while they all tried to get to the root of what was going on.

Jack Carson came through the door, crossing to the coffeemaker. He spoke to Savanna. "Can I pour you a cup?"

She'd already met her caffeine quota, but she was so curious about Lauren's statement the other day when Savanna had offered to call Jack or his mother. Maybe he could shed some light on what that was about. "Sure!"

He grabbed her cup and filled them both, asking if she wanted cream or sugar. When Savanna said "Both, please," she cringed inwardly as she watched him pour way too much sugar into her mug.

He joined her at her table, pushing her steaming cup over to her.

"Wait, isn't your prep hour after mine?" she asked.

"It is. But my student teacher is very good." He smiled. "Just giving her a little space."

"Oh, wow." Savanna's eyes widened. She hadn't thought about student teachers. "Jeez, I hope I don't get one. I'm nearly a student teacher myself." She laughed.

"Don't sell yourself short, Savanna. You're a natural at this. The kids love your class."

"Aw. Thank you. I'm really enjoying it." Should she bring up Caroline? Did Jack have any idea what had happened Saturday?

He took the decision out of her hands. "Listen, I want to thank you for being there for my grandmother this weekend—again. It sounds like she'll be okay."

"Oh, good, you heard?"

"Yesterday. My uncle called to let us know what happened. Crazy, huh?"

"It is. She's tough," Savanna said.

"My mom and grandmother have clashed for years. You're over there a lot since you've been back. You might as well know."

"Ah. Well…" She was at a loss for words.

"Uncle Thomas called my mom from the hospital. The relationship is...tricky, but we went over yesterday to see her."

"All families go through things," she offered.

"It's fine. It isn't a new issue."

Savanna was shaking her head. She barely remembered Jack's mother. She thought Elizabeth was a little older than Thomas. "Jack, you don't owe me any explanations."

"I know. But I wanted to say thank you. My uncle said you even came to the hospital. Anyway." He stood. "I'd better get back." Jack picked up his coffee cup and started toward the door. He paused, turning back to Savanna, and raised a hand as if giving a short wave goodbye, and then exited quickly.

Savanna watched him go. She liked Jack Carson, but somehow conversations with him were always a little awkward. He just seemed to have trouble being personable, though he definitely tried, she thought as she finished her too-sweet coffee.

A Carson Village police car was sitting in the drop-off/pick-up circle when Savanna left for the day. She walked past the car on her way to the teachers' parking lot, not thinking much of it until an officer got out and approached.

Savanna stopped and waited for him. Well, this was new. "Can I help you?"

The man was dressed in a standard black suit, badge clipped to his belt. "Savanna Shepherd?"

"Yes." It was a good thing the kids were gone. What if she'd left school on time today? How long had he been waiting for her? How the heck did he know what she looked like?

"Nick Jordan. Do you have time to come answer a few questions?"

"About?" She knew what it was about, but he was making her nervous. This must be the detective Skylar had said she'd call.

"About the incident at Caroline Carson's house."

"Which incident?" Oh, man, why was she being difficult? "Never mind. Yes, I can answer some questions. Now?"

She spotted two teachers walking her way from the building. Rosa was a third-grade teacher, and she was pretty sure Tricia taught first grade. They gawked at her. Savanna closed her eyes. Great. She was already dreading the teachers' lounge gossip she'd have to dodge tomorrow morning.

"Now is good," Nick Jordan said. "Do you know where the station is?"

"Yes. I...I need a little time. I'd like to bring my sister."

"No problem. You aren't being charged with anything," the detective said, his posture relaxing somewhat as he reached inside a breast pocket and took out a pack of gum. "We're trying to get some details about the night Eleanor Pietila died." He offered her the pack.

She shook her head. "Okay, good. Great. So you believe Eleanor was poisoned?"

The detective took a piece and put the gum away. "I can't discuss details. Why don't you call Skylar and have her meet you at the station? The whole thing shouldn't take more than an hour of your time."

"Sure."

"Great. I'll see you there, Ms. Shepherd. Just ask for me." He handed her a business card.

She looked down at the card as he walked back across the circle drive and climbed into the patrol car. Savanna scowled, glancing up to catch Rosa and Tricia with their heads together, still looking at her. It would have been nice if Detective Jordan could have at least shown up in an un-marked car. Small town precinct budget limitations, she was sure. Patrol cars were probably the only type of police vehicle.

Savanna turned her back on the two teachers, got in her own car, and drove directly to Skylar's office on the other side of town. Her sister had better be in.

Savanna stood in the reception area, waiting; Skylar's gatekeeper wouldn't let her pass Apparently, there was a Skype meeting going on in her sister's office.

"I'll wait outside," she told the friendly but firm twenty-year-old behind the desk. She knew it wasn't his fault Skylar was inaccessible, but she really needed her.

On the front sidewalk, Savanna texted Skylar:

I need you to come with me to the police station.

Your Detective Jordan came to my SCHOOL.

He was a little scary.

He wants me to come answer questions and I don't want to do this alone.

While she waited, Savanna scrolled through and found Aidan's number; he'd given it to her Saturday as they'd been leaving the police station, and had told her to call him anytime, for anything. At the time, she'd thought it was sweet, and unnecessary. Now, after typing in a message, she hesitated, her finger hovering over the "send" icon. Did she really need to bother him about this? She reread her text:

Hello Aidan, a detective came to my work to talk to me. Have they called you to ask more questions? I don't know why I'm worried, I know they just want to know what happened. I'm waiting for Skylar to come with me.

Savanna backspaced through the whole message, getting rid of all of it. Much too personal and needy. She tried again:

Hi Aidan, a detective came to my work to talk to me. Have they gotten ahold of you since Saturday? Did they make you go to the station? My sister is going to come with me.

Ugh. Why was she so bad at this?

Backspace again.

Hey Aidan, on my way to talk to a Det. Jordan about Eleanor. Just thought I'd let you know.

She hit send before she could reconsider.

Oh, crap. She'd never given him her number.

This is Savanna btw.

Send.

Have a great day. She inserted a smiley, hit send again, and squeezed her eyes shut.

Wow, she was a dork. Texting Aidan like they were good friends, then realizing he didn't even have her number. She pressed a finger and thumb over her closed eyes, shaking her head.

"Nick Jordan is anything but scary!" Skylar stood right in front of Savanna outside her law offices. She took Savanna's hand away from her eyes. "You're adorable today, by the way. There's something vaguely Parisian about this look."

"Will you come with me?"

"What is your issue? Why are you freaking out?"

"How did he know what I look like?" Savanna blurted the first thing that popped into her head. "Do they suspect me?"

Skylar actually laughed—wholeheartedly too. Tipped her head back and laughed. "Oh, Savanna. Why on earth would they suspect you of anything?"

"Because it occurred to me today, talking to her grandson Jack, that I've been at Caroline's both times someone has gotten hurt, and *how* did they know what I look like?"

Skylar shrugged. "Hmm. Maybe because they're *the police?*"

"Fine. Come with me." Savanna took Skylar by the hand and led her toward her car.

Skylar sighed. "Okay. But I have a meeting at six."

Savanna felt a zillion times better walking into the Carson Village police station with Skylar by her side. She handed the desk sergeant the card Jordan had given her. When she and Skylar were ushered into the detective's small office and seated in comfortable brown leather chairs across the desk, Savanna was further relieved. She'd imagined a long, bare table in a long, bare room, with one light fixture hanging overhead. She was sure they had one of those rooms here, but it wasn't meant for her and Skylar.

Her phone buzzed, and she glanced at it just as the detective entered, greeting Skylar and taking a seat behind his desk.

Aidan had texted back:

Hi Savanna, thanks for the heads-up! Just out of surgery, so I might have missed Jordan's call. Call me later to tell me how it goes.

Savanna dropped the phone back into her bag, giving Detective Jordan her full attention.

The detective leaned forward, elbows on his desk. "Ms. Shepherd, thank you for coming in. Do you mind if I record this?"

Savanna glanced at Skylar, who nodded dismissively. "It's fine," she answered for Savanna.

Jordan pressed a button on the small black recorder on his desk and picked up a pen resting on a yellow legal pad. "So, Savanna, could you tell me what you were doing at Caroline Carson's house the night Eleanor Pietila passed?"

"I'd brought Caroline some of my work—paintings—to look at. I'm doing a mural for her."

"And I understand from what you and Dr. Gallager told Detective Taylor, the three of you—Mrs. Carson, yourself, and Mrs. Pietila—were each served a glass of red wine by Mrs. Carson's granddaughter Lauren?" He was jotting notes as she talked.

"That's right. But Eleanor is the only one who drank the wine."

"And why is that?"

"Oh. Uh, Caroline and I were talking, I think."

"Where was Dr. Gallager?"

"Upstairs. At first. But then he came in to talk to Caroline." She and Caroline had been standing at the picture window, talking about her heart, Savanna recalled.

"And which of you noticed something was wrong with Mrs. Pietila?"

"Um...I think we all did. Her glass fell. That's what got our attention. She was slumped over in her chair. She seemed to have passed out. Dr. Gallager moved her to the floor and put a pillow under her legs." It had been so awful, watching poor Eleanor, lifeless and pale as Aidan had tried to save her. Savanna felt shaky all over again, remembering.

"Did she ever regain consciousness? Did she speak at all?"

Skylar spoke up. "That would be a question for Dr. Gallager. My sister took Mrs. Carson out of the room at that point."

Savanna looked gratefully at Skylar. "The doctor suggested I take Caroline to the other room and call 911. Which I did. I mean, I called 911 while we were walking to the living room. I didn't see Eleanor again. The ambulance came...we called Caroline's granddaughter to come back...then when I went to go check on things, Aidan—Dr. Gallager—was coming to talk to us. It was over." Savanna shook her head. She still remembered how defeated he'd looked that night.

"Back up, please. You said you called the granddaughter to come back. She'd left?"

"Yes. I think that's just her routine. She's there every day helping Caroline. But she doesn't live there."

"So Mrs. Carson told you to call her to come back when this happened with Eleanor?"

"Oh." Savanna remembered. "No. Actually, Lauren called the house."

"The granddaughter who'd just left called the house?"

"Yes."

"For what purpose?"

"She... I don't think she said why she called."

"So the granddaughter, Lauren, called, and who answered the phone? You?"

"Yes."

"Why?"

"It was the house phone, in the kitchen. I guess I wanted to save Caroline the walk. She's almost ninety, and she was very upset," Savanna said, irritation coloring her tone.

The detective either didn't notice or didn't care. "What did Lauren say when you spoke to her?"

"She asked if Caroline was all right, and then I told her what had happened to Eleanor. She said she'd come back."

"Just to be clear," Jordan said. "You said the granddaughter asked if Caroline was all right before you told her something had happened to Eleanor."

"Yes."

"Why would the granddaughter have called to ask if Caroline was all right? She'd just left her."

Skylar interjected. "Jordan, anything my sister answers to that is going to be speculation on her part. You know that. She can't guess at intention."

Jordan pursed his lips. "Sure, right." He scrawled another something on his notepad, illegible to anyone but him. He looked back up at Savanna. "Can you think of anything else I should add?"

"I assumed," Savanna said, "when Lauren asked if Caroline was okay that she was probably asking simply because she was surprised to still find me there."

"Sure. Is that part of Lauren's routine, to call her grandmother at night shortly after she's left?"

"I have no idea. Maybe."

"Okay. Did you happen to see the bottle of wine Lauren served from?"

"No...but she talked about it being a unique, pretty bottle. It came with the grocery delivery that day."

Jordan scrawled on his pad. "From Happy Family, I assume? The smaller store doesn't offer delivery, I'm fairly sure."

"Yes, Happy Family." Savanna paused. To mention Amber or not? Well, if Amber was completely uninvolved, it couldn't hurt to mention her, right? "Caroline's delivery girl is named Amber. I passed her on my way in."

"Good to know. Savanna, other than the grocery delivery service and Dr. Gallager, who else has access to Mrs. Carson's home?"

Savanna glanced wide-eyed at Skylar. "Well, everyone," she said, Skylar murmuring her agreement. "She's renovating right now. There are always people in and out. I can't even begin to say who exactly has access...but Caroline makes it clear that she expects people to just come in and take care of their business."

Jordan sighed, looking at the sisters. "She doesn't lock her doors?"

"I've never found them locked," Skylar said.

"In the days surrounding Eleanor Pietila's death, can you tell me who exactly was in and out of Mrs. Carson's house? Can anyone?"

"Um," Savanna considered. "Caroline's granddaughter probably has the best idea of everyone who was in and out.

In general, it's been family members, me, the grocery delivery lady, a couple of handymen, her friends occasionally...I'm honestly not sure who else."

"Okay." The detective sat back. "One last question. Were you present during the book club meeting that took place earlier in the evening?"

"No," Savanna replied. "I came in as they were finishing up. Everyone left about ten minutes after I arrived."

"And did you notice if refreshments had been served during that meeting?"

Savanna closed her eyes, frowning. Had there been?

The detective, for once, remained quiet, not pushing.

"Lauren was cleaning up when I came," she remembered. "Something must have been served. She was carrying a tray of empty cups and plates, and she ran the dishwasher before she left."

"And how long after the book club members left was it that Eleanor fell unconscious?"

"I'm not sure."

"Twenty minutes? More? How long did you visit with Mrs. Carson?"

"I'm really not sure. My meeting with her was set for seven thirty. And I called 911..." Savanna pulled out her phone, immediately seeing that message from Aidan that she hadn't responded to. She scrolled through her outgoing calls until she found the EMS call two weeks ago. "I called 911 at 8:02 p.m."

Jordan nodded, his pen working. "Good to know," he said again. He pushed his chair back, standing. "All set. Quick and painless, right?" He smiled, and it transformed his face.

Savanna couldn't remember why he'd seemed intimidating now. "Detective," she said, standing with Skylar, "just out of curiosity. Why did you come to my school?"

"Oh." He looked sheepish, and now Savanna thought she must have been crazy to think this man was scary. "Your, uh, sister. Sydney Shepherd. When I pulled your information to come talk to you, you've got Sydney's address listed as your primary residence," he said, glancing from her to Skylar.

"That's right, it's temporary." She still didn't understand.

"Oh. It's just that Sydney and I dated a while ago. And it didn't end in the, uh, best possible way, so I thought...maybe I should find you at work. I'm sorry if I surprised you." He looked chastised, and Savanna hadn't said a word.

Savanna rolled her eyes at Skylar. "We should have known."

Skylar shook hands with the detective as they left. "Thank you, Jordan. I knew we could trust you to get to the bottom of this. Caroline Carson is very dear to us. I hope you'll find that the incident with Eleanor wasn't somehow aimed at Caroline. After her fall on the stairway that I told you about, we're a little spooked."

Jordan walked them out. "It's good to be cautious. I'll look into this further, and I'll keep you updated on any developments. Try not to worry," he told them both.

Savanna dropped Skylar off at her office with plenty of time to spare. She grabbed her and gave her a big hug before Skylar could get out of the car, thanking her.

"Don't worry about it, I'm happy to help," Skylar said. "I was thinking, maybe it wouldn't hurt if we kept a kind of tally of who's in and out of Caroline's house. At least during the times you're there. Just in case…"

Savanna shivered. "Just in case something else happens. Yeah. You're right. I'll be there tomorrow after work. I'm going to talk to Caroline if I can find a way to bring it up. She's too trusting, and it's going to end up getting her hurt."

"Good luck with that conversation."

"I was thinking too," Savanna said, "I really need to look for my own place."

Skylar laughed. "Why, just because Sydney's dated a few of Carson's finest?"

"I can't blame her." Savanna shrugged. "And she's kind of a serial monogamist. I think I remember her talking about a Nick last year. Was he the one she got to adopt that shelter dog from Lake Haven?"

"Oh! He might be," Skylar said. "I'll ask him next time I see him."

"At least she left him better off than he was before, right? Who doesn't love rescuing a dog?" Savanna smiled. "Hey, can you text me the name of your real estate lady? I do want to start looking. There are some really cute Cape Cods close to the lake, at the south end of town. They need work, but they might be in my price range."

"And we know a great contractor." Skylar winked. "So, does this mean you're planting roots? We aren't losing you to Chicago again?"

Savanna shook her head. "Not a chance. I'm so glad to be back where I belong."

Chapter Eleven

"CAROLINE?" SAVANNA PULLED the screen door open and poked her head in when ringing the front doorbell yielded no response. Many people in Carson were in the habit of leaving their doors unlocked; Caroline wasn't the only one. It had never seemed strange to Savanna until she'd moved to Chicago. First in the dorms, and then on her own, she'd retrained herself to always keep her door locked. Nobody in the city left their place unlocked—it just wasn't done. Now, back in her usually safe little hometown, where everyone knew everyone and even her own parents hadn't used a house key in years, Savanna found the practice to be naïve and worrisome. Caroline had probably been leaving her doors unlocked her whole adult life; Savanna doubted she could convince her to change that.

Lauren's car wasn't in the drive today, but Aidan's was. Savanna hated interrupting a medical visit. Aidan was probably here checking on her ankle. She would just say a quick hello without interrupting, and then get to painting. She'd stopped off at home to change, and Fonzie had followed her out the door before she could stop him, so she'd let him come along. He didn't cause any trouble, and she knew he missed her during the day, especially if Sydney didn't have him at the shop.

She entered the foyer, noting the stairway railing had been reinstalled; there was new plaster applied to the holes in the wall, awaiting paint. Harlan had mentioned Sunday night that he'd go take care of the railing, and he sure hadn't wasted any time.

"Caroline," she called again, Fonzie trotting ahead of her as she slowly made her way through the house toward the parlor and her mural. She heard laughter coming from the kitchen.

Savanna found Caroline and Aidan seated at the kitchen table, enjoying delicious-looking chocolate cake.

Aidan was reaching for his glass of milk when he spotted Savanna, his face breaking into a wide smile. "Savanna, hi." He stood, moving toward her for a moment and then, hesitating, he instead settled for pulling the chair out next to him.

Caroline waved her over. "Join us, my dear! Your father brought this from Charlotte yesterday when he came to repair the railing, and it's wonderful. Your mother has always been quite the baker. Dr. Gallager, would you be a doll and get Savanna a piece? I'm a little"—she waved a hand at her leg that was propped on pillows on the kitchen chair next to her—"indisposed right now."

"Sure," Aidan said, grinning at Savanna as he moved past her to the cupboard for a plate. "She insisted I try some. She isn't going to take no for an answer from you either."

"And I thought country doctors exchanging services for baked goods was just a myth," Savanna murmured, smiling up at him.

He rolled his eyes at her. "Shows what you know. I always accept payment in chocolate cake."

Savanna leaned down and hugged Caroline before taking her seat. "You look great, Caroline, as usual. How are you feeling?" She eyed the bulky plastic boot covering her foot and lower leg.

"Not too bad. Please be sure to thank your parents for me. They're so kind to look out for me."

Aidan set a piece of cake and glass of milk in front of Savanna, and added a fork and napkin, taking his own seat again.

Savanna took a bite, acutely aware of Aidan's proximity. Why, for goodness' sake, *why* did she look like she hadn't bought new clothes since she was a teenager every single time she encountered him? Today's painting outfit was different, at least, than the other day: the faded, torn jeans and Harry Potter tee were now replaced with loose green cargo pants and a time-worn Johnny Cash shirt that used to belong to Charlotte. Maybe she did need new clothes.

"You never called last night," he said.

"Oh! I'm sorry." She'd assumed he was just being nice; she hadn't wanted to bother him with a phone call by the time she arrived home last night. He must be busy with Mollie, and it had sounded like he'd had a long day in surgery.

"Did everything go all right?" He tipped his head, watching her. "You know, with the...the thing."

Savanna nodded. "Yes, it was fine. The—uh—meeting

was easier than I expected." Now she wished she'd asked Jordan what exactly he planned to do with the information they'd discussed. If Caroline wasn't in the loop already, she needed to be. He put a hand on Caroline's arm. "Dr. Gallager and I need to talk with you about something, Caroline. About your safety."

Caroline put her fork down. "My safety? A detective stopped by last night to discuss a few matters. This is all a bunch of hullabaloo over nothing."

Aidan spoke. "I don't agree. There's good reason to be concerned."

"We think someone may be trying to hurt you. And it might have started with Eleanor," Savanna said.

Aidan's face was painted with concern, his glance moving to the blood pressure monitor on the table nearby. "We don't want to upset you, but did the detective tell you there were some disturbing results with the autopsy? I don't believe she died of natural causes."

Caroline was shaking her head. "This doesn't make any sense. Eleanor had a heart attack."

"She may not have," Aidan said. "There was a substance in her system that didn't belong there. We think the only explanation is that she ate or drank something that was tampered with."

"But…she was here, with me. With us, for book club." Caroline looked from Aidan to Savanna. "How could she have been poisoned?"

"We aren't sure," Savanna said. "But I think it's likely that whoever is responsible was trying to get to you, Caroline, not Eleanor."

"No. I told Detective Jordan—Lauren and I prepared all of the food beforehand. We only had tea and finger sandwiches. And cookies Lauren picked up from Pop's bakery next to Fancy Tails."

"And wine," Savanna said quietly.

"Wine?" Caroline looked puzzled.

"Lauren served the three of us a claret, after your book club friends left. Remember?"

"Ah. Yes…but we barely had a chance to drink it. I don't think I touched mine."

"I only had a little taste," Savanna lied, just so details would match up with what she'd said to Lauren. "But Eleanor drank hers."

"Her glass was empty when she dropped it," Caroline murmured. "Oh, my." Her hand went to her throat as she stared at Aidan and Savanna.

He leaned forward. "Can you think of any reason someone might want to hurt you, Caroline?"

Her response was immediate. "No! Of course not."

"Do you know what happened to that bottle of wine? Have you seen it at all?"

"No…I haven't seen it since that day. It was on the kitchen counter with the groceries. Lauren must have put it away."

Savanna spoke up. "I asked Lauren. She hasn't seen it either. We also aren't sure exactly what happened with the handrail on your stairway."

Caroline looked sternly at Savanna. "Of course we are. It

was an accident. These century-old walls aren't always the sturdiest. I don't blame anyone for that."

"It was just a thought," Savanna said, putting her hands up. "My dad says Bill Lyle knows his stuff, that he'd have known how to correctly secure that railing."

"So you're suggesting...what? That Bill conspired to poison Eleanor, and then rigged the railing so I would fall?" Caroline was shaking her head.

"No," Savanna said, "not necessarily." She looked at Aidan for help.

"We're just worried about you, Caroline," he said. "Maybe the railing incident was just an accident. But you have to admit, it seems strange, in light of Eleanor and the autopsy results."

"We don't want anything else to happen to you," Savanna said, taking Caroline's hand in hers. She knew she'd upset her. "I know you can't imagine anyone trying to hurt you. And I know you trust Bill and Maggie. I heard them arguing outside, the morning he was here working on the stairs. She was angry at him for not doing something he'd promised."

"That could be over anything." Caroline rolled her eyes. "Those two fight all the time. You don't need to worry about me. Maybe Eleanor's results are wrong."

"The police are looking into it," Aidan said. "They'll figure it out, but in the meantime, we don't want you to be in the dark if something sinister is going on here."

"Something sinister," Caroline repeated. "That sounds crazy."

"Caroline," Savanna said, "maybe, just until this all settles down, would you consider locking your doors, please?"

Caroline huffed out a sigh. "Nobody in Carson locks their doors. Even that detective knows that. I have no idea where my house key is anymore. Do you really think that's necessary?"

"We really do," Aidan said. "Just as a precaution."

She sighed, giving up. "All right. I'll ask Lauren to start looking for my keys. I honestly haven't locked my doors in decades."

"Where is Lauren?" She'd promised Savanna she'd push Caroline to let her help out at the house more.

"She's at Happy Family. She canceled my delivery service. She got some wild notion that she should be doing all the shopping. Oh." Understanding dawned on the older woman's face. "It's because of Eleanor, isn't it? Oh, my. You've already spoken to Lauren about this, haven't you? So how on earth am I supposed to know who I can trust?" She took off her glasses and set them on the table, her hand trembling.

"Caroline," Aidan said, standing and coming over to her, "I'm sorry. We are both sorry. We didn't mean to upset you. None of this is good for your health, and you have a whole team of people looking out to make sure you will be fine." He met Savanna's eyes over Caroline's head, sympathy furrowing his brow.

"Very true," Savanna agreed. "And other than starting to lock your doors from now on, there isn't a thing you should do differently. Listen, I wanted to work on where the sailboats should go in the mural today. Would you help me?

I need your input." She stood too, holding a hand out to the woman.

She looked up at them, from Savanna to Aidan. "Nice distraction technique," she said wryly. "But yes. I want one of them to have the same sails Everett's boat had."

Aidan helped her up, and Savanna moved her new walker over to her.

"This thing," she murmured, patting the walker, "is going in the trash the moment this boot comes off. Until then, I know I'm stuck with it."

With Caroline on the move, slowly, the poodles lazily stretched in their sun spots on the kitchen floor and got to their feet, followed by Fonzie, leading the procession into the parlor. Caroline's family had set up a twin-size bed against the far wall, and a proper bedside table next to it, with everything Savanna imagined Caroline normally had upstairs in her bedroom: table lamp, small clock, a couple of hardcover books, her pillbox, a bottle of strawberry-scented hand lotion, even a purple satin sleep mask.

"This is nice, Caroline." Savanna gestured at the bed as they passed it on the way to the set of wingback chairs. "Your family thinks of everything."

"That was Lauren, of course. She got a few of the grandkids over here and they set it all up, until I have my leg back in working order. She tried to move herself in for a few weeks—just ridiculous. She's a quick phone call away if I need her."

The doorbell rang as Savanna followed Caroline and the dogs.

"Do you mind getting it, Savanna?" Aidan asked, carrying his black bag. "I want to check her blood pressure before I leave, once she's settled."

"Sure." Savanna backed up, letting Aidan take her place behind Caroline. With the boot on, she wasn't exactly steady; her gait made Savanna nervous. She watched Aidan's hand hover a few inches behind Caroline's back, a reflex measure just in case, as she turned to go see who among Caroline's visitors would actually ring the bell.

The gentleman she'd met a week or two ago, Caroline's art dealer, stood on the porch, along with a younger man she didn't recognize.

"Mr. Thiebold, please, come in." Savanna held the door open for him.

"Felix, please," he corrected. "This is my assistant, Ryan. Caroline has us picking up a piece."

"Of course. Why don't you follow me? She's not quite...mobile at the moment." Savanna led the way to the back of the house.

"Felix!" Caroline clasped her hands together, leaning forward in her chair when she saw him.

Aidan had his stethoscope in his ears, the bell on Caroline's arm, midcheck. He smiled and released the cuff, stepping back.

"Oh, my, I'm sorry." Caroline looked up at him. "I'm supposed to be still. Try again, Dr. Gallager. I'll be good, I promise."

Aidan placed the bell of his stethoscope on Caroline's arm again, glancing at the trio—the gallerist, his assistant, and Savanna. "One minute, and she's all yours." He put his head down, listening. Getting a valid reading this time, Aidan removed the cuff from Caroline's arm and straightened up. "Still a little high. You need to take it easy. Sit, read, watch the paint dry," he said, winking at Savanna at his own little joke. "Relax. You've got one more week until you're done wearing the monitor. I'll be back to take all the equipment next week, okay? And do *not* overdo it on the leg," he said sternly, pointing to the boot.

She nodded obediently. "Yes, sir. You have my word." Caroline glanced past him at Savanna and gave her a wide-eyed look.

Savanna laughed. "I'll walk you out," she told Aidan, leaving Caroline to talk to Felix. "I think," she told Aidan once they were outside on the wide front porch, "you're the only person I've ever seen boss her around effectively."

"It's just the white coat." He grinned. He still looked doctorly, despite the lack of a white coat; today he wore black dress pants and a crisp lavender button-down with sleeves rolled up, tie loosened now at the end of the day but still around his neck, along with his stethoscope.

"No white coat today," she noted. "So it's just you. You have magical powers when it comes to Caroline Carson."

"Well, maybe it's the threat of the white coat," he said. "Whatever works. So, you're staying for a bit to paint?"

"Yes. I haven't gotten much done and I know she wants it finished for her party."

"I love it. I guess I hadn't seen what you've done until today. You're very talented, Savanna."

"Oh." She shrugged. "Well, thank you, I appreciate that. I'm still a little rusty. I hardly painted at all in Chicago."

"I'd never know," Aidan said. "I think it'll be beautiful when you're finished. We're lucky to have you," he said, and then clarified, "teaching at the school. I mean, art teacher doesn't necessarily mean you have the skill too. The kids are lucky to have such a well-rounded teacher. I know Mollie's happy in your class."

Savanna smiled. "I just love her. She's such a little sweetheart."

Aidan's eyes lit up. "I think so too. But I'm biased. Thank you." He started to head down the front steps and stopped, turning back. "Wait, when is Caroline's birthday again? A few weeks still, right?"

"First weekend in October," Savanna said. "A little less than three weeks from now."

"She should be in good shape by then," he said, still in doctor mode. "I can probably graduate her to an ankle brace before that. I need to put it in my calendar." He pulled out his phone, tapping the screen.

"October fifth," Savanna offered.

"Oh, I almost forgot," he said. "The youth event this weekend at the Carson Ballroom. Are you involved in that at all, through the school?"

"No, I don't think so?" Savanna wasn't sure what he was talking about.

"Mollie was reminding me this morning. It's called Fall Fun Fest. The library and the ballroom have sponsored it the last couple of years. Saturday night...it's not a big deal. They just have booths set up, used books for sale, activities for the kids, face painting, music. That kind of thing."

"How cool! I guess I've been so preoccupied lately I must have missed the information. The ballroom is the next block down from Fancy Tails. I wonder if Sydney knows," she mused.

"She might. They usually try to get input and donations from local businesses. Anyway, I just thought maybe, since you're the art teacher, the committee might have hit you up to help or something."

Savanna shook her head. "Nope. I wish they had though. I'd have loved to help! I'll see what my sister knows."

"You should. It's a nice event. I know Mollie and her friends are excited. Maybe I'll see you there?" His tone was odd, Savanna thought, and that was a question, not just an offhand statement; one look up at him confirmed that. He was waiting for her response, keys in hand. Aidan wanted her there. Didn't he?

A little zing shot through her and she felt her cheeks warm. "Sure," she said. "I'll definitely be there. It'll be fun to see my kids outside of class. Thanks for letting me know about it!"

She watched Aidan's car drive away. Had she misread that entire exchange? She hoped she hadn't. Either way, she was glad he'd mentioned it to her. She'd ask Skylar and Nolan to come with her—it sounded like something her little nephew would love.

She went back into the house; the fall air finally held a chill, a welcome break from the too-warm eighty-degree weather in early September. Caroline's huge maple tree out front was all gorgeous reds, oranges, and yellows now.

As she passed the living room just off the foyer, she spotted the young man who'd accompanied Felix tying up a large, brown-paper-wrapped painting with string. In the parlor, she found Felix seated across from Caroline in the other wingback chair. He pressed a check into her hand, covering it with his other hand. "It was an excellent sale, Caroline. You gained about twelve percent above the purchase price Everett paid."

"Wonderful." She looked up as Savanna entered. "Savanna, you and Felix met the other day, didn't you?"

"We did. Is that the Laurant you sold?"

"Yes," Caroline said. "I know you loved it, dear."

"I love all of them. But I'm glad to hear you've done well finding it a new home."

"A private investor in Hartford fell in love with the pair," Felix said. "That one and the one he bought in August. He was happy to pay top dollar. And"—Felix clasped his hands together, leaning forward—"I may have a buyer for one of your Sergei Minkovs."

Savanna gasped; she couldn't help it. Caroline and Felix both looked at her. "I'm so sorry." She looked down, embarrassed. The Minkov in Caroline's library was priceless. The last known value of that piece was over 2.5 million dollars. She glanced up. "I just love that piece so much. I thought you were keeping it, Caroline?"

"I had planned on it," Caroline said. She was clearly conflicted. "I didn't know there was interest in the Minkov,

Felix. We were focusing on the works I have by Laurant and Rothman."

The gallerist nodded. "Absolutely, that's my plan. I actually—"

"The Minkov in the library was Everett's forty-fifth anniversary gift to me," Caroline said. "I'm just not sure I can part with it, not for any amount of money."

"It's off the table. Don't worry, I completely understand. I was actually speaking of the smaller piece you have in the dining room."

"Ah," Caroline and Savanna both spoke at the same time, and then laughed, looking at each other.

"I've never loved that piece," Caroline said, relief in her voice. "I think that would be fine if you feel it's a good deal. I haven't heard anything lately from Everett's other gallerist friend, Mr. Banfield, so have at it."

"I'm still working on it. I want you to be careful who you trust, Caroline," he said, reaching over to place a hand lightly on her forearm, his demeanor serious. "I don't mind handling these sales for you. I'm seeing the interested party again on Friday, so I'll let you know. And I'll be sending Ryan next week to pick up your Rothman, the one that was hanging in the foyer, if you're still on board with that plan? Different collectors, a married couple in Santa Rosa."

Savanna shook her head. "You certainly must travel a lot. I know it can be the life of an art dealer, but you're on both coasts in the same week. You don't seem to mind."

Felix gave a little shrug with one shoulder. "I love it. It's the only work I know. I'm not cut out for anything else," he said, tone humble as he ran a thumb over his knee on the crease in his slacks. "And I meet the most interesting people." He smiled at Caroline.

"Likewise, Felix." Caroline reached a hand out, and he took it. "We're so fortunate Everett found you."

Felix patted Caroline's hand as he stood. "I really must go. Oh, paperwork, I almost forgot. Might I get the provenances, Caroline? For the Laurant today, and I'll take the one for the Rothman Ryan will pick up next week, if you have it here."

"I do, but the Rothman document is still filed away in Everett's desk. Savanna," Caroline said, "could I bother you to fetch the envelope on the credenza over there? That's the certificate for the Laurant, I had Lauren get it ready."

"I can get the other one," Felix told Caroline, "if you tell me where to look."

"Oh, don't trouble yourself." Caroline waved a hand. "My granddaughter will have it ready when Ryan comes back for the Rothman, don't worry. I'll make sure...as you can see, I'm not going anywhere. I'll be available." She tapped the plastic walking boot for emphasis.

Savanna handed Felix the manila envelope with his name on it.

"Thank you, my dear." He turned to Caroline. "I'll see myself out. You be careful, young lady. No more accidents," he scolded. He took her hand and planted a quick kiss on it. "I want to see you looking lovely and safe and sound when I return with good news about the Minkov—the one you don't love."

Savanna took Felix's seat in the wingback chair when he'd gone. "What a charming man."

"He's quite the gentleman, isn't he? He's such a good friend to help me out with the collection he and Everett built all these years. I'm sure he has more important things to do, but he never seems to mind visiting with me."

Caroline looked comfortable and content, bad leg high in the air in her recliner, propped on pillows. Savanna imagined if Aidan was here to check her blood pressure now, it would be perfect.

Chapter Twelve

SAVANNA WAS THE first to arrive at Fancy Tails and Treats Thursday. She came into the grooming salon backward, carrying a deep-dish pizza from Giuseppe's down the street. She crossed over to the gourmet treat side of the large shop and placed the pizza on the round red and chrome table, setting paper plates, napkins, and three Mary Ann's sodas next to it.

"Savvy?" Sydney called from the back.

Savanna went over and stood in the doorway to where the magic happened: Sydney was standing at a long stainless-steel table trimming a Shih Tzu mix. She put the electric clippers down and picked up small hairdresser scissors, snipping here and there to make sure the dog's ears were trimmed evenly. The dog, for his part, stood perfectly still and stared at Savanna with a *save me* expression.

"Oh my gosh, what a cutie!" Savanna loved watching Sydney do her job. She would be terrible at it; she'd be constantly worried she'd accidentally hurt one of the dogs, plus there were so many that had special issues...hip dysplasia or diabetes or skin allergies. She'd end up wanting to take them all home. Sydney was cut out for this: she knew every animal on sight, gushed over them, loved them, and happily sent them on their way looking and smelling beautiful.

"I'm starving. What did you bring?" Sydney finished with the little dog and gave him a hug as she unhooked his collar and carried him over to his kennel.

"Pizza from Giuseppe's. Veggie on one side, pepperoni on the other."

"Yum! I can't wait." Syd deposited the dog in his little room, gave him a biscuit from her supply, and closed the half door.

"Skylar's running behind. She just texted," Savanna said.

"She'll be lucky if I leave her a piece. Ringo's pick-up is in a half hour, just enough time to eat." She untied her apron and threw it on the rack, then stripped her scrub top off, leaving a fitted pink tee underneath. She moved to the separate small sink against the back wall, calling over her shoulder, "Let me wash up and I'll be right out!"

Savanna took a piece of the pepperoni and opened her pop; she'd chosen the root beer this time.

Sydney came zipping out of the grooming area, drying her hands on a clean towel, hair piled high on top of her head. She flipped the St. Bernard sign on the door to the Closed side and joined Savanna at the table. "Oh, wow, this looks amazing." She took a piece of the veggie side. "So, I know you don't have much time either. Tell me what the heck is going on at Caroline's!"

"Well, you know about her ankle. And my chat with the police—I'm so glad Skylar could come with me for that. Aidan and I followed up with Caroline after Detective Jordan visited her. She doesn't know everything, like what drug they found in Eleanor's system, but we tried to make sure she'd take things seriously and try to be more cautious. The whole thing is strange. And it's still bothering me how that wine bottle just disappeared."

"So, you and Aidan handled things, huh?" Syd opened her bottle of blueberry-flavored pop.

"She didn't really agree…but by the time he left, I almost wished we hadn't tried so hard to convince her. She was a little shaken up."

"And you and Aidan are making sure she stays safe."

Savanna set her pizza down and looked at her sister. "Um, yes, we're trying to."

Sydney nodded. "I'm just wondering when 'Dr. Gallager' became 'me and Aidan.'"

Savanna's cheeks burned. "Never. We haven't become anything. He's just around…a lot, I guess. Between Caroline's and school, we run into each other."

"Mm-hmm." Sydney polished off her first piece of pizza and grabbed a second. "That's so nice." She smiled sweetly at Savanna.

"Okay, I'm sure I have no idea what you're insinuating, but that's a very creepy smile, Syd. Aidan's a great guy. He's a good doctor, and he really cares about Caroline. But there's nothing going on. The last thing I need is another man running my life. And he's all wrapped up in work, and his daughter…" She stopped, cutting herself off. She'd just remembered. "Hey. Do you know anything about the thing going on this Saturday at the Carson Ballroom?"

"Sure, Fall Fun Fest. It's every year. You'd know, if you

hadn't abandoned us for the glitz of Chicago."

Savanna rolled her eyes. "Yeah, yeah. I'm here now, so fill me in on this new custom."

"There will be music, food, and stations set up for kids to get their faces painted and play carnival-type games to win prizes. Violet Lyle runs a bake sale, the library donates a bunch of books for fifty cents each, most of the businesses up and down Main Street donate something for the silent auction, and if it doesn't rain, they usually have hayrides for an hour or so at dusk." Syd popped the rest of her second slice in her mouth and went behind the long glass treat display case, hefting a large shrink-wrapped basket with a dog-bone-patterned ribbon around it up onto the countertop. "This is Fancy Tails' contribution to the auction."

"That's seriously awesome, Syd!"

She shrugged. "I've had it ready for a week or so. I do the same donation every year."

"Are you going?" Savanna sat back, a hand resting on her belly through the bell-sleeved navy dress she'd finally liberated from her closet this morning. She'd added a few of Sydney's jangling bracelets to spruce up the boring color, which her students today had loved. "I am so full," she groaned.

"I'll stop in for a while," Sydney said. "Kate is teaching mini yoga—fifteen-minute yoga sessions—and I promised to relieve her at some point. Why, are you going? I'm sure a lot of your students will be there."

"Yes, it sounds like it. I'll be there. Maybe I'll take one of your mini sessions."

"Really? You should!"

Savanna checked the time on her phone. "I have to go soon, and I wanted to ask Skylar about something..." She leaned back in her chair and looked out the front window. "Syd, are you going to be at Caroline's at all in the next few days?"

"I don't think so, why?"

"I volunteered us to make the punch for her birthday party. She remembered Mom always making it for Christmas parties, and I was thinking, we could mix up a couple of small batches to see which flavor she wants."

"Oh, the punch. I miss that. We haven't had that in a few years. Let me get the recipe from Mom, and maybe I can stop by. When are you there next to paint?"

"Tonight and Saturday morning. I've got to get the mural finished. I'm running out of time."

"Tonight isn't good. I'm going out with Brad. Saturday then," Sydney said, taking her seat again across from Savanna and biting into another piece of pizza.

"How is Brad?" Savanna said his name in a singsong voice, and then realized she was just as bad as Syd when it came to talk about boys.

"Brad is adorable, as you know. You met him." Sydney sighed, smiling. "He's just...amazing. He treats me so well."

"That's awesome, Syd. I'm so happy. You deserve that."

"Yes I do!"

"Okay, I've got to get back to school." Savanna stood, gathering her things, just as the bell over the door jingled and Skylar arrived, followed by Jack Carson.

Jack paused, stopping to read the out-to-lunch sign on the door. He stepped half into the shop. "Sorry, are you closed right now?"

Syd waved him in. "No, no, we're finished. Come on in." She met him at the door and flipped the sign back around.

"I'm so sorry." Skylar hurried over to the table, dumping her briefcase, purse, and a stack of folders onto the over-stuffed aqua chair behind Savanna. "Sometimes I have no control over my schedule. I'm sorry—looks like I missed lunch."

Savanna gave her a quick hug. "You're fine, don't worry. We saved you some. Sit. Hey, Jack." He was mulling over choices at the counter.

"Do you know which kind she meant?" Sydney asked him.

Jack shook his head, bending to look closer. "She just said to get the new flavor you have." He scratched his head. "Hmm. Too many choices."

"Do you want a package of each? There are no preserva-tives in them, but they'll last about two weeks, refrigerated. My three newest flavors are Steak Sticks, Turkey Jerky, and Chicken Churros."

Jack hesitated, reading the price sheet on the countertop. He pulled out his wallet and thumbed through the cash inside.

"Cash or credit is fine," Sydney added.

"Um...maybe we could give her a sample size of each one? For now, at least? That should be enough to figure out which one Princess and Duke prefer. Then I can stop back in and get that flavor once we know. How much would that be?"

"Of course. Let's see." Sydney nodded, scooping a generous sample of each into three individually marked paper packages and ringing it up. She placed those into a brown box and wrapped it with thin white string, and handed it over the counter to Jack.

Jack smiled gratefully. "Perfect. Thank you, Sydney." He handed her a few bucks, and Syd gave him change in return.

Savanna stopped at the exit to wait for him. "I'll walk back with you. Skylar, I need to pick your brain about something. Can you call me when you have a minute?"

Her older sister didn't look up from what she was working on at the table. "Sure, on my way to Lansing later." Tonight was her overnight for court tomorrow.

Savanna and Jack walked in companionable silence for the first block. She'd miss this gorgeous weather when the snow fell, but she figured she could still walk into town on lunch, she'd just have to unpack her winter things.

"You three meet up for lunch regularly?"

"We shoot for once a week. It's nice having Sydney's place right in the middle. I love being home. And look at you, spoiling the poodles." Savanna pointed at the box in his hand.

"I'm trying to help a little... Lauren kind of put out a distress call. She wants as many of us as possible to stop in and check on Grandmother when we can, since her accident. She keeps telling Lauren she doesn't need her there so much.

She's worried about being a burden. So maybe with a few of us taking turns, it'll worry Grandmother less."

"That's actually a great idea."

"I saw your mural. It's beautiful," Jack said.

Savanna grinned. She loved hearing good things about her work, especially after all this time. "Thank you! I'm so glad you like it. I think she will too. It's coming along well."

They parted ways at Jack's classroom, kids already milling around the hallway after lunch.

"I'm sure Princess and Duke will love those flavors. My dog does," she told him.

She was somehow heartened that Jack was being included in the "distress call" for family to pitch in and check on Caroline. She knew Lauren's siblings were each involved in the Carson real estate and investment companies in varying capacities. Lauren's father ran the Indianapolis branch in addition to the western Michigan branch. She thought Jack's mother handled the Toledo and Detroit area, but that had been years ago, and there seemed to have been a falling out between Caroline and Jack's mother, Elizabeth. In any case, it seemed to make Jack happy to be included.

Savanna checked her phone as she walked into her classroom; it had dinged and buzzed three times while she and Jack had been walking back from town.

Sydney had texted her, several times in a row. Typical for Syd:

How weird was that?

Jack Carson can't afford dog treats? He seemed so concerned about what those little samples would cost. I felt bad for him.

Is everything okay with him, Savvy?

Savanna had wondered the same thing as she'd witnessed the exchange at the counter in Fancy Tails. It was a bit strange, the thought of a Carson having money troubles. She'd have to get back to Sydney later. She dropped her phone in her purse and put it away in her bottom drawer, picking up a box of rainbow-colored pipe cleaners to distribute.

"You guys won't even believe the fun project we have today with these!" She smiled down at Zoey. The little girl beamed back up at her, lining her seven pipe cleaners up on her desk in neat rows, legs swinging furiously under the table. Man, she wanted Zoey's boundless energy.

Skylar called Savanna as she was pulling up to Caroline's house that evening, around six. Fonzie was snoozing in the sun spot on the passenger seat. She turned the car off and sat in the driveway while she chatted with Skylar. She knew her sister probably wouldn't have time to talk again until tomorrow.

"So, I just wondered, what's the process with these paintings Caroline's selling?" Savanna asked.

"What do you mean? Let me switch you to Bluetooth; there, that's better. Can you hear me okay?"

"Yes, perfect. Be careful, I know traffic can be bad this time of day. I guess I want to make sure she's being treated fairly, especially since Everett is the one who built their collection, and now he isn't here to help with thinning it out. Does she get, like, receipts every time her art dealer sells one? How does she know she's getting fair market value? I spent most of my time at Kenilworth on the third floor, authenticating paintings and sculptures; I'd consult once in a while on purchases the museum was considering, but I was never directly involved in private party sales when I worked there. I don't know how it works."

"Presumably, Caroline trusts the gallerists she uses...the one gentleman you met is a longtime friend of Everett's, isn't he?"

"He is. And I know of him. I'm not disparaging him at all. He's got an impeccable reputation. But the value of these pieces she's liquidating is pretty...extreme. I know the provenances go with each piece, so that verifies authenticity, but then does Caroline receive documentation in return on the buyer and the actual selling price? She does have certificates for everything Everett bought, doesn't she?"

"She should," Skylar said. "She keeps the originals at the house, and I have copies in my office. Everett was smart—he wouldn't have purchased anything without the provenance. I doubt a gallerist would have assisted with that kind of sketchy sale, so that's not a concern."

"True," Savanna agreed.

"With private sales of any kind of high-value piece, art or otherwise, detailed receipts are the norm. I'm sure her current dealer—What's his name again?"

"Thiebold."

"I'm sure Mr. Thiebold takes a standard fee. You'd know better than I what that might be, and Caroline reaps the rest of the profit from the sale."

"So she'd have all that documentation at the house too, or has she given that to you?"

"No, this is all pretty recent," Skylar said. "She started renovating and decided she didn't want the abundance of some of those paintings anymore. She's keeping her own sale records, at least so far. I'm sure she'll bring it all in at tax time. I'll see it then."

"Okay." Savanna felt a little better. "Just wanted to check. And I know she's still sharp. I don't think anything would get past her anyway."

"Agreed," Skylar said. "But let me know if you have reason to worry about anything. As you said, a lot of money is changing hands. I can always double-check the copies Everett sent to me over the years."

"Okay," she said again. She was sure it was all fine. "Last thing, Skylar. Would you and Nolan like to come with me Saturday night to the Fall Fest thing in town? I just found out about it. Or if you're busy, I could take Nolan."

"Oooh," Skylar said. "That sounds so great. Travis and I haven't had any face time in forever. Are you sure you wouldn't mind if it was just Nolan?"

"Absolutely! I'll pick him up on my way. Syd and I will keep him overnight. You and Travis can have the whole night off." She smiled, already mentally planning a late-night Disney movie slumber party in Sydney's living room for after Fall Fun Fest.

"You're the best, Savvy," Skylar said.

"Oh, I've got to go. Another car just pulled up." There was a small beige sedan beside her. Getting out, she saw it was the Happy Family delivery woman—Amber. She was wearing her standard apron and cap. Maybe Lauren had reinstated delivery service?

"Hello," the woman said uncertainly to Savanna. She stood beside her car, no grocery bags in hand, only a bouquet of flowers and a long, slim box of chocolates.

Savanna came around her car to greet her. "Hi, I'm Savanna. I think we passed each other here a while back. Are the flowers for Caroline?"

"Yes. My boss said Mrs. Carson doesn't want the delivery service anymore, and I just kind of…feel bad, I suppose. For her accident. I heard she fell down the stairs? Is she doing okay? I wouldn't wish that on my worst enemy."

Savanna was suddenly on guard. This was strange. Why would Amber feel bad…did she think she'd done a poor job? Or did she feel bad for something else? "She's hanging in there. Would you like me to give those to her?" Savanna wasn't sure if she wanted to offer Amber the opportunity to see Caroline. That missing bottle of claret was on her mind.

"Yes, would you? That would be great." She handed the flowers and candy to Savanna.

"Amber," Savanna said, and when the woman looked surprised, Savanna pointed to the embroidered yellow name on the front of Amber's green apron. "A few weeks ago you brought a fancy bottle of wine with the groceries. Do you remember bringing it?"

"No, Mrs. Carson never orders wine."

"Oh. Well," Savanna pressed on. It couldn't hurt to push, could it? The woman either had something to hide or she didn't. "There was a really pretty bottle of wine left on the counter with the grocery delivery that day. We thought it was from the store, maybe, or you." She braced herself for Amber's defensive response, or false cluelessness. She got neither.

Instead, the woman looked mildly confused. "I don't think so. I didn't bring wine. I never do. I pack my own orders, and she never orders wine or cocktail fixings like some of our customers. Sometimes Mr. Frank will send a gift to our regular customers, like, as a thank-you, but never alcohol. He says that would be inappropriate. He usually just sends flowers." Amber tapped the box of chocolates now in Savanna's hand. "Those are from me, but the flowers are actually from him. I should have said that," she added sheepishly.

"Ah. Okay. Well...that was very nice. Thank you, for both." Now Savanna didn't know what to think about the wine. Unless, of course, Amber was lying. "I'll give them to Caroline."

Amber nodded. "Thank you. Oh, here." She handed a small white envelope to Savanna. "A get-well note."

Savanna watched Amber leave. As she turned to go in the house, she caught sight of Maggie Lyle at the far side of Caroline's property, standing on the easement. Staring. Frowning and staring right at Savanna.

Savanna turned quickly and glanced behind her; the woman was staring so intently in her direction. Nothing was there. She looked back at Maggie and tentatively raised a hand in greeting.

Maggie Lyle crossed her arms over her chest and turned abruptly, heading back toward her own house.

What on earth was that about?

Savanna carried the flowers and chocolates up the front steps, pausing to type in the four-digit code on the brand-new front door lock. Harlan had struck again yesterday, this time installing new polished brass handles with digital locks on the front, back, and kitchen doors. Harlan had written down the code for Caroline and told her to put it in her purse, and with permission, he'd given his girls the code. Savanna assumed Lauren had shared it with any of the other grandkids who were checking on her. At least the new locks would eliminate unlimited access for all, Savanna thought. She was so glad her dad had made some room in his schedule to step up and take care of Caroline this week.

She opened the box of chocolates and dumped them all into the sink, running water and hitting the garbage disposal switch. No way was she taking the chance of giving Caroline more tampered-with items from Happy Family. It seemed a shame to waste good candy, but it was better than the alternative.

She cut the stems of the flowers and arranged them in a vase. She'd taken two steps out of the kitchen when it hit her—had she just destroyed possible evidence in the garbage disposal? She lurched back to the sink and stuck her hand into the garbage disposal, cringing. Why did every scary garbage disposal scene from every horror movie ever play in her head anytime she dropped something down one of these? The thing was switched off; she was just being silly. She blindly groped but found nothing at all except the blades of the machine. Not even a scrap of chocolate. Savanna groaned. She dreaded confessing her mistake to Detective Jordan, but she'd have to.

She carried the flowers in to Caroline. "Look what your grocery delivery lady brought."

"Amber? Oh, my! They're beautiful! And a card too?" Caroline opened it, two kittens with the message *Get Well Soon!* adorning the front. She read aloud, "'Mrs. Carson, I heard about your accident and hope you are feeling better soon! I'm sorry I won't be delivering anymore, but any time you need something, I'm happy to bring it, just call. I know there were some hard feelings after your husband bought our diner, but I want you to know I understand it was just business. Roy is doing better. We are both doing better lately. He'll be home in a month if everything goes well. Please know that you're in my prayers. Take care, Amber.'"

That was certainly a change from how Amber had sounded that day in the grocery store. Maybe the woman had just been blowing off steam? Or maybe she'd had a change of heart, hearing about Caroline's accident? Things seemed encouraging as far as her husband was concerned, in any case.

"How sweet." Caroline set the card on the side table next to her. "I still don't know why Lauren felt it necessary to cancel the grocery delivery."

Chapter Thirteen

"**D**ID YOU GET the sherbet?" Savanna called out the open kitchen window to her sister.

"No, I thought you would!" Syd shouted from the rear deck.

Sydney burst through the kitchen door at Caroline's for the second time that morning, dropping three more heavy grocery bags on the counter. "I got the sherbet." She smiled at Savanna.

"Ugh, you're such a pain," Savanna groaned. "I thought you'd forgotten it."

"No, you're just fun to mess with." She stopped to kiss Savanna's cheek on her way to the freezer, and Savanna gave her wavy braid- and bead-filled ponytail a light tug.

"Cranberry juice, orange juice, 7UP, red Faygo, Rainbow Sherbet, French vanilla ice cream, frozen lime-aid, raspberries, blueberries, kiwi. Man, I'm hungry." Savanna popped a raspberry in her mouth.

Syd smacked her hand. "No sampling the supplies!"

Savanna stuck her tongue out at Syd and ate another one, scooting around the other side of the kitchen island out of her reach.

Lauren was upstairs vacuuming, cleaning for the party,

just two weeks away now. She'd come through this morning and had opened all the windows to the sunny seventy-degree day outside. Days like this in late September were few, and Savanna breathed in the refreshing lake air.

She moved to the coffee maker and poured a steaming cup, adding creamer for Caroline. "I'm going to ask where she keeps the punch bowl. You can get to work peeling kiwi," she ordered.

Syd sat on one of the stools at the counter and pulled her phone out, scrolling through. "You're not the boss of me."

Savanna couldn't help laughing. "Pain in the butt," she murmured on her way to the parlor. She set the coffee on the side table by Caroline's wingback chair, leaning over to see what she was working on.

"It's just another blanket," the older woman said, moving the knitting needles effortlessly as she worked her way through a dark burgundy spool of yarn. "Keeps my fingers from stiffening up and my mind occupied. One can only watch so much television." She looked up at Savanna.

"I know…I'm sorry you're housebound at the moment. I know you're used to a much more exciting day-to-day."

"I really am, as funny as that sounds at my age. But this is temporary." She flapped a hand at her boot. "I know I'm lucky. I'll be up and running again soon. Your friend says so." She winked at Savanna.

Savanna felt her cheeks flush. "My friend?" She had to ask, but she knew who Caroline meant.

"Oh, you know. You and my Dr. Gallager seem to have struck up quite a friendship." She set her knitting needles down and captured Savanna's hand in hers, looking her in the eye, suddenly serious. "I think it's very sweet, so you know."

Savanna patted Caroline's hand. "Thank you. We are friends. He's a very nice man. He thinks a lot of you."

"He thinks a lot of you as well. I hope..." She broke off, hesitating.

Savanna's heart raced a little at Caroline's words. Had Aidan said something about her?

Caroline nodded, seeming to have decided to say what was on her mind. "I hope that, when you're ready, when your heart is ready, you might give love a chance again. It won't always turn out the way it did in Chicago. And as for our Dr. Gallager, I believe he's had to do his own share of mending too. We never know what the future might hold, do we? But we must be brave enough to make the journey."

Savanna leaned in and hugged Caroline. "You're the wisest person I know. Thank you," she whispered.

Both their eyes were glistening when Savanna let go.

"So." She cleared her throat. "I was wondering, where do you keep your punch bowl?"

SAVANNA FOLLOWED THE long hallway around to the formal dining room, probably the most infrequently used room on the main floor these days. A regal, dark cherry wood table ran the length of the room down the center, complete with three wide leaves and twelve chairs. Against the far wall, on a matching buffet, sat Caroline's large crystal punch bowl and ladle, surrounded by twenty or so petite crystal cups. Lauren, or someone, certainly did a wonderful job caring for the Carson mansion and everything inside. There wasn't a speck of dust anywhere.

As Savanna carefully dispersed the cups so she could pick up the bowl with both hands, she studied the Sergei Minkov painting hanging above the buffet. *Storm in Sochi*, one of the more obscure pieces. She still recognized it; she'd done her thesis on Minkov's work. How could Caroline let this go? It was a study in rich, opulent color, done in oils as was the norm for late-nineteenth-century work; this piece was simple, a distant view of a village with a tumultuous sea beyond. Two figures skipped through the foreground, the entire work fairly abstract, but Savanna knew they were children; Minkov depicted them as such not just in stature but posture and carefree attitude, on their way home to the village. The overall tone was a contradiction, also as Minkov had intended: humble, light-hearted, and foreboding all at once.

The painting lacked the size and presentation of the much-larger piece in Caroline's library; this was from the artist's early work, void of pretention and ego. To Savanna, it was even more stunning than that gorgeous piece in the library, because of its simplicity. She took a step back, and then another, without thinking, her time in school coming back to her, the fine nuances of works done with oil over a century ago.

And then she saw it. The child's dress... Savanna stood

stock-still, the dining room chair now touching her back, as she let her vision relax and she took in the painting, the children, the vague shapes of clothing, the trail they skipped along surrounded by some type of farming fields. She felt her heart race as she gasped.

Moving forward quickly, Savanna leaned in, over the punch bowl, until she was just inches away from the painting, peering at the child's dress. The pigment in the dress—the emerald-green sheen of the painted fabric—the texture—it was wrong.

She pulled her cell phone from her back pocket and focused the camera on the spot and zoomed in, waiting until the mechanism made sense of the pixels and the lines sharpened. The texture had minute vertical cracks, rather than the typical grid or cross-hatch lines normally seen in a Minkov and other work from the same era. She snapped a photo, zooming in further and studying the screen. Could this piece be a forgery? Something was just not right.

What she had, what she knew, was nothing. A slight variation in pigment, the pattern of age lines in the paint. Neither of those things proved a thing without diagnostic equipment.

"What happened to you?" Sydney appeared in the doorway. "Do you need help with the punch bowl? You've been gone forever."

Savanna shook her head, rubbing her eyes and frowning. "No, I'm fine."

Sydney came and stood next to her, facing the Minkov. "What's up? Do you know this picture from Chicago?"

"I thought I did," she said slowly.

Sydney was quiet.

Savanna turned to find her staring at her instead of the painting.

"What is up with you?"

"I think this piece is a fake," Savanna whispered.

Sydney's eyes widened. "What? For real?"

"Yes. I think so. I don't know." She looked at the photo she'd snapped on her phone, the close-up that showed texture. "I don't know," she repeated. "I can't tell for sure. I'd need my equipment, X-ray, or at least a microscope to start with."

Syd leaned on the buffet, taking care not to disturb the crystal. "So what does this mean?"

"I don't know. It could mean Caroline's house is filled with fakes? Or maybe just this one? If I'm right, and it is a forgery?"

"Have you looked at the others? She still has a lot."

"No. I mean, not really. Not closely. But there was that corner in the Laurant," she suddenly remembered, the discordant area where the lighter paint led into the dark, in the piece that was above Caroline's piano in the living room. The piece she'd just sold. Ugh! It was gone now, with no way for her take a better look at it. But what about the rest of the collection, the fortune in fine art Caroline had throughout her house? "I need to check the rest," she said quietly. "I really can't though. Some of them are hung so high I doubt I'll be able to see anything. But I need to try."

Sydney was nodding. She carefully picked up the punch

bowl between both hands. "Let me make the punch. Go take a closer look."

"How?" Savanna's eyes went to the ceiling. "I know Caroline isn't mobile right now, but Lauren's here cleaning."

"Well, she's vacuuming at the moment. You'll hear when she stops. And if she comes downstairs before you're back in the kitchen with me, I'll just say I sent you looking for something. A footstool. Because I'm short, and we all know I can't reach the top shelves, and that's where all the supplies we need are. Right?"

Savanna laughed softly. "Right. Okay. I'll try to be quick."

As Sydney headed back to the kitchen, Savanna moved quietly from room to room. Caroline had one stunning piece in almost every room. Savanna studied the large Minkov in the library for a long time. She pushed the rolling ladder to the center of the room and climbed it so she could view the painting head-on. With the Laurant gone from the living room, she moved through to Caroline's office at the far south end of the house. It felt wrong being in here, even though she and her sisters had had run of the house when they were little. A Rothman adorned the mantel over the fireplace, and two more hung on each of the adjacent walls. Caroline's office was light and pretty, but very full, the result of seventy-odd years of adulting, Savanna supposed, along with helping run the lucrative Carson businesses. It made sense that Caroline was liquidating some of her art collection. As regal as the three Rothmans were, the room would appear less cluttered with them gone.

Savanna studied each one carefully. She only recognized the large one over the mantel. The two smaller paintings weren't familiar to her, but she didn't know Julian Rothman's work nearly as well as Minkov's. She took photos of each one to research later.

The house suddenly became very quiet. Savanna no longer heard the vacuum. She walked on stocking feet back toward the doorway; Caroline's office was all the way at the opposite end of the house from the kitchen, where she was supposed to be. She listened for footsteps overhead, creaking floors, anything. Silence. Where was Lauren? Savanna's heart raced as she stood perfectly still, frozen. What could she say if Lauren found her in here? That Caroline had sent her looking for something? That wouldn't work. Lauren might mention it to her grandmother later.

She wasn't technically doing anything wrong. She was looking out for Caroline's best interest. But she also didn't know anything concrete right now. Not yet. She worked up her nerve and crept down the hallway. The library. If she could just get to the library, she'd be in the clear. Anything looked better than being caught coming out of Caroline's office.

Savanna heard footsteps on the stairs and pinned herself to the wall, panicking. Lauren would see her if she decided to go in any direction other than the kitchen.

"Lauren?" Sydney's voice rang out, and Savanna was flooded with relief. "Hey, Lauren, could you help me with something, if you're down here?"

"On my way," Lauren called, descending the stairs on

the left and exiting toward the kitchen.

Savanna could have kissed her sister. She tiptoed over to the front door, pulled it open, and then closed it, loudly. Now she proceeded the rest of the way down the hall normally, pulling a pack of gum from her pocket as she walked into the kitchen. "Got it. I knew I'd left it in the car. Want some?" She set the pack on the counter.

Syd winked at Savanna as Lauren closed a drawer and handed her a peeler. "Ah, I thought I looked everywhere for that! Thank you," Syd told her.

"This looks really good," Lauren said. There were four bowls on the counter, with different mixtures in each one. The punch bowl sat on the kitchen table, waiting.

"We'll finish up, and then we can have you and Caroline do a taste test."

"You two are so great to do this. It's important to her that everything be perfect, and she hasn't stopped talking about your mother's punch. You have to let me reimburse you for all these supplies." Lauren went to the little nook where Caroline kept a to-do list, calendar, coupons, and the like. She returned with a checkbook and pen, looking from Sydney to Savanna. "How much were the groceries? Did you go to Happy Family?"

"Oh!" Sydney grabbed Savanna's arm across the counter, jarring the knife in her hand as she was slicing strawberries.

"Hey!" Savanna stared at her.

"Sorry! But I just remembered, I checked out the wine while I was there."

Savanna made settle-down motions with her hands, her

finger to her lips. "I don't want to get her blood pressure up again, shh."

"Okay, right," Sydney said much more quietly, looking from Lauren to Savanna. "Happy Family doesn't sell any kind of claret that looks like the fancy bottle you described. Their selection is very small, all domestic, and some of it local. No cute, fat, round bottles with gold vines. Nothing imported."

"I'm not surprised," Savanna said. "That's basically what Amber said too. I just wasn't sure whether to believe her."

"I think we can believe her. I even asked Mr. Frank—you know, the owner—if they ever get different types of wine in, like maybe an occasional holiday claret, odd-shaped bottle, any imports. He said no. Well, he said absolutely not. They carry the same sixteen brands year-round; it never varies."

"That's good to know," Lauren said. "So we still don't know where that bottle came from. And now I'm even more freaked out, thinking about someone sneaking around in here, planting a bottle of poisoned wine. You have to thank your father for us, again, for installing new locks. My dad wants to pay him for his time."

"He won't take it. He wanted to do it. I think it was the only way to get her to keep her doors locked." Savanna laughed.

"Okay," Sydney said, "the finishing touch." She scooped the Rainbow Sherbet into two of the bowls and the vanilla ice cream into the other two, all of them fizzing from contact with the carbonation in the mixture.

Savanna distributed the berries according to Charlotte's instructions.

Lauren produced a serving tray, holding it out for Sydney to place each four-ounce cup on, all with just enough punch to get an idea of the flavor, four sets of four. "Ready?" She led the procession into the parlor and set the tray in front of Caroline. "For your consideration, Grams. The Shepherd sisters have been creating concoctions all morning from their mother's recipes."

The women picked up the first round of sample cups.

"Cheers, girls," Caroline said, clinking with each of them.

"Taste tests are the best." Sydney grinned, taking the first sip.

SAVANNA WAS STILL able to squeeze in a few hours of painting before having to clean up and head home. She had to change and go pick up Nolan for the Fall Fun Fest. Syd had left to relieve her assistant, Willow, at Fancy Tails the moment Caroline had decided on her favorite punch. The red Faygo pop and 7UP with sherbet and kiwi had won, hands down, the only alteration being an addition of raspberries to the mix. Savanna and Sydney had promised to keep the punch bowl filled two weeks from today for Caroline's party.

Savanna needed to figure out what to do about the Minkov in Caroline's dining room. It had been on her mind all day. And nothing else had happened this week; she wondered if the immediate threat had passed. She had no answers. But as pressing as that was, she couldn't keep her thoughts on a possible solution.

Throughout showering, drying her hair, applying makeup, adding blush and just a hint of eyeshadow to dress up her usual mascara-and-nothing-else look, and then choosing what to wear, Aidan keep creeping into Savanna's thoughts. Five days had passed since she'd seen him. Five whole days. It seemed like a very long time. He hadn't even been in the after-school pick-up line this week; she'd spotted Mollie getting into a car with an older couple, likely her grandparents. She realized how little she knew about Aidan, other than he was from New York.

Would she see him tonight? The event went from six to nine p.m., and it was kind of a "come and go as you please" thing, as far as she could tell. It was entirely possible that she'd not see him. He and Mollie might come later, or she might be tied up with Nolan or in the middle of a mini yoga session when he did show up.

How could she miss someone she'd only known for three weeks?

The thought bothered Savanna more than she cared to admit. She'd come home to heal, to rediscover the person she wanted to be. She'd lost herself in the relationship with Rob, and she was never going to let that happen again.

But maybe things didn't always have to work that way. Her parents were very distinctly their own people, with their own opinions and interests, and yet, they somehow seemed to complete each other when they were together. And as independent as Skylar was, what she had with Travis looked like it worked well.

She and Aidan had the beginnings of a lovely friendship. That thought alone warmed Savanna to her toes. It was enough.

Chapter Fourteen

THE CARSON BALLROOM was lit up inside and out. Housed in the town's largest space, the ballroom was basically a huge banquet hall with pale, gleaming oak floors and redbrick interior walls. The adjoining building, through a majestic set of double doors that were now permanently sealed, was once a theater for live shows. That half of the building had been in disrepair since the 1980s, sitting empty and unused. Skylar had mentioned the other day that the five-year lease was expiring soon on the entire building, wondering aloud whether it would ever be restored or renovated.

The banquet hall was, by default, a catchall venue for most of Carson's events—weddings, wakes, proms, and the handful of town-spirited events like this one. Tonight, multicolored globe lights were strung across the ceiling to match the carnival-themed games and bounce houses.

Savanna paid her $3 admission fee; Nolan was free. They were hardly in the door and he was tugging at her hand, looking up at her through white-blond bangs.

"Auntie Vanna, come *on!*"

She laughed, letting him lead her. She was so happy he'd begun saying her name, though she wished he'd latched on to any other part of it—Savvy, Savanna, Anna. But she could learn to be content being Vanna to Nolan.

She should have guessed: first stop, bounce house. Nolan was experienced at this. He was already on the floor kicking his shoes off. She bent to help him, tying the laces together and stringing them through her purse handles so they wouldn't be lost in the pile.

He paused, looking back at her from the little mouse-hole opening he had to enter through. "Auntie Vanna, you come too!"

"I'm too big." She waved him in and went to stand near the mesh side where he could see her. "But I get to see how high you can jump!"

She cringed as she watched him get jostled when a little girl bounced past him, but he fell onto his back giggling, loving it. The age cutoff was seven for this one, with older kids in the adjacent bounce house.

Savanna took in the room from her safe observer's spot in the corner; she still felt a little like an outsider here, having been gone so long. She wasn't sure how to dress for this, so she'd chosen what she'd be comfortable in: dark formfitting jeans, black leather boots, and a soft, fuzzy black V-neck sweater. She'd added the necklace her parents had given her when she'd graduated college, a delicate gold compass on a fine chain, and equally fine dangling gold earrings; checking her mirror on the way out, she'd liked how they glistened against her long, dark hair. No side pony or messy bun tonight—she'd actually had time to dry it, and it fell to the middle of her back.

Looking around, she'd done okay; she was neither under-nor overdressed. Most of Carson was in jeans and sweatshirts or jackets, a few of the women in skirts or dresses. She scanned the room and found the silent auction tables and the yoga station, Sydney's friend Kate conducting a mini class with a handful of kids and one good-natured adult. No Sydney yet.

"Ms. Shepherd!"

Savanna jumped, startled, as a little girl threw herself at the mesh wall, bouncing off and landing in the center of the bounce house.

The girl hopped back over to Savanna, pressing her little face into the mesh and grinning. "Hi, Ms. Shepherd!"

Savanna laughed, putting her hand against the girl's through the mesh. "Hello, Zoey! Are you having fun?"

"Yes!" Zoey shouted before pushing off and rolling to the other side, giggling wildly. Second grade, Wednesdays and Fridays, Savanna remembered. The girl was exactly the same in her classroom. She was so joyful, Savanna could never be irritated with her.

"Auntie Vanna, watch!"

The next ten minutes were spent watching all of Nolan's amazing superhero moves; he demonstrated bounce house Spider-Man, Batman, Buzz Lightyear, Thor, and Wonder Dog for Savanna until he was sweaty and worn out. She helped him slither limply out of the mouse hole and get his shoes back on, brushing his damp bangs back and planting a kiss on his forehead.

"So. Thirsty." Nolan panted, clutching his throat.

She scooped him onto one hip and carried him to the food and drink tables they'd passed on the way in. "Apple juice box and a water, please," she told the woman handling the money at the end of the line once they had their hot dogs and chips.

"Savanna Shepherd. I heard you were back!"

Savanna shifted Nolan, who had his tongue hanging out of his mouth, one chubby little hand thrown dramatically across his forehead, and did a double take, staring at her good friend from high school. She wore her hair short now, and glasses had replaced contacts, but Savanna would have known her instantly. "No way. Mary?"

"Oh my gosh." The woman across the table from her squealed, reaching over to hug her, whining toddler between them and all.

"Here, honey, I'm sorry." Savanna popped the straw in the juice box and held it for Nolan so he wouldn't spill it. "How *are* you? I haven't seen you in...I don't even know. Has it really been ten years?"

"Longer. At least eleven, I think. Savanna, you look fantastic. The same as the last time I saw you! And you have a baby!"

Nolan scowled at this woman who'd just insulted him. "Not a baby!"

Savanna gave him a little squeeze. "Nope, not a baby at all. You're a big boy, Nolan."

Mary held out a chocolate chip cookie, a conciliatory gesture. "Here you go, buddy. You're definitely not a baby, I'm sorry. Only big boys can have these cookies. But you have to eat your hot dog first," she warned. "I have three," she told Savanna. "Two girls and a boy. He's just adorable. Not adorable," she backtracked. "Handsome. A very handsome boy."

"Thank you! I can't take credit—he isn't mine. This is my nephew. He's Skylar's son."

"I heard she had a little one. Nolan, it's nice to meet you," she said.

Savanna set him down. "I think we're going to need another juice box. We have to catch up. I really miss you!"

Savanna remembered senior year, she and Mary had planned their classes so they'd both have seventh period free. Mary's car had been perfect for the quick ride to the beach; her parents had bought her a convertible for her birthday that year. They'd beat everyone else to the Lake Michigan dunes most days, claiming the best spot, close enough to the waves but far enough to stay dry—until Sydney and her friends had shown up and somehow always convinced them to go in. Syd had always traveled in a pack, an abundance of friends, both boys and girls; Savanna had been content with a few close friends. Boy, they'd had a lot fun. How had a decade gone by?

Mary gave Savanna another quick hug, returning to her cash box and the growing line of people waiting. "Come back when the line dies down. I want your number!"

Savanna called over her shoulder, "I will!" She followed Nolan and set him up with a hot dog and chips, dropping the extra juice box and cookie into her purse and taking her seat next to him.

Nolan tapped her hand. "Auntie Vanna."

"Yes, honey?"

"That lady gave me the cookie."

She was confused for a moment, and then understood. "Of course she did! I was just holding on to it for you, for later."

Nolan bumped her arm with his head. "That's what Daddy says about candy."

She laughed. "Oh, my. You're so smart." She took the cookie and set it on the table in front on him. "But you have to do what the lady said. You have to eat your hot dog first."

"I know." He sighed, rolling his eyes like he'd heard this a hundred times before, and bit into his hot dog.

Wow, she loved this kid.

Piano music drifted to her from somewhere in the room. It was hard to hear from where they sat, close to the bounce house, but it was nice. She spotted several of her kids from school at the carnival game booths and face painting.

"Ms. Shepherd," she heard whispered behind her and turned.

"Mollie!" The little girl wore her trademark bluebird barrettes in her fine strawberry-blond hair. "Are you having fun?"

Mollie nodded, smiling shyly at Nolan.

Savanna looked up at the older woman who was with her; her blond hair was cut into a pretty bob, and she looked to be around sixty. Savanna held out a hand. "I'm Mollie's art teacher from school."

"Mollie talks about you all the time," the woman said,

taking Savanna's hand. "She loves your class. Oh, I'm Jean. Grandma Jean."

"Nice to meet you. Mollie is a wonderful artist. I'm sure you've seen her work."

"Oh, yes. We practically have a gallery on our refrigerator. And in your grandpa's study." Jean looked at Mollie. "He collects the bunnies she makes—drawings, paintings, clay, all of it."

Savanna's heart swelled; she swore she could feel it. She was so happy this sweet girl had a loving support system that wasn't just Aidan. No one should have to raise a child alone, and he clearly wasn't. She wasn't certain whether Grandma Jean was his own mother or his late wife's, but Mollie was obviously treasured. "Your grandpa must be a smart man. You make the best bunnies I've ever seen," she told Mollie.

She resisted the urge to ask if the little girl's dad was here. Grandma Jean was Mollie's chaperone tonight, which meant Aidan wasn't. Maybe he was working—called into an important surgery. Or maybe he was on a date.

She shook off the thought. She glanced at Nolan, who was polishing off the cookie. His hot dog and chips were gone. She ruffled his hair, leaning down. "Nice work, honey. Thank you for waiting until last to eat that."

He hopped off the bench. "I can be a tiger now?"

Savanna grinned widely at him, standing to gather their wrappers. "You can be a tiger now!" She looked down at Mollie. "We're going to get our faces painted, Mollie. Would you like to come? If it's okay with your grandma?"

"Sure, if you don't mind," Jean said. "We didn't mean to

intrude. You deserve your family time."

Rather than make another correction about who Nolan was to her, Savanna held out a hand to Mollie, Nolan already tugging on her other one. "We don't mind at all. Even tigers need friends." She winked at Mollie.

The music volume slowly increased as they headed across the ballroom to the face painting station, and Savanna saw why. A beautiful black baby grand rested near the far wall. As they moved closer and rounded the tall lid, she saw that Aidan Gallager was seated on the bench, playing his heart out.

Savanna stood, dumbstruck, staring. She dimly registered Nolan and Mollie letting go of her to file in line.

Wow, could he play. His head was down, hands moving deftly across the keyboard. The song she'd heard earlier was upbeat and quick; he'd slowed the tempo for this one, a mellow tune she recognized from some George Winston album.

Savanna drifted closer without meaning to, her gaze going to his fingers on the keys. Surgeon's hands, she thought. She'd noticed Aidan's hands before, his long fingers, the wide grip; she'd categorized them as capable, strong doctor's hands. Of course they were musician's hands as well. She watched as his body swayed on the piano bench, just slightly, with the flow of the music. He looked at home, peaceful. In this enormous room full of people and noise and bright lights and laughing children running everywhere.

Aidan looked up as the song neared its end and found Savanna watching him. Her breath caught in her throat and for a moment she couldn't breathe, and she couldn't tear her gaze away from his. Her pulse pounded in her ears.

"Savanna," he said, and suddenly she could breathe again.

"Hi," she replied, her voice coming out breathless and shaky. Her legs felt the way her voice sounded.

He rose and crossed the ten feet or so between them, one hand smoothing the deep blue sweater he wore.

She looked up at him. Something was happening in her chest, tingles, zings. *No. No, Savanna. Stop this right now.* Her own voice echoed in her head, the words contained there. Everything about this man was overwhelming.

"Are you all right?" He put a hand on her upper arm; she could feel the warmth through her light sweater.

"Auntie Vanna! I can be a tiger!" Nolan's voice broke the spell; Savanna blinked, turning to look back at her nephew. He was sitting on the chair in front of one of the teenagers doing face painting.

The teen boy was watching her expectantly. "Is that okay? It's a lot of black and orange paint."

"Yes, totally okay." She gave Nolan a thumbs-up. "Sorry." She turned back to Aidan, now unable to meet his eyes for more than a second or two. "You play beautifully. I had no idea," she said quietly, looking at his left temple. Oh, jeez, this was bad. She always had trouble making eye contact with anyone she was attracted to. It was an infallible sign. And once she was aware of it, it just got worse.

Aidan gave her a sheepish half smile. "I was kind of hoping you'd show up here."

"Why didn't you tell me you were part of the entertainment?" Where to focus her gaze? Her eyes rested for a moment on the white V of cotton at his neck, under the collar of his sweater.

"Oh, I'm not, really. I mean, it's only background music… The kids don't care about it. I just enjoy playing."

"You're really good. I mean, like, really good."

"Like, really, *really* good?"

She met his eyes. He was teasing her. Okay, she could overcome this. *Maintain eye contact; don't make it weird.* "You keep too many secrets. Or maybe I just don't ask enough questions."

"Ask away. I'm all yours."

Savanna opened her mouth to speak, no clue what to say. Mollie chose that moment to crawl over to them on all fours, face painted like a cat, meowing; she pawed at Aidan's leg, circled him, and then sat down on his feet, making loud singsong meowing noises.

He reached down and scratched her head behind her ears. "Good kitty. I seem to be trapped—there's a cat on my feet. Someone else will have to play the piano now. Maybe Ms. Shepherd?"

Savanna laughed. "Oh, believe me. Nobody wants that."

"Mollie, where's Grandma?"

The girl looked up at him and meowed, and then jumped to her feet. She sprinted toward her grandmother, who was crossing the room toward them. Mollie brought her Grandma Jean over to them and slipped her hand into her dad's. "Grandma says I can spend the night at her house,

Daddy, okay?"

Aidan turned to Savanna. "Savanna Shepherd, this is Jean Beckett, my mother-in-law. Jean, my friend Savanna, Mollie's art teacher."

"We met." Jean smiled at Savanna. "Ms. Shepherd was nice enough to take Mollie for face painting."

"Did you really invite this schemer to spend the night?" Aidan rested a hand on top of Mollie's head, and the girl turned in silly circles under his fingers like a music box dancer.

"We did! Grandpa promised her bunny pancakes tomorrow morning."

"Shaped." Aidan leaned down and murmured to Savanna, "Bunny-*shaped* pancakes. We aren't monsters."

Savanna laughed. "I sort of figured."

"So," Jean said, "we'll take her with us, and bring her back after church tomorrow. Mollie, one more time in the bounce house? Are you finishing up here too, Aidan?"

He shook his head. "I promised to play until the end, another hour."

"Okay," she said, glancing again at Savanna and then back at him. "I hope you can get some rest. I know this week was a lot for you. It was nice to meet you, Ms. Shepherd."

Aidan gave her a hug. "Kiss Mollie good night for me, would you?"

Jean nodded and turned to follow Mollie, who was already on her way to the bounce house.

Savanna looked up at Aidan curiously, wondering what his mother-in-law had meant. It seemed somehow too personal for her to ask. She was still considering when Nolan came roaring up to her, in full tiger face paint. She let out a quiet little shriek and backed away, doing her best terrified impression.

Behind Nolan, Savanna spotted Sydney, just arriving with Brad. Syd snuck up and scooped Nolan into her arms, swinging him around in a circle amid giggles and roars.

"I'm stealing your tiger, and there's nothing you can do stop me!" Sydney perched Nolan on her shoulders.

"Balloons," Nolan shouted, now at a much higher vantage point and making grabby hands at one of the carnival games across the room.

"We have balloons to slay," Syd told them, and took off toward the far wall with Nolan and Brad.

Suddenly without any distractions, Savanna was tongue-tied. She dug around in her purse for gum, for something to do.

"I should probably get back to work." Aidan tipped his head toward the piano.

"Sure, don't let me stop you from doing your job." She could go three-wheel it with Syd and her boyfriend at the balloon animal station. Fun.

"Want to join me?"

"What? At the piano?"

"Come on," he said.

Savanna followed him, finding herself shoulder to shoulder on the small piano bench with him. "I really can't play. I wasn't kidding," she warned.

Aidan turned and grinned at her, stirring up a brand-new

series of zings and tingles in Savanna's rib cage, electric butterflies. He rested his fingers lightly on the keys, and she saw his brow furrow as he decided. Scott Joplin's *The Entertainer* filled the air, a lively tune. She found it impossible not to tap her feet, marveling at Aidan's fingers flying over the keys.

"I love that!" She clasped her hands together, beaming at him when he finished. "Your musical taste is very eclectic. Did you learn as a kid?"

"Yes, we had to choose an instrument. My brother was so much cooler than I was. He chose guitar. We took lessons until—" He broke off. "Well, until we were twelve and fourteen, I guess."

"You have a brother? Younger or older?"

"Younger. Finn."

"And is he still in New York?"

"No, he's…at the moment, I'm not sure. Phoenix, I think? He's a Med Flight paramedic. He moves around a lot, doing these temporary assignments that last six months or a year each."

"That sounds so cool. He doesn't mind all the moving around?"

"He loves it. He makes huge bonuses each time he moves, and he's seen more of the country than I ever have."

"You've been here awhile now."

"We love it here. It's the best place for Mollie."

"Her grandparents seem really great."

Aidan nodded. "They are."

"What did your mother-in-law mean?" she asked haltingly. "About this week? I noticed you weren't at after-school pick-up."

"You did?"

Savanna shrugged, wishing she hadn't admitted that.

"I was gone for a cardiothoracic conference in Lansing for a couple of days. Busy week. Sad week." He paused. "It was our tenth anniversary yesterday; I'm not sure if you know this, but my wife died two years ago."

Her eyes widened. It was the first she'd ever heard him say about his wife. "Oh. I'm so sorry, Aidan. I knew you were widowed, but... I can't imagine how hard this must be on you, especially when special dates come up."

"Thank you." He glanced at her. "I'm okay. I worry about Jean and my father-in-law too. They were a close-knit family. Kind of like yours."

"You don't have to talk about it. I didn't mean to bring it up."

"I don't mind. Really. People are afraid to mention it, but it doesn't change what happened. We were happy." He looked at Savanna. "She was a great mom. Time doesn't make the loss any easier, but it makes the edges less sharp, if that makes sense. I'm okay now. I'm good. Mollie is good. Mollie is fantastic." He smiled.

"Mollie is really fantastic," Savanna agreed. She rested a hand on Aidan's forearm. "I'm sorry that happened to your family."

He met her gaze, saying nothing for a moment. "Thank you." He covered her hand for just the briefest moment, his large and warm over hers on his arm. "I appreciate that,

Savanna." He let go, resting his fingers on the keys again, head tilted, considering. "Hmm. Any requests?" He gave her a sideways glance, eyebrows raised expectantly.

She took a deep breath. "Oh, boy. Let me think. What do you know?"

"A little of everything."

"Everything? Really? Okay." Savanna tapped her knee, wanting to choose well. "Do you know anything from musicals? Like…*Once*? Or *Phantom of the Opera*?"

Aidan laughed. "That's a pretty wide range, *Phantom* to *Once*. Yes, I think I do." Head down, he moved his fingers over the keyboard, making a couple of false starts; he scowled and shook out his hands. "Hold on, let me try again."

To her delight, the strains of her favorite tune from *Once* rose from the piano. She smiled, cheeks flushed. He glanced at her quickly before returning his attention to the keys.

"I'm a little rusty," he murmured, concentrating.

"I love it," Savanna said softly, fully aware of Aidan's shoulder lightly brushing against hers as the crisp, sweet notes of "Falling Slowly" flowed from his fingertips into the air.

Chapter Fifteen

As the Fall Fun Fest wound down, Savanna had stalled, giving Nolan a little longer in the bounce house while she filled Aidan in on what he'd missed this past week. She covered Lauren canceling all deliveries from Happy Family, and then the delivery lady bringing get-well flowers and candy; Maggie Lyle's strange, silent scowl at Savanna from the easement that day; Sydney learning that the grocer didn't even carry the type of fancy wine bottle the claret had come from; even the problem she'd discovered in Caroline's smaller Minkov, hanging in the dining room.

Aidan was nodding, listening, as he and Savanna helped carry folding chairs to the supply room in the ballroom. "How is all of that connected?" he asked her.

"I have no idea. Maybe it isn't." She sighed. "Maybe none of it means anything. I just don't want her to get hurt again. I feel like there's something I'm not seeing."

"Well, this isn't only up to you. Skylar's friend Jordan is looking into it too. He called me the other day with a few questions after he'd talked to you."

"That's good. Maybe he can make some sense of things."

"When will you be seeing her next?"

"Monday or Tuesday, maybe both. Her party is so close,

and I know she wants the mural finished. I'm going to try to wrap it up this week."

"Maybe I'll run into you. I have to see Caroline this week," he said.

They'd parted ways unceremoniously, Savanna laden with Nolan and his collection of balloons, prizes, and a double-layer raspberry torte he'd won in the cakewalk, and Aidan having been captured by Tricia Williams, Mollie's first-grade teacher. He met Savanna's eyes over Tricia's head as Savanna gave him a quick wave goodbye from the doorway.

When Savanna woke the next morning, in the blanket fort she and Sydney and Nolan had made in Syd's living room, the Glen Hansard song from *Once* was still playing in Savanna's head. She'd loved "Falling Slowly" from the first time she'd heard it, but she would never hear it the same way again after last night. She closed her eyes, reliving the music, sitting with Aidan on the little piano bench, the way he'd looked at her in the opening notes when he'd started to play. Had he chosen that song on purpose? Savanna knew she wouldn't be able to get it out of her head all day.

She stretched out flat; Sydney had set up surprisingly comfy memory foam mattresses for the three of them, and Savanna had slept like a rock. Maybe she could fall back asleep. Her phone buzzed somewhere in the blankets near her feet. She kicked at it, turning on her side and resting a hand ever so lightly on Nolan's warm little leg; he was snuggled up against her.

When Savanna opened her eyes again, the sun was much

brighter through the blankets. She must have fallen back asleep. Now, Nolan was sprawled between her and Syd, arms and legs flung out to his sides. He was the cutest little boy Savanna had ever seen. It was fact; she'd feel that way even if he wasn't her nephew.

Savanna very carefully moved Nolan's foot off her hip and half slid, half crawled out of the fort as quietly as she could. She crept in sock feet to the kitchen. Thank goodness Syd remembered to set the coffee maker timer. Savanna poured herself a steaming cup of hazelnut coffee, added two heaping spoons of sugar, and headed to the sunroom.

Her current painting sat neglected on the easel, waiting for her. She'd been so busy between work, the mural, and scrambling trying to figure out who might be trying to hurt Caroline, she hadn't gone back to this piece in over a week. There were two others she'd started when she'd first come home, propped against the wall, but the one on the easel was more abstract than her usual style. Caroline's Minkov was weighing on her mind—all of the Carson house artwork was, and she could see the influence of it now as she doled out the paints onto her palette, picking up her brush. As she worked, she delved into her current piece, with its deep, rich tones, broad strokes, and a paring down of her usual fine detail. She recalled the same thing happening to her when she was sixteen or seventeen, absorbing the artwork that even then had been abundant at Caroline's house, and then returning to her paintings. All of her time spent in the Carson house growing up had helped shape her love of fine art.

Savanna perched on the stool, working, her mind wandering. She must figure out what was happening in Caroline's house. There was something she was missing—she just knew it.

"Auntie Vanna, breakfast!" Nolan spoke from the doorway behind Savanna, jolting her from her thoughts.

"So, what's Skylar making tonight?" Sydney asked her once they were seated at the kitchen table.

Breakfast was bacon, scrambled eggs, and cinnamon rolls. Nolan dug in, making a face as he pushed the eggs to one side of his plate and concentrated on the swirled, sticky cinnamon roll.

Savanna shrugged. "I haven't talked to her. She was getting all fancy last night when I went over to pick up Nolan. How's everything going with Brad?" She couldn't keep the childish singsong out of her voice as she asked Syd about her boyfriend.

"Brad is fabulous." Sydney grinned. "We had a lot of fun last night while you were with Dr. Gallager." Syd's voice carried the same inflection Savanna's had, and she smirked at her.

"How wonderful," Savanna said, sipping her second cup of coffee.

"Was he teaching you to play piano? It looked pretty intense over there."

"No, he was not teaching me to play piano." She glared at her little sister. "We were just talking. He's a nice guy."

"Definitely. Definitely." She imitated Savanna, picking up her coffee and sipping demurely. "It's so nice," Syd said, "when handsome doctors make googly eyes at you, and it's especially nice when they play you sappy love songs."

"There was no googly anything, Sydney! We were just talking. Stop it."

Syd was uncharacteristically quiet. She put her hands up in surrender. "Okay. Sorry," she said sincerely.

It was a perk of sisterhood, even after years apart, knowing when it was okay to tease and when to stop. Savanna was grateful Sydney knew where the line was. The whole topic of Aidan unsettled her.

"Hey," Syd spoke up, "why don't I run Nolan home after breakfast and let you flex your creative muscles? You've got a bunch of pieces back there that are half finished."

"I'd love that. But I don't know if I'm willing to let this monkey leave." She scooped up Nolan, a piece of bacon hanging out of his mouth, and kissed him on each temple. He giggled and dropped the bacon, and Fonzie was instantly under Savanna's chair, cleaning up.

Syd stood and started clearing dishes, setting Savanna's phone on the table in front of her. "Here, you might want to check this. Someone's trying pretty hard to reach you. I found it cleaning up our blanket fort."

Savanna glanced up at Syd, detecting a strange tone to her voice. She tapped the screen, seeing she'd missed a call and some text messages. She swiped to unlock the phone, and sucked in her breath.

Missed call from Rob Havemeyer.
Voicemail from Rob Havemeyer.

She touched the envelope icon flashing at the top of the screen and saw her ex-fiancé had also texted her. Oy. What in the world? She hadn't heard a single word from him since

August ninth when she'd left Chicago.

Her eyes rose to meet Sydney's.

Her sister looked irritated, angry, annoyed…nothing good. "What does he want?"

"I don't have a clue." She scanned the text message from him.

Savanna, please call me when you get a chance today.

"Ugh!" She turned the phone toward Sydney. "What the heck does he even want?"

Syd raised one eyebrow and looked at her. "You haven't reached out to him at all?"

"No! Why would I? He was a jerk. He had to go find himself…which apparently you can't do unless you travel around Europe for weeks on end, and make sure to dump your girlfriend before you leave."

"Fiancée," Sydney corrected.

Savanna gave her a sharp look.

Syd shrugged. "Well? You were more than a girlfriend. I just don't want you listening to some stupid voicemail from your stupid ex-fiancé with rose-colored glasses on, romanticizing what you had. What if he wants you back?"

"No." She cringed at the thought. "Oh, jeez, no. That isn't it. Rob is way too self-involved to have second thoughts."

"And even if he did…" Sydney prompted, looking worriedly at her older sister.

Savanna rolled her eyes. "Even if he did want me back, there's no way that's happening. Pigs will fly first. Fonzie will suddenly decide he hates bacon. Nolan will give up eating sweets."

That got the little boy's attention; he slapped both palms to his temples, staring at her. "*What*, Auntie Vanna? Why?" He looked pained.

They cracked up.

"So dramatic, buddy." Savanna grinned at him. "Don't worry, your sweet tooth is here to stay. You got it from your mom…from all three of us!"

He popped another piece of cinnamon roll in his mouth, looking relieved.

"Okay, so you'll stand firm when you call him back." Sydney nodded at Savanna.

"Of course." Savanna looked at her phone. "But later," she finally said after a long pause. "I'm not dealing with this now."

"I get that. If you want me there for moral support when you do listen to the message, let me know."

"I will. I'm not quite ready to ruin my mood by hearing Rob Havemeyer's voice. Later."

"Hey," Sydney said as Nolan hopped down from his chair and headed toward the living room, followed by Fonzie. "What did you decide to do about that painting at Caroline's? Was it just that one that you think was a fake?"

"I haven't really decided anything." Savanna sighed. She found the photos she'd taken in her phone and scrolled to the Minkov, zooming in again on the suspicious area. It was so hard to tell on a screen; it was even hard to tell in person with the naked eye. She zoomed out and scrolled through the others she'd snapped photos of, Syd looking over her shoulder: three Rothmans, two Laurants, a Matisse, a Monet, and the two Minkov paintings.

"You don't think Mr. Carson knew he was displaying a knockoff, do you? Maybe he was trying to cut corners, save money?"

Savanna looked at her, thinking. "I don't think so," she said slowly. "But if he was, Caroline's going to be in for a rude awakening. That smaller Minkov, if it's genuine, is worth close to seven figures. I really need to get a look at the authentication certificates and go from there. But I can't upset Caroline; she's been through so much lately. I can't put a damper on her birthday preparations."

"What about the other pieces? Did they all look okay to you?"

Savanna shook her head. "It's impossible to know for sure. I don't know them as well as I do Sergei Minkov's work. I have to do some research."

Syd began clearing the dishes. "Well, let me know if I can help at all."

HARLAN WAS WORKING in the large pole barn he called a garage when Savanna arrived that afternoon for dinner. He collected and restored old vintage motorcycles in his spare time, and was adjusting something underneath a handsome gold-and-black Triumph as she waved to him.

Savanna followed the delicious scent of something cooking around to the rear of the house, finding Travis at the grill on the two-tiered patio, Skylar kicked back in a deck chair with her feet propped up while he worked.

Savanna gently nudged the big orange tabby, Pumpkin, out of his chair, and sat opposite her sister. "Mmm. Steak?"

"Steak, pepperoncini pasta salad, and the last of Dad's asparagus from the garden," Skylar replied.

"Sounds amazing. I'm starving!"

Travis stabbed one of the steaks, turning it. "Another few minutes, and we should be good. I'm gonna go grab that seasoning," he said, handing the spatula to Skylar. "Can I get you anything?" He addressed them both.

"Oh, I'd love some more iced tea, Trav, thank you. Savanna?"

"Yes, that would be great, same for me, please."

Skylar handed Savanna the spatula as her husband headed into the house.

"What am I supposed to do with this?"

Skylar shrugged. "Try to not burn the steaks? He should know I can't be trusted." She laughed.

Savanna stood and moved to the grill. She was better at barbecue than she was at actual cooking in the kitchen; she'd learned from Harlan, and he was the master. "Oh," she said, "I brought the torte your son won last night in the cakewalk. I should have told you that you didn't need to bring dessert."

"Mom made cookies with Nolan earlier, so we'll have a couple of choices. I don't think anyone's going to complain. Hey. I meant to ask you, when are you seeing Caroline next? I was thinking I might check in with her and see if she'd like me to secure any of her paperwork from the paintings she's sold so far."

"I'll be there Tuesday after school." Savanna lifted one corner of a steak, peeking underneath before turning it. "I think that's a good idea. I need to talk to her about a couple of the pieces. Did Sydney tell you what I found the other day, when we were over there making punch?"

"Yes! That's crazy, the idea that Caroline could have a forged piece of art in her collection! Do you really think that painting is a fake?"

"I'm honestly not sure now. I'd need my tools; ideally, I'd need some of the diagnostic equipment I used in Chicago. There's nowhere around here that I could even take it, except for Lansing or Detroit. Even Lansing is too far to do it without giving Caroline more to worry about. I'd have to find the right time."

"I can pull my copies of the provenances, if that might help," Skylar said. "At least to compare with the originals she has, maybe. I think I can wrap things up at work by around four thirty Tuesday. Stop and pick me up on your way."

Travis reappeared, setting a glass of iced tea on the table by Skylar and handing Savanna hers. He was shaking his head, smiling. "Charlotte has Nolan sitting on the kitchen counter icing cookies. There's at least an inch of frosting on them, and chocolate chips piled on top of that."

"Ugh." Skylar laughed. "So it's a good thing we have the torte he won."

Savanna handed him the spatula. "I saved them from your wife."

"Good call, thanks." Travis pulled the seasoning from his

shirt pocket and liberally peppered the meat on the grill.

"So Tuesday? And you'll bring copies of her certificates?" Savanna asked.

"Absolutely," Skylar replied.

Savanna finally felt some weight lift off her shoulders. She'd have answers Tuesday, one way or another.

She intended to head home right after dinner; she had a handful of projects to finish grading, and Rob's voicemail was weighing on her mind. But full of steak and pasta, a piece of untouched raspberry torte on a plate in front of her, Savanna was just too comfortable to move. Plus, she loved listening to the banter between Skylar and her husband over the *Star Wars* movie trilogies, Travis finding a way to draw a parallel to the *Lord of the Rings* trilogy; as a casual fan, Savanna didn't really get either of their points. Harlan finally got involved, telling them they were both wrong and launching into a zealous explanation of why.

Charlotte took control after the dishes were cleared and the dishwasher was running, setting their old Michigan Rummy game in the center of the table. They played with plastic chips, and Nolan delighted in having the job of depositing each player's chips into the right pot. Whenever anyone won the kitty, Nolan meowed loudly as he emptied out that compartment for the winning player.

Charlotte won...she always won, probably because she had the best poker face.

It was after ten by the time Savanna and Sydney pulled into their own driveway.

Syd stopped her as they separated at the end of the hall

to go their separate bedrooms. "Are you going to check his voicemail?"

Savanna groaned. "Yeah. I have to. There's no way I can sleep if I don't."

"Do you want moral support?"

"*Yes*," she said, following Sydney into her bedroom.

Syd's room reflected her personality, done in muted shades of aqua and orange. Savanna hopped onto the high, queen-size bed, and Syd joined her, pulling the sheer, billowy curtains closed around the four poster sides once Fonzie had jumped up, settling against Savanna's hip.

She looked up, smiling at the tiny white fairy lights. "A grown-up blanket fort."

"Exactly." She tapped the phone lying between them on the bed. "Do it."

Savanna sighed. "Okay." She dialed into her voicemail and put it on speaker. Hearing Rob's voice after all this time was jarring.

"Savanna, hi, I uh, I just wanted to call and say I hope you're okay. I'm back, and"—a pause, an audible sigh—"and I don't know, it feels strange here without you. Anyway. I found a couple of things of yours—a book, your winter coat, a necklace. Stuff you need. I'm going to be in Lansing next week and thought I'd find you and drop them off. Give me a call."

Savanna hung up and flung the phone away from her into the pillows. "What? Why does he have to come here? He doesn't belong here. What in the world *was* that?" She looked at Sydney. She felt shaky and sick.

"He's a jerk. Call him right now and tell him to mail your stuff. He doesn't need to come here."

Savanna groaned. "Ugh! I don't want to call him. I don't want to talk to him at all!"

Sydney picked up her phone. "I'll tell him."

"No." Savanna grabbed her phone from Syd's hand. "I have to do it."

Sydney stared at her, waiting.

"I don't want to talk to him," she said again. She shouldn't have checked the voicemail, not right before going to bed. Now she'd never fall asleep.

"Then text him," Sydney suggested.

Her hopes lifted a little. "Hmm. Text him? You think?"

"Sure. He doesn't deserve a call—just text him."

Savanna shook her head. "No. I'm not twelve. I'm not going to deal with this over text. I'll call him. Tomorrow. I'll call him tomorrow right after school."

Sydney looked at her skeptically.

"I will! Trust me, I will. The last thing I want is for him to show up in Carson."

Chapter Sixteen

Rob's voicemail stayed with Savanna through the entire school day on Monday. She'd been certain she wouldn't sleep last night, but she'd slept soundly; she'd woken with that feeling that the night had passed in a minute, but had seen on her bedside clock that she'd slept a solid seven hours.

The day seemed to drag as she scripted what she'd say to him in her head, revising it over and over. And then somehow the last two hours of her day flew by in an instant, and before she knew it, she was home, standing alone in Sydney's kitchen, staring at Fonzie staring back at her.

"Okay, okay, I'm going to call him," she told her dog.

Savanna clipped on Fonzie's leash and headed through town toward the park and the lake beyond. She'd find her spot on the dunes where she used to go as a teenager whenever she needed to think. The waves and the sand and sky made everything going on in her life seem small, manageable. Maybe it would still work, that Lake Michigan magic.

She found a spot on the beach, looking out over choppy blue waves, and let Fonzie go—he loved it here. She should come more often, she thought as she watched him kick up sand and bark at the seagulls. Her little section of beach was deserted. Not surprising, given that it was the end of September and the weather had settled into a brisk fifty-five-degree average. The cold wouldn't stay; they'd get another several days of warm weather in the next month, but swimming was over for the season for all but the hardiest. She spied two surfers in full wetsuits a half mile or so down the beach. No way. She was glad she'd thought to bring a blanket to spread out on the cold sand, and her red-checked scarf and gloves.

She hit dial and had the phone to her ear before she could talk herself out of it. As it rang, she watched Fonzie race back and forth at the water line, pouncing on the waves rolling in and trying to bite the water.

"Hey, Savanna!" Rob's voice came on the line.

"Hey." So many things ran through her head, things she should have said to him that day. He'd come straight from a board meeting for the museum, full of himself and all hyped up about a high-end deal he'd been part of negotiating. Rob was smart—he'd broken up with her at their favorite restaurant, the same one he'd proposed to her in. He knew Savanna well, had known she'd never make a scene in public.

She hadn't. They'd cut their dinner short, her appetite ruined after he'd explained that he needed space. He needed to find himself. They were just too different, he'd said, and he'd never imagined himself settling down so young. Rob was thirty-one. She'd have pointed this out to him, but she'd been too disgusted by then.

"Savanna?" Her name coming through the phone in his voice sounded wrong to her.

"Rob, don't worry about my things. If you really want to, you could mail them. What book is it?"

"Uh, I can't remember. I'm not home right now. Some thick hardcover."

She sighed. She hated losing a good book. And she really didn't want to buy a new winter coat. "Okay. Could you please just put everything in the mail? I'll give you the address."

"Well, I thought it would be nice to catch up in person."

She laughed. "I'm not an old friend who just moved away. I don't want to catch up. I'm good here. I'm doing fine. I should actually thank you."

"What? Why?" He sounded hurt.

"Why what?" Savanna felt a sense of calm come over her. This wasn't hard at all. Yes, hearing his voice pushed all of her buttons and instantly took her back to the day he'd broken up with her. But now? It was okay. It was all okay. She didn't care enough about him anymore to be angry at him, on the other end of the phone.

"Why should you thank me?"

"I needed to come home. I'm happy here. I'm not happy with the way we ended things, but I'm so glad to be back in Carson. So thank you for whatever it was that led you to break off our engagement. I wouldn't have been happy. You were right to do it." She meant every word.

There was nothing but silence on the other end of the line.

"Rob?"

"I'm here. I actually wanted to talk to you about that,

Savanna."

Savanna had an inkling…almost a premonition, a prickle across her shoulders. *Don't say it.*

Rob said the words that, just a month ago, Savanna would have given anything to hear. "I think I made a mistake." His voice was quiet.

Fonzie bounded over and stared at her, whining.

"What," she whispered at the dog, motioning for him to go play.

The dog pawed at the ground and barked, obviously wanting her to come play too.

"Savanna? I hear Fonzie. Where are you? I miss our dog."

"He wasn't *our* dog. You know that."

"Well, I helped walk him sometimes. I miss him. Where are you? Are you working at all? Did you move back in with your parents?"

Wow. The idea he must have of her in his head: sad, distraught, barely functional without him. So broken-hearted she was unable to secure a job, find a place to live, or even exist on her own. "I'm on the beach right now. The lake is gorgeous on this side. I'm working, and I'm staying with my sister for the moment. But there are some really cute houses I'm looking at." She couldn't help it—she needed him to know she'd landed on her feet. And she *would* be looking at houses.

"Wait, so you're staying there?" He sounded incredulous. "You still have subletters in your apartment. We still haven't filled your position at Kenilworth. It's yours, Savanna, if you want it. I guess I thought you'd be back."

She swallowed hard, stunned. "Rob. I moved. I only have subletters until my lease is up. I'm sorry you've held the position at work but...I'm done. I made that clear when I turned my notice in to your father."

"Okay, listen. I want you to think about this seriously. You had a future here, in Chicago and at Kenilworth. What are you even doing now? You always made Carson sound tiny. Are you commuting all the way to Lansing for work? Wouldn't it be better to be back in the city?"

"I'm working in art. I had no trouble finding a job. I have a future here. Don't worry."

Silence.

"Rob," she said, softening her voice. She wouldn't have believed it possible a month ago, but now she actually felt a little sorry for him. He sounded so shocked that she wanted nothing to do with his olive branch. "I'm honestly happy now. I hope you can find a way to be too. Please just mail me my things. I'll text you the address."

He was so quiet, she pulled the phone away from her ear, making sure the call was still connected. It was.

"Goodbye," she said and pressed the end call button.

Savanna lay back on the blanket, looking at the sky. She didn't know what she'd expected, but that whole conversation had certainly surprised her. Rob's end of it, and her own.

Fonzie barreled onto the blanket and flipped onto his back, rolling around and pushing off of her with his sandy paws.

"Oh!" The smell of dead fish assaulted her senses. "Oh,

Fonzie, you reek!" She leaped up, brushing the sand off, and he jumped up with her, running through and around her legs. *Now* it must be time to play, right? "You need a bath," she told him. "You're not going home smelling like that!" She shook the blanket out and reached for him, trying to clip the leash onto his collar without actually touching him.

He darted away from her, running along the water's edge with his nose down, obviously looking for whatever it was that had given him such a pungent aroma.

"Fonz!" Savanna shouted in her best disciplinarian voice.

"Fonzie! Come here, boy!"

Savanna whipped around to see Skylar several yards away from her, making her way through the dunes. She put two fingers to her lips and whistled, loud, and Savanna's traitor dog ran directly to her. Skylar covered her nose with one hand as Fonzie wagged his whole body, waiting to be petted. She reached down and gingerly patted his head, making a face.

"Sorry about that," Savanna called, heading toward her sister.

"He stinks! Ugh!"

"I know. He rolled in something." She quickly hooked up his leash and straightened up again. "What are you doing here?"

"Syd saw you leave; she had a feeling you were heading to your spot to call Rob back. She told me about his voicemail. Are you okay?" She frowned, expression full of concern. "Because I will so kick his butt for you. I don't mind. Someone needs to. And better me than Dad, right?"

Savanna hugged her older sister, kissing her cheek. "I'm totally fine. I swear. I'll tell you about it on the way, I'm stopping at Fancy Tails to throw him in the tub." She pointed at Fonzie as they started back toward the park and town.

"Oh, thank goodness." Skylar laughed. "That's pretty awful. And you wonder why I don't want a dog."

Savanna rolled her eyes at Skylar. "Nolan would love a dog, you know. It's worth the work. Get a rescue, like Fonzie. They're wonderful. It's all about unconditional love."

"Nolan gets that from us. Maybe we'll start with a fish."

Chapter Seventeen

S AVANNA DRESSED MORE carefully after school Tuesday, changing to go work on the mural. Every time she was at Caroline's working, wearing grungy ten-year-old painter's clothes, Aidan showed up. Well, almost every time. She pulled on a nice pair of dark slim-fit jeans she'd accidentally spattered a few drops of bleach on at the right ankle, and a plain pink tee. The T-shirt wasn't from her collection of painting clothes, but it was old. She liked the color and the way it followed the curve at her waistline. She was willing to sacrifice it for the sake of not looking horrible every time she was Caroline's. She pulled on black-and-white Converse high-tops and a black sweater on her way out the door.

Savanna stopped in front of Skylar's law office, her sister getting in before Savanna even had a chance to call and tell her she was here.

Skylar threw her briefcase and purse in the back seat. "I've got all of Mr. Carson's paperwork. Copies of authentication certificates, bills of sale, everything. I haven't had a chance yet to look through it, but I thought we could go over it with Caroline while we're there. It's really a bookkeeping measure that we should have been doing since August, anyway, when she started selling off some of her collection. We need to get everything in order for the upcoming sales she's making, and file the ones she's already sold."

"Perfect," Savanna said. "I have an idea too. I'm going to ask if she minds if I check out that smaller Minkov in the dining room a little closer."

"You're going to take it to Lansing? Will she let you do that? I mean, you said it's worth a ton. I can probably find her purchase price in the paperwork I brought."

"I won't have to take it offsite, not at first anyway. I still have my Firefly—" She broke off, glancing at Skylar. "It's a handheld microscope that connects to my computer through the USB port. I'd have to calibrate it first, and bring my laptop for imaging, but I might be able to authenticate that Minkov with just that. But I can't just take her priceless painting off the wall and set up my equipment on her buffet without asking her. So I'm going to ask."

Skylar nodded. "Okay. Does she know you saw something odd in that painting?"

"No. I haven't mentioned anything to her, but maybe I can blame it on my neurotic eye, or my former job...say that I just want to take a closer look at the work. She knows how much I love that artist."

"That sounds like a great idea. Do it. Did you bring it today?"

"No. I have to run this by her first, but it's not a big deal for me to get the equipment and run it over there this week to check it out."

"Perfect." Now Skylar echoed Savanna's earlier sentiment. "That should put your mind at ease. Hopefully."

As they turned onto Caroline's street, Savanna gasped, grabbing Skylar's hand. Two patrol cars were in the Carson house driveway. She automatically looked for Aidan's SUV but it wasn't there. Which might mean nothing medical had happened…?

Savanna rang the bell, looking at Skylar. "Should we go in?"

Princess and Duke came skittering into the foyer, barking.

Skylar peered through the screen door. "The door's open."

"Caroline?" Savanna called as they stepped inside.

"Hello?" Skylar put a hand on her forearm. "Hold on a sec."

They were quickly met by a police officer coming down the hall. She was imposing, wearing the Allegan county dress blues, chrome nametag reading D. Zapelli. One hand rested on her belt near the holster.

"Sorry," Skylar spoke. "We should have waited at the door. Is Mrs. Carson all right?"

Zapelli frowned. "You are…?"

"I'm Mrs. Carson's attorney. This is my sister, Savanna. She's working on a project for Mrs. Carson."

The officer stood still, considering for a moment. "Come with me." She stood to one side, motioning them to walk ahead of her down the hallway toward the kitchen.

They were relieved to find Caroline sitting at the big kitchen table. She appeared fine, plastic-booted foot propped up on a pillow on one of the chairs.

"Girls! Oh, my, you've no idea how glad I am to see you." She held out her hands.

They each leaned in for a quick hug. Savanna stayed close, shaken up at being greeted by the officer; for a second, she'd assumed something else had happened to Caroline. She rested one hand on her shoulder, looking around the kitchen.

Lauren and her father, Thomas, sat adjacent at the table, and Detective Jordan leaned against the island, arms crossed.

Skylar spoke first. "What happened?"

Jordan raised an eyebrow at her. "There was a break-in."

"Oh, no," Savanna said, giving Caroline's shoulder a light squeeze. "Are you okay?"

"I'm fine," she replied. "I wasn't home when it happened."

"Thank goodness for that," Lauren said.

Detective Jordan spoke. "I just have a few more questions, Mrs. Carson. Is there someplace more private we can finish up?"

"No," Caroline said, "you can speak in front of the girls. I've known them all their lives."

Jordan sighed. "Fine." He looked down at the notepad he'd been writing on. "So you changed your locks on what date?"

"Oh, I'm not quite sure." Caroline glanced at Lauren.

"It was a week ago yesterday. Our dad installed new exterior door handles with digital locks," Skylar said.

"And who has the entry code?"

"Just us," Lauren said.

"'Us' who?" Jordan looked at her.

Thomas said, "Myself and my daughter." He gestured at Lauren.

"And us," Savanna added. "Caroline gave it to me for when I come over to paint, and to Sydney so she can pick up the poodles for grooming."

Jordan jotted that down on his notepad.

"I don't understand why you're concentrating on who knows how to unlock the doors, when it's clear the burglar came in through the living room window," Caroline said.

"We have to cover every angle," Detective Jordan told her. "And I'm not sure that was the actual point of entry."

"What do you mean?" Thomas asked.

"It makes the most sense," Jordan acknowledged. "And it wouldn't have set off any alarms, since the doors are alarmed now, but you don't have any alarm system set up on the windows or screens. But the broken glass doesn't leave a large enough hole for someone to climb through."

Savanna glanced wide-eyed at Skylar. Detective Jordan thought Caroline knew the person who'd broken into her house?

"So, maybe they reached up and unlocked the window, to open it. To climb in," Lauren said.

"Okay," Jordan said. "Except the lock mechanism is still engaged."

Thomas shook his head. "Why is that important? Maybe the guilty party closed the lock when he closed the window, after climbing through."

"Why would someone do that after breaking the window?" Jordan asked.

The room was quiet.

"And then there's the displaced glass pattern that Detective Taylor took photos of before he left. We'll know more after we analyze that, as well as the fingerprints forensics collected. Mrs. Carson, we have to entertain the possibility that whoever is responsible already had a way into the house."

Savanna realized they'd arrived well after the incident. It sounded as if there had been a whole team of law enforcement at Caroline's house.

Caroline cleared her throat. "I don't believe that someone I know could have done this. But I'll be honest, Detective. Until recently, I've never locked my doors. It's never been an issue. So, I've given the lock code to the people I rely on to help me here. I'm eighty-nine years old. I'm still fortunate enough to live on my own, in this rambling old house, because I have help."

Detective Jordan nodded. "Is there anyone else you'd like to list as having access to your house?"

Caroline sighed. "Sure. But I think the notion that this could become a list of possible suspects is ridiculous. Anything of real value that I own is still here, from what my son's been able to glean so far. Don't you think it's likely that this is along the lines of that rash of car break-ins last summer? Just kids, bored and looking for something to do?"

The detective pulled out a chair and joined them at the table. He closed his notebook, setting it down with his pen.

"To be frank, Mrs. Carson, I believe someone has an agenda where you're concerned. I don't have the motive yet, but after speaking with Ms. Shepherd"—he glanced at Savanna—"and Dr. Gallager last week, I'd like to get this wrapped up quickly. Before you or anyone else gets hurt again."

The color drained from Caroline's cheeks. She listed a handful of additional people she'd already given her new lock code to: Bill and Maggie Lyle, her other handyman Marty Dawsley, Jack Carson, Lauren's sisters Lucy and Rebecca, Felix and his assistant Ryan, and even Amber.

Lauren looked shocked at that. "Grandmother. I canceled deliveries from Happy Family. You knew that!"

"And I reinstated them, my dear. I understand your concern, but Amber has delivered my groceries for the last two years. I trust her. I do still make my own decisions."

Lauren sighed. "Okay. I know you do."

The mood after the detective and Officer Zapelli left was somber.

Thomas and Lauren chatted and agreed to do another walk-through, to assess for any additional missing items. Savanna and Skylar offered to help, but Lauren stopped them. She pulled them into the hallway, away from Caroline.

"If you two could help Grandmother to the parlor, and maybe get her a cup of lavender tea, that would be even better," she said quietly. "I don't think she's even had lunch yet, and it's almost dinnertime. She's probably starving. We were out getting her hair done when all this happened...in broad daylight. I can't stand this, and I feel helpless. Who would torment her this way?"

"I don't know what to think," Savanna said. She wondered how Caroline's blood pressure was, with all of this. "Dr. Gallager mentioned he might stop by…has he yet?"

Lauren shook her head. "He came late yesterday to take off her heart monitor; the test period was up. Are you thinking I should call him? Maybe he should check her out."

Savanna shrugged, making sure her motives were purely about Caroline. She was disappointed she'd missed Aidan; she'd just been too out of sorts yesterday, with that phone call to Rob, to do much else other than wash the disgusting smell off Fonzie and head home for dinner with Sydney. She'd hoped they'd cross paths today. "I think it's up to you if you feel you should call him. I was just thinking of her blood pressure; I know he mentioned something about it before, so maybe he should know about what happened today."

"You're right. I'll run upstairs and grab her electric blood pressure cuff. We can check it first, and I'll call and update him either way."

"Good idea." She hated to admit it, but part of her had hoped Lauren would just call Aidan. She knew it probably wasn't necessary, and checking Caroline's readings themselves made more sense. No need to make her doctor come out here unless they had to.

Helping Caroline navigate to the parlor with her bulky plastic boot, now Savanna and Skylar saw the result of the break-in today. While the kitchen was relatively untouched, aside from a few drawers standing open, the rolltop desk at the entrance to the parlor was completely broken. The thin wooden slats of the cover were strewn all over the floor, and the compartments had been rifled through.

While Lauren put the blood pressure cuff on Caroline's arm and waited for the machine to do its thing, Savanna threw together a sandwich and hot lavender tea, carrying them on a tray into the parlor.

Lauren straightened up, wrapping the electric cuff up and storing it back in the case. "Grandmother's blood pressure is fine, probably better than mine—122/70."

Caroline spoke. "Good." She captured Lauren's hand before her granddaughter headed upstairs to help her father. "You see? I'm fine. I still have my wits about me, and my heart is good. I'm not a helpless old lady quite yet."

Lauren leaned down and hugged her. "I know, Grams. I know. I only want you to be safe. That's what we all want."

Savanna left Skylar sitting with Caroline and followed Lauren down the hallway to the front entryway and staircase. "What was taken?" Savanna asked. She could see beyond Lauren into the living room, noting the broken glass on the windowsill and floor by the piano. The piano bench was turned over, its contents of sheet music spilled out.

"The television in the living room is gone…and her Victrola, which she's really upset about; I guess she's had that since she was young. Upstairs, they went through her dresser drawers and took some jewelry she kept there. I'm not sure yet what else. My dad is going through both their offices. My grandfather's is on the second floor across from their bedroom, and Grandmother's is through the living room. I know they ransacked her office, but I haven't been in his yet."

"Wow," Savanna breathed. "This is just crazy. I mean, I know I'd mentioned my worry about Amber, but this seems kind of beyond anything I imagine her capable of."

"I agree. And I can't fight Grams on the household decisions she makes. It was probably a waste of time, your dad coming over and changing all her locks."

Savanna's thoughts were spinning. "Has Bill Lyle been back over here at all since her accident?"

Lauren shrugged. "I honestly don't know. Not while I've been here. Why?"

"I'm not sure if it's even worth mentioning. I guess there had been some kind of property dispute in the past between the Lyles and your grandparents."

"That." Lauren rolled her eyes. "I know what you're talking about, but I think that's long over. Maggie checks in on Grams all the time. She calls me anytime she doesn't see the shades go up in the morning." Then understanding overtook Lauren's features. "You aren't thinking the railing was anything other than an accident." She made it a statement rather than a question.

Savanna put her hands up. "I don't know anymore. I wondered, when I heard about the easement issue. But then, I know they've been neighbors forever. It was probably just an accident."

Lauren was frowning. "I think so. And as for the other handyman who was taking care of the leak in the basement, we found him in the church newspaper. I can't imagine why he'd have anything to do with this."

"What about her art dealer?" Savanna was mentally click-ing through everyone who had the lock code.

"Mr. Thiebold? He's been here dozens of times, even more when Grandfather was alive. He's their friend. I know," she said, "I'm doing it too, going through every possibility, everyone who has access. But that also includes family. Me, my dad, my sisters, Jack…and you and your sisters too. Do you really think someone who knows Grandmother could do this?"

Savanna glanced around as Lauren made a sweeping mo-tion to accentuate her point. She shook her head. "I don't know."

"I've got to help my dad clean up," Lauren said, heading toward the stairs. "One of us will be staying here with her for a day or two, to make sure she's safe."

Savanna headed back toward the parlor, making an im-pulsive left at the kitchen. She just had to check on the Minkovs; she couldn't help it. Lauren hadn't listed any of Caroline's artwork among the items stolen, but perhaps she wouldn't have missed them yet. Savanna went through the butler's pantry to the dining room, recalling using the semiconcealed passageway as a kid to her advantage in hide-and-seek. Emerging through the other swinging door into the dining room, she was immediately relieved to spot the Minkov hanging in its usual spot above the buffet.

She moved through the dining room, taking care to stay quiet, and poked her head around the corner into the library. The large Minkov was also present and accounted for. She couldn't very well march into Caroline's office to take inventory of the Rothmans there, but if the Minkovs were untouched, then the rest of the collection must be too.

Savanna slinked back to the parlor, feeling a little paranoid. Today would, unfortunately, not be the day for Skylar and her to dive into the provenances with Caroline. The poor woman had already been through enough. But she had to get a handle on whether she was right about the small Minkov being a forgery, and soon, before anything else happened in this house.

She saw that Skylar had found a way to take Caroline's mind off the events of the day; she'd set up a folding table between them and had rummaged the old chess set from somewhere. The opposing troops faced off against each other on the board. Skylar glanced up, catching Savanna watching them. Caroline was deliberating her next move.

Savanna stood in the doorway, deliberating hers.

Chapter Eighteen

S AVANNA PAUSED OUTSIDE the teachers' lounge Thursday morning, just about to turn the doorknob. The hallway was empty; it was still early. She looked down at her empty coffee mug. "I could come back after the bell," she murmured to herself. The excited speculation was awful after any kind of town drama, and the town matriarch's house being broken into and ransacked was definitely drama.

Glancing again her empty cup, Savanna smoothed the full A-line skirt of the black and white polka-dot dress she'd paired with a cropped red sweater today, and pushed through the door into the teachers' lounge. The principal, Mr. Clay, sat alone at one of the tables, and two of the fifth-grade teachers chatted on the bench by the window. Savanna said her hellos and moved to the coffee maker.

When she'd gotten her refill, Mr. Clay motioned her over to his table.

"I was hoping to catch you or Jack. I wanted to ask you about something." The older man leaned forward, speaking quietly. She guessed him to be in his sixties; today he was dressed in a blue argyle sweater vest and white shirt, his navy blazer draped over the back of his chair.

Savanna joined him, setting her coffee cup down.

"Tell me if I'm overstepping, please. You've been painting a mural for Caroline Carson, haven't you?"

"Yes, I have."

"My nephew Marty mentioned it. He's handling her basement issues, sealants, new plumbing, and the like. Mrs. Carson's son, Thomas, is a friend of my nephew. They attend the same church."

"Right, I did know there was some work being done in the basement…she's renovating a few things for—uh—just things in need of repair." Did Mr. Clay know about the party? Savanna didn't want to mention it; she had no idea who was on the party guest list. Lauren and her sisters were handling all of that.

"My nephew told me there were police cars in the driveway the other day. Marty went over to finish the last of the pipework, but he didn't go inside after seeing that. Is Mrs. Carson all right?"

Savanna kept her voice quiet like Mr. Clay's. "She's okay. Someone broke in while she was out. She isn't hurt, and her family is still figuring out what was taken."

Mr. Clay shook his head. "That poor woman." He sat back, sipping his coffee.

"I know," Savanna agreed. "Are you close to her?"

"No, not really. Though, we will be at the party, my wife and I. She's quite admirable, isn't she? Mrs. Carson deserves to celebrate her ninetieth. I'm sure she hasn't had an easy time of it, after losing Everett."

"I'm sure. She's been through a lot. But she's pretty resilient."

"Well." Mr. Clay stood, taking his coffee cup and pushing his chair in. "Let her know we're thinking of her, would you? We're looking forward to the party. A lot of the town is. Carson is what it is because of Caroline Carson and her family. I hope she knows that." He smiled.

"I'll tell her you said so," Savanna said. "I think she needs to hear it right now, with all she's been through. Thank you, Mr. Clay."

"You're quite welcome, Ms. Shepherd. Oh, and I'm hearing delightful things about your classroom, by the way."

Glowing with Mr. Clay's praise, Savanna sat at the table and waited a little longer in the teachers' lounge. The first bell would ring in twelve minutes. She had some prep work to do, but her first set of students, Mrs. Condor's third-grade class, didn't arrive until nine. She'd hoped to run into Jack Carson this morning; she wanted to ask him if he'd heard anything else yesterday about the break-in. By the time she and Skylar had left Tuesday night, Lauren and her father had been joined by her sister Rebecca, and Jack, all acting as cleanup crew, and Jack hadn't been at work yesterday. He was probably still pitching in at the house.

By three minutes before the bell, and with the teachers' lounge emptied out, Savanna refilled her coffee and went to start her day. Maybe she'd catch him later.

She stood outside the library, waiting, at the end of her first hour. Mrs. Condor's third-grade class went straight from Art to Computers on Wednesdays. Jack was always here, standing in the doorway to greet them when Savanna ushered them over. Today, the library was dark and locked.

"Ms. Shepherd, should we go back to our class?"

Savanna smiled at Calvin. "No, not quite yet. Let me see if I can track down Mr. Carson." She pulled her phone out and scrolled through, looking for his number to send him a text. He'd given it to her after Caroline had been in the hospital, in case she had any need to reach a family member in the future. She didn't love the idea of going to the office to let them know Jack wasn't where he was supposed to be.

I have your 3rd graders ready for you. Is everything okay?

She hit send and watched her phone, waiting. What if something had happened to Caroline? Was that why he was absent yesterday? And late today?

"I can go get Mr. Clay," another student spoke up, trying to be helpful.

Savanna spotted her next class on their way down the hall, teacher Tricia Williams heading up the line of first graders trailing behind her. Mollie's class.

Savanna's phone buzzed in her hand:

Walking in now, so sorry.

She addressed the class, the kids milling around getting antsy now. "Children." Savanna put a hand up. "Volume, please. Mr. Carson will be just a moment." Tricia passed her, giving her a questioning look. "I'll be right there, Mrs. Williams, thank you." Tricia could wait with the first graders an extra minute, she was sure.

At the end of the line of Tricia's students, Mollie gave Savanna a little wave, and Savanna waved back. She spotted Jack coming down the hallway behind the girl, thank goodness.

"Hello, hello." Jack approached and unlocked the library

215

door. "Everyone in, let's go." He met Savanna's eyes as the third graders filed through the door between them.

"Ms. Shepherd?" Tricia stood in Savanna's classroom doorway, staring at both Savanna and Jack. "Shall I get them started?" The teacher's voice dripped with irritation.

"No, thank you," Savanna said sweetly. "I've got it." As she stepped into her own classroom, she saw Jack make a hasty exit into the library before he had to deal with Tricia's scathing look any longer.

Jack found Savanna while she ate lunch at her desk. She'd brought a sandwich with her today and was fine-tuning details on the computer for two upcoming projects her classes would be working on. She looked up, mouth full of slightly soggy BLT, to find Jack hovering in the doorway.

She motioned him in, chewing and swallowing quickly. "Sit, how are you? Can I offer you half a substandard BLT?"

Jack pulled up a chair and sat across from her at her desk. "I owe you an apology. I had a meeting this morning and I underestimated how long it'd be…and how long the drive back to town would take."

"Don't worry about it," Savanna said. "I was just concerned that something else had happened with your grandmother."

"Not that I know of. She seemed fine yesterday. We got most of the house put back together."

"Did you have far to drive from your meeting this morning?" Savanna was thinking of Skylar's early-morning commute every Thursday. Her sister always complained about the traffic in Lansing.

Jack looked surprised.

"Oh! Well, that was rude, wasn't it? I guess that was a little personal, I'm sorry," Savanna said. "I just meant, it sounds like you had a very busy morning before you even got to work."

"I did, yes."

Savanna waited, thinking he'd say something more about it, but he didn't. He was dressed differently, she noticed. His daily khakis and button-down were now replaced with a nice suit and tie. His hair was even different, no fly-aways or sticking-up pieces. "Well," she said to fill the awkward silence, "I appreciate your apology, but it's not necessary. I'm glad to hear Caroline is all right. What an awful scene to come home to; it's lucky that she was out getting her hair done when it happened. Your grandmother is one tough lady."

Jack stood. "That's for sure. She mentioned you'll be back this afternoon to paint? Are you going right after school?"

"Yes, actually, I brought a change of clothes with me," Savanna said. *And my Firefly*, she thought. She'd packed a bag with her USB microscope, laptop, and painter's clothes... She was prepared. Even if her art background was making her overly suspicious about something funny going on with the Minkov in Caroline's dining room, it wouldn't hurt to check it out. She was still kicking herself for not looking into that odd spot in the corner of the Laurant before Thiebold's assistant had packed it up and taken it. She wasn't going to miss her chance a second time.

Normally Savanna would have run home to grab Fonzie, but Sydney had offered to drop him off. She was meeting her fireman, Brad, on the beach beyond Caroline's house for a picnic dinner and marshmallow roast later tonight.

"Great, that's great," Jack said as a notification came through on his phone; a little bell jingled. He pulled it from his pocket, checking it. The phone rang while he held it and he instantly silenced it, looking from the screen back to Savanna. "I'll let you get back to your lunch."

"Okay. I'm glad everything went well with your meeting this morning."

"Sure," he answered on his way out of her classroom, the picture of distraction as he typed something into his phone.

Savanna stared at the doorway after he'd left. Every time she thought she had a handle on who Jack Carson was, he turned that notion on its head. She sighed, taking a bite of the remaining half of her sandwich and turning back toward her computer. Her fifth graders would be here in ten minutes. She needed to wolf down the rest of her lunch and run to the copy room.

JACK REAPPEARED JUST after the last bell. "Savanna."

She gave a start; her back was to the doorway, and she was hanging still-damp projects from the last class on a long clothesline strung a few inches out from the wall. "Hi again." She smiled at Jack.

"I wonder if I could convince you to take my after-school

pick-up duty today?" He looked desperate as he held the orange and yellow apron out to her.

Savanna groaned inwardly. She'd wanted to get the rest of the projects hung and skedaddle out of here. She had so much work to finish up still at Caroline's. "Sure." She crossed the room and took the apron from him.

"Thank you! I owe you one. Just ask, anytime. I'll return the favor, I promise." He turned to leave.

"Jack!"

He stopped, looking back at her.

"Are you all right? Is there something wrong, possibly? Anything I can help with?" She dropped the ugly orange apron over her head.

"No. I've just got to run. Thank you again!"

Savanna pulled her classroom door closed behind her, mentally resetting her expectations; by the time she finished after-school pick-up, and then hung the rest of the projects, she wouldn't actually be on the scaffolding painting until at least five. Or five thirty.

Which would be fine, she told herself, walk-running down the hall toward the pick-up circle at the front of the building. Jack really should have given her more notice. She was supposed to be out there by now.

After-school pick-up was controlled chaos in a nutshell.

Savanna waved three cars through, around two others that were clustered together because the parents were chatting through open windows, cars idling next to each other. From the looks of it, their respective children were already collected and buckled in.

She hated being the bad guy, but she approached the car closest to her; she'd have to remind them to keep the line moving. The woman in the car met her gaze, immediately put her car in gear, and pulled away, the other car following.

She smiled, happy not to have had to issue her gentle reminder. The school held around 284 kids. All it took was one inconsiderate person in the pick-up line, and the whole thing fell apart.

Mollie came bounding down the sidewalk, holding hands with another little girl. "Bye, Ms. Shepherd!" she called as they skipped by Savanna.

Savanna lifted a hand in a wave as she watched Mollie pass the three cars closest to her and head toward the fourth in line: Aidan's dark SUV.

Aidan sat behind the wheel, and he had a hand raised in a return wave.

Oh, jeez. She hadn't been waving at him; she was waving at his daughter.

The cars in line nearest Savanna efficiently loaded their passengers and went along their way, smoothly bringing Aidan right up alongside Savanna.

Aidan rolled down his window, ducking down a little so he could see her. "Hey there! How are you, Ms. Shepherd?" He smiled at her.

She grinned back at him. "Very well, thanks. How are *you*, Dr. Gallager?"

"I'm okay. A little worried about this pick-up procedure, you know. I've heard the people who run it are pretty strict. I wouldn't want to end up in detention for not following procedure."

Savanna laughed; she couldn't help it. "I think you're well within standard protocol, Dr. Gallager."

"Good to know!" Aidan winked at her. "Any news on the Caroline mystery?"

"Nothing since Tuesday, but I know the detectives are still checking out fingerprints and broken glass patterns."

Aidan's eyes widened. "Fingerprints and broken glass? Savanna, what? What happened?"

Savanna glanced past him; the cars were stacking up, two deep, parents looking irritated. "Ah, shoot, Aidan, I can't talk right now. I could call you later?" She straightened up, backing away and waving Aidan and the other three adjacent cars through. His vehicle moved away from the curbside spot, followed by a few others.

Savanna walked a few car lengths down, trying to get on top of the small-scale traffic jam. Ten minutes later, the circular drive in front of the school nearly empty and the lineup of cars looking pretty sparse, she finally took a deep breath. She glanced over her shoulder; sometimes when the traffic circle was insane, Mr. Clay would come out and take over. He'd done this once when Savanna had been on duty, the second week of school, and it had made her feel terribly inadequate, even though she'd known that wasn't his intention.

No Mr. Clay today. As she turned her attention back toward the circle, she spotted Aidan's SUV in one of the short-term parking spaces. He'd exited and was walking toward her. He turned and gave Mollie a one-minute sign, and the girl nodded. Savanna could see just her little blond head. She was drinking a juice box; Aidan must bring her one when he picked her up from school.

Savanna looked up at him, glancing out the corner of one eye at the remaining cars she was responsible for.

"They'll figure it out," he told her. "Don't worry."

She laughed. "Okay. This whole process is taken so seriously. I try not to shirk my responsibility!"

"Trust me, you're not a shirker. I've met some excellent shirkers, and none are as on top of things as you."

"That's good to know."

"What did you say about detectives…and fingerprints?"

"Oh. Lauren said she was going to call you; she didn't?"

"No." Aidan shook his head.

"Oh, boy." Savanna bit her lower lip. "There was a break-in yesterday. Caroline is fine," she added quickly. "They took her television, an antique record player, some jewelry, and I'm not sure what else. Her family was over there yesterday cleaning everything up. Detective Jordan asked a lot of questions about who has the code to her door locks. They aren't sure the broken window was how they actually got in."

"So, whoever broke the window is trying to make it look like a random robbery," Aidan said. "Why?"

Savanna shrugged, frowning. "I don't know. I keep going through possibilities in my head, everyone who comes in and out of her house."

Aidan cocked an eyebrow at her. "I'm above suspicion, aren't I? What about those Shepherd sisters? Do we trust them?"

Savanna grinned at him. "I think we're all off my short list. But honestly, it's got to be someone who has something to gain. Either by hurting Caroline, or by taking something she has in the house. Somehow, I don't think they were after her electronics and gold."

"You're probably right. Too much has happened, especially if we go back to what happened with Eleanor. That's someone trying hard to take Caroline out of the picture."

"Or get rid of something incriminating in her house," she added. "If the Eleanor incident and the fall on the stairway actually were related, then attempts to hurt Caroline haven't been successful, and maybe they've now decided to go at it from a different angle."

The paintings, Savanna thought instantly. But that made no sense. If someone was after those, they'd have been taken in the robbery. And if there were fakes in her collection, then no one would even be interested in stealing them.

"Hey." Aidan leaned closer to her. "Where did you go? I can see the wheels turning."

She met his eyes, suddenly oblivious to the stragglers in the pick-up line. He seemed to peer right into her soul with that blue-eyed gaze. And why did boys always have the longest, blackest lashes? It wasn't fair at all. Savanna shook her head to clear it. "I...I still have some ideas," she said vaguely. "I have to check something out tonight."

He frowned. "You aren't going to tell me, are you?"

"I have nothing to tell," she said truthfully. "How about, if I learn anything else while I'm there, I'll give you a call when I get home?"

Aidan tipped his head. "Will you though?"

She smiled. "I will. I promise."

Chapter Nineteen

SAVANNA MET LAUREN at the front door as she was leaving.

"Savanna! Grams said you might stop by. The mural is looking amazing." Lauren smiled, trotting down the front steps. "I just set her up with dinner. You could join her. She's so stubborn; I've spent the last two nights here but she's sending me home tonight. She's discouraged that she still isn't very mobile. I reminded her that Dr. Gallager is going to graduate her from her walking boot this weekend. She'll be so happy to be back upstairs in her own bed."

Savanna nodded. "I'm sure this has all been frustrating for her. She's normally so independent. I'm happy to keep her company while I paint."

"You look nice today, by the way," Lauren called over her shoulder.

Savanna laughed; Lauren only ever saw her in faded or stained painting clothes. Her polka-dot dress and red sweater was nicer than that any day. She locked the door behind her in the foyer and set her backpack, laptop case, and purse with her change of clothes on the entryway table.

In the parlor, Caroline had some kind of delicious-looking soup on the folding table in front of her, a piece of baguette, and a steaming cup of tea. "I was just imagining," she said as Savanna took a seat in the other wingback chair, "that I was on that little boat, sailing out into the sunset."

"I can imagine that. It looks like Mr. Carson's boat, doesn't it?" She'd painted the sails exactly to match Caroline's late husband's favorite sailboat, down to the number imprint on the sail.

"It does. You've done such a beautiful job. I think it must be nearly finished, isn't it?"

Savanna shook her head, sitting back and crossing her legs, studying the mural. "No, not quite yet. I have another few hours to do, maybe more. I've really enjoyed it, though, Caroline. I'm so happy you asked me to do it."

"You're not painting today, are you? Not in that lovely dress."

"I did want to spend a little time on it, yes. If you don't mind? I think I can have it finished by this weekend, a whole week ahead of schedule for your party."

"Whatever you'd like, dear. I'm so looking forward to celebrating here, to seeing everyone I love. It'll be almost like the parties we had when you were a child."

"I can't wait." Savanna stood and gave Caroline a quick hug. "I hope I'm just like you when I'm ninety. I'll be back. I'm going to go change clothes."

She wound her way through the house, fetching her things from the foyer and crossing through the living room to the small half bath adjacent to Caroline's office. She gasped as she was passing by and glanced through the doorway. As crowded as the office had been last week when

Savanna was snooping, it had been impeccably neat and organized, everything quite obviously in its place. Now, Savanna stood and surveyed the mess: open boxes along one wall held stacks of papers and binders; two of the drawers from Caroline's desk sat on top of the large coffee table in the center of the room, the wood splintered and broken, the drawers no longer usable; a broken floor lamp was dissembled and in a stack of other debris obviously meant for the trash. The framed mirror behind Caroline's desk was pulled out from the wall on one side, and Savanna saw it was on a hinge, with a wall safe behind it. The lock on the safe was broken but still attached, hanging by three wire cables. She took two steps into the room, turning in a circle, stunned at the damage. Her gaze found the spot over the mantel where Caroline's largest Julian Rothman painting had been—the void the piece had left was darker than the surrounding wall.

Savanna was speechless. So they *had* stolen some of her collection. The empty, bare area over the fireplace was more visually disturbing to Savanna than all the rest of the damage in the room.

She backed out of the office, hastily changing into painting clothes in the little bathroom next door. Her mind was reeling. Poor Caroline. Savanna dug around in her backpack and pulled out the case with her Firefly. Instead of going back to the parlor through the living room, Savanna went the other direction into the dining room, setting the Firefly and her laptop on the buffet below the still-present Minkov. Who in their right mind would steal a Rothman over a Minkov or even a Monet? Leaving her equipment there to use later, she cut through the butler's pantry and kitchen to get back to the parlor and Caroline.

She hated to ask, but she had to know. "Um, Caroline?"

The woman looked up from her book.

"I saw your office. Accidentally," she added, "when I went to change. I can't believe they stole your Rothman. I'm so sorry."

Caroline looked surprised. "The Rothman? Oh, the big one, over my mantel? No, no. That one sold. Don't worry, I got a nice deal on that one. Felix sent his assistant this morning to pick it up."

"Oh! Oh, that's so great. So none of your artwork was taken with the break-in?"

"No, it's all accounted for. You're such a sweet girl to be concerned."

She was flooded with relief. For goodness' sake, the woman had enough to worry about without also having just lost part of her valuable collection. "I'm so glad to hear it's all still here. I'm sorry about your office—it's awful how they tore it apart. I hope Detective Jordan finds out who did this."

"I'm sure he will. It's all right," she said earnestly, leaning forward in her chair. "I don't want you to worry so. No one was hurt, especially not my babies." She patted Princess on her furry white head, the poodle alongside her in the wing-back chair. "It's all just things, and things are replaceable."

"You're right. As you always are." Savanna matched the woman's posture, leaning in as well, and gave her hand a quick squeeze. She was so wise.

She was high up on the scaffolding, reworking the pink-ish evening sky near the ceiling, when both poodles barking startled her, making her jump. Her paintbrush flipped out of her hand and hit the grate under her feet; she snapped it up before it could fall through.

Princess and Duke tore out of the parlor down the hall, toward the front door.

"They heard the doorbell." Caroline rolled her eyes. "I have an excellent canine alarm system."

"I can go get it," Savanna said, starting to climb down. The outside sky through the parlor windows was now a darker pink than in the mural; she always lost track of time when she was painting.

"Don't bother, I'm not expecting anyone. If they belong here, they'll just come in, and if not, then they won't."

Savanna laughed. There was a weird kind of logic to her reasoning.

That was confirmed when Sydney's voice called out from the foyer. "Hello? Caroline? Savanna?"

Savanna continued down the ladder on the side of the scaffolding, stooping to catch Fonzie when he came skitter-ing through the parlor, his whole body wagging. She laughed, hugging him and letting him say his hellos, first to her and then to the poodles and Caroline.

"He kind of missed you," Sydney said.

"Thank you for bringing him. I miss him when I'm at work all day," she said as Fonzie bounded back over to her, Princess and Duke clamoring to be part of the fun as she sat down on the huge round rug in the center of the room.

"Well, I guess he misses you too," Syd said, "though he doesn't act like it at the shop. He spends all day greeting my customers; he thinks he owns the place." Sydney greeted Caroline, bending to give her a hug. "You look gorgeous," she said to the woman. "Did you get your hair done?"

"I did. You look stunning as always," Caroline said. "How's business?"

"It's good. You were right. I had to allow for a dip in revenue in the first two quarters, but reinvesting my..."

Savanna was already tuning out the conversation; she knew Caroline had helped Sydney immeasurably with her business model when she'd opened Fancy Tails and Treats, but finances were so not Savanna's strong suit. She stood, spilling Fonzie off her lap, and made a quiet exit, cutting back through the butler's pantry into the dining room.

This was just the opportunity she'd hoped for. Savanna pulled her phone from the large pocket on her cargo pants, quickly typing in a text to her sister.

Keep her busy, I need like 10 minutes please!

Savanna set her phone on the buffet and opened her laptop, pressing the power button. Working fast, she unzipped the case for her Firefly microscope and plugged it into the port on her laptop. She tapped the mousepad; the screen remained black. Her battery was dead.

She crouched down, peering behind the buffet for an outlet. Nothing. She moved around to the other side. Still nothing.

Savanna groaned. She turned around, scanning the room for the closest outlet. There was one on the other side of the dining room table. She grabbed her laptop and microscope, and carried them around. Once she had the computer plugged in, she hit the power button again and let out her breath when she heard the whir of the laptop powering on. She touched the on button on the microscope, and the green LED on the side blinked on.

"Okay," she whispered, moving back to the buffet and the wall over it with the Sergei Minkov painting. She'd tried to work up the nerve to just ask Caroline if she could check it out; she'd been thinking of how to phrase it all evening. But every version led to Caroline asking why. And then Savanna explaining that she thought…maybe…possibly…Caroline's piece of art valued at over a million dollars might be a fake.

No version of the conversation ended with Caroline remaining calm and relaxed, book in her lap, blood pressure perfect. Not even after hearing the woman declare that her belongings were just things, and things could be replaced.

Savanna's phone on the buffet buzzed and made her jump—again. She was a little on edge tonight. Sydney had replied.

Ooh, why, what are you doing? Where are you?

Savanna picked up her phone.

Dining room. I brought my microscope, checking out the Minkov. Just keep her occupied!

She stared at the phone for a moment, but there was no response. Good.

Savanna took a deep breath and carefully, carefully took the Minkov off the wall. She carried it over and set it on the dining room table gingerly. *Same as being at work*, she told herself. *No different. This isn't even the highest-valued piece you've handled. Stay calm.*

Savanna ran her Firefly slowly over the canvas, starting with girls' dresses, the discrepancy she'd sworn she'd seen in the work. She stopped and clicked through the settings on the scope, choosing the capture option; this way, she'd have a record of what she was viewing. Savanna watched the computer screen populate with a closely magnified image of the Minkov, very tiny section by section. The green of the smaller girl's dress varied from one side to the other, in and of itself not necessarily significant, but it wasn't so much the pigment as the sheen. The darker sheen, under the Firefly, stood out slightly from the canvas. An area Minkov had amended in the creation of the work? Savanna wasn't sure.

But. The brushstrokes were wrong.

Sergei Minkov used what was commonly known as broken brushwork, a technique some artists employed to show movement in still work, whether in cloud formations, water, or grass, as in this piece. The long grass in the field surrounding the two girls on the trail was similar in appearance to winter wheat, thick, lush, and tall. It would have moved in the breeze or as the girls brushed against it as they walked. In Minkov's other works, his signature brushstrokes contributed to the viewer feeling as if movement in the scene was nearly detectable.

This piece, the supposed *Storm in Sochi*, lacked that sense of movement, and through her Firefly, the brushstrokes were a poor imitation of Sergei Minkov's broken brushwork technique. When she pulled up the piece online and compared it side by side in a new browser window with Caroline's painting, the two looked identical. But, in person and under the microscope, they were not.

Savanna knew it wasn't enough. Just because Minkov had employed a specific brushstroke style in his later works didn't quantitatively mean that he'd started out that way. This piece was from 1869; the majority of Minkov's work dated between 1882 and 1903.

Savanna needed two things now.

She had to get the copy of the provenance paperwork from Skylar. Tomorrow, if not sooner; she needed to research just exactly where and with whom this painting, or the actual painting, had been. And the only way to prove this painting was a forgery was by radiograph. For that, Savanna would have to take it offsite.

And to do that, she'd have to come clean with Caroline about what she'd done.

Savanna's phone was dinging like crazy over on the buffet. She forced herself back to the here and now, quickly packing up her microscope and laptop. She carefully carried the Minkov back to its spot and hung it, both vindicated and disappointed at her discovery. Now she couldn't help wondering about the large, imposing Minkov hanging in Caroline's library, but that would have to be a project for another day.

She glanced at her phone screen as she went back through the butler's pantry and kitchen toward the parlor:

Are you almost done?
I'm supposed to meet Brad in 10 minutes.
Savvy, hurry up, she has to use the bathroom!

OMG I steered her away from the dining room but I have to leave SOON.

Dude.

Oh, poor Syd, Savanna thought, rushing into the parlor to find Sydney sitting on the floor in front of Caroline, holding her hand, palm up. The dinner dishes were gone, the folding table stored against the wall, and Sydney was telling Caroline something about a past life.

"I am so sorry." Savanna put a hand on Caroline's shoulder. "I got a call. I had no idea how long I'd be!"

Sydney gave her a look—*the* look—the sister look, the one Savanna had used on Sydney just last week when she'd asked Savanna to mind the shop for a minute while she ran across the street to the yoga studio to change the schedule, and hadn't returned for over an hour. That look.

Savanna pulled the corners of her mouth down in remorse, mouthing *I'm sorry* to Syd as she stood at Caroline's side.

"Well." Sydney stood. "Caroline, we can pick this up when I come to get Princess and Duke this weekend; your house isn't the only thing getting spruced up for your birthday. And, tonight, I have a very sweet fireman waiting for me on the beach."

Caroline clapped her hands together. "Go, dear girl! Never keep the good ones waiting—he is a good one, isn't he?"

"He's a very good one." She leaned down and kissed Caroline's cheek. "Maybe I'll make him my plus-one at your party so you can meet him."

"I would love that," she said. "Now scoot."

Sydney pulled Savanna by the sleeve toward the hallway as she left, whispering, "I'm waking you up later so you can tell me what you found!"

Savanna moved to her scaffolding, packing up paints and brushes for the night. She was dreading talking to Caroline about the painting, but she had to. Finished cleaning up, her supplies now corralled in the large multipocketed canvas bag, Savanna finally sat back down opposite Caroline in the empty wingback chair.

"You must be tired," Caroline said. "Go get some rest. I'm starting to feel guilty keeping you here."

"I love visiting with you. Don't feel guilty; I'm going soon. But…I have to ask you something."

"Anything."

"You and Mr. Carson put so much of your efforts and heart into your art collection. You have some incredible pieces here. You know I worked as an art authenticator in Chicago. It was my job to know characteristics of fine art, and the artists who created those works. So, sometimes unfortunately, even without meaning to, I don't always see works of art in the way others do. Sometimes a piece speaks to me differently, especially if it's a work by an artist I know well."

"Of course. That makes sense."

"I'd like to take your small Minkov to Lansing to authenticate it," she blurted. She cringed inwardly, wishing she knew a better way to approach this.

Caroline tilted her head, looking at her curiously. "Are you doubting that piece?"

Savanna leaned forward. "I don't know," she said quietly. "I know Minkov. And that piece. And there is just something…off with it, Caroline." She didn't want to rat herself out just yet; Caroline didn't need to know she'd set up a mini authentication station in her dining room.

"Savanna, you know I trust you implicitly. If you think it's necessary to take a look at that Minkov, then absolutely, do it."

Her words warmed Savanna. This was why she'd thought Caroline was actually her grandmother until she was eight, and Skylar had corrected the notion: the woman treated Savanna and her sisters as if they were family. She'd hoped she could convince Caroline to trust her with such a potentially valuable piece of art, but she shouldn't have worried.

"Okay," Savanna said. "There's one other thing. Has your family checked on your important papers after the break-in? You'd said you have the originals of the provenances for your collection here, in Mr. Carson's study, I think. Is your paperwork still intact here? Is anything missing?"

Caroline shook her head. "No. Fortunately, Mr. Carson was a shrewd businessman and, if I might say so, a little overzealous in protecting his assets. Those provenances are all fine, along with our other important papers, in a safe built into his desk." She smiled. "He never left a thing up to chance. Whomever broke into my house had quite a tantrum in our offices, but that hulking old cherrywood desk of his upstairs has barely a scratch."

Savanna let out a sigh of relief. "Amazing," she breathed.

"He was smart, wasn't he? I may want to see the certificate for the Minkov at some point, or perhaps I should look at all of them, but for now, Skylar has your copies and that's good enough for my research."

"I appreciate you looking into this for me, Savanna."

"Of course. Don't tell anyone where those papers are kept. Not a soul, please. And try not to worry. It's always possible I'm wrong."

Caroline sat back in her chair and picked up her book. "I dare say, I doubt you are often wrong. We shall see. I'm not worried, no matter what you find. You shouldn't worry either. But could you do me one small favor before you go?"

"Anything," Savanna echoed her from moments earlier. She should have known it would take more than the chance of a forged painting to ruffle Caroline Carson.

"I'd love a cup of lemon tea, if you don't mind." She reached over to pat Savanna's hand.

Savanna made the tea, disposing of the soup and bread Caroline hadn't eaten and loading the dishes in the dishwasher. She moved through the house collecting her things; she hadn't meant to, but she'd gotten a little scattered, what with her secretive antics in the dining room. She gathered her backpack, laptop, bag of brushes to clean, and leaned down to hug Caroline goodbye. She picked up her keys from the entryway table and whistled for Fonzie once she'd made it to the front door.

Back at Sydney's less than ten minutes later, Savanna flounced onto the plush, comfy couch in the living room, Fonzie turning in three circles before snuggling up next to her. She picked up the remote for the television, then thought better of it and tapped the screen on her phone. She'd promised to call Aidan if she learned anything new tonight at Caroline's house.

It was 8:58 p.m. He was probably putting Mollie to bed. She hated to bother him, but he had taken note the last time she was supposed to call and didn't...so she called.

Aidan picked up on the first ring.

Savanna smiled into the phone and began.

Chapter Twenty

FRIDAY MORNING, BARELY a minute past eight, Savanna typed in the code to Caroline's front door and pushed it open, poking her head in. "Caroline?" She'd walked right in plenty of times before, but never this early.

Savanna had discovered as she was leaving for work this morning that she didn't have her purse. She'd gone back and checked her bedroom, then retraced her steps to the living room, where she'd sat last night and talked to Aidan until past her bedtime. Then she'd checked her car.

And then she'd remembered: when she'd changed out of her polka-dot dress at Caroline's yesterday, she'd been so focused on checking the Minkov that she'd piled her clothing and purse on the bathroom countertop to retrieve later. And had left them there.

She'd called Lauren on the way over to Caroline's; Lauren had reassured her that it was fine to stop by and grab her purse, as Caroline was always an early riser.

Now, calling through the open door and hearing nothing from inside the house, Savanna quietly entered. Maybe Caroline was still sleeping, and she could be in and out without disturbing her.

Princess and Duke raced up to her, prancing and whining.

"Well, hello guys." Savanna bent to pet them. "Do you need to go out?" She held the front door open, but they stayed where they were, right by her side, wiggling and antsy. "Okay." Savanna shrugged. "Suit yourself."

She went through the living room and turned the corner where Caroline's half bath was, and sure enough, found her black and white dress and red sweater folded neatly on top of her purse on the bathroom counter. She tucked the clothing under one arm and slung her purse over a shoulder, heading back out toward the foyer, and nearly tripped over the poodles.

Savanna crouched down, giving them equal scratch-behind-the-ears attention. "Listen," she whispered, "we're trying not to wake your mom, okay?" She frowned, considering. Maybe they were hungry?

Savanna hung her purse over the front door handle so she wouldn't forget it a second time and followed the poodles down the hallway toward the kitchen. Princess and Duke veered off into the parlor; Savanna skidded to halt on the polished wooden floors in her stocking feet, motioning to them. They were standing on the big round rug, staring at her. She knew Caroline was sleeping in the parlor until her walking boot came off tomorrow.

"Hey! Come on, guys, I'll feed you," Savanna told them in her loudest whisper, waiting.

Duke came over to her, prancing in a circle around her legs, then darting back into the parlor.

A sick feeling sprang up in Savanna's stomach. Caroline

should be up by now. She would see the poodles acting strangely, even if she hadn't heard Savanna.

Now Princess and Duke both ran over to her, pawing at her legs, and this time, she followed them into the parlor.

Caroline was in bed, against the far wall. Her temporary bedroom had two sets of four-panel room dividers decorated with cherry blossom branches, partitioning her sleeping area off from the rest of the parlor; her family had thought of everything. But she was quite visible in her bed, and she wasn't asleep. She was murmuring something.

Savanna ran over to her. "Caroline? Caroline!" She took the woman's hand in her own, patting it vigorously.

Caroline appeared drugged. It was Savanna's first thought and had nothing to do with the memory of Eleanor in this same room. Caroline was groggy, eyes barely open, hand limp in Savanna's.

Savanna dialed 911, and when the operator's voice came on the line, she shocked herself by bursting into tears. She held on to Caroline's hand, squeezing it, and quickly gave details to the operator.

"I'm sending an ambulance right now, ma'am," the voice on the other end of the phone said, and Savanna was flooded with relief.

"Hurry!"

The dispatcher stayed on the line with her, and Savanna registered the woman giving her instructions on what to watch for, what to do, should Caroline worsen. Savanna heard the words and dismissed them, filing them away somewhere else, in a little corner of her brain where she wouldn't need them, because Caroline would be fine. She had to be.

"You're going to be okay, Caroline, I promise." Savanna squeezed her hand, putting the back of one hand against the woman's forehead. She was cool, no fever.

Now she heard the sirens. She shouted for the first responders to come in. There were four of them this time. Savanna stepped back out of the way and let them work. She found Lauren's phone number and hit call with shaking fingers.

Lauren arrived within minutes, still wearing cupcake-print pajama pants, and put a call in to her father. Savanna hovered in the doorway with Lauren, both relieved and even more afraid once the team had Caroline loaded onto a gurney to take her to the hospital.

"What can I do?" Savanna called to Lauren as she followed them out the door. "Should I come? Should I call anyone else?"

"Thanks, Savanna. Could you let Dr. Gallager know she's on her way in to the hospital? So he'll watch for her? Oh, and I texted my sisters, but could you tell Jack?"

Savanna watched the ambulance scream down the quiet street. How much could one person endure? Sure, Caroline's last ambulance ride had been only for a sprained ankle, but what in the world had happened to her just now? She'd been fine when Savanna had left her last night.

Drifting back into the house, Savanna called and got Aidan's voicemail. "Aidan, this is Savanna. Caroline is on her way to the hospital. She's—I don't even know. She was semiconscious this morning, I stopped by the house and found her. Oh, it's, uh..." She glanced at the clock on Caroline's stove. "It's 8:25. I hope you can help her," she finished, voice shaky.

Savanna hung up and looked around the kitchen in a daze. She spotted a plate on the counter, a piece of untouched toast in the center of it, and half of another with a few bites missing. A small, empty juice glass sat on the counter next to the plate, and a smaller plastic medication cup next to that.

Savanna had run the dishwasher last night and left Caroline with tea, just before she was going to turn in. So she had gotten up this morning, early as Lauren said. She'd come in here, picked at her breakfast, taken her morning medication, and then...what?

She went back through to the parlor and scrolled through her contacts in her phone to Jack's number. Savanna heard the second ring in two places, the phone to her ear and the kitchen behind her. She turned and walked back to the kitchen. A phone rested on the island countertop, ringing. She held her phone in one hand, looking down at the ringing phone. The screen read *Incoming Call Savanna Shepherd.*

Savanna hung up. When had Jack been here? She picked up his phone and went back into the parlor. She stood between the two partition screens, frowning at Caroline's temporary bedroom. On her bedside table was a lamp, a lipstick, her weekly medication box, a clock, and her book, the same book she'd been reading last night when Savanna had left her. Savanna bent and peered at the face of Caroline's small analog clock; the little gold arm for the alarm clock time was set to 6:30. Caroline had fallen asleep reading last night and woken at her usual time this morning. She'd gone into the kitchen, where she'd eaten, although not very much, and had drank her juice and took her pills. And then, for some reason, she'd gone back to bed. Which seemed very unlike Caroline Carson.

Shouting came from the front of the house. "Hello! Lauren! Anyone!"

Savanna moved through to the front door to find Maggie Lyle standing in the foyer, hands on her hips, long pink housecoat on, hair piled on top of her head in a disheveled bun.

"What happened? Where is Caroline?" she demanded.

Savanna shook her head. "They took her to the hospital."

"Again? For what this time? Was it her heart?"

Savanna looked sharply at Maggie. "What did you say?"

Maggie backed down. "Her heart. I just meant, I know that doctor's been over here checking her heart."

"How do you know that, Maggie?"

The older woman straightened her back, scowling at Savanna. "Because we're neighbors, that's why. What are *you* doing here?"

She didn't have time for this. "Oh, no." She sucked her breath in. "School. I've got to go." It was now 8:40, just minutes away from the first bell. She looked down and saw she was still holding two phones in her hand. And Princess and Duke were dancing around her legs.

She dropped the phones into her purse, scooped up her discarded clothing from yesterday, and held an arm out to Maggie as she moved to the front door, ushering the woman out.

"No," Maggie said, stepping back, out of reach. "I'll stay and take care of the dogs. I'll lock up. I know the code."

"No," Savanna said firmly. "That's okay. My sister is coming to pick them up," she lied. Well, Sydney would, when she called her. And her next call would be to her dad, to change the lock code. The doors needed to stay locked, even if it meant nobody had the code but Caroline and Lauren. "Come on, I'll fill you in as we walk."

Maggie gave up, letting Savanna lead her out onto the front porch and lock the door.

"I came by early this morning and found Caroline not feeling well," Savanna said as Maggie was standing, waiting for details. "I honestly don't know what was wrong. But the ambulance got here really fast, and I called to tell her doctor she's on the way to the hospital."

Maggie sighed, seeming satisfied at that paltry explanation. "That poor woman. I just can't imagine, being her age and still struggling to live on my own, in a big old house like this. I'd have thought one of her kids would take her in once Everett went." Maggie made a tsking noise.

Nice, Savanna thought. Use Caroline's second trip to the hospital in as many weeks as a platform for why she was too old and feeble to live alone anymore. "Maggie, last night, did you happen to see anyone coming or going here?" If anyone had, she was positive the woman would know. She was tuned in to the goings-on here 24-7.

"I saw *you* leave," Maggie said.

Savanna nodded, exasperated. "Yes, that's right. I left a little before nine. Anyone else?"

"It's not like I'm just sitting and watching out my window. I don't keep tabs on my neighbors," she informed Savanna.

"Of course not," Savanna agreed, biting her lip.

"But that young man came by, the one who's helping her with the paintings. And then I saw her grandson's car early this morning, around seven."

"Wait, what man? You mean Felix Thiebold—her art dealer? He's probably in his fifties or so. He was here last night?"

"No, the young one. He's thin, maybe in his twenties. His hair is too long. You know, I've seen him carrying paintings out."

"Ryan?" Felix's assistant had been here last night?

"I don't know his name. I told you, I don't camp out and spy on everything."

"And then you saw which grandson today? Was it Jack?"

"Yes, the school librarian. Jack."

That explained his phone on the counter. And now Savanna had a panicky feeling that the Minkov was gone.

She'd reached her car. She had to get to school. Her first class arrived at nine. She opened the car door and got in, starting the engine and apologizing to Maggie for rushing off to work. It was disconcerting how much that woman knew about everyone and everything. Savanna waited a minute, then another, tapping her foot impatiently as she watched Maggie cross the wide Carson front lawn toward her own house.

It was 8:48.

When Maggie was nearly at her easement, Savanna hopped out, shutting the door quietly, and sprinted back up onto the porch. She zipped through the house, making a big circle through all the rooms and taking a super-fast inventory of Caroline's paintings. Both Minkovs were there, as well as the others; the Monet and Matisse were fine too. Darn it, she wished she'd dug her hard-sided portrait case out of her storage bins this morning. She'd take the questionable Minkov with her if she could, but there was no way she was carting around a potential million-dollar painting in the back seat of her car, to mingle with dog fur and Nolan's Cheerios.

She did discover that Caroline was down to one Rothman in her office. There'd been three to begin with; Felix had sold the large one over the mantel earlier this week, Savanna recalled. Now the one closest to the desk was gone—that had to be what Ryan had taken. Savanna groaned inwardly. She wanted time to check out all the remaining work in Caroline's house.

She locked the door again as she left, a futile measure, and called Harlan on the way to school. "Dad! I have a favor to ask. Could you please go over and change the lock codes on all the doors at Caroline's? I can explain later, but can you go do it right now, pretty please?"

Harlan's laughing voice came through the phone line. "Can I at least grab a cup of coffee first?"

"No!" Savanna slammed on the brakes; she'd almost run a red light. It was 8:59. "Dad, I'm sorry I don't have time to explain, but it's so important, please. Please just go do it now. I would have done it but I don't know how. Caroline isn't there, she's at the hospital. I'll call you on my lunch break, I promise."

"Got it. I'm on my way," he assured her, and Savanna heard his car start on the other end of the line.

"Thank you, Dad." She dropped the phone into her pocket and raced into the school. She'd never been late before. She walked past the office, head down, ignoring the secretary's stare. Well, she'd been spotted. Now Mr. Clay would know. Nothing she could do about it.

She set Jack's phone on her desk and set about passing out the supplies to her third graders for today's project. Savanna stood at the front of the room, looking over the students and finally settling on Paige, a quiet, serious girl in the third row. "Class, I have to go next door to the library for two minutes. I'll be right back, but while I'm gone, Paige will be in charge. Is that clear?" Paige looked surprised but pleased.

Reaching for Jack's phone, as she wanted to let him know right away about Caroline, Savanna was startled when it rang. She paused, hand in the air above it. The screen was lit up with the words *Call From Private*. The call ended and the phone dinged, signaling a new voicemail message.

Savanna grabbed the phone and winked at Paige. "Thank you. I'll be back in a sec. If there's any problem, come get me next door, okay?"

Just outside her classroom door, the phone jangled like a bell: a text message notification popped up on the screen. The phone displayed the first line of the message, as hers did, even with the lock screen on. Savanna had never cared enough to go through the settings and change them to hide everything on the lock screen. Apparently, Jack hadn't either.

Without even meaning to, Savanna read the text.

We lose everything if you don't get the money. It's the only way to—

Savanna stared at the screen. What on earth was this about?

Entering the library to find Jack in his usual spot behind the counter at a computer, Savanna set his phone on the counter, and he looked up in surprise.

"Thanks! Where did you find it?"

"At your grandmother's this morning," Savanna said, watching him.

He picked up the phone and came around the counter. "Thank you so much. I couldn't remember when I'd had it last."

"Maggie Lyle said you stopped by this morning." Savanna wanted to see how he answered her. Did he know Caroline was ill?

"Yes." He looked at Savanna curiously. "I did. I had to drop off those treats for Princess and Duke. Grandmother said they devoured the Steak Sticks from Fancy Tails, so I picked up a larger bag. What was Maggie doing there so early?"

"She stopped by as I was leaving."

Jack shrugged. "Well, at least it's nice Grandmother never has a chance to get lonely." He smiled. "Oh! You have class, don't you? I'll let you get back. Thanks so much for my phone."

She felt a little pang of guilt. If he had any inkling that something was wrong with Caroline, he sure was hiding it well. "Jack, your grandmother was taken to the hospital this morning. I tried to call you and found your phone on the counter. Lauren wanted you to know she was on her way to Anderson Memorial."

Jack stared at her. "No. Oh, my... What happened?"

"I'm not sure. I stopped by to get something I forgot last night and found her not feeling well. You should call Lauren. Or maybe you should go the hospital? I'm sure Mr. Clay will understand."

He took a deep breath in and let it out slowly, shaking his head. "I can't believe the year she's had. Did she seem... How bad is it? Do you think I should be there?"

Savanna's eyes widened. She certainly didn't want that kind of decision on her shoulders. "That's up to you. I'm not sure how serious it is."

He reached over the counter and grabbed his jacket. "I think I should go. I'll stop in the office and let them know I'm gone the rest of the day."

"I hope she's okay, Jack." Savanna watched him head down the hall, her worry for Caroline sitting in her stomach like a stone.

She found her third graders still in their seats, working on their projects. She stopped at Paige's desk and deposited a blue plastic token in front of the girl to use at the school store; it was a little shop the school ran in the lunchroom on Wednesdays. "Thank you, honey. Nice job."

When the lunch bell finally rang, Savanna bolted out the front doors of the school. Her mind was working overtime and she couldn't shut it off; she needed the walk to Fancy Tails to clear her head. She buttoned a few of the buttons on her royal blue sweater and stuck her hands in the very cool pockets of her bright color-blocked A-line dress. There was just something about a dress with pockets, not to mention it kept her hands warm against today's chill in the air.

Savanna pushed through the door to Fancy Tails, the bell over her head jingling.

"Hey!" Syd greeted her from behind the treat display case.

"Would you mind picking up Caroline's poodles a day early?" Savanna had thought about them all morning; she knew they were fine, but they must be worried about Caroline.

"Hello to you too." Sydney smiled at Savanna.

"I'm sorry. It's already been quite a day. Did you hear what happened? Have you talked to Dad?"

Sydney motioned Savanna over behind the display case with her, pointing through the window into the grooming area. Sydney's assistant had one little white poodle on the steel table, in the middle of a trim. The other one was already washed and primped, wearing a new red bandana and curled up on a purple fleece dog bed in one of the holding pens.

She impulsively hugged her sister. "You. Are. Awesome.

Thank you so much. They look happy. Well, that one, not so much." She giggled at the one being trimmed. She couldn't tell Princess from Duke unless they were side by side, but the one on the table looked anxious to get the haircut over with, prancing impatiently on its front paws.

"Dad called me from Caroline's. I ran by and got them this morning. I figure we can just keep them through the weekend. I'm sure that'll help Lauren so she won't have to leave them there alone. Oh, and we already called her with the new lock code."

"That's a great idea. Fonzie will love it. Did Lauren say how Caroline was? Do they know anything yet?"

"Not really," Sydney replied. "She said she's in the Cardiac ICU. See now, aren't you glad your Dr. Gallager is her doctor?"

"He's not 'my' anything, Syd. Stop it."

Sydney shrugged, returning her attention to restocking the display case. "Sheesh. I meant 'your' as in your friend. But I see where your head is at."

Savanna gave Sydney's long red braid a yank. "Whatever. I'm going to grab a sandwich from the deli before my break is over. Do you want anything?"

"Yes! A chicken fajita wrap—two of them. One's for Willow." Sydney pointed through the window at her assistant.

After work, after twenty minutes in Sydney's basement rummaging through boxes she still hadn't unpacked from Chicago and another twenty minutes at Caroline's house, Savanna stood in the lobby of Skylar's law office holding a large brown leather case in each hand.

Skylar's receptionist pressed a button on the office phone on her desk. "Your sister is here. She says it's urgent and she must speak with you right now."

"Send her in," Skylar's voice came over the speaker.

Savanna set the cases on Skylar's long conference table and opened them, carefully folding back the layer of polyethylene sheeting to reveal the paintings she'd taken from the Carson house.

"Wow," Skylar breathed. She turned and stared at Savanna.

"It's okay," Savanna said. "She said I could take the Minkov to Lansing to authenticate it. I know it's a forgery, just from what I saw yesterday with my Firefly. At least, I'm almost positive it is."

Skylar nodded. "Syd filled me in. And Caroline said you could take both these pieces from her house?"

Savanna bit her bottom lip. "Well. She said I could take the Minkov."

Skylar groaned, pulling the white sheeting back over the Rothman, the only remaining painting from Caroline's office. "I really didn't need to know you took both. I didn't see anything." She raised an eyebrow at Savanna.

"Ah, yes, okay. Got it. So, I took the Minkov and I'm taking it to Lansing first thing tomorrow. I already talked to their authenticator. He knows I'm coming and they said I can use their equipment."

"What are you thinking? I'm trying to see how this could be related to why Caroline keeps landing in the hospital."

"I've thought a lot about that. If she has forgeries in her

house, someone knew about them. Either Everett, or their art dealer Felix, or Ryan, Felix's assistant. Or maybe all of them. Ryan came and picked up the counterpart piece to that one"—Savanna pointed at the now-covered painting—"last night. Caroline's gallerist is helping her thin the collection and they're slowly finding buyers. I couldn't leave the other Rothman at her house. It's my best chance at finding out if the first two Rothmans were genuine."

"Okay, I can see why you needed to do this. But what can I do? We never looked over the certificate copies." She moved to her desk.

"We need those. I do want to sit down and go through all of them. Just like I want a chance to look at each of the pieces still hanging in Caroline's house using my Firefly. But I brought the paintings here, because...you're going to call me paranoid."

Skylar shook her head. "Try me."

"Your office has a security system, right? Alarms, cameras, all of that?"

"Yes. All of the branches do. It's protocol from corporate in Lansing."

"Can we please lock these in for the night? They can't stay in my car, and honestly, I won't sleep if I have to keep 1.5 million dollars' worth of art in the house overnight. At least here, they'll be safe, and I won't worry. I can meet you here first thing Saturday morning to get them."

Skylar took a deep breath, looking at Savanna. "Of course. I understand. I hope you're wrong about the paintings. That's a ton of money."

"I don't think I'm wrong."

Chapter Twenty-One

SAVANNA STOOD AT the coffee kiosk in the lobby of Anderson Memorial, waiting. She'd told Skylar she was stopping off at the hospital this morning to see Caroline before meeting her at the law office, and Skylar said she'd join her. Savanna had gotten two large coffees, black for Skylar and a caramel mocha for herself. She'd chosen one of her favorite dresses this morning, telling herself it had nothing to do with the possibility of seeing Aidan. She wanted to look nice when meeting with her friend and colleague Britt at the Lansing Museum of Fine Art.

"Mine?" Sydney tapped Savanna on the shoulder and took the frothy, whipped-cream-topped coffee out of her hand, taking a sip. "Thanks!"

"Hey! I didn't know you were coming." She turned to the barista and ordered a duplicate of the one her sister had just stolen.

"I want to see Caroline too. I'm taking Skylar's car from here and going to babysit Nolan. Travis has a meeting later. Skylar wants to come with you to Lansing."

"Cool." Savanna checked her phone. She'd texted Aidan a few minutes ago, hoping he might be on-site at the hospital. She was so worried about Caroline.

Skylar arrived, giving them each a hug. She looked with disgust at the whipped-cream-topped confection the barista set on the counter but picked it up anyway.

"Mine?" She looked doubtfully at Savanna.

"No." Savanna laughed and traded her, handing over the plain black coffee. How Skylar could drink that, she'd never know.

Savanna spotted Aidan across the lobby, coming down the wide staircase. He wore the doctor uniform well, long white lab coat over blue scrubs today.

Sydney poked Savanna in the ribs and whispered in her ear, "So hot."

Savanna elbowed Syd, hard.

Aidan crossed the shiny linoleum, smiling and greeting each of them. "I take it you came to see Caroline?"

"We were hoping to," Savanna replied.

"They only allow immediate family in the CICU," he said. "I'm so sorry. But," he added, reading their disappointment, "I can tell you she's doing much better. We'll probably move her to the stepdown unit by tonight as long as she remains stable."

"Do you know what happened? Was it something with her heart? Was it what you'd been checking her for with the monitor?" Savanna took the role of spokesperson, standing between her sisters.

"Not exactly," Aidan said. "Why don't we sit? I wanted to talk to you about something," he said to Savanna.

Savanna glanced at her sisters as they followed Aidan to a small round table by the wall of windows that made up the front of the building. Something was up; she knew it. Her stomach turned over as she wondered if Caroline was once again here in the hospital because someone was trying to hurt her. She never should have assumed the woman was safe, even temporarily.

Aidan leaned forward, arms resting on the table, keeping his voice low. "I ran a few extra labs yesterday when she came in. It looks like an overdose of digitalis—a cardiac medication."

"What? But how? Caroline knows what she's on. She's sharp. She'd never take something you didn't prescribe her."

"She is on digitalis," Aidan explained. "But her blood level was through the roof. It triggered a dangerous arrhythmia, which we're getting under control. Digitalis toxicity can cause a host of symptoms—nausea, poor appetite, fatigue...eventually death, if the level is high enough. Did you happen to notice anything when you saw her Thursday? Was she acting normal?"

Savanna was quiet, thinking. She remembered cleaning up Caroline's half-eaten dinner plate to put it in the dishwasher. And then, yesterday morning, that empty pill cup alongside a barely eaten breakfast. "She wasn't eating—at least, not very well. Her appetite had dropped off. And Friday morning, it looked like she'd gone back to bed after having breakfast and taking her pills. Caroline doesn't nap."

"Digitalis, her form of it anyway, is a tiny yellow pill. It's smaller than a pencil eraser. As the dose increases, the pill gets slightly bigger, but not much." Aidan lowered his voice even further, and all three sisters leaned in to hear him. "I'm thinking somebody switched out her pill for a much-higher dose. She'd probably have never noticed."

"Oh my God," Savanna breathed.

"I'm calling Jordan." Skylar fumed, bright red color high on her cheekbones, her brow furrowed in anger. "This has gone too far. Caroline could have died. We'll find out who did this."

Sydney shook her head, looking as if she might cry. "Caroline has tried so hard to stay healthy. She does everything she's supposed to do. You bet we'll find out who did it."

Savanna grabbed Aidan's arm. "Her pillbox. It's been sitting out in plain sight since her fall. Her family moved her bedroom into the parlor. Anyone could have tampered with it!"

Aidan's eyes lit up, suddenly struck with a light bulb moment. "Aspirin," he murmured, pulling his work tablet from his lab coat pocket. "I think I have her on a baby aspirin. Let me check."

The sisters were quiet as he worked, glancing at each other. Why would it matter if Caroline was on aspirin?

"She takes a baby aspirin every day." He looked up from his tablet at Savanna, then at Skylar and Sydney. "That's another small yellow pill. Whoever tried to kill Caroline could have easily quadrupled her cardiac med dose over just a couple of days, replacing both those pills with a high-dose digitalis. Who sets up Caroline's pills? Does she do it herself? Or does Lauren?"

"I'm not sure," Savanna said.

"We need the pillbox," Aidan said. "Better yet, Detective Jordan needs the pillbox; I just need a photo of the open pill compartments so I can see what's in there."

Savanna stood. "We'll go get it right now."

They were heading toward the door when Aidan called to Savanna, catching up with them. "Be careful. So many people have the lock code. The pillbox could be gone. It might be too late. Oh, here." He pulled a set of purple latex gloves from his pocket. "Don't touch it. Use these."

"It's not too late," Sydney said, taking them. "At least, I hope it isn't. Our dad changed the lock code yesterday, right after Savanna sent Caroline to the hospital. No one has access now except for Lauren."

"And," Savanna added, "we may be narrowing things down to just a few people. This has something to do with the forgeries, I know it."

"Alleged forgeries," Skylar said.

"We'll know soon enough." Savanna looked up at Aidan. "I'll send you pictures of the pillbox, and we'll get it to Detective Jordan before we head to Lansing."

"Call me later and let me know what you learn at the museum," Aidan told Savanna.

Outside in the parking lot, Sydney told them firmly that she was taking Skylar's car to get the pillbox from Caroline's house. "You guys need to go. We need to know what's going on with her artwork, to either factor that in or figure this out another way. I'll take care of the pillbox."

Skylar put a hand on Sydney's arm. "The only way we're letting you do that is if you call us from the driveway before you go into the house. I want to hear your voice the whole time you're there, until you get to the police station."

"Wait," Sydney said, "what about Nolan? When does Travis have to be at his meeting?"

"He's got time. I'll call him now and tell him you'll still be a bit."

Savanna and Skylar hit the expressway after a quick stop to grab the two hard-sided cases from the office.

Sydney's call came over the Bluetooth system in Savanna's car; she and Skylar listened as Syd executed every step of the plan. "I'm on the porch... I'm unlocking the door... I'm walking to the parlor... Hello, are there any dangerous bad guys in here?"

"Not funny!" Savanna and Skylar both shouted at once.

"No sense of humor," Sydney muttered. "Okay...putting the gloves on. Oh, boy, I feel like a doctor now. Got the pillbox... Walking out the door... Locking the door... Getting in the car. I'm hanging up now. I'll take photos from the Carson Village police station parking lot and send them—oh, wait, I don't have Dr. Gallager's phone number with me. It's in his file at Fancy Tails. Only Savanna has it." Syd made Savanna's name into three drawn out singsong syllables.

Savanna rolled her eyes, glancing at Skylar. "Hold on, Skylar will look it up in my phone and send it to you."

"That's a pain," Sydney said. "Besides, he wants to hear from you. I'll send them to you."

Savanna opened her mouth to argue, but her sister had already hung up. "I always thought she'd get less annoying when she grew up," she said.

"Yeah, I always thought you would too." Skylar grinned at Savanna.

Savanna pulled up to the security guard booth at the Lansing Museum of Fine Art. She'd bypassed regular visitor parking in favor of the small employee parking lot closest to the side entrance. "I'm a guest of Britt Nash. I think you have my name? Savanna Shepherd," she told the pretty security officer.

The woman consulted the screen in front of her and hit a button, speaking to Savanna and Skylar. "All set. Ring the bell at that door"—she pointed—"and a guard will answer. Have a nice day."

The yellow-and-white-striped parking arm rose up, allowing Savanna's car through.

Skylar cocked an eyebrow at her sister. "Ms. Fancy Pants, huh? How do you rate front-row parking? Do they know you here?"

Savanna laughed. "Their authenticator and I sometimes crossed paths in Chicago at events. When I told them what I was bringing in, they thought it best to put us in the employee lot. Guards and surveillance." She pointed overhead to one of four cameras mounted on light posts throughout the lot as she pulled into a space.

"Ah," Skylar said. "I thought you were a little over-the-top last night, bringing the paintings to my office to be locked up, but I was wrong. I think I'm seeing what a big deal this could be."

Savanna nodded. "Museums like this don't take any

chances—one stupid, petty theft or mugging in an unguard-ed parking structure could mean the loss of millions. Kenilworth has a secure system too, for any artwork coming in or out of the building." She handed Skylar one of the cases and rang the bell at the side door.

A man in the same uniform the guard booth officer was wearing opened the door. "ID, please."

"Oh!" Savanna handed the other case to her sister and fished around in her purse, pulling out her wallet and handing the guard her driver's license. "Sorry, here you go. We're here to see Britt Nash."

The guard ushered Savanna and Skylar to the visitors' desk, and less than a minute later, Nash rounded the corner.

"Savanna!" Tall and lanky, Britt approached with open arms, and Savanna matched their quick, friendly hug. Britt's bowtie matched their pink and black wingtips, lending a bit of fun to the otherwise conservative black suit. Those shoes never would have flown at Kenilworth, Savanna thought. Good for them.

Britt caught her looking and grinned. "I just got them. They're fabulous, aren't they?"

Savanna laughed. "They really are! It's been way too long, Britt. Thank you so much for helping me out. This is my sister, Skylar. Skylar, Britt Nash."

"Don't believe a word she's said about me," Britt warned Skylar, shaking her hand. "Shall we?"

Five minutes later, Savanna and Skylar were standing in a state-of-the-art diagnostics lab, housed on the third floor of the museum. Nash, Lansing's authenticator, had escorted them to the lab and left them alone to work after eliciting a promise of a lunch date soon from Savanna.

Skylar turned around in a circle. "Amazing. I never thought about the scientific side of the art world."

The Lansing museum's lab was large, clean, and rather dimly lit, due to the special lighting required when handling and authenticating sometimes centuries-old pieces. A track ran across the ceiling, holding the bulky, heavy radiograph equipment for the X-ray, confined to one end of the room, an L-shaped partition around it. A long countertop ran the length of one wall, with optical microscopes, cameras, a mass spectrometer, and long wavelength UVA lamps among the work spaces. Two large square desks took up the center of the room, and on one was a disassembled frame being restored.

Savanna set to work. Skylar maintained a respectful distance, asking questions as Savanna set up the X-ray and handled the imaging. She then took both the Rothman and the Minkov to the UV lamp, jotting notes on a pad and snapping photos as she went.

"Very high-tech, Savanna. This is what you did at Kenilworth?"

"A lot of the time, yes."

"Do you miss it?"

Savanna looked sideways at Skylar, from her position peering through a lens at the Rothman. "I miss parts of it."

Skylar nodded, quiet.

"I was right." Savanna straightened up suddenly. "I was right!" She clapped her hands, looking at Skylar, and then her heart sank. Despite being fairly certain after checking the painting with her Firefly, this wasn't something she wanted to find. "Oh, no, I was right. Look at this."

Skylar looked through the microscope. "I'm not sure what I'm supposed to see?"

"Never mind, it doesn't matter. This is what really proves it, with the Minkov." She moved back to the light screen where her radiographs were displayed. "See this?" She pointed at the X-ray film on the left. "This is a pentimento. A painting under another painting."

"It is?" Skylar leaned forward, trying to see. "What does that mean?"

"It means that this isn't the original artwork on the canvas."

"So it is a fake!"

"Well, not always; a pentimento doesn't automatically mean forgery. Often artists painted over their own work, because of money or short supply. So, we compare the underlying work with the visible one, looking for stylistic differences, techniques specific to the artist."

"And if they match, then the artist just painted over his own work, so it could still be authentic," Skylar guessed.

"Yes, or, if the underlying image is obviously not from the artist, as in this one—it's definitely not a Minkov underneath—then we look for clues to when that image was made, where, using what medium—paint types."

Skylar took a deep breath, frowning. "Okay, spell this out for me, Savvy, so I understand it. What do you see?"

"The underlying image in this supposed Minkov is much

more recent, likely from the last fifty years. Minkov died in 1917. There's no chance at all that this is a genuine Minkov. It's a pretty good fake."

Skylar stared wide-eyed at Savanna as she continued.

"The Rothman"—she moved back over to the UV lamp—"is also a forged piece. The luminescence in sections of the work doesn't match; it's newer, and a different type of paint than portions of the underlying paint. I wondered if maybe it had just been touched up, but even the brushstrokes in the original sections don't match Julian Rothman's signature style. Brushstroke technique can give away a forgery more often than almost anything else."

"What the heck," Skylar breathed.

Savanna moved to the center of the room and sat abruptly in a chair at one of the square desks. What the heck was right.

Skylar joined her, quiet, both sisters thinking.

Savanna's phone buzzed. She turned the screen toward Skylar. "Syd's the best. She took one photo of the med box with the little doors open, so you can see the fine print on each tablet. Then she took a picture of her purple latex-sheathed finger, flipping over a pill in one of the compartments. And then the last picture"—Savanna looked again at the phone—"is the same compartments and pills, but showing the opposite side of each pill, to capture any additional imprints on each tablet and capsule."

Skylar took the phone from Savanna. "That's a great idea. Caroline isn't even on much; Travis's mother takes more than this. There are only five pills per compartment.

Ah, and she just texted that she delivered the pillbox directly into Jordan's hands an hour ago." She handed the phone back.

Savanna saved each photo and forwarded them all to Aidan. "I think I was wrong," she said, looking at Skylar. "I think it was crazy to believe that the Happy Family delivery lady would try to hurt Caroline. And, as much as I really, *really* don't like Maggie Lyle, I doubt she or Bill would have the nerve, or even the…resources…to know enough to tamper with Caroline's meds."

"I agree," Skylar said. "So you're thinking it's the art dealer's assistant who came to pick up the most recent painting? The counterpart to that one." She pointed at the Rothman. "But why?"

Savanna shook her head. "I don't know. I'm not sure it is him. I'd hate to think it's Thiebold's assistant…or even Felix himself; he's been friends with Caroline and Mr. Carson for years. And I still haven't told you about Jack."

"No. What about him?"

"I think he's having money problems. Sydney and I picked up on it when he stopped by Fancy Tails to get some treats for the poodles. And he has honestly been acting very strange this week."

"Strange, how?"

"He was gone Wednesday. Everyone takes sick days now and then, so I didn't think much of it. But Thursday, he came into school over an hour late, and he was all frazzled. Plus he had to leave early," Savanna recalled. "I had to cover the pick-up lane."

Skylar looked skeptical. "I don't know. I've had days like that. We all have."

"Okay. You're right. But yesterday he stopped by Caroline's house early, way before school, and he forgot his phone there. I found it after I'd sent her to the hospital. When I went to take it back to him at school, a text message came through and I read it. I didn't mean to!"

Skylar's skeptical expression hadn't softened at all.

"Listen. The phone was in my hand, and I was carrying it into the library for him. You know how part of the message will show up on the lock screen? That's what I read. I couldn't not read it. It was right there in front of me. It said, 'If you don't get the money, we lose everything,' or something like that."

Skylar was staring at her now. "Whoa."

"I know! See what I mean?"

"All right. This is what we do. You need to use your lightning bug microscope thingy to look at all the rest of Caroline's artwork. And we need to go through those provenances. We still don't have much. The only way we're going to find out who made an attempt on Caroline's life yesterday is to figure out who has the most to gain. I think."

Savanna stood, nodding. "That makes sense. But I can't go over there while Caroline's gone. I can't see Detective Jordan thinking that would be a good idea. I'll have to wait until she's home, and then level with her. Everything in her house should for now be safe, right? Since Dad changed the locks?"

"I'd hope so." Skylar helped pack up the paintings and

they walked out to the elevators. "I'm tied up tonight, taking Nolan on a play date at Bounce World. Can you meet me at Mom and Dad's tomorrow before dinner, and we'll go through the certificate paperwork? Syd can help."

Savanna shook her head. "We're doing brunch tomorrow, remember? Mom has that trip to Seattle, so we changed the time. I'm cooking—don't worry, I already know what I'm making and it's amazing. Let's set aside some time afterward to check out the papers. I'm going to do some research of my own tonight on our two confirmed forgeries. Maybe we'll have some answers before Caroline gets out of the hospital."

"Let's hope she's better and home quick," Skylar said. "Lauren will probably have to postpone her party."

"That is not going to sit well with Caroline," Savanna said.

She and Skylar walked through the museum lobby and adjacent hallway, greeting the guard once again at the employee exit.

He held the door for them. "You'll need your ID for Wanda to let you out." He motioned to the guard shack.

"I'm impressed," Skylar said as they loaded the large cases into the back of Savanna's car. "You've got some serious skills, little sister."

Savanna shut the hatch and turned to look at Skylar. The parking lot had emptied out since they'd arrived, and only a few cars remained. She glanced over her shoulder—she had the oddest prickly sensation.

Skylar frowned. "What's up?"

"Nothing. I don't know." She took one more look around as she and Skylar got in the car.

"Are you okay?" Her sister put her seat belt on, frowning at her.

Savanna shrugged. "Yeah. It's nothing. For a second I just had the weirdest feeling of being watched."

Skylar looked out her side window and then back at Savanna. "Well…we are. Guards and cameras everywhere."

Savanna laughed. "That's not what I meant. But yeah, I'm sure that's all it is."

Chapter Twenty-Two

HALFWAY THROUGH THEIR hour-long drive back to Carson, Savanna began to think she hadn't been imagining things. The outskirts of Lansing gave way to farm land, miles and miles of open fields and rolling hills. Four lanes eventually narrowed to just two in each direction, and traffic was sparse, making the posted seventy-mile-an-hour speed limit feel like nothing.

"I think this guy is following us." Savanna checked the rearview mirror for what felt like the hundredth time in the last few miles.

Skylar turned around in her seat to look out the back window. "Really?"

"He's been behind us for I don't know how long." Savanna turned off the radio and adjusted her side mirror, getting a better view.

"Are you serious?" Skylar stayed in position, watching the large black SUV several car lengths behind them.

"Let me try something." She signaled and moved over into the right lane. Besides her car and the one behind them, there were only a few others in her line of sight.

The SUV changed lanes and stayed behind them.

Savanna slowed down and watched the vehicle maintain

its distance, matching her speed. She looked at Skylar, beginning to feel tendrils of panic creeping up her spine.

"Okay, maybe you're right," Skylar whispered. "Why am I whispering? What do we do? Should I call the police?"

"I don't know. And tell them what?"

"Um, I don't know, that we have evidence of forged priceless paintings in our car and some freak is following us? How long has he been back there?"

"I'm not sure. I didn't notice him until we got out of the city."

Skylar checked the back window again. "Well…I mean, maybe it's just coincidence. He isn't trying to do anything. Maybe it's just someone heading the same way we are."

Savanna accelerated back up to the speed limit, and then past it—75, 78, 82, 84. Her little car rattled as she pushed toward ninety, and she saw Skylar reach for the hand grip above the passenger door.

"Too fast, Savvy! I get what you're doing, but slow down."

"He's still behind us! He's definitely following us." She eased up on the gas pedal; she obviously couldn't outrun the SUV.

"Okay," Skylar said, "we'll get off at the next exit. We'll go into a store or a gas station or whatever we find. No one's going to mess with us around a bunch of people. If he follows us off the expressway, we'll call Detective Jordan. I'm sure he can do something. When's the next exit?"

"A while, I think." Savanna racked her brain, trying to remember what they'd passed a few miles earlier. There were long stretches of nothing between Lansing and Carson.

Skylar was tapping the screen on her phone. "Oh my God. The next exit isn't for another twelve miles."

Savanna met her sister's eyes. She was at a loss. "I mean, he isn't technically doing anything. We keep driving, I guess. We'll call the police if he tries something. Watch him."

Skylar had turned around backward in the front seat, watching the SUV.

"Okay, that's not safe. You need to stay buckled," Savanna admonished.

"Really, Mom? That's your biggest concern right now?"

Savanna shot her a look.

"I'm fine. See?" Skylar shifted sideways and made an exaggerated show of displaying the still-fastened seat belt for Savanna to see.

"Thank you." She checked the rearview mirror; the vehicle was still back there, maintaining the same distance. They drove in tense silence for a while. Savanna signaled and moved back over to the passing lane to go around a slower car in the right lane.

"He's staying," Skylar said.

"What?"

"He's still in the right lane. Maybe we're just paranoid, Savvy. Look, he hasn't changed lanes to stay with you. Speed up. I think we can lose him."

Savanna pressed the gas pedal, her quick check in the rearview telling her Skylar was right: the SUV was receding in the distance and still hadn't changed lanes. "Okay, we're officially loons. No one is following us. I'm sorry, I don't know what got into me."

Savanna kept an eye on the mirror, relief building as the SUV got smaller and smaller behind them. This whole experience was making her jumpy. It was probably just someone on a long drive, not paying attention to their own speed but matching hers without realizing it. She was sure she'd done that before too, her mind wandering while behind the wheel.

"It wasn't just you," Skylar said. "I was running through possibilities in my mind, like, why don't you have handfuls of thumbtacks in your glove box for us to throw on the road, or how fast would the police actually be able to find us if the guy tried to hit us? It was all that high security at the museum. It made us paranoid."

Savanna laughed. "That's probably it." The landscape had gotten hillier, and traffic continued to thin out. The SUV was nowhere in sight now. Besides Savanna's car, only one other was visible, up ahead.

"I think he's gone," Skylar said.

"So we keep going, right? We shouldn't get off now." Savanna pointed to a green sign bearing the words *Little Bear, Pop. 3,205, ½ Mile.*

"Right, keep going. Just in case, so we can make sure he's long go—" Skylar's words broke off and she grabbed Savanna's arm. "No. Savanna—is that him?" Skylar's voice rose at the end.

Savanna looked at her sharply and then at the rearview mirror. "No," she breathed. The black SUV was now behind her in the left lane, and gaining fast. Very fast.

"Get off. Get off!" Skylar shouted, pointing at the exit they were approaching.

Savanna made a quick check before switching lanes and moved over to the right, steering to follow the yellow car in front of them off the expressway. In her peripheral vision, she caught a flash of black, and the SUV was suddenly right beside them, next to Skylar in the passenger seat, driving on the shoulder and preventing Savanna from taking the exit.

The entirety of the vehicle had dark-tinted windows. Whoever was behind the wheel was barely visible to them. Savanna tapped her brake, hoping she could slow down enough to zip behind the SUV and still catch the exit ramp she was just about past.

The SUV immediately dropped its speed and veered over into her lane, hitting the passenger side of Savanna's car and sending her to the left. Savanna let out an involuntary shriek and wrestled for control, straightening out on the left shoulder just in time to avoid going into the trees in the median of the divided highway. Her car was filled with the loud growl of rumble strips on the shoulder before she moved back into the left lane.

Skylar's window was shattered and the passenger door caved in, somehow still miraculously closed. The glass hadn't yet fallen out of place but was a mass of tiny pieces, ready to crumble. Skylar had moved as close as she could to Savanna in the front seat, leaning away from the door.

Savanna glanced quickly at Skylar, noting her sister's wide-eyed stunned expression. "You're okay. Are you okay?" She heard her own voice shaking.

Skylar nodded.

"Call Jordan, call 911."

Skylar was already dialing, her phone in her hand on speaker as it rang.

The SUV had slowed when Savanna had, and now it was once again encroaching into Savanna's lane.

"Jordan." The detective's voice came on the line, and Skylar squeezed Savanna's shoulder, getting her words out in broken bursts.

"It's Skylar. We're being followed—on westbound I-22—A black SUV—Jordan, he hit us!"

"We just passed the Little Bear exit," Savanna shouted, pushing her car to speed up as much as it could, now going ninety-four miles an hour.

The interstate widened by a lane, the trees down the median thinning to only a wide, grassy expanse, and Savanna could now see the opposing eastbound lanes on the other side of the expressway. Traffic was denser heading that direction; a sparse but steady stream of cars whizzed by. She eased off the gas, her little car protesting the high speed, and had a momentary rush of relief when the SUV abruptly dropped its speed and fell behind them. Savanna glanced at Skylar, and then her rearview mirror. The black vehicle matched her speed, but from two or three car lengths back.

"We can see other cars now, Detective," Savanna said, "on the eastbound side. Whoever hit us backed off a bit, but he's still behind us."

"Stay with the traffic if you can," Jordan said.

"I'll try." Savanna took deep breaths, trying to slow her

breathing. This was crazy. She moved over into the center lane, wanting to get away from the edge of the freeway.

A long, thick stand of pine trees dotted the landscape up ahead, the road curving into an incline on a hill. They wouldn't be visible to the other cars soon, probably less than a half mile.

Skylar saw it too. "Jordan, we're going to lose the traffic in a minute. And there are still no cars on our side."

The SUV was now almost alongside them again, this time on Savanna's side of the car.

Savanna steered away, cutting the wheel a little too hard to the right as she tried to stay as far over in her lane as she could. Skylar, perched precariously near the console in the center of the car, lost her grip on her phone and it bounced out of her hand, landing somewhere out of sight.

"—state boys on their way now. Hang in there." Jordan's voice came through the phone from under Savanna's seat. "Don't engage. Do what you can to stay away from the vehicle. Do you see any exit signs? Rest stops, anything?"

"Nothing," Savanna yelled to make sure he would hear her. She wasn't taking her hands off the wheel for a second. "No exits, and westbound is empty—wait, I think I see a car way up there! Do you see it, Skylar?"

Skylar peered into the distance. "Maybe? It's past the trees, hard to tell."

This stretch of highway was always sparsely populated, Savanna thought. How fast could the state police possibly show up to help? Should she just pull over and give them the paintings? But would the people in the SUV let them go free after that? There was no way. Not after they'd obviously seen her carrying the paintings in and out of the museum.

They were now completely blocked from eastbound traffic by the thickening trees down the median.

Skylar screamed as the SUV, now slightly ahead of her and moving into their lane, nearly made contact with Savanna's front end. Savanna hazarded a glance into the cabin of the vehicle. There were two figures in the front seat, but she couldn't see anything beyond that through the dark windows.

Detective Jordan's voice came from under the seat. "Do not stop, do you hear me? Stay calm. I have troopers eastbound approaching your location and another about a mile back, west of the Little Bear exit. Help is almost there."

Savanna felt the impact as the SUV sideswiped her little car a second time, and she gripped the wheel as tightly as she could, struggling to stay on the road, but the other vehicle was bigger, heavier, and she was losing ground. Sparks flew past her window as the SUV steadily nudged her off the road again onto the right shoulder. Skylar's window gave way, thousands of pieces of safety glass falling into the car.

Skylar shrieked and braced herself with one foot on the door. "I love you, Savanna!"

"Don't say that!" That made things so much worse. "We aren't going to die! Stop it!"

Louder than the grass and vegetation under her tires, louder than the horrible scraping noise the SUV made as it refused to give up, Savanna's heartbeat filled her ears, roaring over everything else.

And then she heard the sirens. Was she imagining them? Drawn-out and high-pitched, they filled the air, and Savanna couldn't tell which direction they came from. But they were getting louder.

"Look!" Skylar pointed ahead of them, across the median on the eastbound side: two glorious blue state police cars, speeding with lights and sirens right toward them.

And another in Savanna's rearview mirror, red and blue lights flashing, impossibly, wonderfully close.

Skylar was laughing. "Oh, I love you, Jordan."

"We love you, Jordan!" Savanna shouted.

Savanna finally took her foot off the gas and came to a stop, nose end of the car pointing down the hill and the evergreens she'd have ended up in the middle of if it weren't for Detective Jordan.

She watched the SUV speed effortlessly away. There was no license plate.

The two eastbound police cars used a utility-vehicle turnaround to cross the expressway median and went after it.

Savanna put her car in park and turned off the ignition, the keys jangling in her shaking hand. She looked at Skylar.

Skylar threw her arms around Savanna, and Savanna hugged her sister back fiercely. Hot tears overflowed onto her cheeks, and she swiped at them as they separated.

"I'm so glad we're okay," she whispered.

"Me too. Oh my God, that was scary."

Savanna sniffled and cleared her throat. "I really thought we were done."

Skylar squeezed Savanna's arm. "I knew we'd be okay."

"Really?" Savanna laughed. "That's why you had to scream 'I love you' at me?"

"Shut up." Skylar pinched her where her hand rested on her arm. "You could have said it back, you know."

"I love you too." Savanna rolled her eyes. "You know that."

Skylar reached under Savanna's seat and pulled out the phone she'd lost in the commotion. "Jordan? Are you still there?"

"Still here. I'm glad to hear you love each other. And me. Is the state trooper there with you?"

Savanna turned and saw the uniformed officer approaching her car. "Yes. We're all set, Detective Jordan, thank you so much. I don't know what would have happened without you."

"No problem. You aren't all set though. I'll arrange a tow truck, and I want you to let the deputy bring you, and the paintings, straight here to me at the station. Unless either of you needs medical care? I had dispatch send an ambulance to check you out."

"I think we're okay, actually," Skylar said.

"All the same, let them take a look. I heard the impacts." His voice was firm. "I'll see you both when you get here."

Savanna's legs felt like wet noodles when she got out of the car. She let the paramedic lead her and Skylar over to the ambulance behind the state police car, but not before handing the trooper the two evidence-filled cases from her car.

Half an hour later, on the way to Carson in the back of

the police car, Savanna called Sydney, and she and Skylar took turns recounting what had just happened. Sydney was at work, but she told them Detective Jordan had just stopped in to see her and informed her he'd be stationing police officers outside Caroline's hospital room and each of their houses.

"This all sounds terrifying," Sydney said. "I'm hope you're both okay!"

"We're okay," Savanna said. "Really. We're almost back in town. Do you want to pick us up at the station? My car is out of commission for a while."

"I'm in the middle of grooming a collie. But I'll have Dad come get you, don't worry."

"No!" Both Skylar and Savanna spoke at the same time.

"Don't tell Mom and Dad about this, please," Skylar said. "There's no reason to worry them."

"Um." Sydney was quiet on the other end of the line.

"Oh, Syd," Savanna said. "You already told them?"

"Guys! I had to! You were nearly killed!" The line went silent for a beat. "Sorry."

"It's okay. We'll see you soon," Savanna said.

Both sisters rode in silence for a while after they'd hung up with Sydney, hands linked on the seat between them.

Skylar looked at Savanna. "She's always been a tattletale, you know."

Savanna burst out laughing. "I know!"

Skylar laughed with her, leaning her head back on the seat as they rolled into downtown Carson, both of them laughing too hard for longer than made sense.

While waiting for Harlan to pick them up, Skylar and Savanna filled Detective Jordan in on the details he wasn't aware of: Savanna's findings at the Lansing Museum of Fine Art.

Jordan took custody of the paintings and told them he'd already been in touch with Caroline at the hospital and had gotten her permission to remove the rest of her collection from the house this evening as a precaution. They'd be secured here, at the station. "I heard back from the captain at the Michigan State Police post outside of Lansing. They unfortunately lost the vehicle."

"What?" Skylar was incredulous. "How?"

"You know that multi-highway interchange at Grand Rapids? They lost track of it there."

Grand Rapids was the only major city between Lansing and Carson. Their unknown assailants were smart—they'd chosen that long, deserted stretch of road to attack them, and then had taken advantage of city traffic to get lost in further on.

HARLAN PULLED INTO Sydney's driveway, coming around to open the door for Skylar and then Savanna. "I'm not dropping you at home," he told his eldest daughter. "Nolan's here. Sydney picked him up. We're going to stay together, right here, until Travis comes to get you two."

Skylar raised a hand to point at the patrol car sitting fifty feet from Sydney's front door, but her father shook his head.

"No. I don't care if the cops are keeping an eye out. I'm not leaving you here alone. No arguments." He cast his gaze sternly from Skylar to Savanna. Neither of them argued.

Charlotte rushed in, breathless, as they were cleaning up from dinner. Wordlessly, she grabbed and hugged each of her daughters tightly. "I'm so sorry, I was in Indianapolis. I canceled the rest of my meetings over the next few days. Are you okay?" She placed a hand on Savanna's cheek and then Skylar's. "You look okay. You aren't hurt?"

"We're fine, Mom. I promise," Savanna said.

"You're stepping back from this," Charlotte said. "Let the police handle it from here. I'm serious, Savanna. Look what almost happened. You could have died! You both— what if—" Their normally reserved mother clapped a hand over her mouth, tears welling up in her eyes.

Harlan's arms were instantly around her, but she pushed back, shaking her head. "I'm fine. I am. But I'm not kidding; this is the end of your involvement. I know you're too old to be told what to do but I'm your mother and I'm telling you anyway. Please."

The break in her mother's voice at the end made Savanna's throat swell. "Okay. It's all right, Mom. Jordan's got it from here. I'm done." She needed her mom to stop looking at her—at them—this way. She couldn't stand knowing she'd caused her parents this much sickening worry.

"Good," Charlotte said. She swiped her fingers impatiently under her eyes, clearing her throat.

Harlan's hand remained on the small of their mother's back and now she leaned into him, resting her cheek on his chest. He finally spoke. "I'm staying here tonight, and your mom is going home with you," he said, nodding at Skylar. Travis hadn't left her side since he'd gotten there just before dinner.

"Dad—"

"No." His voice softened as Nolan sprinted into the room after Fonzie. "I've got plenty of subcontractors; this is my job right now until I'm sure you're all safe. It's how it's going to be. Let's put this to rest for now. Hey, buddy," he addressed Nolan. "Grandma's going to have a sleepover at your house tonight, how's that sound?"

Harlan stepped outside to see Skylar's family and Charlotte off, bending down to have a few words with Travis before they left. Savanna turned away from the window to find her younger sister silently judging her.

"What?"

"Are you really out? You're going to let Nick handle things from this point?"

"That's what I told Mom," Savanna replied.

Sydney pursed her lips, saying nothing.

"I was almost finished anyway. Jordan has everything he needs, and if he doesn't, it's not going to hurt me to just share information with him. I didn't lie," she added, hating the defensive tone in her own voice.

"I haven't seen her that upset since she caught me drinking at your grad party, like, twelve years ago," Sydney said. "Dad is Dad. But don't mess with Mom, Savvy."

"I won't—I'm not."

While Harlan and Syd watched TV in the living room,

Savanna took an excessively long, hot shower, washing away the traumatic day. Leaving her hair to air dry, she settled under her cozy comforter in bed and opened her laptop.

She logged into her account through Kenilworth, holding her breath and hoping Rob's family hadn't thought to disable her access yet.

They hadn't. She clicked through to the search feature and typed in Minkov's name and the painting, *Storm in Sochi*. The screen populated with items from the database. Savanna scrolled down, going through each listing of the provenance information online. One of Savanna's professors had best explained what a provenance really was by comparing it to a CarFax for works of art: documented, certified proof of every location and owner a piece had, every change of hands, every new authentication, and every expert who'd ever certified it as genuine.

There were six documented points in time at which *Storm in Sochi* had come into contact with an expert or a new buyer. The last known location of the piece was listed as Brussels, in 2001. When Savanna changed the search criteria to show current disposition of the piece, the screen again displayed the sale in 2001. So either the 2001 buyer still had possession of the piece, or Felix had failed to register online when he'd sold to the Carsons. Based on the pentimento they'd found today, Savanna knew the truth about the painting. But the paper version of the Minkov provenance might offer answers in terms of how the forgery had made its way into the Carson collection. Had Mr. Carson been tricked by Felix? Or had Felix been duped by a dishonest seller? Or, Savanna hated to entertain this idea, had Everett Carson known he was collecting forgeries?

And what about Jack? What if, during the break-in, the thieves had actually been after the original provenances? What if Jack somehow thought he might liquidate a high-end painting to get the money he so desperately needed? He'd have needed the provenance. Or he'd have needed Caroline eliminated, assuming his portion of the estate was substantial, and Savanna guessed it probably was. But. She liked Jack. Was he really capable of attempted murder?

And with everything that had happened this afternoon, she had to consider how serious this situation had become. Whomever was responsible was willing to go to extreme measures to protect what they'd done.

All things considered, Caroline was probably safer than ever right where she was tonight: in a hospital bed, surrounded by people, a police officer stationed at her door, far away from forged artwork, thieves, murderers, and anyone with ulterior motives.

Chapter Twenty-Three

"YOU'VE GOT TO give me this recipe," Charlotte said, reaching for a second serving of Savanna's Cinnamon Crunch Coffee Cake. "It's delicious!"

"It's so easy. I started making it in Chicago when we'd have friends over. It's just cream cheese mixed with a little sugar and pralines layered a couple times across the dough, then glazed while it's still warm and sprinkled with cinnamon and sugar.

Nolan was on his second piece too, and even Sydney had some, breaking her no-dairy-before-noon rule; Savanna had trouble keeping track of Syd's healthy eating plans, but it was one of the few things she didn't tease her about. Whatever she was doing obviously worked. Syd always looked and felt fantastic.

Harlan had taken over and made the western omelets Savanna had planned, the green pepper and onion flavor balancing out the sharp cheddar.

When they'd all finished, Travis scooped up Nolan and carried him toward the back door upside-down. "We're going out to play," he called over his shoulder.

Savanna rose and got the coffeepot from the counter. She refilled cups around the table, along with her own. She hated to admit it, but she was a little sore from the impacts yesterday. She'd noticed Skylar was moving more slowly than usual too.

"So," Charlotte said, looking from Savanna to Skylar, "we need to talk about yesterday."

"We already did," Savanna said, and instantly regretted it. Her mother's gaze spoke volumes.

"You were followed, someone hit your car, and the police came. You've each got patrol cars outside your house. What does the detective say is happening?"

"Someone was obviously trying to hurt you," Harlan said.

"We aren't so sure they were after us," Savanna said.

Harlan looked at her sharply. "I took a look at your car this morning at Andy's shop. I disagree. You two are lucky to be here."

Sitting next to him, Skylar linked her arm through Harlan's on the table, giving him a squeeze. "Dad, she means we think they were after the paintings, not us. I don't think they were actually trying to hurt us. I think they hoped to disable our car long enough to get the paintings."

He shook his head, meeting his wife's eyes across the table. "That doesn't make us feel any better about what happened."

"You girls need to do better." Charlotte's voice was stern, and this morning the threat of tears had passed. "We understand this seems to have escalated rather quickly, and maybe you didn't realize the danger involved. But you do now. We just got you back, Savanna." Charlotte softened, and she

TRACY GARDNER

placed a hand on Savanna's. "And Skylar, you're a mother. You don't have the luxury of irresponsible behavior."

"Ugh." Skylar let her breath out in a huff. "Mom. Dad." She looked at Harlan. "We thought we were being very responsible. With Detective Jordan involved now, nobody is going to get hurt. But we were only trying to protect Caroline."

Charlotte spoke. "I know."

Sydney got up and wrapped her arms around Charlotte from behind, kissing her temple. "We love you, Momsie. They're safe, Caroline is safe, and the paintings are safe. Please don't worry." She let go and sat on the other side of Harlan, leaning her head on his shoulder.

He put an arm around his youngest daughter's shoulder. "Always the peacemaker, aren't you," he grumbled.

Charlotte sighed. "Does anyone have an update on Caroline? Is she improving?"

"I heard from Lauren last night," Savanna spoke up. "She said they transferred her to a stepdown unit. She's out of the ICU. They might send her home tomorrow."

"That's great! So she's doing a lot better then?" Charlotte asked.

"It sounds like it."

"Did you send Dr. Gallager those pictures?" Sydney asked. "Could he read the imprints on the pills all right?"

"Yes, and he said he'd guessed correctly. There was no baby aspirin at all in her daily setup, even though there should be. It was two yellow digitalis tablets, much higher than Caroline's dose."

"Your buddy Jordan yelled at me," Sydney said to Skylar, making a pouty face. "He said I shouldn't have taken the pillbox out of her house, that I should've called him to come get it."

Skylar rolled her eyes. "If you'd have done that, he would've said you weren't supposed to be at her house in the first place. It's fine. They can verify that it's Caroline's pillbox if they have to. He's a detective. He's very by the book."

Sydney shrugged. "He's all right. He was glad we came to him with the information, and he said he's going to call Dr. Gallager—Aidan to *you*," she said to Savanna, smiling.

Skylar spoke up. "When Caroline had me draw up her living will, you know, medical power of attorney papers, she made sure it was clear that she handles all her own medical care. She fills her own prescriptions, she communicates with her doctors directly, that kind of thing. She's perfectly competent to handle her pillbox. But I can see how somebody switching out her yellow baby aspirin and digitalis pills with two slightly larger yellow pills could slip by her."

Sydney agreed. "For sure. Look at the supplements I take every day." She pulled a little plastic carrying case from her purse, snapping the lid open. There's, like, seven things in there. I just open the box and take them. I don't inspect each one; I know what I'm on. Caroline probably does the same thing."

"Her pillbox moved to the parlor two weeks ago, along with that bed her family set up. It would have been easy for someone to tamper with it," Savanna said.

"Absolutely," Sydney said.

"So where are we with the artwork? Are we thinking the forgeries are related to Caroline's precarious health lately, or just a coincidence?" Skylar asked.

"Definitely related," Savanna said.

Charlotte paused while clearing dishes and frowned at them. "And you're doing what with this information?"

"A phone call to Jordan, Mom. That's it," Savanna promised. "I can help without risking anything. This is exactly my wheelhouse; this is what I'm trained to do. I need to help."

Charlotte was silent, finally giving her the smallest of nods.

"Once is coincidence," Harlan said. "Twice is a little odd. Three times—her best friend being poisoned, her fall on the stairs, and now the medication overdose—three times is not coincidence. Add to that what happened to you girls yesterday, and I believe this is all connected." He followed Charlotte to the sink and slid an arm around her waist, kissing her temple and taking the sponge from her hands to wash.

"He's right. I think we can all agree someone has an agenda where Caroline and her collection are concerned," Savanna said. "Did you bring the copies of the provenances?" she asked Skylar.

"I did." Skylar stacked the last of the dishes and deposited them by the sink, leaving the room and then returning with her briefcase.

Sydney wrapped up the tablecloth and tossed it toward

the laundry room off the kitchen, and the three sisters spread out the art provenance copies, separating them into distinct little piles, one for each piece of art. There were eleven in all.

"She's down to seven, which Detective Jordan confirmed when he and his partner packaged them up and took them last night. There are the two Minkovs, a Laurant, a Rothman, a Monet, and two Matisse pieces," Savanna said. "Just since I've been there, she's sold"—Savanna paused, counting in her head—"four of the pieces. She sold two—no, three—Rothmans, and the Laurant over the piano. But Felix also said he has a potential buyer for the small Minkov."

"Look," Skylar said, pointing at the document closest to her, and then the next one. "According to this, the two Matisse paintings and the Monet were acquired decades ago, in the nineties. Mr. Carson must have started their whole collection with those. She has an actual Monet? Even I know Monet. Wouldn't that be her highest-value piece? Why is she having Felix sell the lesser paintings?"

"Is the Minkov, the one you proved has another newer painting underneath it, is it part of a set with the bigger one you mentioned? Are you worried about that one being a forgery too? What do the certificates say?" Sydney was moving around the table, leaning in to read this or that as she went.

"Hold on, one question at a time," Savanna said. "I see a pattern. She hasn't gotten rid of the Matisse or Monet pieces at all, and there's no reason why she would have. Both those artists' works are highly valued. The Laurant..." She went quickly around to the other side of the table, picking up the copies of the certificates for the Laurant paintings, one of which Caroline still owned, and set them out side by side. She located the small Minkov documents, *Storm in Sochi*, and carried them over next to the provenance for the large Minkov in the Carsons' library. She laid out all four Rothman certificates in a row, first the three that had sold, and then the last remaining one in Caroline's office.

Savanna stood back, surveying the table. All that was left were the two Matisse documents and one Monet. She laid those provenances out one by one on the buffet, separate from the Laurant, Rothman, and Minkov documents.

She had the three certificates for the Monet and Matisse paintings on the buffet, out of the way, and all of the others—the Rothmans, the Laurants and the Minkovs—on the dining room table.

Minkov first. Savanna dove into the documents for *Storm in Sochi*, seeing right away that the paper version didn't match what she'd seen online last night. The next set of hands the piece had landed in following the 2001 acquisition in Brussels was noted on the provenance as a Victoria Griffin, and the next name after that was Felix Thiebold, and he'd had the provenance updated, certified genuine by an authenticator named Kiernanski, and sold to an owner in Michigan, name undisclosed. She followed the signatures down with her index finger, then moved to the larger Minkov, shaking her head.

Savanna carried the provenance copy for *Storm in Sochi* over to the Rothman documents, laying it down and reviewing signatures on each of them, side by side with the small

Minkov certificate. "All of the Rothmans," she murmured, moving now to the Laurant certificates and setting the *Storm in Sochi* document down between them, peering closely at the papers. She pulled out her phone and typed something in, scrolled down a few times, and then set the phone on the table.

"What's she doing?" Sydney leaned over to Skylar; both sisters had taken a step back and were now standing near the buffet, watching Savanna work.

Skylar matched Syd's whisper. "She's looking for the flaw. I think she thinks since Felix Thiebold hasn't had any interest in trying to sell the Monet or Matisse pieces"— Skylar gestured behind them at the paperwork laid out separately—"that he was possibly dealing in forgeries with these specific artists, just Rothman, Laurant, and Minkov."

Savanna's head snapped up. "Yes. He was. Hold on." She moved behind Skylar and Sydney to the buffet with the Monet and the Matisse paperwork, quickly examining their certificates. She then went back to the table, picked up the provenance for the large Minkov, and turned and placed it next to the Monet and Matisse documents on the buffet. She straightened up.

"Felix Thiebold acquired most of these pieces for the Carsons"—Savanna gestured at the dining room table—"but not the ones on the buffet. The Monet and Matisse paintings, and the large Minkov in Caroline's library, are all authentic. Two other art dealers helped Mr. Carson acquire those four pieces." She pointed behind her sisters at the buffet.

"Okay," Syd said slowly. "So…all of these are fakes?" Sydney's eyes were wide as she moved to the dining room table, looking at the certificates.

Savanna shook her head. "I can't say for sure, not without taking them all to the lab, but look at this. This is crazy." She gathered up the top piece of paper from each painting's little pile, except for the large Minkov, and pushed the rest of the documents out of the way. She laid the six certificates out in a row. Harlan and Charlotte had joined them now too. "Look at this name here." She pointed. The signature below Felix's own name, on all six documents, was scrawled on the authenticator's line with the name printed underneath it: Ivan Kiernanski.

"So Felix used the same art expert for the deals he brokered," Skylar said. "Don't a lot of gallerists do that? Use the same person or services as long they provide good work?"

"Sure. But I'm not positive this Ivan Kiernanski exists." She tapped her phone and showed them her Google search. "The only site his name appears on is a gallery in Florida called The Masters Gallery, starting in 2008. There's no record of him at all other than that."

Harlan looked skeptical. "I'm not sure that proves anything. Type my name into Google. I doubt I'll come up."

Savanna set her phone down. "Well, as an example, I'm searchable; I checked it out. Just by typing my name into the browser, it shows my time at Kenilworth and, before that, at school as an undergrad. And besides, it's not just that. Look at this one." She picked up the certificate for the Laurant that had been over the piano, the one Caroline sold a few weeks ago. "Read Ivan Kiernanski's name on that one, and then look at the spelling in all the rest of them."

"What?" Sydney looked up from the certificates incredulously. "He spelled his own name wrong?"

Skylar took the paper from her and peered at it. "Okay, yeah, that's crazy. This one says Ivan Kiernaski. Only one *N*. In both the signature and the typed name below it."

"Yes. I think Felix acquired nothing but forged artwork for the Carsons. And I think, after Mr. Carson died and Caroline decided she wanted to thin out the collection, Felix got very nervous about the possibility that he might be found out. Especially knowing that Caroline had put feelers out to a couple of the gallerists who'd acquired work for them. Felix knew he had to liquidate these pieces himself, or be exposed as a fraud. He's internationally known; his reputation is his livelihood."

"So, why not just take all the pieces out of her house at once? Then there's no proof of any crime," Skylar said.

"How? There's no way he could do that," Savanna said. "No one in their right mind is going to just hand over millions of dollars' worth of art, and provenances, and then wait for the dealer to sell them off one by one. The way Felix has been doing it is standard—he finds a buyer, sends his assistant to pick up the piece and provenance, Felix delivers them to the buyer, then Caroline gets paid, minus Felix's fee. His way arouses the least suspicion. Until Caroline mentions bringing in another dealer. Which she did. I was there that day. Felix told her he had a potential buyer for the small Minkov, which we know now is a fake, and she said she hadn't heard anything back from Banfield about his buyers. Kevin Banfield is a lesser-known dealer, though still quite legit; he's the one listed as the acquiring gallerist for the large Minkov. And to think," Savanna mused, "I always thought Felix Thiebold was legit too."

"I wonder how many others he's sold forgeries to," Sydney said.

"I'm calling Jordan." Skylar was already scrolling through the contacts in her phone.

"Now? It's a Sunday," Charlotte spoke up. "Will you even get through?"

"Yes," she said. "I have his personal cell. We're thinking Thiebold or his assistant tampered with Caroline's medications, right? Do you think Ryan might have been involved? We can't wait on this."

Savanna nodded. "I'm thinking Felix or Ryan switched out the digitalis doses, and also brought the poisoned wine. And who knows, they could have somehow even rigged that railing so Caroline would fall. I think the whole idea was to get rid of Caroline, so there was no chance he'd be exposed and his career ruined. For all we know, Ryan was part of it too."

Skylar gasped. "What if it was Felix and Ryan yesterday in the car that hit us?"

"There were two of them. But that's all I could see. The windows were too dark."

"Wait," Sydney said. "About the poisoned wine that killed Eleanor. What happened to that bottle if Felix or Ryan left it at Caroline's? Would they have gone back to dispose of it after the fact?"

Savanna shrugged. "Lauren said it was gone when she looked for it. She didn't know what happened to it."

Skylar put the phone to her ear and left the room to talk to Detective Jordan.

Sydney spoke. "Caroline is staying put at Anderson Memorial until tomorrow, right? She shouldn't come home until this is all taken care of. Felix will be furious once he knows his plan didn't work."

"Yes, Aidan said tomorrow is the earliest she'll come home."

Skylar reappeared. "Jordan's on his way over. He wants to see what we're talking about, and he said he talked to Dr. Gallager yesterday about the digitalis; the tablets in Caroline's pillbox are three times her normal dose, and she was getting two each day rather than just one. She's lucky she's alive."

Chapter Twenty-Four

DETECTIVE NICK JORDAN sat opposite the Shepherd sisters at the dining room table still covered with artwork certificates. "We have enough to bring Thiebold and his assistant in for questioning. The originals for all of these are still at the Carson house?"

"Yes, they should be," Savanna said. "I can tell you exactly where—in a compartment in Everett's desk upstairs. Caroline told me."

"We can pursue charges for trafficking in forgeries, but we don't have evidence to support that this dealer or his assistant actually tampered with Mrs. Carson's medications, or chased you yesterday."

"What about the pillbox? You have that," Sydney said.

"We do, and forensics is trying to pull fingerprints off it, but I'm just warning you, I don't have enough right now to show attempted murder."

Savanna groaned. "Okay, well, at least Caroline will be safe when she comes home from the hospital. You can hold Felix?"

Jordan nodded. "As soon as I get the originals for these. I don't believe copies will hold up once Thiebold calls his lawyer."

"Let's go now and get them," Savanna said. He cocked an eyebrow at her. "After we stop by the hospital and get Mrs. Carson's permission."

"Right, isn't that what I said?" She smiled.

"I'm sure the detective can handle that without you," Harlan said, leaning on the counter. Charlotte had stepped outside to take a call, and Savanna had nearly forgotten her father was still in the kitchen, catching all of this.

Detective Jordan nodded. "True."

Of course he'd side with her dad. "I'm going. I'm literally going to have the police glued to my side, Dad."

Syd stood, pushing her chair back. "Okay, I'm going to go take the dogs out, and I have two grooming appointments this afternoon. I'm unfortunately out, at least for a little while. But"—she looked at Savanna—"will you keep me updated? I won't be too long."

Savanna gave Syd a quick hug. "Absolutely."

"So." Savanna looked at Skylar and Jordan. "Just us?"

Skylar cringed. "Just you two, I'm afraid," she said. "Trav and I got tickets to take Nolan to the LEGO convention today. They've been waiting for me to finish up here."

Jordan shrugged. "No worries. I'll shoot you an email to sum up. You're going to end up involved in prosecuting on Mrs. Carson's behalf, assuming everything breaks down the way we think it will. Are you ready?" Jordan turned to Savanna.

"I am." She gathered up the copies of all the provenance documentation, handing them to Skylar. "Thank you so much for that. I hate to go confirm to Caroline that so much of her collection is not authentic... You're sure we have to bother her again to do this?"

"No way around it," Jordan replied. "But from everything I know about Mrs. Carson, I have a feeling she'll take it better than expected."

Probably true, Savanna thought.

AT CAROLINE'S BEDSIDE, Savanna perched on the edge of her bed, holding her hand. The first thing she noticed about the woman was her lipstick: if Caroline was wearing her lipstick, things were righting themselves. She broke the news about the paintings to her, and she calmly listened.

"I suppose that makes a strange kind of sense," she said. "No wonder Felix got all flustered when I mentioned Kevin Banfield might be able to help with liquidating the pieces. I thought at first he was just being possessive, trying to be a good friend to me...but he was never our friend."

"I'm so sorry," Savanna said.

"Well, at least my Everett isn't here to learn of this betrayal. He truly believed we were in great hands with Felix as our art dealer."

"You had no reason not to believe that."

Caroline gasped. "Oh! Oh, my, I almost forgot. Lauren said Ryan is coming to pick up that small Minkov today at five. I've lost all track of time in this blasted hospital bed."

Savanna's gaze went to Detective Jordan. Would everything that happened yesterday change that? What if Ryan was in on what Felix Thiebold was doing? She wasn't certain how much Caroline had been told in order for her to agree to let Jordan lock up her collection.

The detective subtly held his hand out in a tamping motion at his side, a cautioning signal to her. He turned back to Caroline. "That's perfect. We can meet this Ryan at your house. He's the assistant, right?"

"Yes. Lauren was going to meet him there. She had to get the provenance for him."

"Thank you, Caroline," Savanna said. "I'll call her right now. We'll meet Ryan instead. Right?" She was watching Jordan.

"Yes," he agreed. "Call and cancel Lauren going."

Savanna leaned down and hugged Caroline, giving her a quick kiss on the cheek. "We're off. We'll get this taken care of and make sure you're safe. And, as soon as you're home, you and Lauren can sit down and find a later date for your birthday party."

"Excuse me? The party is happening as planned. I will not postpone."

Savanna stood looking down at Caroline, lying in the hospital bed, hair disheveled, wires and leads and IV tubing connected to her on all sides. She smiled sweetly at Savanna, her lipstick a rich shade of red.

Savanna spoke. "Okay. I'm sure that'll be fine. Don't worry." Let Lauren talk to her, Savanna thought; she was as stubborn as ever, lipstick or no lipstick. Or maybe Aidan could talk some sense into her.

She patted Savanna's hand. "I'm not worried a bit, dear. You be careful. Thank you for looking out for me."

Jordan stopped to speak with the deputy stationed outside Caroline's room, and then he and Savanna headed to the elevator.

"Do you think Ryan will still show up today?" Savanna took an offered stick of gum from him while they rode down to the lobby.

"It'll depend on whether or not Ryan was involved in your chase from Lansing yesterday…and if Thiebold is arrogant enough to think we haven't figured things out by now. Would he be aware that Skylar had copies of the provenances? If not, he may believe you have suspicions, but no way to connect anything back to him."

"I don't see how he'd know about Skylar's copies. He does know the originals are somewhere in the house. I think that's what the break-in was about, in light of all of this. Both Caroline's and Everett's home offices were ransacked. Caroline says Everett has a concealed, locked compartment in his desk; she was certain the provenances were untouched."

Jordan held the door open for Savanna as they walked out to the hospital parking lot. "Then let's hope Felix Thiebold's arrogance outweighs his caution, and he allows Ryan to come for the painting."

Caroline's house was only six blocks from Anderson Memorial. Jordan informed Savanna that he'd be riding with her, leaving his police vehicle at the hospital to avoid cluing Ryan in that something was up before he'd made it into Caroline's house. As they were leaving, she caught sight of Aidan's SUV pulling into the parking lot.

Savanna pulled up next to him, rolling down her window. "Hi there."

"I was hoping to catch you here. I just came from Fancy Tails. Sydney said you were with Caroline." He peered through to her passenger seat, where Jordan raised a hand in a brief greeting.

"Aidan, you remember Detective Jordan. Detective, Dr. Gallager." She said to Aidan, "We're going to Caroline's house to meet Felix's assistant, Ryan. He thinks he's picking up a painting…the detective hopes to have a chance to talk with him."

Aidan nodded. "I'll follow you. I was hoping for a way to check on what the medication situation is before Caroline comes home tomorrow. I've got a new pill planner to leave her… I'd like to double-check her prescription bottles."

Jordan spoke up. "That's not a good idea, not right now."

"It's okay. My car's over there at least a few times a week. It won't cause a problem."

Savanna felt instantly better as she rolled the window up and pulled out of the parking lot, knowing Aidan was following them.

"No reason to make this a circus," Jordan said gruffly.

"It's all right, Detective. Dr. Gallager has taken excellent care of Caroline. I think he just wants to make sure everything goes seamlessly when she comes home."

"Fine." His tone was terse.

Savanna told her car to call Lauren as they drove to Caroline's.

Over the Bluetooth system, Lauren's voicemail picked up. Savanna tried to explain as briefly as possible, knowing she probably wasn't making much sense. "Anyway," she said as she pulled into the Carson house driveway, "no need to come to the house today. Detective Jordan from the Carson Village police department is with me. We're going to wait here to meet Ryan."

Within ten minutes, they'd retrieved the locked, firesafe box of provenances from the compartment under Mr. Carson's desk, Savanna and Detective Jordan sitting in the living room off the foyer, waiting. Aidan was in the kitchen, where Caroline kept her prescription bottles.

Jordan tapped the locked box. "Not all of these will need to be kept for evidence. I'll get everything back to her except for the ones needed to prove Thiebold brokered deals on forgeries," Jordan told Savanna.

"Of course," she said.

Aidan joined them. "Okay, all good. Her new pillbox is set up correctly with the couple of changes we made at the hospital."

While they waited, Savanna went through the events of the weekend with Aidan. He listened, stunned, as she recounted making the discovery of the pentimento under the Minkov, the brushstroke giveaway in the Rothman, and the error in the authenticator's name this morning with her sisters.

Another ten minutes crawled by. Savanna crossed, un-crossed, and recrossed her legs. Checked her phone. Went to the kitchen and returned with a glass of lemonade for her and the two men.

Jordan sat still, in his chair, waiting. He finally looked at her. "You know, if you have somewhere to be, you can go. It's not necessary for you to be here. Either of you."

Savanna glanced at Aidan. "I just realized you were prob-ably coming to the hospital for a reason. I didn't mean to take you away from work. Do you need to go?"

Aidan shook his head. "I was already there early this morning to make rounds. I'll go later and check on Caroline, don't worry. Do you have somewhere to be?"

"No, not at all. I'm fine. Just nervous. I wish he'd get here."

"You told Lauren what was going on," Jordan spoke. "It's possible she tipped Ryan off."

Savanna looked at Jordan like he had three heads. "*What?* That's crazy. Lauren's fine. She's Caroline's biggest advo-cate."

He shrugged. "You never know. People are unpredicta-ble, and very predictable, when it comes to money."

Savanna thought once more of Jack and let it go. There was just no way he was involved. She might never find out what that odd text message was about, but Jack was no monster.

A car door closed outside, and footsteps sounded on the porch. The trio in the house stood.

Savanna looked at Jordan when the doorbell rang.

He put a hand up, frowning at her. "Wait, I want to see something."

They remained seated, and a minute later heard the tones on the push button lock being pressed, followed by a long beep, meaning an incorrect code had been entered.

"He doesn't know the locks have been changed," Savanna said. "He hasn't been here since Friday."

The code was tried a second time, to no avail. The doorbell rang again.

Jordan motioned to Savanna. "Go ahead, answer it."

She stared at him. He waved a hand for her to go, standing out of sight behind the door. She took a shaky breath, and opened the front door. "Ryan! Come in!"

"Hi," he said, looking confused, his gaze moving beyond Savanna to the foyer. "Sorry, I didn't know there must be a new lock code. I'm meeting Lauren here?"

"Right, Caroline told me."

"I'm, uh, supposed to pick up a painting?" Ryan wore tan Levi's and sneakers, a black canvas jacket, and a backward baseball cap over shoulder-length brown hair. Savanna hadn't noticed before how young he was; he looked to be around twenty-five.

Savanna closed the door behind him, revealing Detective Jordan, and Dr. Gallager beyond, in the living room.

Ryan looked curiously at the three of them.

"Lauren isn't here," Jordan said. "We'd like to talk to you."

Savanna saw, from the corner of her eye, Jordan's right

hand no longer visible, resting near his belt under his suit coat. *He's waiting to see if Ryan is going to run*, she thought.

Ryan nodded agreeably. "Okay, sure. But if I can't pick up the piece today, I'll have to let Felix know so he can reschedule the buyer."

Jordan led him into the living room. "Sit." He motioned at one of the chairs.

Ryan obediently did so.

Jordan held his badge out for Ryan to see. "I'm Detective Jordan. You might be acquainted with Savanna Shepherd, and this is Dr. Gallager. Lauren won't be joining us today. Mrs. Carson is in the hospital at the moment."

"I heard that. Felix told me. Something with her heart? I'm sorry to hear it."

"What is your last name, Ryan?"

"Nelson."

"Ryan, I'm investigating a few incidents that have happened here, at Mrs. Carson's house. Were you aware she was on heart medicine?"

"No." He shook his head. "But she's old, right? I mean, that happens when you get old."

"Have you ever handled any of Mrs. Carson's food or medication, Ryan?"

"What? No! Why would I?"

"Ever been in the parlor where she's been sleeping recently?" Jordan barely allowed time for Ryan to answer before peppering him with the next question.

"No. Look, man, I come, I package the paintings and take them to Felix, and I get paid. The only rooms I've ever been in here are the ones where the paintings are. Like this room"—he looked up—"she sold a piece that was over that piano. And her office, around the corner there."

Savanna saw that Jordan was jotting notes in a small leather-bound notebook. He hardly glanced at Ryan, completely ignoring how flustered the young man was becoming. "And Ryan, what about the stairway? Have you ever had occasion to be on the second floor of the house?"

Ryan stood up. "No. Never. I don't know what this is about, but I think I should go."

Jordan remained seated, looking up at Ryan. "Sit. Down."

Ryan sat. He leaned forward, elbows on knees. "Listen, what are you looking for? I've spent like, twenty minutes tops in this house. I haven't done anything. Did something happen with one of the paintings?"

"How long have you worked for Mr. Thiebold, Ryan?"

"Five or six years. Six years."

"And do you travel with him, to act as courier for the artwork?"

"Yes, sometimes."

"So." Jordan jotted something else in the notebook. "You meet the buyers as well as the sellers. Have you been to The Masters Gallery in Florida recently, Ryan?"

"Where?"

"An art gallery in St. Armand's, Florida. It appears Mr. Thiebold often uses an authenticator there to verify authenticity before pieces change hands. So, Ryan, you'd have traveled to The Masters Gallery in St. Armand's with Mr.

Thiebold, wouldn't you?"

Ryan shrugged, looking confused. "I don't know, man. I work for Felix a few months a year, and he flies me to wherever he's making art deals. I carry the paintings. Sometimes things get boring, and he sends me for coffee. I don't keep track of where the deals are. So, maybe?"

Jordan looked at Ryan. "You work as Mr. Thiebold's assistant a few months a year? What do you do for work in your off time?"

"I, uh, don't. I don't need to. I mean, Felix pays really well. I get pay raises every year, and sometimes a bonus. But it's not an easy job," he added, looking from the detective to Savanna to Aidan. "He relies on me for everything when I am working."

Jordan nodded, silently writing notes in his book. "Interesting. Ryan," he said, not glancing up, "where were you yesterday at four thirty in the afternoon?"

"What?" Ryan looked confused. "Why? What was yesterday, Saturday?"

Jordan now met the younger man's eyes. "Yes, Ryan. Saturday. Where you Saturday at four thirty?"

Ryan was looking at the ceiling, ticking off something on his fingers, one at a time.

"Ryan?" Jordan pushed him.

"I'm thinking. I was gaming. My friends and I play an online game together. I think I logged on around noon."

"And you were still playing this game four and a half hours later?"

Ryan sighed, appearing exasperated. "I was still in the

309

game, like, nine hours later, man. Unless I've got something going on for Felix, there isn't much else to do when we're traveling."

Savanna caught Jordan's look—was Ryan not involved at all in Thiebold's crooked dealings?

"Ryan," Jordan said, "I assume there would be a record of your activity online? And if my tech guys were to check into it, they'd find you were active in this game. What game is it?"

"*Space Bug Colony.* It's a multiplayer game I play with a bunch of guys from all over the country."

Jordan finished his question. "They'd find you were active in *Space Bug Colony* from noon until well after four thirty yesterday?"

"Yes, for sure," Ryan replied, relief painting his features.

"One more question, Ryan. Are you aware Mrs. Carson's friend was poisoned and killed earlier this month with an overdose of the medication Attendall?"

The relief was quickly replaced by shock; watching the exchange, Savanna felt a little sorry for him. He stared wide-eyed at Jordan. "*What?* No, I had no idea. That's awful." He huffed out an impatient sigh, giving up. "Okay, you're the police. You probably already know, I take Attendall. I've been on it since I was fifteen. I lost my prescription bottle a few weeks ago and had to have it replaced."

"You lost it? The whole bottle? It never turned up? What date did you lose it on?"

Ryan shrugged. "I don't know. It's not on me. Wait, I get text notifications when my prescription is ready." He pulled out his phone, tapping the screen. "I got the replacement prescription on...hold on, let me find it...okay, I got the replacement on September third. I lost it the day before. I'd just had it filled, so it was almost full when I lost it."

"That's convenient," Jordan said. "Eleanor Pietila was poisoned on September fifth."

Ryan looked at the detective sharply. "I have a real prescription from my doctor. I'd never do anything shady with my medication. I don't know what you're getting at."

Jordan glanced at Savanna, then back at Ryan. "You've never shared your medication with anyone? Could anyone else have had access to it?"

Ryan sat back, hands out in front of him, fingers out straight. "No. Oh, no, no, no. I haven't done anything. I don't think this is okay. Should I have, like, a lawyer or something right now?"

"Have you done anything illegal, Ryan?" Jordan stared at Ryan, poker-faced.

Savanna bit her lip. It was all she could do to sit still and remain quiet. Her knee shook with small movements, jittery, and Aidan moved his hand from his own knee, placing it lightly on hers; she felt instantly calmer as he gave her a barely perceptible nod. She stilled her knee under the light touch of his palm, and he took his hand away, looking back at Ryan and Jordan.

Savanna saw what Jordan was doing, but she felt awful for this young man.

"No!" Ryan answered Jordan's question without hesitation. "I've done nothing wrong. I never found the missing pill bottle, and I always keep it in the same spot in my luggage. And," he added emphatically, looking at Savanna and then back at Jordan, "I did not use it to poison anyone. Ever. I would never do that. I wouldn't do whatever you think I could've done yesterday either. I was in my hotel room online all day. I'm not a bad person. This is just a job, man. I just pick up and deliver paintings!"

Jordan stood up. "We're done here. You can go, Ryan, but don't go far. I may have a few more questions."

Ryan looked like he might cry; his whole face was flushed and his breathing was rough from his impassioned outburst. He dug his keys out of his pocket, and left without another word.

Savanna stared at Detective Jordan. "Wow."

Jordan glanced at her.

"You just… You don't actually suspect him, do you?"

He shook his head. "Of course not. Has he seen things he probably shouldn't have? I'm sure of it. Was he involved in trying to kill Mrs. Carson? A firm no. But he's the bait. He's going to take our conversation to his boss, and I think I'll have a fascinating discussion with Felix Thiebold later tonight, when we pick him up. I've already got two officers waiting to bring him in as soon as he shows up at his hotel."

Aidan volunteered to drop Jordan off back at the hospital, at his car, along with the locked box of provenances, and Savanna could have kissed him. She could see how shrewd Jordan was, but right now she felt like she needed a shower, and some distance from the detective.

Jordan leaned down and spoke to Savanna through her

car window before getting in Aidan's car. "Thanks for your help, Savanna. Your eye for detail broke this whole thing open."

"Detective," she said, "would you let me know what the outcome is, please? I need to know Caroline is safe—that we're all safe, actually."

"I'll keep you updated," he said. "You did great."

Savanna pulled up at Fancy Tails, put a hand on the door and then thought better of it, and crossed the street to the coffee house. She ordered two green teas and took them back across the street.

Pushing through the door to Fancy Tails, Savanna immediately went to her spot in the corner, flouncing into the big aqua chair and basking in the loving attention lavished on her by Fonzie. Princess and Duke came over and sniffed at her ankles, then curled back up in the sun spot by the front door.

"You look like you were hit by a truck." Sydney joined her, taking a seat at the red and chrome table.

Savanna passed her one of the green teas, sipping on the other. "I was. It was a truck named Nick Jordan."

Sydney tilted her head at Savanna. "Tell me."

Savanna was halfway through the recap to Sydney when the bell over the door jangled.

Aidan stood in the doorway. "Are you all right?"

Savanna let out a huge sigh. Why did she always feel better with him around? "I'm okay."

He joined them in the corner, taking a chair opposite Sydney at the table. "Okay. I just had to check. Did she fill you in on the interrogation we just came from?" he asked Sydney.

"She did…most of it. I mean, I see what he was doing. But that poor guy."

"Definitely," Aidan agreed. "He was shaken up. I'm sure he's going to be in contact with Thiebold. He's got to be figuring Thiebold took his prescription."

"What about the digitalis?" Sydney wondered.

"If Felix was able to steal Ryan's Attendall out from under him," Savanna said, "and was sneaky enough to change around the pills in Caroline's pillbox, I'm thinking he probably has whatever resources he needs. She probably isn't even the only person he's bought and sold forgeries to."

"I'm sure you're right," Aidan said.

"Well, at least we know they're bringing Thiebold in tonight. Jordan said he'd keep us updated. Hopefully it'll go well; I just want Caroline to be safe," Savanna said.

Chapter Twenty-Five

J ACK CARSON WAS waiting for Savanna Monday morning when she got to school. As she passed the library, he spotted her and followed her to her classroom. "I owe you an explanation," Jack said, perching on the community table closest to Savanna's desk.

"For what?" Savanna put her purse away in the bottom right drawer and hung her sweater up. The last day of September, and it was already brisk and chilly this morning. It would be seventy-two degrees by this afternoon, but was definitely sweater weather right now.

"For my strange behavior last week. I know you wondered what was wrong. And I'm sorry I let my problems affect your schedule. You shouldn't have had to worry about why I was late, or cover for me."

Savanna sat opposite him. "Listen, don't worry about it. I never mind helping out a friend. I did wonder, though"— she paused—"why you seemed so frazzled last week."

"I can tell you now. I finally got some good news this morning. I developed a business plan with a friend of mine. We wanted to purchase the Carson Ballroom that's coming up for lease renewal."

"Jack! That's quite an undertaking! Purchase, not lease?"

Jack nodded. "We plan to renovate it. I already love the banquet area, and Carson needs that space for exactly what it's used for. But there's a lot of time it stands empty too. With just a few changes to the space, it could double as a small concert venue. We could attract local and regional music acts, which would bring in more revenue for the town and give the kids something to do as well. And the adjacent space, the old movie theater, well, that's a no-brainer. Carson needs a theater. Can't you imagine, strolling through town on a Friday night, maybe you've already picked up your gourmet treats for your dog and a hot cup of coffee, maybe even a nice Italian meal at Giuseppe's, but you're not ready to go home yet? Wouldn't it be great to have movies in town? With two screens, bottomless popcorn, and reclining, heated seats?"

Savanna sat back in her chair, dreaming of what Jack described. "It sounds wonderful. I would go every week! So…you're doing it?"

"Yes!" Jack clapped his hands together, animated and happy. "We met with the potential investor Saturday morning. I pushed the meeting back, from Friday. I couldn't leave town not knowing if Grandmother would be all right, but it went well. He just emailed to tell me he's in. My partner and I will be able to purchase the space, the whole ballroom and theater. It's ours, as of December first!"

"I love it! Congratulations, Jack. I think it sounds like a fantastic addition to Carson."

Savanna had a feeling he'd be smiling the rest of the day. "Oh." He stopped in her doorway, looking back. "And I was thinking, if you might be interested, I'd love to commission you to do some artwork in the theater portion, once it's renovated and ready. Just something to keep in mind," he said, turning and heading down the hallway with a new spring in his step.

Savanna moved about her classroom, setting out the items she'd need for her first set of students, lost in thought. It made her feel good to see Jack so passionate about his endeavor. The idea of beautifying the new theater was exciting. Savanna was almost finished with Caroline's mural. She needed one more hour or so to add a few finishing touches, but she'd begun feeling that tug, the little pang of sadness that it was almost done. Painting transported her in a way nothing else really did.

So, apparently, she would have more projects ahead. She couldn't wait.

That strange, seemingly incriminating text she'd seen on Jack's phone popped into her head. Now it all made sense. Sometimes even she connected the dots in the wrong order. She was so relieved that, in all of this, Jack really was the nice guy she thought he was.

Savanna was up on the scaffolding for the last time that afternoon when her phone rang. She scrambled down, grabbing it from her supply bag just before her voicemail picked up. "Hello?" she said breathlessly.

Lauren poked her head around the corner into Caroline's parlor, checking on her. "Are you okay?"

Savanna nodded, giving Lauren a thumbs-up. Caroline was being released tonight, and Lauren had let Savanna come in to finish her mural while she zipped around the house, cleaning, changing bedding, setting fresh flowers out, and sprucing up the place for her grandmother.

"Hello, Skylar?" Savanna said again, this time hearing her sister on the other end of the line.

"They just brought Thiebold in," Skylar said, talking fast. "Jordan called to let me know. They're waiting for his lawyer to arrive, and then they'll question him, but Jordan said they've already read him his rights. He's been arrested on four counts of fraud, for now. I can explain more when I see you. I need to observe the interrogation, as Caroline's attorney. I know you're dying of curiosity about what Felix has to say for himself. I can arrange for you to observe with me through the two-way mirror. You were instrumental in cracking this case, so you should be there to see it tied up."

"Yes!" Savanna didn't even need to think about it. "Yes. Can you pick me up? I walked here."

"I'll be there in five minutes."

Savanna stood back and looked up at the mural. It was finished. It had probably been finished before the last half hour she'd just spent, but it was so hard to stop. She packed up her supplies, leaving the bag at the foot of the scaffolding to collect later. She'd bring Harlan back tomorrow morning to disassemble it and take it away.

She found Lauren in the kitchen, scrubbing the sink. "Skylar just called. They arrested Felix Thiebold and brought him in to the police station. She's picking me up, but I'll be back soon."

Lauren turned off the faucet and leaned against the counter. "Oh, my. Thank you, Savanna. Thank you for everything you've done. I don't know if Grams would still be here, if not for you."

Savanna gave Lauren a quick hug. "You're so welcome. I'm glad we were all able to take care of her. She's worth it."

When Savanna let go, she saw tears in the woman's eyes. "Sorry." She sniffled, swiping under one eye. "I'm just a little emotional today. Grams will be home by the time you get back. She's so happy to be coming home. You *are* coming back, aren't you?"

"Absolutely," Savanna said. "I'll be back soon, and Syd's bringing Princess and Duke home around seven. She got them all fancied up for your grandmother's party, but she'll gladly do it again in a week or two if you decide to postpone."

Lauren let out a long sigh. "I honestly don't know if she'll allow that. I was going to ask Dr. Gallager to put his two cents in. She might listen to him."

"She might. Or she might not." She laughed.

Lauren smiled. "You know her well. She does what she wants."

At the Carson Village police station, Savanna and Skylar stood with Detective Jordan in a darkened room on the other side of the wall from the holding cell where Felix Thiebold sat.

"He can't see or hear you," Jordan told them. "I'll start with a few questions to put him at ease, make him think this is all about one painting. But we've already fingerprinted him, and the lab has pulled three sets of prints off Caroline

Carson's medication box. I'm hoping one of them is his. We've got Ryan Nelson in our back pocket to use as leverage if all else fails."

"What do you mean? I thought you didn't suspect Ryan was involved," Savanna said.

"I don't," Jordan said, "but I do believe Ryan probably saw things he shouldn't have over the years, things Felix likely glossed over or swept under the rug. Thiebold will be very, very worried when he sees Detective Taylor walk Ryan past the room where we are. We're bringing Ryan in for a few more questions. He may ultimately end up in protective custody depending on how this goes; we aren't aiming to put in him in danger. But seeing him should trigger Thiebold to automatically recall all the questionable situations Ryan observed. He'll assume it's over."

"That all makes sense," Savanna said.

"Yes," Jordan said. "Oh, there's Thiebold's lawyer. Here goes."

Savanna and Skylar watched through the two-way mirror as Jordan went out into the hallway and into the holding room with Thiebold and his attorney. The lawyer was a tall, dark-suited, solid man in his midthirties; he sat straight-backed in his chair, arms folded over his chest. His dark brown hair and mustache were impeccably groomed. He leaned over to Felix and said something inaudible, then straightened up again, adjusting his glasses.

"So," Jordan began, "we need to talk about the Sergei Minkov painting belonging to Caroline Carson."

Thiebold sat back in his chair and crossed his legs.

"What about the Minkov?"

"We've had our authenticator assess the piece, and it's been determined a forgery."

Felix scoffed. "You may want to get a second opinion. I personally handled that piece and had my own authenticator evaluate it. It is, indeed, a genuine Minkov."

"It's a forgery, based on more than one marker. In fact, there are three separate issues with the piece alone that identify it as a fake, and that's not even mentioning the provenance."

"The provenance is fine. Have you even viewed the original, or are you basing this on what's online? Because the internet is notoriously unreliable when it comes to up-to-date provenance information."

"Oh, we've viewed the originals. We've actually done diagnostics on more than one of the pieces you brokered deals on for the Carsons, and we've done extensive research on each hard-copy provenance," Jordan said calmly.

"Then you would know," Felix said, equally as calmly, "that several methods of authentication are used now, and often one must use more than one medium or protocol to certify a piece."

Felix's attorney spoke up. "My client obviously has no knowledge of any issue you've found with that painting or any other. We'll need to see the documentation you're speaking of."

Felix added, "I only deal in genuine works, with reputable buyers and sellers. You'll find that's true if you check my references."

"Your references...like"—Jordan flipped his small leather-bound notebook open—"Ivan Kiernanski?"

"Exactly. His signature on the Minkov provenance speaks for itself. It's even notarized."

"Really?" Jordan asked, glancing down at his notebook. "I'll have to check that out," he said, pulling a pen out and jotting something down. "We noticed you used this Ivan Kiernanski for all the pieces you've acquired for Mrs. Carson."

"I have. When one identifies a well-qualified art authenticator, one has reason to continue to use those services," he said haughtily.

"If that's all," the attorney said, "we need to know what the bond will be. These charges are ridiculous; I doubt they'll hold up. Mr. Thiebold will not be a guest of Carson Village tonight." The attorney said "Carson Village" as if the words tasted cheap and disgusting on his tongue.

"Sure," Jordan said, starting to stand, and then paused. He placed a hand on the table and leaned forward. "But you know, I almost forgot to ask you, Mr. Thiebold. How much did you pay your assistant to help you with eliminating Caroline Carson? We know you bonused him occasionally. Was this one of those circumstances that warranted a bonus?"

Felix looked pale. "What?"

"Your assistant. Ryan Nelson." Jordan consulted his book.

Savanna suddenly knew exactly what he was doing. She grabbed Skylar's arm, shaking it. "He knows Ryan's name.

He knows every detail of this case," she hissed. "He's playing Columbo to throw Thiebold off. He's good."

"Oooh! You're right." Skylar grinned.

"My assistant? I'd hardly call him my assistant," Felix said. "He's a delivery boy. He packages and acts as courier for the pieces I deal in."

"Hmm. That's odd. Because when we talked to Ryan, he told us he travels everywhere with you when you're working on a deal. To the seller, the buyer, and The Masters Gallery in St. Armand's each time you need to see Mr. Kiernanski. Or…is it Kiernaski? Well, I can ask him soon enough. We're talking to him again tonight."

"Ryan is just a kid," Felix said, looking slightly panicked. "He doesn't know the ins and outs of the art world, all the steps in the process of buying and selling. Even if he thinks he can tell you anything of importance, he'd be wrong. He doesn't understand the intricacies of the transactions; questioning him won't help you with this…this wild-goose chase."

"Ryan understands quite a lot, I'd say. He explained in detail the step-by-step process he's assisted you with. Oh! And I almost forgot to mention, there's also the bottle of wine planted in Caroline Carson's house, spiked with the medication Attendall. Mrs. Carson's best friend was the unfortunate victim of that wine, though our theory is that the wine was meant for Caroline. Are you aware your assistant is on Attendall? Wait"—Jordan looked at his notebook—"I'm guessing you are, as the two of you travel so often together."

"This doesn't concern us," the attorney said, leaning forward and placing his hands on the table. "You can deal with Ryan Nelson on your own time. Now, about that bond."

"Oh my gosh, his lawyer is so arrogant." Savanna rolled her eyes.

"He isn't really," Skylar said. "He's got to play things like his client is not guilty no matter what. Jordan is pushing; it's his job to push back."

"Huh. I wasn't looking at it like that." That made sense. Nice to have a little insight from an attorney's point of view, Savanna thought.

"I'll go look into the bond," the detective said. "If they do decide to grant it, you'll need to remain in the state, Mr. Thiebold."

Felix's complexion was now an unattractive shade of pale gray; he looked nauseated. Savanna noted a sheen of sweat covering his brow. The attorney put a hand on his arm, but Felix shook it off.

The attorney leaned over again and spoke into Felix's ear, and Felix glared at him.

An officer entered the room, and Jordan went over to him, nodding and listening intently. "Excellent! Mr. Thiebold, Mr. Lloyd, excuse me for a moment."

When Jordan exited, he left the door standing wide open. Savanna saw Thiebold glance at the open door, and then at the uniformed patrol officer standing in the corner.

Felix turned to his attorney, clearly flustered as he demanded, "You'd better do something! You said you'd make this all go away and we'd be out of here tonight!"

The lawyer looked unconcerned. He leaned forward, speaking quietly, turning his back on Savanna and Skylar through the two-way mirror; they still heard his words. "Keep your voice down. The detective's bluffing. They've got nothing. If they did, they'd have arrested your assistant on the spot yesterday instead of telling you they're continuing to question him."

Felix rested his elbows on the table, his hands cradling his head. "You'd better be certain. I'm not sure exactly what Ryan knows. He's my right hand for these deals. I try to be discreet but…"

"Watch yourself." The lawyer smacked the table, interrupting Thiebold. "This is neither the time nor the place."

Jordan appeared in the doorway of the darkened room where Skylar and Savanna stood. "Showtime," he whispered and shut their door. At exactly that moment, Detective Taylor, from Savanna's first time here in the precinct, walked past Thiebold's holding room with Ryan Nelson. One large hand was wrapped around Ryan's skinny upper arm; as they passed the doorway, Ryan glanced into the room and lost his footing for a moment, then continued on with the detective to the next room on the right.

Savanna and Skylar watched Detective Jordan return to Thiebold's room.

"Looks like your client will get to be our guest tonight after all," Jordan said, sliding a paper across the table to the attorney.

Felix peered at it. "What is this?"

"Maybe you can explain to me," Jordan said quietly, "what your fingerprints are doing on Caroline Carson's pillbox?"

Thiebold's eyes were huge. He looked up at his attorney, and finally, Mr. Lloyd looked worried. "It isn't what it looks like," Felix said, no heart behind the statement. "It's, uh, she asked me to fetch it for her when I was there last week."

"Mm-hmm," Jordan said. "And the full print of yours that we lifted from the inside of one of the compartments?"

Felix Thiebold deflated before their eyes. He shook his head. "This wasn't supposed to happen. It's not what I planned."

Mr. Lloyd stood. "That's enough," he barked, looking down at Felix. "If you won't take my advice, then at least know when to shut up. Mr. Thiebold has nothing further to say," he informed Jordan. "We're finished here."

"We aren't," Jordan said. "Not quite yet."

The lawyer grudgingly sat back down, giving Thiebold one more warning glance.

"Perfect," Skylar whispered to Savanna on the other side of the glass.

"They've got him," Savanna said.

"I just want to make sure I understand how you did it," Jordan said. "Because this is how it looks: Ivan Kiernanski—or perhaps Kiernaski, impossible to know which is the actual misspelling, since the name is an alias either way—acted as your forger and authenticator. We'll find out who he really is, but he was classically trained and is very good, re-creating famous works for you on commission out of a gallery in St.

Armand's, Florida. The Carsons aren't the only clients you've procured art for. That should be an interesting thread to follow, but the FBI will take over on that. Ryan will be a great resource for them."

Thiebold's lawyer shook his head. "You're not going to gain anything from this. My client isn't going to incriminate himself."

Jordan shrugged. "That's fine. The evidence speaks for itself. Thiebold's signature follows Kiernanski's on every provenance for every piece he sold to Everett Carson; your client contracted with Kiernanski to create the works and fraudulent certificates. But I don't think Thiebold caught the one instance where his so-called authenticator misspelled his own name. Twice, in both print and signature. When Mrs. Carson decided to liquidate some of her paintings after losing her husband last year and reached out to the three gallerists who have purchased for her in the past, your client panicked. In spite of Thiebold's best efforts to make sure Mrs. Carson used only him to thin out her collection, the woman wasn't all that cooperative. She made efforts to involve other dealers—Kevin Banfield, for one, and another gallerist from New York—to help find buyers for her work. Thiebold couldn't allow that to happen. Your client resorted to desperate measures to protect his reputation, and his livelihood."

Felix Thiebold looked at his lawyer and then back at Jordan.

"Your fingerprints on Mrs. Carson's pillbox, and *inside* the pillbox, are enough to prove attempted murder, even without your fraudulent dealings. We're still working on a way to tie the death of Eleanor Pietila to you, Mr. Thiebold, but we've already been granted a search warrant for your last several points of residence. We'll find the proof we need. Looks like we have quite a few options as far as the charges we'll pursue."

"Incredible," Savanna said, watching. She gave Skylar a squeeze around her shoulders. "Look at Thiebold. He's done. Jordan seems so relaxed, laying all of the details out, and every time he drops another bomb, Thiebold looks like he wants to sink into the floor. I'm glad you got him involved, Skylar."

Skylar nodded. "He's the best."

"Yes, he is." As defeated as Thiebold appeared, slumped in his chair next to his lawyer, Savanna didn't feel bad for him at all. She was still trying to reconcile the sweet, respectful gentleman she'd met weeks ago at the Carson mansion with this conniving criminal in the interrogation room through the two-way mirror.

"I just have one question for you, Mr. Thiebold," Detective Jordan was saying. "Your friendship with Everett Carson. Was that real, or did you cultivate that relationship as a means to an end?"

"Everett and I were friends. At least, we started out that way," Thiebold blurted, his voice cracking. "I didn't set out to hurt anyone. I just loved dealing in fine art."

"And the fortune you gained doing it, especially once you could pocket the majority of the profits for forgeries."

Another uniformed patrol officer entered the room, and

Thiebold's lawyer pushed his chair back, placing his hands on the table.

Jordan stood. "Now we're finished. Check back in the morning, Mr. Lloyd," he said, "and you'll be given the time of the arraignment hearing tomorrow. Have a nice night," he added, leaving the officers to deal with Felix.

Skylar elbowed Savanna, grinning. "*Have a nice night.* Gotta love him."

"He's the best," Savanna agreed. "Thank you for this, Skylar. Felix Thiebold put Caroline through so much; he cost Eleanor her life. Mr. Carson would turn over in his grave if he knew the man not only faked the artwork he sold him, but his friendship on top of it. I'm glad we got to be here for this."

Chapter Twenty-Six

CAROLINE CARSON WAS the perfect hostess at her ninetieth birthday party. When Savanna arrived, Caroline was circulating in the parlor, not a trace of a limp or any sign she'd been in the hospital five days ago. Her silver hair shone, complementing her shimmering navy blue gown; Savanna spied rhinestone-laden silver shoes peeking out from beneath the hem.

Caroline pulled Savanna into a hug the moment she saw her. "Thank you, my dear, for coming home to us. You've been my guardian angel these last few weeks."

Savanna planted a kiss on the woman's cheek. "You look beautiful, Caroline. I still can't believe you wouldn't consider rescheduling this. Are you feeling all right?"

"I'm feeling wonderful. This is all I wanted." She spread her arms out as if to embrace her family and friends. "You worry too much. All of you. I even have my doctor on-site, just in case." She smiled. "I'm very well cared for."

"I can see that," Savanna agreed.

Jack came to Caroline's side. "Grandmother, may I steal you for a moment? Sorry, Savanna."

"Of course."

Caroline linked her arm through Jack's, letting him lead

her toward the foyer.

"Mom is here. She got your invitation. I thought you might like to…"

Savanna lost the rest of Jack's sentence as they were out of earshot. She knew nothing of the guest list, or the somewhat strained relationship it seemed Caroline had with her daughter, but she was happy to hear that none of the family had been excluded from the event.

Caroline's house looked gorgeous; the temporary bedroom was gone now from the parlor, the wooden floors gleamed, and overhead—Savanna had no idea how or when it had been done—hundreds of small white twinkle lights were strung across the ceilings.

Savanna moved to the punch bowl. She and Sydney had prepared it this afternoon and had left instructions for Lauren to just add the ice cream at the start of the party. Savanna saw that it was getting a bit low; she served herself a cup and went to the kitchen to replenish the mixture and fruit.

Sydney was leaning against the counter, one hand on the arm of her fireman, Brad, laughing at something he'd just said. "Savvy! It's an amazing party, isn't it? Mom and Dad are on their way now."

Nolan came sliding on sock feet through the kitchen, giggling like crazy as the poodles pranced around him. He fell onto the floor and let them sniff and paw at him as he rolled around laughing.

Skylar followed closely after Nolan; she bent and scooped him up, passing him to Travis behind her. Nolan wiggled around on Travis's shoulder, reaching for the poodles.

"He needs a dog," Savanna murmured to Skylar as she passed her by the counter. "Right?" She looked up at Travis.

Travis nodded. "Seriously. I'm working on her, don't worry."

"Good!" As Savanna was carrying a large pitcher out to refill the punch bowl, she spotted Detective Jordan at the other end of the dessert table. He came toward her, accompanied by a pretty brunette in a pink dress.

"Savanna Shepherd, this is my wife, June. June, Savanna Shepherd, Carson's new honorary private eye."

Savanna laughed self-consciously. "Well, I wouldn't go that far."

"I would," Jordan said. "You caught details others would have missed, and it's a good thing. None of us would be here celebrating tonight if you hadn't." He glanced over Savanna's head at someone and she turned to look. Maggie and Bill Lyle were just arriving. "I meant to tell you, I did question those two, in the interest of leaving no loose ends. That stairway accident was exactly that—an accident. Mr. Lyle is still beating himself up over missing the stud when he installed the top bracket for the railing."

"Well, I kind of figured, but I'm glad you're sure he wasn't involved."

"Even if circumstances were right, I highly doubt those two are capable of a carrying out a complicated plan to hurt anyone." He chuckled.

"I guess nosy and ornery doesn't necessarily mean murderer." She laughed, poking fun at herself and the conclusions she'd leaped to.

"Listen." Jordan turned back to Savanna. "We found the vehicle that tried to run you off the road. It was abandoned in long-term parking at the airport; all the damage was consistent with the report you gave. No leads on the driver though. And"—he paused for dramatic effect—"I heard this morning that they've tracked down the forger Thiebold used. He was on-site at that gallery in St. Armand's, Florida. The FBI grabbed him. They're still identifying all the work he forged over the years, but apparently, Felix Thiebold was just one of the art dealers he contracted with. This is far-reaching, Savanna. Thiebold and his forger have been doing this for years, in several countries."

"Wow," she breathed. "That's incredible."

"You bet it is."

Jordan and his wife moved to the chocolate fountain. Savanna noticed a few people pointing up at her mural, chatting. Savanna was pleased with how it turned out, but more importantly, Caroline loved it.

Savanna drifted toward the far wall, heading out toward Caroline's back deck overlooking the dunes. The October chill had remained, the days warm and the nights brisk. Savanna stood at the railing, tiny white lights strung over-head twinkling against the night. Someone had even used strands of small, clear light bulbs to create a trail along the tree line toward the dunes and the lake.

Savanna closed her eyes, tipping her head back, and breathed deeply. How she loved the lake air. She wrapped her arms across her chest, running her hands over the bare skin of her upper arms. The royal blue dress she'd chosen for tonight was elegant and classic, but she should have brought a sweater.

She opened her eyes to Aidan draping his suit jacket over her shoulders, pulling it snug around her. Savanna's breath caught in her throat as she met his eyes.

"You look cold," he said, his voice deep and quiet.

"I'm not," Savanna answered, "anymore. Thank you."

He smiled at her, and she forgot all the rest of her words. "It's a beautiful party," Aidan said.

Savanna nodded.

"Savanna," Aidan said, leaning in just a little closer, "can I ask you something?"

"Yes."

"Would you go out with me? Tomorrow? Or some day? On a date?"

"Yes." She smiled, her cheeks flushing hot. "I'd love that."

"Good." He nodded, grinning down at her.

"But," Savanna said, finally finding her words, "it can't be at a hospital, or a school, or in this house."

Aidan laughed. "It's a deal."

The End

Murder on Display
A Shepherd Sisters Mystery (Book 2)

S AVANNA SHEPHERD ENTERED Fancy Tails & Treats
backward, carrying three steaming coffees and a white
bakery box of frosted cinnamon rolls. Her dog's leash was
looped over a wrist, and papers were sliding out of a folder
sandwiched under one arm.

Savanna's younger sister, Sydney, came around the display counter of the grooming salon, relieving Savanna of the
food and coffee and taking everything over to the round red
and chrome table in the corner.

"Thank you!" Savanna unclipped Fonzie's leash and followed Sydney.

"What's all that?" Sydney nodded at the papers now scattered on the tabletop just as her phone rang. "Wait, let me
grab this first." She zipped through the wide daisy-decorated
archway that divided the establishment to her desk, flipping
her long, loose red braid over one shoulder.

Savanna took a sip of her caramel macchiato, watching
Fonzie dig through the toy basket for his favorite. The shop
was strangely quiet, devoid of the usual yipping, barking
patrons. Sydney didn't take customers until nine a.m.

Fancy Tails & Treats doubled as a grooming salon and organic treat shop for Carson's canine population. Sydney had hit a much-needed niche in their small town's Main Street businesses; Fancy Tails had been successful from the day she'd opened. On this side of the shop, along with the gourmet treat-filled display case, Syd had created an inviting waiting area for her patrons in front of the windows, complete with overstuffed aqua couch and chair, café table, and mini-fridge stocked with complimentary drinks.

Sydney typed something into her computer, finishing the call, and then joined Savanna. "There's only a week left of school. Don't tell me you have all this paperwork?"

"No, though I do have papers at home waiting for me," Savanna said. As Carson's elementary art teacher, she still had a lot of grading to finish before summer break. "This is for the Art in the Park festival."

Sydney clapped her hands together. "Ooh! I'm so excited for that. I'm so glad you won the event for Carson. So." Syd poked through a few of the papers as Savanna put them in order. "Do you have all the details figured out?"

"I've got very little figured out. But with the planning banquet tonight, I arranged to meet with some of the committee this morning in the park to talk about logistics."

"I can help. Let me know what I can do," her sister offered. She popped a piece of icing-covered cinnamon roll in her mouth and closed her eyes. "Mmm, so good!"

"I'll need to circulate tonight and chat with the business owners who haven't volunteered goods or services yet. Maybe you can help with that?"

"That is a job I'm cut out for. I know everyone."

"I'm not surprised," Savanna said, smiling.

The bell over the door jingled and they looked up and Skylar Shepherd entered, out of breath. She tapped the smart watch on her wrist. She wore matching pink and navy workout gear and running shoes, her shiny blond hair pulled back into a short ponytail. Two years older than Savanna, four older than Sydney, Skylar was always perfectly coordinated, whether on a run or in a courtroom trying a case. She joined them at the table.

"You look cute today," Savanna told her. "I've got to go. You'll be at the banquet tonight, right?"

"Wouldn't miss it. Where are you running off to?" Skylar waved off the cinnamon roll box Sydney pushed over to her.

Savanna straightened the lightweight black blazer she'd worn today over a bright yellow shell and grabbed her coffee and notes. "I'm meeting a few folks from city council and the state committee in the park; we need to have the festival tables and thoroughfare mapped out before tonight. Can Fonzie stay, Syd?"

Sydney scratched Savanna's little Boston Terrier behind the ears. "Does it look like he wants to go with you?" He was lying on Sydney's feet, chewing on a stuffed green lizard.

"Not even a little." She and Fonzie had returned home to Carson, Michigan, last fall from a decade spent in Chicago, after losing her fiancé and her job on the same day. Starting her life over at thirty wasn't something she'd planned, but Savanna loved being here with her family as much as Fonzie did.

"Hey, hold on!"

Savanna glanced at her older sister and tapped her phone, checking the time. "Britt's on their way, early as always. I should go."

Skylar sighed. "Okay, but I wanted to hear how things went with Aidan yesterday. How was your dinner date?"

"Thank you," Sydney said to Skylar. "Savanna never tells me things. How was your date with Dr. Gallager?" She drew out his name in a singsong voice, cocking an eyebrow at Savanna.

"I don't tell you things because you do *that*," Savanna said pointedly. "We had to reschedule." She tried to keep the disappointment out of her tone.

"What? Why?" Syd's voice carried enough disappointment for both of them. "That stinks." Her expression was all pout and concern.

"He got stuck in New York. They had a trauma case come in and he had to stay."

"Until when?" Skylar asked.

"I didn't want to ask. I mean, we only had a couple of dates before this whole flying-back-and-forth stuff started. He doesn't owe me any explanations."

Sydney huffed her breath out in frustration. "He can't be the only doctor there. He couldn't tell them no?"

Savanna was slowly backing toward the door. "He feels like he has to help. He says they're still so shorthanded." Aidan had called her from the airport yesterday when he'd learned he couldn't come home yet.

His former employer in New York had tapped him a few months ago and begged him to lend them some time, as the hospital had just lost their chief of cardiothoracic surgery unexpectedly. Aidan had declined an offer to step into the position full-time, not wanting to uproot his seven-year-old daughter, but he'd agreed to help out while they looked for a replacement.

He'd explained to Savanna, over a delicious candlelight dinner at Giuseppe's in town two months ago, that the hospital, and his mentor and boss specifically, had done a lot for him. He couldn't let them down. Aidan's in-laws were more than happy to care for Mollie the two or three days each week he was in New York.

Between Aidan's absences, his family commitments, lengthened clinic hours when he was home, and Savanna's own schedule, they'd had limited time to really get to know each other. Savanna cherished the friendship they'd struck up working together to save the town matriarch, Caroline Carson. And she was in no rush to fall into a new relationship, less than a year after Rob had left her to "find himself."

But she missed Aidan. She sensed he missed her too...he'd sounded disappointed on the phone yesterday.

"Guys," she said, noting both her sisters' faces painted with sympathy. "It's okay. Things will work out, or they won't. I'm sure we'll eventually get some time to catch up."

Sydney's brows rose. "That's very chill of you, Savvy."

She laughed. "Maybe you're rubbing off on me. I've got to go," she said, halfway through the door now. "I'll see you both tonight!"

Savanna tried to push Aidan from her mind as she walked the three blocks to the park. She was still a few minutes early. Her friend Britt Nash, a colleague from Savanna's former life as an art authenticator, would likely be the first person to arrive, but she couldn't see anyone yet in the large, inviting community park that sat at the end of Main Street.

The park was lush and green now in June, with a decent stand of mature trees at the far end, a gazebo near the town statue at the other, and plenty of room to picnic, play on swings, or toss a ball in the middle. Savanna had always loved relaxing here. On quiet days, it was even possible to hear the waves of Lake Michigan through the trees. The beach was only a short walk down a sandy trail past the park.

As she approached, Savanna noticed something seemed off with the view, but she was still a block away. Her mind ran through her to-do list. She pulled a rough sketch of the park from her folder. The meeting this morning would involve herself, Britt, city councilman John Bellamy, and a liaison from the Art in the Park state committee that had awarded the event to Carson after Savanna's months of campaigning. She'd been surprised at how much competition she'd been up against, and even more surprised when Carson had finally won.

Today, the four of them were tasked with assessing the space to come up with the best layout for each of the Art in the Park facets: artwork display tents, concessions, live music stage, judges table, and more. Savanna had a rough sketch, but she wanted it firmed up by the time the planning banquet kicked off tonight. Art submissions from all over the state had been coming into Carson's parks and recreation department, which was really just an extension of Councilman Bellamy's office. Savanna and John Bellamy had been meeting every Thursday to review submissions, and she'd recently enlisted Britt to help; there were so many aspiring artists in Michigan! The first place winner of Art in the Park would be awarded a nice monetary prize and a handsome scholarship to the prestigious Michigan Art Conservatory, as well as a round of a high-visibility interviews at local and state media outlets.

Now Savanna saw what was wrong with the view. As she walked around the gazebo into the park, she stared up at the twelve-foot-tall statue of Jessamina Carson on her pedestal. Jessamina wasn't quite twelve feet tall any longer. Savanna gasped, covering her mouth in shock.

Jessamina Carson's head was missing.

Acknowledgments

The Shepherd Sisters series wouldn't exist without my agent, Frances Black. Thank you, Fran, for never giving up on me.

Thank you to my husband and best friend, Joe, for being my constant. From age six at the Detroit A&P, waiting in line at the twenty-five-cent cartoon booth while your mom and my grandma grocery shopped, to meeting for real at age seventeen, to this very moment, our amazing, surprising, beautiful ride through this thing called life is greater than my wildest dreams. I love you.

My kids bring me joy and make my heart full. Katy, Joey, and Halle, thank you for being mine and for being you. I love you all immeasurably.

Thank you to Meghan Farrell and Kelly Hunter of Tule Publishing for falling in love with the Shepherd Sisters and allowing me to continue spending time with them in their little lakeside town. Thank you to the entire Tule Publishing team for an abundance of skilled support and for providing this series a fantastic new home.

Several friends and family had a role in bringing this series to life. Thank you, Ann Sullivan, my lifetime friend, for being such a dedicated concert wife, beta reader, style consultant, and seasoned critique. Thank you, Rocsana

Oana, for expanding my world view and allowing me to see the beauty in this world through your eyes. Thank you, Jimmy Doyle, for your boundless vocabulary and support. Thanks a million, Suzette Nelson and Talia Wiley, for allowing me inadvertent use of some cool names. Thank you, Stephanie and Sandy Simonson, for being such dedicated friends and readers. Thanks, Josh Howe, for very helpful law enforcement advice. Thank you, Thia Homer, for insider information on elementary art projects.

My mom, Joni Gardner, has been a writer ever since I can remember. Thank you, Mom, for cultivating the writer in me. And I believe my dad, David, an English teacher with a deep love of books, would be happy knowing all those books I read at the dinner table and well past bedtime finally led to me writing my own.

To my lifelong friend and fabulous sister, Julie Velentzas, thank you for giving me the foundation and tools to create these three loving sisters and their relationships. There's a little of us in each of them.

Lastly, thank you to everyone who's read, talked about, reviewed, shared, or in any way loved these books and characters the way I do. Thank you to countless readers who've reached out and asked when, for Pete's sake, there'll be more Shepherd Sisters books. Today is that day! xo

Savanna's Cinnamon Crunch Coffee Cake

Cake:

2 eight-count crescent roll tubes

1 egg, separated

2 eight-ounce packages cream cheese, softened

1 cup granulated sugar

1 teaspoon clear vanilla extract

Glaze/topping:

2 cups powdered sugar

3-4 tablespoons whole milk

1 teaspoon clear vanilla extract

½ cup granulated sugar

1 teaspoon ground cinnamon

½ cup pralines or pecans, chopped

Preheat oven to 350°F. Lightly grease 9 x 13 baking dish.

Unroll one (8 count) crescent roll dough from the tube and press to the bottom of the baking dish, pinching the seams to form an unbroken layer.

In a large bowl, beat together the softened cream cheese, 1 cup sugar, 1 teaspoon vanilla, and 1 egg yolk until light and fluffy. Spread over the first layer of crescent rolls.

Unroll another (8 count) crescent roll tube and pinch the seams closed. Add to the top of the cream cheese layer, pinching at edges to cover as much of the baking dish as possible. Brush with the egg white.

Bake for 25-30 minutes. Top should be golden brown. Allow to cool.

Topping:

In a medium sized bowl, add the powdered sugar, 3 table-spoons milk, and 1 teaspoon vanilla into the bowl. Slowly whisk together until the glaze is smooth. If it is too thick, add more milk one teaspoon at a time. Drizzle over cooled cake.

Combine the ½ cup sugar, cinnamon, and praline pieces or pecans in a small bowl. Sprinkle over the entire coffee cake.

Enjoy!

If you enjoyed *Death by Deception*,
check out the other books in the

The Shepherd Sisters Mysteries series

Book 1: *Death by Deception*

Book 2: *Murder on Display*

Book 3: *Still Life and Death*

Available now at your favorite online retailer!

About the Author

Tracy Gardner is an Edgar Award nominated author of two cozy mystery series, one recent novel earning a spot on New York Public Library's Best 100 Books list. Tracy also writes book club fiction with heart and grit under pen name Jess Sinclair. A Detroit native with one foot in the sand of Florida's Gulf Coast, Tracy is a mother of three, the daughter of two teachers, and works as a nurse when not writing. She lives with her husband and a menagerie of spoiled rescue dogs and cats who inspire every fictional pet she writes.

Thank you for reading

Death by Deception

If you enjoyed this book, you can find more from all our great authors at TulePublishing.com, or from your favorite online retailer.

TULE
PUBLISHING